Books by Sue Hardesty

The Truck Comes on Thursday
Book One of the Loni Wagner Crime Fiction Series

Bus Stop at the Last Chance Saloon
Book Two of the Loni Wagner Crime Fiction Series

Taking the Long Road Home
Book Three of the Loni Wagner Crime Fiction Series

Running Through Fire
Book Four of the Loni Wagner Crime Fiction Series
(forthcoming)

The Butch Cook Book
Co-Editors: Nel Ward and Lee Lynch

The Truck Comes on Thursdays

Book One
The Loni Wagner Crime Fiction Series

Sue Hardesty

Launch Point Press
Portland, Oregon

ISBN: 978-1-63304-2070
E-Book: 978-1-63304-2216

THIRD EDITION
Re-edited and Revised 2019

Editing: Alexa Hoffman, Nel Ward,
and Luca Hart

Cover: Lorelei

Published by:
Launch Point Press
Portland, Oregon
www.LaunchPointPress.com

I dedicate this book to my partner, Nel,
for the amazing life she has given me

Acknowledgments

I would like to acknowledge Lori Lake of Launch Point Press who is willing to publish my works. And I thank you. And to the late Roxanne Jones of L-Book, who first published my writings, you are sorely missed. To my best bud Lee Lynch, whose kind nudging inspired me to finish this book. To my dear friends Taylor West and Lynn Evarts, who suffered through vetting every page. To my professional editor, Alexa Hoffman, who patiently corrected all my mistakes in the first edition. And most of all, to my editor and wonderful forever partner, Nel Ward, who decided I didn't have enough to do and so insisted I write something! Here is the result. Peace.

Sue Hardesty
July 2019

CHAPTER ONE

Loni, you there? Gotta plane down south end of Wagner Airstrip." The radio crackled with sharp static followed by Bobby's slow, Western drawl. "Your last name there. You related?"

"My uncle. I'm on it." With flashing lights and screaming siren, Loni sped around an abandoned Shell station and raced along the east end of the small Arizona town of Caliente. Coco pushed against Loni as she whipped her Highway Patrol SUV onto Old Highway 85. She pushed back against the dogs' brown wooly body that fell again against her as the car fishtailed. "How'd you get so heavy?" Loni complained.

The standard poodle panting in her ear dripped drool on her bare arm. The dog was sheared down to a bare cover with just enough wool left to protect her from sunburn except for her ears and a small ball on the end of her stub tail. Loni shoved the gas pedal to the floor as she raced along the ancient concrete patched road for the next three miles. The car clickity-clacked over the bumps like an old passenger train as she clenched her teeth to keep from biting her tongue. "Jesus!" she grumbled, "Will the department ever get us new shocks?" Spinning the car off the highway, she grabbed Coco as the car slid onto the dirt road parallel to the airport runway.

Dawn light filtered into dark places from the breaking day outlining spiraling black smoke ahead. Loni fought to control her panic as she thought about her uncle and cousin. They were airplane mechanics and could be testing a plane. "Oh, God, don't let it be one of them," she prayed. They often worked before dawn to escape the July summer heat turning the hangar into an oven.

Swirling clouds of hot dust billowed behind her as the car headed toward a line of dense, dark-green salt-cedar trees clumped so close that only their huge trunks separated them. Fierce flames shot through the black smoke into the sky above the tree line. Loni couldn't stop repeating, "Don't let it be Daniel or Uncle Herm. Don't let it be Daniel or Uncle Herm."

Loni rounded the end of the runway and speed-bumped under wrought-iron arches with tall letters spelling "Caliente Cemetery." She slammed to a stop beyond the arches and froze, gawking at the scene. A small plane nestled softly on the remains of a fallen tree in the center of the cemetery. The tree was split from its trunk, cradling the plane. The bottom of the naked tree pointed a jagged, crooked finger into the sky.

Both white wings were ripped from the top of the single-engine plane taking the roof off the cabin with them. One was fizzled to black, and the painted numbers were eaten away by the flames. Dry green needles of the thirsty tree popped and sputtered as they fed the fire. The other wing hung upside down in a fork near the top of an adjoining tree. Diesel fuel dripped down the tree trunk, the overpowering smell stung her nose and burned her eyes. Loni rubbed the knot from an old break on her nose in an effort to stop a sneeze.

The impact twisted the Cessna's 172 propeller like a pretzel and shoved it through the branches of the tree into the ground. "Damn!" Loni muttered to Coco as she glanced around at the scattered and broken tombstones. "How weird is this?"

She didn't observe any flames from around the smoking engine. Yet. Dread forced her out of the SUV, and she ran to her uncle's Ford truck in front of the plane. The sight of her uncle gave her a tremendous feeling of relief. He and Paul, a high school kid who hung around the hangar, were pulling on the crumpled door of the passenger's side. Loni stopped to snatch a crowbar from the bed of her uncle's truck and ran to the plane, ducking to avoid the acrid black smoke oozing out of the engine. "Where's Daniel, Uncle Herm?"

"Don't know," he grunted. "How about a little help here. She's still alive!" Uncle Herm shouted in a high, strained voice as he snatched the crowbar. "I saw her hand move."

Loni eyed the smoking engine as she snaked around shattered tombstones to the other side of the plane. She crawled through branches and pulled her way up the side of the plane. Shards of sharp metal from the wing struts gouging her bare arm left a trail of skin and dripping blood, and she cursed the short-sleeved summer uniform.

A branch catching at the gun on Loni's belt nearly jerked her to the ground as she tasted salt from the needles of the tree slapping her in the face. She used the pilot's door handle to pull herself up onto a large limb and peered into the cabin. The open staring eyes didn't belong to Daniel, she slumped with relief.

The lifeless eyes belonged to the school district's superintendent, Rene Garcia who was piloting the plane. He was sandwiched into his seat by the buckled engine, and the instrument panel hung in his lap. A tree limb peeled back the shattered windshield.

Loni felt his neck, but there was no pulse. His head was turned at an unnatural angle, and his skin was turning purple. She knew the face of death from her seven years as a Los Angeles cop before she moved back home weeks before.

Even dead, he reminded her of how much she hated him and his putdown macho bullshit when he taught history in high school. He used to pitch chalk at slot between the breasts of a black papier-mâché female torso on a file cabinet in his classroom and smirk at the girls.

She remembered how he loved to talk about cars. One day in class he said, "I had an old T-bird when I was in high school. Named it the Mayflower. Anybody care to guess why?"

"Because it was so old?" a boy ventured.

"No." He smirked. "It was because so many girls came across in it." Loni could still see the smug smile he gave the boy as he rocked back and forth in his huge padded oak desk chair. Well he's not laughing now.

A young woman was beside Rene. Long, bleach-blonde hair covered part of her face. Rene always liked the blondes. They always made the best grades in his classes. Half-breed Indians like her didn't have a chance. He even flunked her once after she called him a pervert. The "F" was worth it.

Loni reached past Rene to check on the woman. Her head was slanted toward Loni, and her eyes were closed. Loni reached over to check on a pulse. "Who's the woman, Uncle Herm?"

"Name's Rosa something or other. Rene's secretary, I think," he grunted. Loni felt a faint thready pulse. "You're right. She's still alive." Herm's muscles bunched as he doubled down on prying open the buckled door as sweat soaked his blue work shirt. Loni watched his muscles bunch as he pried on the buckled door, amazed at the strength of the big, dark German. The engine's smoke and diesel smell grew stronger. Loni called for Paul. "Get the fire extinguisher from Uncle Herm's truck and hose down that motor."

Rosa's dark eyes slowly opened, and she tried to reach for Rene. Loni took her hand and shook her head. "Can you breathe okay?" Loni noticed the woman's eyes glaze over with pain as she gripped Loni's hand.

"Got it!" Her uncle yanked the protesting door open.

An ambulance siren screamed in the distance. "Don't move." Loni held Rosa as she groaned and tried to lift her head. "Help is almost here."

Blood dripped down from Rosa's lopsided nose and ran across her lips and down her mauve silk blouse. Loni pulled a red-checkered bandana from her back pocket and held it gently against Rosa's nose. "Don't move," Loni repeated. The side of Rosa's uneven swelling face was turning purple. Maybe a broken jaw, Loni thought and hoped that was all. "Hang on." She brushed Rosa's hair aside to study her face for signs of shock. She might have some broken ribs.

"We ran out of gas," Rosa mumbled. Loni released her hand and checked the gas gauge on the hanging panel, careful to not break the wires. One tank still registered full. "Don't talk. Focus on me. Listen to me." She kept smoothing Rosa's hair with one hand as she reached out with the other to undo Rosa's seatbelt.

As Rosa tried to move, she turned grey and cried out, "My legs. Oh, god. They hurt so much!" Rosa was going into shock, and Loni hoped she wasn't bleeding out.

The ambulance pulled up behind Uncle Herm's truck. Loni stepped onto a tombstone and jumped down while two paramedics in white overalls scrambled out of the ambulance cab. Judy was as short as Big Lu was tall, and Judy was as bubbly as Big Lu was dour. They grabbed their cases and hurried to the plane. Judy trotted to keep up with Lu's long stride.

Loni moved toward Uncle Herm and took his huge hand. He towered over her five-foot-ten height as they watched Judy check Rosa. Loni took a deep breath to shake off her fear. It would have been so easy for her uncle or cousin to be in that plane.

Judy's kinky strawberry hair bounced as she stood on Rene's lap to help Lu tighten a neck brace on Rosa and gently lift Rosa up and onto a body board. Judy strapped her down to the board as Lu pulled her tailored skirt down over her thighs. Rosa was passed out, blood dripping from one foot still wearing a strapless high heel shoe. Sliding the board down between branches to the gurney, the paramedics strapped Rosa to the gurney and shoved her into the back of the ambulance. Judy clambered in to help Rosa as Lu jumped in the driver's seat.

"Maybe Rosa has a chance," Loni spoke softly to Uncle Herm as they watched the howling ambulance speed away.

Paul kept circling the engine, hugging the long-empty red fire extinguisher as if it were a baby. Flashing lights and clouds of dust were highlighted against the rising sun as cars and trucks followed the yellow fire truck racing toward them.

Loni questioned people standing in a small group around the plane. The quiet women worried cloth belts and collars of robes and housecoats with constantly moving hands. Men in undershirts and Levis wandered among them.

One woman called out. "Rosa? Will she be okay?"

"She was awake and talking." Loni didn't know anymore. "Any of you see the crash?"

"I did," Paul announced like a small child. He had left the engine to stand by her uncle still clutching the empty fire extinguisher in his arms.

"The motor sputtered and quit as he turned in to land. It fell. Then it plopped in a that tree. Like a toad jumpin' into a pond. Plop." The young man peeked at Herm for confirmation.

Plop? Loni glanced at Uncle Herm, working hard to resist a nervous giggle.

"Where he came from, they traded DNA a little too close," Uncle Herm whispered to Loni as he gave Paul's dark crew-cut head a knuckle rub. His faint grin faded. "I was in the hangar and heard it come down, but I didn't see it crash."

"I was over there." Paul pointed his skinny arm at the archway. A bicycle leaned up against the iron post with an empty basket hanging off the handles. "Just finished deliverin' newspapers and was headed home when it started sputtering. Came in right over my head and scared the crap outta me." Suddenly aware everyone was staring at him, Paul ducked his head and moved closer to Herm, who slid a protective arm over his shoulder.

Loni's eyes roved around the growing crowd. "Anyone else? Anything?"

"Is Rene really dead?" a man asked.

Another voice asked, "Rene? Did he suffer?"

Before she could answer, an old man pushed his way to the front and into Loni's face. "That plane's sitting on my wife," he spat belligerently.

Loni backed away, but he came with her. Old Man Calvin. He hadn't changed much. She heard he had sold the drugstore. He must be retired now, she figured. He was old as dirt and smelled as bad. None of his clothes matched, not even his shoes and socks. He wore a tie without a shirt. Somebody said his wife had died. She wondered if the new owner ever filled in the hole this mean old bastard dug in his drugstore parking lot so no one could park there.

"Well?" He stayed in her space and shouted again, spraying spittle on her face.

Loni jumped and wiped. "Listen . . ." Loni stopped herself in time. "Sorry. We'll move the plane as soon as we can."

She edged around him to stand in front of the group as they fixated on the top of Rene's head that was visible. Loni waited for eye contact, hoping something would pop. "Anybody know anything about this?" She watched for any reaction, but all she got was Dorothea Rodriquez smiling at her.

Dorothea had gained weight since high school. She had four kids, according to Loni's grandma. Loni refused to respond, and Dorothea's smile slid off her face as she nervously pulled down her tight show-everything-I-have thin shirt under an open purple robe. She should squirm! Loni thought as she recalled Dorothea shoving her against the locker room wall and kissing her.

Loni liked the kiss, but she didn't trust Dorothea, with her history of play and tell. Loni knew she left herself wide open for it. Her teen rebellion came with stomping boots, a chip on her shoulder, and short, spiky hair sprayed with rainbow colors.

That was in the past Loni reminded herself. Her workouts changed her from skinny to muscular, and her coal black hair was now twisted in a single braid hanging down to her waist. A scar running through one eyebrow turned some of the hairs white. A second thin white scar ran ear to ear across her throat, left over when a horse bucked her off onto a barbed wire fence. The two times she broke her nose left it slightly lopsided and bumpy.

When she turned away from Dorothea, she came face to face with Old Man Calvin who was still trying to stare her down. Wailing sirens closing in on them drowned out his voice. She sidestepped him and walked off to watch the bright yellow fire truck pull up. Volunteer firefighters, already sweating in their yellow rubber uniforms and hard hats, swarmed off the truck. They pulled hoses spinning out of the truck and turned on the water churning the area into a black mush.

Her cousin James jumped down from the driver's seat and snatched a hose from one of the volunteer firemen. With a cruel expression he turned and aimed it at Loni. She avoided the spray by jumping behind her uncle. James didn't dare spray his uncle. As hot as she was in her polyester uniform, she knew the water would feel wonderful, but the powerful water spray would knock her down. She knew James badly wanted to humiliate her.

"James!" their uncle reprimanded. "Stop screwing around and get the diesel diluted in that tree before it explodes on you!"

James reluctantly pointed the hose through the dancing branches. The wing slowly dropped out of the tree from the force as the water dissipated the acrid diesel smell.

"Did Rene live in the park?" she asked her uncle as she lifted her heavy French braid off her neck. Her hair came loose, and long black waves fell in her face, temporarily blinded her. Damn! Coco must have chewed on the rawhide strap again. She did that every time they were on a long boring patrol. Loni tried to concentrate on her uncle's voice as she fought her hair and swore under her breath at Coco.

"No, he lived up on Walker Heights with the hoity-toity. He kept his plane here, though."

Loni pushed the hair away from her broad forehead and high Apache cheekbones. "Did you know he was coming in this morning?"

Uncle Herm shook his head. "Didn't call a flight plan in to me." Pulling a stained kerchief from his back pocket, Herm hesitated a minute as he scrubbed at the sweat running down his face. "Engine trouble must've happened fast. I sure didn't hear a distress call." Loni decided Rene didn't have time to call. Refocusing on the steadily growing group, Loni noted they were mostly old timers who didn't have to get to work. She recognized Mister Spinzolli walking up to join the crowd. A short, swarthy man with a strong Italian accent who everybody called Spin. He was the only Italian immigrant who ever settled in Caliente. She loved his green corn tamales, best in the world although she didn't dare tell her grandma.

His wife ran a small Mexican food stand in front of their house near the school where kids who had a few bucks in their pockets would hang out. Summertime in the cooling dusk he pulled a two-wheeled cart up and down the streets with a large stainless-steel pot, crying "Tamales!" Young boys followed him, and he sent them to the doors with the orders. Somedays their rewards of free tamales were all they had to eat.

Suddenly a dust devil swirled into Loni, tangling her mass of hair and shooting dirt up into her eyes and nose. The sharp needles of sand stinging her crawled into her hair, neck, crook of her elbows, even down inside her shirt. The dust devil let go and passed on into the firefighters who scrambled to safety, laughed at her as she scrubbed the hot silt out of her eyes between sneezing bouts.

Loni ignored their ridicule by walking over to the fallen tree breaking off a twig. She stripped away the soft needles, making a long pin to fasten a hunk of her hair into a knot on the back of her head. The sweat streaks on her shirt caked into mud she couldn't scrape off.

Everyone but James ignored her as they murmured and pointed around at the broken tombstones. "That's Bessie," a voice quavered. Loni spotted Old Man Forrester. Everybody called him Rooster, not because he had a chicken ranch, although he really did, but because he truly resembled a rooster. His huge Adam's apple bobbed constantly under his chinless face and huge beak of a nose always sunburned and blistering. He wore a red-striped Western shirt with a red round no bill cap.

"Hey, Loni? Who is that?"

Loni Watched Jake Sly push his way to the front of Old Man Forrester, remembering how he took storytelling to the extreme. Wherever he was, drugstore, meat line, café, it didn't matter. Everybody could hear his high, clear voice as he told one whopper after another. She thought about the time she sat beside him at the drugstore counter. "Hey, Sly. Tell me a lie."

"Can't," he'd claimed. "Sold them all to television."

He was an old-time cowboy, working wherever he could, mostly breaking horses. Loni hated the way he treated them. He lost a hand when he roped a bull and the hand got caught in the rope. The bull won. Without a hand, he wrapped a whip on the stub. He used spurs sharp enough to cut and rode a horse until he broke the horse's spirit. She picked him up on the road a few times, drunk. As he lifted his good arm at her, she noticed a cast from fingers to elbow. She had to wonder . . . no, no, no. I'm not going there.

"No," Sly insisted impatiently to the group around him. "That Bes on the tombstone goes to Bessard."

"And you know that how?" Forrester questioned. "Looks like Bess to me."

Loni heard a snort, and Sly insisted, "Cuz it's on the right side of the stone, o' course, you idjt."

"Well, crap. Y'all know Sly knows everything. You hear that too, huh, Pat? Who was it told us how smart Sly is? Who was that? Don'tcha remember? Oh, yeah, it was him!"

She heard snickers as someone asked how the tombstones would get glued back together. Another voice said, "Might as well dig a hole and bury Rene now seeing as he's already here." Loni heard a small laugh. "Won't even have to embalm him," someone else added. Loni knew cops used black humor to cope with tragic experiences. But it sounded as if other people weren't too fond of Rene either.

"No can do," Spin reminded them. "He's Catholic, and they have to have mass and haul him around awhile first."

Loni moved back to Uncle Herm. "Who does maintenance on the plane?"

"He did. He was too cheap to hire anyone." Herm sounded half angry. "Guess he wasn't as good as he thought." He rubbed his arm. "Careless. Always in a hurry to get somewhere." Herm wiped the sweat out of his eyes, smearing grease across his face. "Have you worked on this plane lately, Daniel?" Loni turned, grateful to see her other cousin.

"No, not for a very long time." His warm chocolate eyes matched his caring grin as he reached for Loni.

Loni backed up a step to avoid the whisker burn he always tried to give her. "Could you go through the engine? Paul there says it quit in the air and fell."

"Plopped." Her uncle corrected her.

"Sorry?"

"Just a sick joke, son. Forget it."

Loni jerked on Daniel's arm to get his attention back. "Gas gauge read one of his tanks was still full. With all the diesel running down that tree I tend to agree."

"Sure." He punched her back in affection. He was the spitting image of his dad except for a few aging lines and sags on Uncle Herm's big German face and a few gray hairs.

Loni knew the plane would not crash if her cousin Daniel worked on it. In high school, she did his homework while he rebuilt whatever he got his hands on in their granddad's barn. James, on the other hand, pretty much ruined everything he touched. As the oldest, Daniel watched after both cousins Loni and James over the years. But James took advantage, hot wiring Daniel's cars whenever the mood took him. James, however, refused to step where Loni lived, making the barn a great place for Daniel to work.

Daniel was Loni's protector in high school until he graduated a year ahead of her. With him gone, things got dicey, and her grades went to shit as she spent her time avoiding James and his friends waiting around every corner to bully her.

Loni watched Uncle Herm and Daniel walk away, admiring again how much they were alike. Both big men, Daniel walking just like his dad, wide shoulders swinging and elbows out, slue footed. People parted to give them plenty of space.

The firefighters had thrown their rubber suits onto the top of the truck, the yellow legs hanging helter-skelter over the side. Three of the men used a helmet to play football in the shade of a salt cedar. Her uncle and Daniel stopped to talk to James.

Loni recognized Rene needed to get out of the heat soon. The coroner better hurry. She herded the grumpy old men back through the arch, some more reluctant than others, so she could wrap the yellow tape around the scene of the wreck. "Jeez! You're worse than herding cats!" They tittered like little girls and slowly moved on while she kept them from collecting souvenirs.

The fire truck followed the crowd out, and Loni climbed back up onto the plane and photographed the scene. She leaned over the body and moved Rene's striped tie aside to take a small notebook and cell phone out of his shirt pocket. They might tell her why he tried to land so early.

A middle-aged man in Levis and a Western shirt walked up behind her with a medical bag in his hand. "Anybody alive in there?"

"No. Rosa went in the ambulance. Only Rene left. You must be the coroner."

Smiling, the man held out his other hand. "Doctor Benjamin, at your service."

Loni grinned at the formal introduction. "Loni Wagner, Highway Patrol at your service."

"Good. Would you call the mortuary for me? I left my cell home in the charger."

"Sure. It'll take a bit. I need to go back to the hangar to find a phone book. Can I do anything else?"

"That should do it." The doctor surveyed the plane. Using his bag as a shield, he climbed through the branches.

Loni finished photographing the scattered trash and pieces of metal. Luggage hung out of a split in the side of the plane. She carried the luggage and Rosa's purse over to the back of her SUV and went back to bag the smaller debris.

The ground was already hot to the touch. Too bad the town couldn't afford to water, Loni reflected, seeing the desolate brown around the tombstones. It could really use some green grass and a few wild poppies.

Loni circled made one last search and tripped on a broken marble statue of a young girl. The crash tore the mass from a tombstone and shoved it into the dirt. She caught herself on a limb, gouging a broken piece into her hand. Swearing under her breath, she sucked at the splinters as she scanned the crash site. She felt like a fish in a bowl as the watchers examined her every move. Still sucking on her hand, she checked for any suspicious objects to give her clues relating to what happened.

Back at her SUV, Loni unlocked the tailgate and piled the evidence bags into the back. The smell of diesel lessened but still burned her nostrils.

Ordering Coco into the front seat of the SUV, she got into the driver's seat next to the dog and immediately rolled the windows down, hating she had to leave her windows rolled up to protect the twelve-gauge Remington shotgun and Colt M4 rifle hanging on the rack in the back window. Pushing Coco's wet, dripping muzzle away from her, Loni slowly drove through the stragglers from the crowd and the cars lining the dirt road until she could pick up enough speed to cool off in the hot wind. The painted letters on the front of the huge corrugated tin hangar grew steadily larger until she could read "Wagner Airport." The name was everywhere, the legacy of a pioneer family, and she hated it. Growing up, all she heard was a disgusted "You're just like so-and-so," or "Why aren't you more like so-and-so?" Or the worst, "Must be the breed in you."

In the shade inside the airport hangar, Loni wound around small planes, wings, engines hoisted on blocks, and other airplane parts to her parking spot. With Coco close on her heels, she headed into her uncle's office tucked in the back corner. She silently walked past Uncle Herm and Daniel lounging in overstuffed chairs to stand in front of the swamp cooler hanging in the window. Lifting the front of her shirt to let the air blow around her body, Loni sighed in relief.

Daniel teased her. "You deserve it for living in someone else's country too long."

"Listen." Loni pointed a finger at him. "You got cotton on. Try wearing this godawful polyester crap."

"I don't hear James complaining," he teased her.

"I don't either since he's a town cop and wears cotton shirts and Levis."

"You should go upstairs to your apartment and shower." Her uncle nodded toward the stairs hanging on the other side of the office wall. "Cold water's best way to cool down. You done with your shift?"

"Not yet. I need to get Rene out of the sun."

"You do look like crap." Daniel grinned at her affectionately. "You get down and roll in pig shit?"

Ignoring him, she stood awhile in the cool air before she picked up the phone book.

"Did you find out why Rene crashed?"

"Not yet." Loni opened her phone.

Uncle Herm's big shoulders shrugged. "Only thing come to mind is when he realized the engine problem too late."

"Probably. Still, something doesn't feel right." Finding the number to Kister's Mortuary, she called Wilber to come and get Rene.

"Bout time you called," echoed a voice on the other end. "Heard about it hours ago. Can't be helped how he's gonna smell. Coroner's gonna be mad."

"Coroner's there. He told me to call." She hung up. Shaking off the irritation of the complaining voice, she called the public electric company for a boom to deliver the plane to the hangar. Already on their way, they told her.

Loni used the copier in Uncle Herm's office to copy the five pages in Rene's notebook. The cover had a unique geometric design, and she decided to copy it, too. On the back of the copy she wrote down the numbers from the cell phone's history.

Turning back to Daniel, she joked, "Come to think of it, Dannie boy, why are you up at this ungodly hour? I remember how hard it was to get you out of bed before noon."

Her mind moved on to the five pages she copied, lists of names followed by sets of numbers. Maybe money amounts? She didn't recognize any of the names. Were they listed in his phone? Maybe a combination of something? Streets? Cities? The rest of the notebook was blank.

"It's called too hot to work any other time." Daniel's voice broke into her musings as a middle-aged, thin man stormed into the office.

Wet, stringy hair hung in long strands down his back, and curls of gray hair stuck out of the top of his undershirt as he waved a knobby bare arm toward the runway. Sticking a demanding finger into Daniel's chest, he was nearly frantic. "You got to get me out of here now!"

Daniel stepped back regaining his space. "You know what, Larry? If you don't get a haircut soon, you're going to have to climb up on a limb to shit."

Loni burst out with a guffaw before she could stop herself. Larry glowered at her until he saw the notebook in her hand. The fire quickly bled out of his eyes and his freshly shaved face smoothed out. Pulling his eyes away, he raised his hands in retreat. "Okay, okay, I know I'm out of line. I'm sorry. But this is a really important meeting."

"I know, Larry. Your plane's ready." Daniel's voice was condescending. "Has been for a while."

Uncle Herm studied the runway. "Good time to leave before it gets too hot to get lift. Wind's down this morning. Been having heavy cross-winds from this heat lately." Loni saw the heat from the tarmac was already bouncing water mirages.

Larry's face took on a furtive expression as he nervously turned away, pulling on the black suspenders holding up carefully creased dress pants. Loni followed him out of the hangar and watched him jump into a golf cart, hair flopping, and whirl down the runway into the garage of the third house. She thought she identified Dorothea's purple robe on the woman standing outside the garage door.

Loni turned back to the office and asked Daniel. "Tell me about Larry."

"Like what?"

"What he does for a living, his interests, family. You know, that kind of shit."

"Well," Daniel finally admitted, "he married Dorothea Rodriquez and has a bunch of kids. You know. We called her Dot in school. Now she prefers Dorothea."

"Yeah," her uncle added. "He's got a teenaged kid from his first wife. Calls him Billyjoesombitch."

"Billy Joe what?"

"Billyjoesombitch." Daniel shrugged his shoulders. "That's all we ever heard Larry call him."

Exasperated, Loni punched him in his rock-hard gut. "Be serious."

Daniel lifted an eyebrow at Loni. "Like I tell James, don't play cop with me. I don't play with these people, and I don't listen to your women gossip. Ask Mom." Daniel waved at a small red pickup driving up. "She knows all the gossip."

Loni's Aunt Mae bounded out of the pickup and hugged Loni with one hand as she handed Uncle Herm and Daniel each a sack. "Your lunch." She turned back to Loni. "Shame on you. I've only seen you twice since you've been home."

"I'm sorry. I'll get by soon, I promise." Loni grinned back at the infectious smile on Mae's chubby face under her short, brown curls. The gray strands weren't there when she left years earlier.

Uncle Herm opened his sack and fished out a sandwich. Peeling back a slice of bread, he smelled it.

Mae patted him on the cheek in fake pity. "Have you seen anyone sniff their food before? He's been doing that ever since he saw the rerun of M*A*S*H where Hawkeye was always sniffing his food." Mae's acerbic comments always put Loni on the floor in stitches.

"Oh, bull crap," Uncle Herm retorted. "That's so not true. I got into sniffing my food when your damn cat came up to a piece of cheese that fell outta my sandwich and tried to cover it up."

She stepped back to Herm and patted his belly. "There, there, dear. Come home and I'll make you a hot lunch."

"How come?" he shot back. "We goin' out to eat?"

"Nah." Mae smirked. "Thought I'd fry your baloney."

Mae hugged Loni again and then Daniel. She was a toucher. "Keep your promise now," she told Loni as she got back into her pickup. "I'll call you about coming for breakfast."

"I'll be there." Loni watched the pickup disappear around the corner before she turned back to the notebook and cell phone, wondering why Larry was so interested in them.

Back at her SUV, Loni searched Rosa's luggage, hoping to find a souvenir, paperwork, new clothes, anything to indicate where they were. Nothing. Even the labels were American. She shoved everything back before she opened Rene's luggage. Nothing there either. She opened Rosa's purse. Again, nothing zinged. She was stuffing everything back into the purse when her phone rang.

"What you doin', girly?" Chief's voice barked in her ear.

"Questioning people and collecting evidence," Loni carefully responded.

"Well, get back to traffic watch. You're not hired to be an investigator."

"I thought since I was off duty and here—"

"Not your job to think, girly. Get on back here and sign out. Tully will be there soon. Git, now!"

"What about the crime scene?"

"Didn't you hear me? Not your job!" He hung up.

Loni wondered how far she could throw the goddamn phone. "Hirciamus!" she snarled.

"What did you say?" Daniel was perplexed.

"Sorry. My grandma hates it when I swear so I'm trying to learn how to swear genteelly."

Uncle Herm laughed. "Well, I'm genteel, and I have no idea what it means."

"I said he was a stinking armpit." She backed up as Tully skidded into the hangar, lights flashing, his fishtailing SUV nearly clipped Loni's SUV. She grumped in resentment at his closed windows. His refrigeration seemed to work fine.

Tully climbed out and slowly strutted toward her, slew-footed on skinny bowed legs. He was so pot-bellied his gun belt disappeared into his gut, and his scraggly beard was a failed try. Dried sweat ringed his armpits. Loni wondered how long it had been since he pressed his uniform. Or even washed it. "Oh, shit!" Loni forgot her promise.

"Be cool, girl," Herm warned her as Tully slammed his door shut. "You can't fix stupid."

"Is the ol' bastard really dead?" Tully stalked up to Loni and eyeballed the cemetery at the end of the runway. His hat was so big every time he turned his head, it forgot to turn with him. Probably a brown color at one time, it turned muddy, shapeless, and tired. "Well," he drawled, staring out toward the plane barely visible beyond the split tree trunk. "Good thing he don't need to fly no more."

"You do like to tell it like it is, huh, Tully," Uncle Herm scoffed as he walked away. "What was that genteel word you used earlier, Loni?"

Ignoring Herm, Tully took out his cell phone. Loni listened to him ask for Roland's Wrecking and gaped at him. "You can't do that. Rene's still in there. It's a crime scene, for god's sake!" Exasperated, she shook her head. "Besides, you need a hoist to lift the plane off the tombstones."

He glared at Loni and sullenly called the mortuary for a body pickup. Loni couldn't find the words to tell him she already called. Tully flipped his phone shut and bared his brown teeth, badly stained from chewing tobacco, and spit at her feet. She stepped back and wondered if he even owned a toothbrush. "It's not a crime scene now." Tully pulled his hat off and wiped at the sweat running down his face. "I suppose if he was bound for hell, at least he found the right day for it."

Loni turned away. Back off, she told herself. It's only your second month home. Don't shoot him yet. She clenched her teeth and turned toward the door of the hangar. "There's the luggage and evidence." She waved her hand. "Coco, come." She followed the dog outside.

The heat of Loni's anger matched the waves from the tarmac slamming into her face like an open oven. She needed the walk before she got in her SUV and drove herself into a ditch.

Loni watched Coco sniff the dead grass and wondered why Rene was landing so early in the morning. Especially without a flight plan and a request for runway lights. And why did Rosa claim they ran out of gas when they still had a full tank? She studied the houses along the runway to see which ones had plane garages and which had open plane ports. They were all single stories and had white stucco walls and red tile roofs to alert pilots when they were landing. She felt a growing sense of appreciation for her uncle's accomplishments.

The heat was making Loni feel sick, and she called Coco before hurrying back into the hangar. Running ahead of her the poodle danced over the burning asphalt. Loni grabbed Coco's water thermos from her SUV and poured water into her bowl. Leaning against her SUV, she watched the dog amazed every time she drank. She imitated a turkey, filling her mouth, she tilted her head back to swallow, slopping water everywhere.

Loni circled the cemetery to check on any progress in moving the plane. The boom on the crane was lifting the fuselage onto a flatbed, and Loni guessed Rene was already moved. A few curious stragglers willing to put up with the heat, huddled under the salt cedars to watch.

Loni reminded the driver to drop the plane off at the Wagner hangar before she headed off to the police station. Hot wind from the open windows burned her face. Her refrigeration unit overheated the SUV, but Chief told her she didn't need it for night patrol. He added she used less gas without it. Wondering if she could get Daniel to help her fix it, Loni was more than ready for her day to end as she parked the SUV in the fenced police parking lot beside her truck. Coco followed her into the police station, and she signed out.

The sun was riding high, burning through Loni's shirt when she arrived back and opened her truck door urging Coco to hurry. "We've got shopping to do." The dog scrambled up into the 1994 Silverado. It had a raised chassis and oversized tires and was once green. At least that's what Maria told her. Most of the truck was covered with patches of gray Bondo from fender-benders and dirt from the desert. Maria bought it from a distant cousin who liked to challenge rocky hills and gullies. It didn't have very high mileage, mostly because Maria was afraid to drive it very far. Loni knew the truck came off silly stuck up in the air, but she didn't care. It was Maria's.

At the general store, Loni ordered a new glass-top stove, refrigerator, and dishwasher for her grandma. She remembered the salesman, from school when kids called both of them "breeds." It gave her a connection with Jessie. "Stove will be in—"

"I know," Loni interrupted, sarcasm dripping. "The truck comes on Thursday." She sketched a square with her finger in the air. "Still the same small town."

"Listen," Jessie teased her. "The population doubled while you were gone."

"Really? Someone had twins?"

"Yeah." He tap-danced a few silly steps and genuflected. "I did."

His antics had Loni giggling. "Good for you. Boys or girls?"

"One of each."

"That's one way to settle the name argument."

Loni stopped next at the plumber before heading on to Spud the electrician, Ken the glass man, and finally Raymond the sheet metal guy. She ordered a swamp cooler and refrigeration unit and a hot water heater from him. Her grandma was going to kill her, but she didn't care. It felt good to do something for her.

The hot sun was still high overhead when Loni headed into the hangar and saw the plane huddled in the back like a woebegone puppy. Still pissed at Chief she ignored the plane as she climbed the stairs. Walking into her cool loft apartment with its cathedral ceiling and window skylights always helped her mood. She polished the wood floor to a high shine during her first few days home when she missed Maria so much she couldn't sleep, aching for her touch. The throw rugs from her aunt Mae splashed color throughout the square, open space. Backed up to one side of the stairwell wall was a small apartment stove, refrigerator, and sink. On the other side of the stairs was a closet-sized space with a toilet and tiny shower.

The antique quilt on her double bed in the center of the loft barely covered the mattress sides. Each bed post sat in a tall quart jar to keep scorpions from crawling up into the bed and stinging her.

Two wooden chairs were pulled up to a small square table in front of a sloping window which opened out on Montezuma Mountain on the distant skyline beyond the desert floor. A large desk under a slanted wall was deep enough to hold her laptop computer.

Loni poured fresh water for Coco and checked the level of dry food in a self-feeder. She tried to quell a small voice of doom about the plane crash.

Visiting her grandparents at the ranch could wait until the next day, Loni decided. She called them and felt the usual sense of guilt. She struggled to pull tan, rough-out boots from her feet and peel off sweat-soaked socks. With the possibility of an emergency call, she folded her slacks over the back of a chair for fast access in case of a call. In the bathroom, she stripped off the rest of her clothes and stayed under the cold shower until she wrinkled and shivered.

Loni wrapped a towel around her long, wet hair and climbed into bed buck-naked and half wet. A few battle scars puckered on her buff body in white lines against her olive skin, and her athletic muscles rippled across her back as she opened her laptop.

> FROM: Loni Wagner
> TO: Sandi@gmailyahoo.com
> DATE: July 1
> SUBJECT: Still here.
>
> I know it's been a few days since I've e-mailed. Things have been hectic. Wanted you to know I appreciate your telling me to move on from Maria. I'm trying, but it's still hard.
>
> I'm helping my grandmother as much as I can. She's getting better, which makes it a good thing I came back home. My granddad is also happy I'm back. Bahb hasn't changed one day while I was gone.
>
> You wanted to know how big Caliente is. An old-timer will tell you that by the time you read the "Welcome to Caliente" sign, you're already out the other side. It's not quite that bad but ranching and mining are pretty much gone since nobody can make a living. So many empty places and worried faces on the old folks as they watch their children drift way. I can't help wondering how large businesses undercutting and breaking the small family businesses, forcing their children into the cities for jobs, can be a good thing for family values.
>
> I'm finally through with my training crap and have become a duly noted Arizona Highway Patrol Officer. They let me patrol by myself. I got assigned the graveyard shift, following drunk drivers around after the bars close,

ticketing speeders, and driving the desert for hours at night. It is deadening.

Sometimes I miss the rush the LA city streets gave me. I usually get to the station in time to watch everybody come to work before I go home, which feels backwards, like so much else. I know. I'm whining. It will get better. Shiichoo tells me so. But I still feel so lost.

Tell the girls I miss them.

Loni

She hit "Send," closed the laptop, and slid down in the bed, too exhausted to pull up the sheet. Her restless brain thought about Maria's sister, Sandi, and her daughters, how much she missed seeing them. Sandi was Maria's favorite sister, and they both babysat the kids. Her thoughts drifted to Maria, always Maria. She missed Maria's smell, like warm, sweet milk fresh in the bucket. And her feel, the soft velvet of a horse's nose. She especially missed the closeness in bed when she would wake up so intertwined with Maria she couldn't tell where one of them began and the other left off. She missed the whispers of love in the dark of the night.

Coco interrupted her reverie with sharp barks in her ear. "What the—!" Loni pushed the dog away. "Stop it!" Coco jumped off the bed and rushed to the door barking and back again. She shushed the dog and heard a repeated ringing vibration from below. As Loni swung out of bed, she grabbed her gun from under the pillow. "Stay," she ordered Coco and quietly opened her door. At the foot of the stairs, she flipped on the light switch and spotted a human silhouette in the light flooding the hangar. A shot rang out.

Loni felt a brush of air beside her arm and flipped off the lights as she dropped to the floor. She heard sounds of running and the side door opening before the roar of a motorcycle. Naked, she jumped up and ran outside, alternating between pissed and scared. There were too many houses around and too many people in them to shoot at the single taillight in the distance. She ran back upstairs before someone saw her and called the shooting in. "No point in sending anyone." She told Bobby who was the police dispatcher. "Shooter's long gone, and I can take care of it."

"You coming to work?"

"Got a reason why I shouldn't?"

"Guess not."

Loni dug the bullet out of the wall and dropped it into an evidence bag. She'd take it into work later.

CHAPTER TWO

A full moon floating high in the summer sky followed Loni to work. She stopped on the side of the road and turned off her lights. Greasewood leaves and cactus needles glittered silver across the desert floor. She waited for peace, but she couldn't shake the adrenaline hangover. Reluctantly she made herself drive on to the police station, arriving as Trevor was coming off his shift. He followed her up to the booking counter where Bobby stood.

Loni had no idea exactly what Bobby's title was. He had at least five jobs she knew about: dispatcher, 9-1-1 operator, booker, interrogator, and office manager. Skinny and tall, he towered over her and peered down with pale blue eyes, cautiously watching her sign in. "You patrol east tonight," he spoke softly to Loni as he acknowledged Trevor over her shoulder. "Just in case the shooter knows your route."

"Wow, you really know how to cheer a girl up." Loni frowned as she took the map from Bobby. She stepped back to let Trevor sign out.

Trevor's open and cheerful face always made her feel better. His uniform hung snug and straight on him, his shoes were shiny, and his face was clean-shaven. She never understood how he stayed the same throughout his shift. She was signing in, and she felt messy already.

"How come you're gonna change my route?" Trevor teased. "Didn't want me stoppin' by your house anymore? Wife told you about us and wants to kick you out?"

"You wish," Bobby bounced back.

"You got that right." Trevor sadly conceded. "Tell her it's your fault I can't get there anymore." He turned to Loni who was scanning her new patrol map. "Your new route has some good speed traps." He reached into his pocket and pulled out his map, falling apart at the creases. "Give me your map, and I'll mark it."

"Hey, that's great!" Loni leaned over the counter to watch. "I never pick up enough speeders to make Chief happy."

"And you never will." Trevor lowered his voice, mimicking Chief. "Got to pay your own way here, boy." Trevor borrowed Bobby's pen and began circling places. "This one is best." He pointed at The Oasis Bar. "It's the only bar not in the town proper. Get down wind about a half mile. You can pick 'em up either hurrying to the bar or hurrying to get home cuz they know their ol' lady's mad." He handed her the map. "Good for five or so of what Chief would like. Best at closing." Trevor chuckled. "Stopped someone leaving there today who had the gall to ask me if the ticket I gave him met my quota. Told him no, I didn't have a quota, I can write as many tickets as I want and would he like another?"

Trevor was wrong. At three in the morning, Loni was still waiting a half mile up the road from The Oasis. She hadn't picked up anybody, drunk or speeding. She knew bars could give drinkers until 2:30 a.m. to finish before they locked the door, and she waited long enough.

As Loni drove by the bar as its large garish sign went dark, leaving the adobe walls bathed in moonlight. Two cars were parked under the salt cedars. She drove on, aimlessly turning wherever the whim led her. Windows down, she enjoyed the dry wind blowing around her head. She smiled at Coco's flying fuzzy ears as she stuck her head out her window sniffing the air.

Behind a small pickup, Loni watched the driver throw a can to the side of the road while four boys riding in the back were beating on the rear window and yelling. She flashed her lights and followed for a mile until the pickup pulled over. Loni handed him a ticket for his illegal passengers in the bed of the pickup. "You go get your girl home now. And slow. I'm following you."

With a disgusted glare, he snatched the ticket from Loni's hand and spat at her, "You're gonna be sorry. My dad is best friends with Chief."

"How nice for your dad." Her sarcasm bounced over the driver's head as she herded the four teenage boys out of the bed of the pickup and shoved them into the back of her SUV.

"Honest to god." The smallest one giggled. "Nobody had more than one can of beer."

"Really?" Loni had a hard time keeping a straight face. "When did they come out with beer in gallon cans?"

Most of them were townies and she finally got them all delivered home, their giggles staying with her the rest of the long night.

The still, numbing dead heat combined with her exhaustion emptied Loni of any emotion. She had picked up only three speeders before she headed back out of Sandhills. The old sand planks left from an ancient road snaked in and out off to the left, sometimes slowly disappearing into the sand beside the empty highway. The rising sun glaring into her eyes painted the sand, turning it from silver to bleached white. She pushed against Coco to fumble with the lock on the cubbyhole and grabbed her sunglasses. Coco leaned back, shoving Loni up against the SUV door,

"Move, damn it!" Loni pushed back. "I'm mad at you anyway." Coco didn't budge. "Oh, shit, oh dear." Loni pushed on the dog, again "How much do you weigh!" she objected. "Oh, bite me! I'm talking to the dog again."

Loni pulled her long black braid over the front of her shoulder, Coco mouthed the thong immediately chewing on it. Tearing up, she remembered how Coco did the same thing with Maria's braid. Loni fought the memories, but the scene dug into her mind as frame after frame flicked into view. She held her partner as the blood drained out of her, begging her to hang on while the backup cop repeated over and over, "Sorry! So sorry! Sorry! I thought she was the perp! Sorry!" Shaking away the image Loni remembered how she had hated LA for some time. People lost their humanity in crowds. How did Bahb put it? "They so close together they sour each other."

Think about something else, Loni told herself. "Damn it, Coco, move!" Ignoring her, the dog continued to lean in, hanging on to Loni's braid. The sun bounced off the hood of the white SUV into her eyes, and the asphalt on the road in front of her shimmered with the rising sun, reflecting a water mirage disappearing as she reached it. In her mind, she saw Maria in front of her. "Damn it! Damn it! Damn it!" Loni finally screamed. Like the mirage, Maria always disappeared before she could reach her.

At the end of her shift. Loni drove into town around the collection of tired, unpainted buildings strung along a dry river bed. The town lay straight with the river, but it rested catawampus to the world, confusing some people because they didn't know what direction they were heading. Loni wondered if the iron in nose hairs really gave a sense of direction. She remembered her dad was so sensitive to his sense of direction he actually threw up when he lost it. She wondered if he had a lot of iron in his nose hair.

Loni circled the courthouse square, thinking about the Southern aristocrat who supposedly founded the town. According to stories, he was so homesick he designed the town exactly like a Southern town. The lopsided courthouse squatted splat in the middle of a town block and stood like a square peg pounded into a round hole.

During the last century, a city and state police department, a small courtroom and judge's chamber, a jail on the second story, and a half-basement for storage were added to the original building. Double doors led out both ends of the building. People went in the north entrance to the police department and into the south entrance for the courtroom and judge.

A huge dirt lot circled the courthouse and drifted down to the sidewalk. Some called it a lawn, but the only green Loni ever remembered seeing was bull-head stickers, ground-crawling plants surviving the Arizona drought. Willow trees leaned against the courthouse walls as if they needed the help to stand. The pale green leaves clung to the branches curled from the lack of water.

Massive branches from the eucalyptus trees lining the courthouse sidewalk reached across the street. Loni felt a little cooling as she drove under them. The branches were two feet in diameter and hung so low they forced tall loads to detour along the railroad.

Loni zigzagged around a dig blocking the sidewalk and part of the street, an attempt to patch the vintage World War II sewer system. She chuckled at the crunching noises made by the truck as it drove over scattered pieces of fragile Orangeburg sewer pipe made of creosote-soaked heavy felt-paper. The thought of the pipes' disintegrating made her reflect on what was feeding the trees.

Later than usual, Loni was more than ready to sign out and call it a day. She signaled Coco to follow her across the street and up the long concrete walk to the double-wide doors. Through the window, she saw a dark redheaded woman pop up behind the booking counter at the sound of the bell. Lola something or other, the dispatcher who followed Bobby's shift, Loni thought as she detected the click of the door's release.

Chief Redneck was standing in the door of his office as Loni walked up to the counter. "Well, girly!" His bloodshot eyes popped out at her, and a smirk spread over his red face. "Tully said you should fill out the report seeing as how you already investigated." He waddled up to her and stuck a blank form in her face. "Go find a desk in the bullpen." Chief grimaced as he rubbed his fat chest and belched. "You got yourself a case."

Loni sighed as she took the blank report. She watched Chief return to his office, his rolling gait reminding her of an old dray horse tired of living. His clothes never fit, and every time he stood, he had to resnap his Western shirt and tuck it back in his pants. His bolo tie, a fancy big turquoise piece, didn't fit with the black and white-striped suspenders holding up his Levis. Loni figured he wore battered brown leather slippers because he couldn't reach down to put on boots.

His bald head stuck out the doorway. "Another thing. I'm fed up with getting calls about somebody's beloved mother or great-aunt Lily's tombstone getting oblibertated. Fix it." He disappeared a few seconds before his head reappeared again. "And get that damn dog out of here."

The head disappeared once more. Wanting to giggle at his slaughter of obliterate Loni waited a few minutes to see if his head would pop out again. She read somewhere most people who bullied when they were young ended up either behind bars or a badge. Or a politician. Loni couldn't tell the difference anymore.

Loni turned back to the woman at the desk and reached out her hand. She was mesmerized by her clear emerald-green eyes. Guys around the station called her Chief's eye candy, but no one warned her about the eyes. Stumbling over her words, Loni finally blurted out, "We met a few weeks back when I was hired. I'm Loni Wagner, graveyard patrol."

Lola returned the hand shake with a firm grip, finally pulling out of Loni's hold. "I remember. If I can do anything to help you, let me know."

"You can. Could you let me know when something comes back on the plane evidence Tully turned in?"

"He didn't turn anything to me."

"Oh, shit, I really need to find out who shot at me."

"You think the shooter might try it again?"

"No reason he wouldn't. Depends on if he got what he wanted." Loni turned and pushed through the swinging half-gate into the bullpen, uncomfortable she had an audience. Hoping to avoid the usual aggravation, she dropped into the nearest empty chair facing away from the watchers. Coco slithered under the desk, hidden by its solid wood front, and was soon lightly snoring on Loni's feet.

Loni heard snickers behind her, especially from James. Bad enough she had to see him outside work, but the town law shared space with the state police, so she was stuck with him at work, too. They even shared the dispatcher and jail.

Chui Castro, James's partner in narcotic investigations, was making kissy-kiss sounds at her back between James's snickers, disturbing her concentration. Loni sputtered to herself, wondering if boys ever grew up?

Fed up, she whirled around to confront Chui. The small, swarthy Mexican had shiny black eyes matching his shiny black hair and a banty rooster attitude. As a detective often undercover, he could dress casually in a brown tee and Levis.

Chui pulled a gun from the hollow of his back and pointed it toward Loni, taking his time sliding the clip out and counting the bullets before shoving it back. Still smirking, he tugged a switchblade knife out of a boot and played with it, switching it open and closed, over and over as he stared back at Loni.

Refusing to play his game any longer, Loni ignored him as she read a poster above his head on his wall. A cold shiver passed through her.

Across the bull's eye in the center of the poster ran the words "IF YOU CAN READ THIS, YOU ARE NOW IN RANGE." Chui's shiny-wet black eyes were even colder than Loni remembered in high school. They reminded her of the dead eyes of the Gila monster. She wanted to forget her serious history with him when he tried to rape her in high school. He kissy-kissed her again, puffed up and flip her the bird. Disgusted, Loni turned away. She should have learned by now to always sit with her back against a wall.

The bull pen was surrounded by cheap forest-green dividers in a failed attempt to create privacy. Not a nice forest-green either, Loni decided. More like the color of a dying plant. She read somewhere green was supposed to be calming, but there was nothing worse than the ugly institutional vomit-green paint and the fluorescent lights hanging by chains from the ceiling. The faded ragged ribbon tied to the cooler vent in the ceiling barely fluttered, and the warm moisture in the stifling room turned everything into a wet, gloppy mess.

Loni avoided the report on her desk by perusing the wanted posters, yellowed with age. No longer able to put off filling out the form, she peeled the paper off her sweaty arm in a failed attempt to anchor the form. The ballpoint pen skipped and smeared on the damp paper. She knew Chief considered the case a slam dunk, but she couldn't leave until Tully got back after his lunch hour. Gossip made out he took long lunches. Was it something about a widow up Dusty Road? Or was that Chief?

Bored, Loni filled in what she could. Nobody would be able to read it, but then what did she care? Nobody would read it anyway. She used the form as a fan and rolled her chair through the swinging half-door to Lola's counter. "Can you tell me why Chief hates sniffers so much?"

Lola half giggled and leaned over closer to Loni. "He didn't used to, but the last police dog we had around here ate the stock on his shotgun, the driver's seat in his car, and the wires to his siren. The kiss of death for that dog was when he ate Chief's Ray bans."

Loni grinned in surprise.

"Oh my god, oh my god, oh my god." Lola leaned back, waving her arms, inciting her bracelets and keys on her arms to jingle like a Greek chorus. "I would DIE for your dimples."

"Tell you what. I'll trade them for your incredible eyes."

"Why would you ever want to trade away your dimples?"

"Because they have been the bane of my existence."

"Really?" Lola stared at Loni like she was crazy. "I have got to know why anyone would hate dimples. They were the single reason I married the most worthless man on earth." Lola rested her chin in her hand, waiting.

Loni took a chance. She glanced around and kept her voice low. "Have you noticed the way James treats me?"

Lola rubbed her arm in sympathy.

"Did you know James and I are cousins?"

"I heard."

"Growing up around here, most of my dad's family disowned me, except for Uncle Herm, his wife, Mae, and Daniel, my other cousin." Loni lowered her voice another notch. "But my Uncle Kirk's family insisted no way could I be related to them. James was the youngest and a year behind me in school." Loni poked at the dimples on her face. "Since none of them had dimples, they played the old milkman joke. They thought it was very funny." Lon leaned back in her chair. "Since I didn't know any milkmen, I had no idea what that meant." She gave Lola a wry grin. "What they really meant was they didn't want to be related to a half-breed Apache mix."

"See these green eyes. See this red in my hair?" Lola lifted it and let it sift through her fingers, the light bouncing off the red highlights. "I may be Mexican, but it wasn't a Mexican gave me these." She lifted her eyebrow, reading Loni's expression. "Wasn't henna either."

"Guess we're a couple of bitch curs, huh?"

"Nah. More like pinto kids."

"That's a new one. What does it mean?"

"That's what we Mex call a mix. Light and dark brown, like pinto beans."

The sound of the door buzzer jarred both of them, and Loni rolled back to her desk as Tully wandered in.

"Hey." Loni stopped Tully. "Chief told me to write up the report on your plane crash case. I need the evidence from the plane and your notes."

"What notes?"

"The plane yesterday morning." Loni pointed her pencil at Tully, holding up her report. "Did you bring the plane records?"

He crossed his arms over his fat stomach and silently stared at her.

"You know, the evidence?"

Tully shrugged. "Wasn't useful to me so I left it."

"You didn't work the case at all?"

"Here." He put a single sheet of paper on her desk.

"And?"

"A drawing of the plane." He pushed it toward Loni. "Want to see it?"

"Not really. I have photos. Did you search for any more evidence under the plane after it was removed? Measure its fall?"

"Why?"

"Because the report requires it. The family may need it for insurance. We may need it if a crime is involved."

"What crime?"

"I don't know, Tully. That's why I need your report."

"I didn't do it."

"Why not?" Loni decided talking to Coco was more productive.

"I don't do numbers is why not."

"What do you mean?"

Tully slid his drawing into a drawer. "Everybody knows five plus five is ten. Always was and always will be. Nothing new to learn there so don't need to mess with it."

"Does that go for car accidents, too?"

"Why not? Easy to see who's at fault. Waste of time."

"Well, damn!" Loni leaned back. "You're fun to work with."

"What?"

"Nothing." Loni turned back to the desk.

"My drawings are good enough for the boss." He snorted behind her back. "Bitch!"

Funny, Loni thought, it sounded different when I called myself that. Maybe I could just shoot him. She collected her paperwork and ordered Coco out from under the desk. Signing out with Lola, she took out her cell phone on her way out the front door and called her cousin. "What's happening to the plane, Daniel?"

"I'm working on it now."

"Somebody really interested in the plane broke into the hangar and shot at me last night. Can you keep an eye out for anything unusual?"

"Oh, shit! Are you okay?"

"Yes. I think it was a warning shot."

"Well okay then." His sarcasm warmed her. "Why don't you hang up now so I can get back to it?"

Loni snorted. "What a good little cousin you are." She flipped her phone shut and reached for the door handle of her truck. "Aww, shit!" she sputtered as her hand burned on the hot metal. She pulled the bloody kerchief from her back pocket and wrapped it around her hand before she tried to open the door a second time. Following Coco in, she started the engine and rolled down the windows. It must have been at least a hundred-sixty degrees inside. A ziplock bag with aloe vera was in the cubby hole, and she squeezed some on her blistered skin. She drove one-handed to the airport, cussing, glad Shiichoo couldn't hear her.

🌵

Back in the hangar, Loni found her cousin already deep into the plane engine. "Any luck?" She held the lid to the water jug for Coco to get a drink. "Ah, hell." She poured water on Coco's head and back before she turned the jug on herself. She was dripping water onto the floor when Daniel got her attention.

His worried voice reached her. "Far as I can figure, the fuel tank selector valve didn't work."

"And?" Loni gave him her full attention.

"Didn't switch to the second tank."

"So he ran out of gas?"

"Yep."

"That's what Rosa insisted," Loni mused as she walked up and leaned into the plane with Daniel. "But his second tank was full, remember? Do you know why the valve failed?" She couldn't identify the object in Daniel hand. "What is that thing?"

"It's a valve. You know. One of those things opens and closes? But that's not the interesting part. Look." Daniel showed her one end of the valve. Hardened epoxy clogged the opening.

"Oh my god!" Loni took the valve, holding it in her hand. "Oh my god! This is murder!"

"That'd be my guess."

Stunned, she inspected the engine where the open ends of the bent and battered gas lines dangled. "This must be what the thief was after. He was banging on the gas lines, trying to break the valve off."

"Pretty stupid, all around." Daniel pointed to the epoxy. "Left a thumb print."

Loni smiled broadly. "Or he was in a hurry." Suddenly she focused on a dark streak above the dangling lines. "Daniel, did you cut yourself on this engine?"

"No. See?" He showed her his knuckles.

Loni was staring at the blood when Daniel's voice finally got through to her.

"What's wrong with your dog?"

Dazed, Loni walked to the tail of the plane where Coco was frantically scratching at a small door. She rubbed the dog's head to quiet her. "What's here?"

"Storage."

Loni pulled the door open and found a dark blue gym bag. Coco went ballistic.

"She smells drugs. From her reaction, my guess is cocaine."

"Wow! I've never seen a dog do that before."

"Anybody else fly this plane?"

"Not that I know of." He was watching Coco. "How long did it take you to teach her?"

"I didn't. She belonged to my partner."

"She the one got killed?"

Loni dodged the question. "Can you find out where he went this trip?"

"I think so." Daniel walked into the office. He searched the computer and told Loni what he found. "He went to San Diego. Scheduled to return later this morning at 9:00 am. He was early."

"Reason lights weren't on, huh?" Coco kept whining and whipping around in circles. "Coco, sit. Enough." Loni ordered before she turned back to Daniel. "Hell, do me a favor and don't let anyone near this plane." She stared at the valve in her hand. "I need to take this." She put it in an evidence bag and rubbed the dark spot on the engine with a Q-Tip. It appeared to be blood.

"Be a bad day when you report it." Daniel nervously rubbed at his stubble. "This doesn't happen here."

Loni waited.

"James isn't going to like this."

"What's he got to do with it?"

"Nothing I can say for sure." Daniel refused to meet Loni's eyes.

"What do you know?"

"Not really anything. Only something he said."

"Maybe he's upset because I'm back."

Daniel studied her. "You do know not everything's all about you, right?" He grinned, taking the sting out. "Anyway, it began before you came home. Something's bothering him." He walked away. "Watch your back." After a few more steps he turned back. "And take care of James. You hear me?" He turned away again.

"Cousin!" Loni called to his retreating back. "Don't mention the valve to anyone."

Daniel kept walking. Flipping a back wave, he climbed in his flat-bed service truck and disappeared around a corner.

Loni opened the gym bag and stared down at bundles of money. Did the valve and money have anything to do with each other? she wondered. Digging around she pulled out a bag of white powder. "Coco, you're right again." She shoved the money, drugs and valve with the copies of Rene's notebook and phone numbers into Uncle Herm's safe.

Loni walked up to the plane and poked around. Rene or someone else had taken out the back seats of the plane to haul something. Leaves, plastic bits, and hair littered the carpet. Loni wondered why someone was transporting plants. She swept up the debris into a bag to send it to the state lab.

Loni sealed off the plane as carefully as possible before she drove to her grandparents' ranch. At the entrance was an old barbed-wire gate wired between tall weather-beaten posts, bleached and rotted. A rust-streaked sign showed the faded, barely readable letters "Wagner Ranch." She opened the gate, drove through, and closed it, cursing the billions of times she had to climb in and out of her truck for a damn gate. Once again, she swore she was going to put in a cattle guard.

As Loni wound around a black hill, she got the same warm feeling she always got at the first sight of the ranch house tucked up inside a crescent-shaped volcanic black hill. She was torn between not wanting to live at home any more but not feeling safe anywhere else.

At the main gate of the ranch, Loni could see the faded and broken boards with missing screens on the dirty windows of the outbuildings scattering the landscape. One was a sandwich house Bahb said was built in the early 1900s. She remembered wishing it had been a hogan, but, even though he was Navajo, her granddad grew up mostly in the O'odham Nation.

Loni drove the last quarter of a mile through pasture land, a homestead belonging to her great-grandfather on her father's side. Old salt cedars and eucalyptus trees raised above her as she neared the circular drive in front of the main house. The reddish-tan adobe house was built Spanish ranchero style with a walled court around the front and kitchen side of the house. On the other side, a screened-in porch filled with bunk beds where she slept many nights begging for a breeze in the heat of the summer. More salt cedars sheltered the porch in a fluffy line of dark-green needles. The giant salt cedars surrounding the house created a small oasis.

Two small boys playing dump truck with empty nail boxes in the silky soft dirt below a salt cedar tree, jumped up to pet Coco. She gave each one a lick with her long tongue before she ran to the screen door. Pima, Loni decided as she noted characteristics. Their teeth were lightly layered with brown from the high fluoride content in the lower Gila River Valley.

A cool blast of air from the water cooler vent in the ceiling hit Loni when she opened the screeching screen door and walked into the cool, dark interior of the large living room. A stone fireplace filled one wall, and straight ahead were two doors leading to bedrooms. To Loni's right was the double-wide archway leading into the dining room. Indian rugs covered the wood floor.

In his recliner under the cooler vent, Bahb sat, reading *The Cattleman* magazine. The thin brass lamp with swirling, brightly colored stained glass feathers highlighted his face. "When did you learn to read, Bahb," Loni teased him.

"Learn teaching you." Bahb's mouth quirked toward a smile.

"Where's Shiichoo?"

"Kitchen." He went back to his magazine.

The heat almost knocked her over when she pushed open the swinging door into the kitchen. "Holy s —" Loni gulped the rest of the word at her grandmother's disapproving scowl. "Shut down the stove before we die in here."

A huge black cooking woodstove stood out from a plastered wall worn through in spots to the adobe bricks. Wooden countertops, grayed from years of cleaning, ran under the open dirty-gray cabinets the same color as the walls behind them. Double windows silhouetted Shiichoo, Apache ramrod straight, in front of the corner sink. Dim lights on a large hanging wagon-wheel fixture flickered like candles. Faded peeling red-and-white-checked linoleum on the floor showed black patches in a path from the sink to the stove and to the back door.

A snow-white braid crowned Loni's grandma's head as sweat poured down her face, darkening the pale blue of her blouse. Gaunt and rope-thin, she fanned herself with the hem of her faded, rainbow-striped apron Loni made in her sophomore home economics class.

"Funny," Shiichoo retorted. "Bring in some wood."

"I thought we agreed you would cook outside."

"Maybe in your imagination. Just as hot out there as it is in here."

"Then don't cook."

"Don't smart-mouth me." Shiichoo glared at her. "I can still whip you."

Loni picked up her grandma and carried her fussing, into the living room, deposited her in her easy chair next to Bahb. Determined to keep her grandma in the chair, Loni got up in her face. "The heat will make you sicker. Dinezaa! Dinezaa! Too hot!" She scolded her granddad. "Can't you keep her out of the kitchen?"

"I'll watch see how you do it." Bahb ducked his head to hide his small grin.

"So what if it's hot?" Her grandma struggled to get out of the chair. "I'm used to it, child."

Loni gently held her down. "You won't have to put up with it after your electric stove gets here."

"What electric stove?"

"The one coming Thursday with a new refrigerator and dishwasher. I wanted them sooner, but I keep forgetting this town doesn't have daily deliveries." Loni babbled. "The electrician's coming next Tuesday. He had to go to Four Corners this week to get his mother."

"Humph! Don't know why anyone would want that mother-in-law there while she's having a baby. She only have to take care of her, too."

Loni laughed. Shiichoo knew everything happening to her neighbors.

Bahb peered into space. "Don't remember any mother-in-law. I think you drink from Hassyampa."

"What does that mean?"

"Come from O'odham maybe. Mean 'Drink its water and never tell truth again.'"

Shiichoo ignored Bahb and kept staring at Loni. Willie quietly ambled in and softly sat on the couch across from Bahb. As tall as Loni's five foot seven, he appeared much smaller as he sank into the broken springs. She was surprised the couch hadn't fallen apart. From the patches of cloth on the once-yellow couch, it wouldn't be long now. But then, she said that twenty years ago.

Facing Shiichoo again, Loni sputtered, "But—but—we've had electricity for—what? A hundred years now? You don't have to live like the Jessups."

"I never!" Shiichoo sputtered back. "I don't have dirt floors."

Solemnly Bahb said, "I miss eggshells behind stove."

"I never!" Shiichoo glared at him.

"One thing," Willie said. "Shiichoo don't hide behind house when anyone come. I saw Miz Jessup do that."

"Isn't she the one who found a couple of rustlers branding her cows?" Loni vaguely remembered something about it.

"Yi," Bahb answered. "Jessups never brand cows. Like us. She knew ever' one. She held rifle on them and said 'Take the runnin' iron and change that to my bran'.' When done, she thank them and took the cows home."

Willie sniggered. "She tell them they did good job."

Shiichoo snorted. "Glass-top?"

Loni relaxed. "Yes, ma'am." She waited a few beats. "And I ordered refrigeration, too. Oh. And a new hot water heater."

All three of them stared at her.

"That all?" Shiichoo finally asked.

"No. I ordered windows, too."

"That all?"

"For now." Loni kept her head ducked.

"Who's paying for all this?"

"I am."

"You rob a bank?"

"Nope. Service station at Salome," Loni shot back. "That's what Sissy Newmire did, right? Got a nice farm out of it, too."

"It was a service station in Phoenix, and she married the farm," Shiichoo snapped back at her.

"Well," Loni retorted. "Never did like her husband, anyway." She fled the room through the kitchen door. Then she poked her head back in. "I had some money saved." And she fled once again.

Through the flapping door she heard Shiichoo say, "Tell me you did not buy a set of encyclopedias!"

Loni stuck her head back in one last time. "Don't forget we're painting the kitchen tomorrow. Don't light the stove."

"I'll think on it."

Loni finished filling the bowls with food from the stove and placed them on the table, hollering through the door, "Soups on." She disappeared out the back door with a handful of tamales from the refrigerator. Driving away with a big smile on her face, Loni chortled on getting in the last word. For now.

FROM: Loni Wagner
TO: Sandi@gmailyahoo.com
DATE: July 2
SUBJECT: Still here

I managed to visit my grandparents. You asked what kind of names Bahb and Shiichoo are. Bahb is Papago for grandfather on my mother's side. Well. He's also got some Navajo from his dad's side and mixes both cultures in strange ways. I would call him Bahb anyway because his Papago part speaks both Spanish and the O'odham language. He also knows the Athabaskan language because Navajos and Apaches both spoke it, but I could never learn Athabaskan beyond a few words he taught me.

Everybody calls him Bob. That's fine with him because the Navajo part of him doesn't like anyone knowing his real name. According to Bahb, the less someone says your real name, the less they can harm you. He could be right, but it makes for a short list of friends.

Shiichoo is grandmother in Apache. Shiichoo doesn't remember much of her Apache life. She was taken to the

Indian boarding school when she was only five, but she had a few fond memories of her own Shiichoo, so she wanted me to call her that. Some sort of spiritual connection to her past.

It was good seeing them today even though I upset Shiichoo. I told her about ordering the electric stove yesterday. And the refrigeration, hot water tank, and dishwasher. And the windows. And a new evaporative cooler. The old one has a wheezing fan, rusted pan, and badly in need of new pads. Time for it to go.

Wait until she hears about the rest, especially the bug man to spray the scorpions. Every time I see one I shake inside. God, do they hurt! It wouldn't be so bad if they didn't crawl everywhere, up bed legs, across the ceiling, into shoes. At least they can't crawl up the glass quart jars my bed sits in. As long as the bedding stays tucked . . . off the floor . . . I'm scaring myself again so I'll say goodnight.

Oh, before I forget. I talked with a really nice woman today at work. She's my day dispatcher. She's Mexican with Irish somewhere. Incredible green eyes and amazing dark red hair. She's sort of nice in a sizzling, over-dressed way—but not cheap. I'm betting that she dresses that way to get what she wants from the redneck assholes around here, and, of course, it works. I think she might be good friend. God knows I could use one.

Give the girls a hug for me.

Loni

Loni checked around her bed for scorpions and tucked her bedding in a little further before she slid in between the cool sheets. Six whole hours before she had to go back to work. She hoped the motorcyclist didn't come back tonight. She was too tired to get out of bed and do anything about it.

CHAPTER THREE

Rumdum, Loni thought as she dragged herself into the station to turn in the evidence she'd stored in Uncle Herm's big office safe. She spent the afternoon, tossing and turning in the warm sticky air dreaming about Maria's death. The best part of Loni was ripped out of her when she watched Maria's blood run down the gutter. The freezing cold settled in her chest that night never left.

Loni cringed at the clomp of her leather-soled boots on the hardwood floor when she walked up to the counter. She kept forgetting to replace the leather with rubber. She dropped the box on the counter as she studied the chubby booking clerk who worked the shift before Bobby. Scribbling away in some book, he ignored her. His name tag read 'Harris.'

Annoyed, Loni opened the door behind him marked 'Property' and dropped in a chair just inside the door. "Down, Coco." Loni stared at rows of shelves holding folder-sized boxes and waited to see if he would follow her. She leaned her head back against the wall and closed her eyes against the glare of the bank of hanging florescent lights.

Several minutes later, Harris stuck his head in the door. "Need this inventoried?"

"Yep."

"Now?"

"Yep."

Harris took a while to carry the box into the property room and set it on a table next to Loni.

"That dog bite?"

"Only if you piss her off." Loni tried not to smile. "Harris? Your first or last name?" She already knew the answer.

"Both." He skirted the dog. "My mom loved redundancy." His round face flamed red with embarrassment as he opened the box. "Need a receipt?"

"Yes." Loni never opened her eyes as she continued to set back, relaxed. "There's a phone and notebook I took off Rene, a shitload of money I didn't count, a blood sample, and drug samples from Rene's plane as well as other debris from the scene. And a valve from the plane. The bullet is from a wall where someone shot at me. Get a request to the state lab to analyze the DNA on the blood sample. I think it's from the person who shot at me. Add lifting a print off the epoxy in the valve. That should be from the person who murdered Rene. Did you get all that?"

Harris's round brown eyes widened at her monotone speech as he picked up the plastic bags with the valve and bullet, rolling them around as he studied the pieces. "Think the valve and bullet are from the same guy?"

Loni shrugged, opening her eyes. "Don't know, but it's very likely."

Harris opened the bag with the money and dropped it like a hot branding iron. He picked it up again and dumped the money out of the bag.

Loni broke the silence, closing her eyes again. "You also need to put a trace on the money so wear gloves when you count it. Add dusting for fingerprints. And identify the plants, and maybe add analyzing the soil. See if the names and numbers in the notebook lead anywhere. Maybe trace the phone calls. And see if they can find a bullet match."

"That all?"

"For now."

"I gotta count it before I give you a receipt." He reached for a banded batch and warned, "You have to watch me. With both eyes." Harris turned red again.

"Fine." Loni settled again in the rickety wooden chair and kept her eyes closed as she listened to his monotone voice counting the money. A half-hour later, Harris handed her the receipt for the evidence and the form to sign for the lab request. "Have a safe night." He blushed again.

Wondering at Harris's severe shyness, Loni pocketed the receipt and walked back to the front of the desk. The wood was cool under her hand as she ran it along the eight-foot length. The nicks and chips dug into the dark surface showed years of use and misuse. One long groove through the center shaped for bullet bore. Loni followed its trajectory to a small hold in one of the filing cabinets behind the long counter.

Bobby appeared, signing her in. Fingering the indentation, she said, "That what I think it is?"

Bobby's slow drawl slowed down even more until he finally explained, "Husband got arrested and his wife followed him in. She had his gun and slammed it down on the counter. It went off and scared the crap outta all of us. Wizzed right below my . . . good thing she only shot the filing cabinet." He snorted. "She wished she had shot him by the time she bailed him out." Bobby finally said, "No extra assignments this morning for you. Bet you're glad about that."

"I will be if you keep it that way the rest of the night."

"Don't count on it!"

Coco kept shoving in front of Loni when she unlocked the door to the SUV. The dog was so excited she scraped her leg on the opening door as she jumped into the passenger seat. Loni started the engine as the dog bounced on the seat, panting in Loni's ear.

They weren't on patrol long before the radio crackled. "Crap!" Loni ended the call with Bobby. Another bar fight. She didn't know which she hated more, domestics or bar fights. Or maybe coyotes. Loni decided Coyotes as she made a U-turn and sped across the desert toward the Oasis bar. She saw the monstrous red and green neon sign from miles away. The land was flat between her and the bar, unusually bare of black dormant volcano hills or tree-lined washes.

Surrounded on three sides by giant salt cedars, the old adobe bar was once part of a string of stagecoach stops. A century ago, they were turned into auto shops marking Old Highway 85 crossing the Arizona desert. Dirt ruts kept cars from going more than fifty miles in a night, and the road was too hot and too dangerous to travel during the day. Long gone were the shacks behind the bar where travelers sheltered from the heat. Also disappeared were service stations and small grocery stores where prospectors and traveling Pimas traded for supplies and locals met to settle world issues.

At the bar, most of the cars were parked in a row across the front, but a few huddled under long branches of the trees in the back. Owners backed the vehicles in until bumpers hit the tree trunks in an effort to keep them out of the sun and cool. Loni could identify repeat visitors by the splotches of paint eaten off by the erosive acid in the salt-dripping trees. She glanced around for any cars or pickups she might recognize. Those tree-bumpers could be mean drunks.

Even after 1:30 a.m., the temperature was still over ninety degrees. Loni slipped around each car and watched for moving shadows in the soft glow of the moon. Finding nothing, she tried to peer in one of the windows of the bar, but it was covered.

Loni kept her hand on her gun butt as she cautiously pulled open the thick wood door. She quickly stepped inside and to the left, crab-walking against the wall. All appeared quiet, even orderly, with no broken or scattered chairs and no overturned tables. She didn't hear any groans or crying.

Six cowboys with their hats on sat at one end of the long bar closest to her. Four couples perched around tall tables dotting the edges of a small dance floor. Large hanging oval fixtures reflected pools of light on the green felt of the three pool tables along the back wall and gave a greenish tinge to the faces of the two couples playing at the center table.

At the bar, two of the cowboys snickered and pushed at each other as they watched her crabwalk along the wall. Loni moved toward them but kept her back to the wall as she glanced around the room again. Old movie posters taped on the windows blocked any outside looky-loo's. Loni dropped her hand from her gun and walked up to the barkeep. "You call for help?"

"Nope." He kept drying glasses.

Out of the corner of her eye, Loni saw Chui come out of the bathroom, smirking. She waited for him. "Did you call in?"

Chui shrugged and climbed on a bar stool in front of her.

Loni decided to leave as a drunk cowboy got off his stool. Chui put a foot out and tripped the drunk, sending him sprawling in front of her. The drunk struggled up off the floor, ready to swing. Chui wore an evil grin. "What'd you want to do that for?"

"Whoa." She apologized to the drunk, who was staggering toward her. "Sorry." The drunk staggered back to his stool and muttered unintelligibly. Loni followed the unhappy cowboy back to his bar stool and relieved him of his keys. She tossed them to the barkeep and attempted to shame Chui. "Too chicken shit to handle it?"

Chui smirked. "Don'tcha know, shit runs downhill and dykes with it." He turned away from her.

Wishing she could just shoot him, she walked out the door.

The rest of the shift was uneventful. She signed out and was on her way to her grandparents' house before Chief got to work and found something else to get mad about.

Loni parked beside the tired barn squatting behind the house. Its plank siding faded rock-hard gray from drying in the incessant heat. Beside the barn, four square shacks squatted beneath a row of eucalyptus trees. Each one had a screened-in porch and a rusty evaporative cooler along with rusted galvanized tin roofs that thrummed with a loud drumbeat during the rare rains.

She left her truck under a salt-dripping salt cedar and stopped to pet Jack. Bahb's old dog was curled up in a hole he dug under tree. Jack was her dog until he was three and she had to go to college. The border collie was once a great heeling cowdog. Loni remembered him racing around the heels of kicking cattle like a fish dodging rocks in a fast-moving stream, never getting caught by the deadly hooves. Those days were gone.

Coco raced circles around him, trying to play. "Cool it, Coco." she warned. "His play days are over." She ran her hands down Jack's sides and along his shaky legs, feeling for hot spots and ticks. "What a good old boy you are." He was relegated to alarm dog and gave out a single woof at Coco to prove he could do his job. With a couple of final rubs on his head, she herded Coco out to the barn. "Stay," Loni told her.

Loni filled three gunny sacks, each cut into a feeding halter, with rolled oats and walked out of the barn. She spotted the horses at the far end of the large corral where it widened out from the barn. The grassy field was surrounded by a barbed wire fence. At a long cement water trough under the windmill, she buried her head in the water and stood up again, shaking herself like a wet dog. The cooling water felt good as it ran down her back and between her breasts.

At the gate into the corral, she took in the once familiar scene. Everything seemed much smaller than she remembered. Two determined mesquite trees at the south end of the corral stood their ground. Their limbs were bent out of shape and stripped of life from years of horse teeth gnawing on them for salt. Small sparse lacy leaves barely fluttered in the slow hot breeze, and even fewer yellow, pea-like bean pods hung from their tops, waiting for a good wind.

Loni was always surprised desert-raised horses preferred the mesquite bean to grain. She knew from experience the beans were bubble-gum chewy without the sticky satisfaction. The only thing worse than its sickly sweet taste was Shiichoo's cactus candy.

Two horses in the pasture stomped and swished their tails against the flies as the hot sun beat down on their backs. Roani was the closest to her. He wasn't the biggest of horses or even close to beautiful, but he had a powerful essence. His big bumpy head sat on a short squat neck, and his knees were so knobby they appeared deformed on his small legs. His rear end, though, was all quarter horse. Heavily muscled legs bowed out on both sides of his hocks all the way down to the knees like an old tired cowboy, but his body flowed with amazing dance steps when he cut cattle.

The other horse, Paint, was Willie's best friend as long as Loni could remember. The beautiful paint was a small desert broom-tail Indian pony with large brown spots over white. The black, flowing mane and arched neck and tail reflected his Arabian ancestors brought in to improve the desert broomtail.

Loni whistled and held the sacks in front of her. She whooped at the two heads jerking up, four ears twitching in unison. It had been such a long time they took a minute to remember before they came trotting, small clumps of dust puffing around their hooves on the well-worn trail through the grass. She stood in the shade of the barn overhang, taking pleasure in the sight of them.

She opened the gate and walked into the corral, hurrying toward the shadow of the lean-to where Stonewall, their old pale-yellow Brahma bull, stood waiting. Both horses followed behind her and pushed their noses under her arms to get to the grain sacks. Loni giggled again as she ducked under their necks to keep from being squashed between them while they vied for the grain sacks.

Maneuvering around the horses, Loni reached Stonewall, watching the gentle bull stomp a huge hoof and flick his lion tail over his back as he bobbed his huge head up and down. She smiled as she recalled her uncle's description of Stonewall's huge ears big enough to eat off. "Looks like a VW bug with both doors wide open."

Roani was always fed first. Loni pulled the sack up around his nose and hung the halter behind his ears before she felt for hot spots on his legs. Roani was a joy to ride. When he worked, he didn't tolerate any interference. He knew what needed to be done before the rider did, and he loved doing it. A favorite tactic was bringing up the rear so he could rush up and bite a cow on the butt if it didn't stay in line. He could spin on a dime and never quit, famous along the Colorado River for running cattle in the brush.

Thieves would sometimes steal Roani for days at a time and return him, so beat up and crippled he could barely walk for weeks. He was eighteen now, too old to work hard again, but he still wanted to go.

Loni pulled on Paint's black mane, leading him away from Roani to get some space. She slid the strap over his ears and studied his teeth. Rubbing his tiny ears, she tried to figure out his age by counting the lines around his eyes. "Bet you're twenty by now, huh old friend? I count twenty lines. Maybe twenty-one." Paint wiggled his ears to listen. "Then again, maybe not." His sweet face reminded her of a trusting puppy.

The original Arabians were too small to work cattle and became a worthless experiment like the camels whose soft hoofs couldn't walk on the hard, sharp rocks and cactus covering the desert floor. Bahb told her about seeing the last camel when he was a child, sometime during the late thirties. That camel spent his last days on the sand banks of the Hassampa River.

Loni turned to Stonewall, patiently waiting. He gently stuck his massive head forward, pushing his nose into the sack. Eyes half-closed, he chewed, a happy boy. Everyone on the ranch learned to ride on him. When anyone slipped, he would stop until they regained their balance or fell off. His huge hump made a natural saddle. She was always sorry he couldn't sire calves. But Bahb never cared. "He come, he stay. This always his home."

Loni gazed around, amazed Stonewall's old shed was still standing. Four forked mesquite branches stuck in the ground held other limbs shaping the roof. The bull's back was patterned from the sun shining through the hundreds of holes in the rust-eaten tin sheets nailed onto the posts. Stonewall could push the shed over if he ever decided to lean on it. Loni hoped he never wanted to scratch his butt on one of the posts.

When they all finished chewing, Loni pulled the sacks off their heads and returned to the barn to hang the empty gunny sacks on the nails. She stared up at the well pulley above her. Maria paid twenty-five dollars for it on one of their trips home. They had taken a side trip to the Verde River up on the Apache Indian Reservation at Fort McDowell. Maria spotted the wheel over a long abandoned well next to a sandwich house. She made Loni stop while she knocked on the door and asked the price.

The twenty-five dollars didn't include taking the wheel off the wood frame and hanging over a deep hole didn't excite Loni one bit. Lucky for her, the ancient wood frame was so old and rotted she was able to yank it off the frame along with the board.

Loni remembered how successful she felt at pleasing Maria until twenty minutes later she got stuck in the river sand and had to find a couple of her Apache brothers to pull her out. Maria never let her forget about that day. Whenever Maria wanted to drive, she reminded Loni of every mistake she ever made, especially the two men pulling her battered truck out of the sand. Loni would give anything to have Maria back, even if she did point her finger in Loni's chest and recite her litany of Loni's mistakes in order to get her way. She was willing to make a million mistakes if it would bring her back.

Loni sighed and signaled Coco to follow. She stuck her head into Willie's bunkroom. "Time to paint."

Willie stood and grinned at her. "Bahb get brush, too?"

"Of course!"

"I paint other side of room then."

"Me, too." They shook hands as co-conspirators and walked back to the house arm-in-arm. Willie was her best friend all her life. Rock-hard wiry, he could hold down a large cow. He came and went around the ranch and across the desert like a ghost. Loni never knew where he was. He just appeared. When he rode Paint through a herd of deer, few would shy away or even lift their heads to watch him.

"I swear, Bahb, I already cleared that gully," she told her granddad when she went out to help them a couple of weeks earlier. "He came out right behind me with a cow. How does he do that?"

Bahb snorted. "Hope you're better at cops and robbers."

"Nah," Loni snorted back. "I always preferred cowboys and Indians. I'm the cowboy."

"Like I said."

After a cold lunch, Loni cleaned the kitchen. Against her grandma's great protest, the wood stove was left unfed since yesterday.

"What wrong with gray? It go with everything." Willie stood in the doorway.

"Those walls are gray from age and soot." Loni was determined. "I want to see sunshine in here."

"Leave door open. I wash windows." Willie dropped paint brushes and tape on the floor in a corner and went out again, mumbling about too much sun already.

"How'd you get those two to help you, Shiichoo?" Loni whispered in her ear.

"Easy," she whispered back. "If you want either of them to do anything, tell them they're too old for it."

Loni helped her grandma pull everything off the counters and out of the cabinets and onto the table and floor. "Lordy, Shiichoo. You have enough cooking stuff for five families." Loni picked up a cut-glass bowl. "You know? I've been looking at this thing all my life and I still don't know what it is."

Swatting Loni with a dish towel, her grandmother took the glass bowl out of her hand. "It's a finger bowl."

"Have I ever seen you use a finger bowl?"

"Have I ever used a finger bowl? Let me think on it." Shiichoo made fun of her as she carefully placed the bowl on the table. "I keep it because it's your history."

Bahb walked in pushing on Coco who was attempting to led Bahb. "That dog have better memory than you. How many times you told? Things from your father side."

"Did I know that?" Loni felt confused.

"Only told you thousand times."

"Where was I when you told me?" Loni took a huge plate from a tall stack. Shiichoo took the plate back from her and returned it to the stack. Bahb picked the stack up and carried it to the table.

"What are those, anyway?" Loni vaguely remembered the dishes but hadn't seen any of them used.

"Chargers," Shiichoo answered.

"What do they charge?"

"If you don't get busy," Bahb warned her, "They charge you."

"Well?"

"Your great-grandmother," Bahb explained. "She from back East where they had big dinners. Your dad remember from when little. Set other dishes on this one at time. Your dad hated how long it took to eat."

Loni gawked at all the dishes. "You kept these for me?"

"Didn't keep them for me."

"Do you have anything from your family?"

"Can't think on it, but no."

"Yes, you do." Bahb watched Willie carry in a tarp and two gallons of paint.

"What?" Shiichoo asked.

"Your mother's rug sticks."

Nostalgia shined on Shiichoo's gentle face as she pulled out the last of the glass dishes and covered everything on the table with a plastic red-checkered cloth that had seen better days. "I forgot those. I can see myself sitting at her feet to keep the wool from tangling." Shiichoo took one end of the tarp and helped Bahb cover the floor. Quietly she concluded, "Never got to stay around learning to use them."

"Is it really true you never saw your family again after you were taken to the boarding school?" Loni spread newspapers on the counter. "If everyone was gone when you got old enough to try and find them, how did you find the sticks?"

Bahb poured pale yellow paint in a small can. "Not ever'one. Remember your aunt Gate? We visited her before we went south to work."

Shiichoo's dark eyes gazed into space. "Of course. She gave me the sticks. Good heavens. That was over fifty years ago. I still remember her tiny house. Sort of half sandwich and adobe."

"I remember, too. It on edge of deep arroyo. Scary."

Shiichoo turned to Loni. "In the high country they threw trash over the banks so they built close to an edge. I think I like that better than the desert trash mounds"

Bahb barely smiled as he eyes twinkled. "What I remember are the chickens sticking their heads up through the holes in her kitchen floor."

"I remember." Shiichoo fussed at Bahb. "She really got mad at you and told us to leave. She accused you of stomping their heads."

"I no kick. I tol' you. I tryin' to feed them her—what that bitter stuff?"

"Acorn bread, I think. She didn't leach it very well. I don't remember you feeding those chickens."

"Well, had to. They kept pecking my toes!"

Willie nearly fell off his ladder in spasmic laughter. Fortunately, Loni was sitting down painting baseboards when she fell over in a fit of giggles.

"She not so bad. I remember she give you rug sticks when we leave." Bahb moved close to paint above Loni. "Bet old coot felt guilty she keep them."

"I remember those sticks now." Loni dodged Bahb's splatters, swatting at him as he grinned down at her. "They're in your closet. You never let me play with them."

"It was all I had from my childhood home. I wish we had culture to pass on to you like your gringo grandparents."

"Gringo? Never known you to badmouth them before." Loni stood and gave Shiichoo a big hug while she fought her tears. "You gave me a home, the best home anyone could have. Nothing else matters." She picked up her brush again before the tears flowed. "Why don't we find a way to display the sticks?"

Pleased, Shiichoo finished covering the counters.

"Shiichoo. What was my mother like?" All anyone told her about her mother was that she was sweet and pretty. And died giving birth to her.

"She not like you were." Bahb teased her. "She easy to raise."

"I don't remember being hard to raise." Loni got another one of her grandma's famous skinny looks and changed the subject. "Bahb? You got anything left from your past?"

"No. They take everting at Indian school. Never got anything back."

"You never told me about the school. How old were you?"

"I a teen before school. Don't know how old. Don't know when born."

"You never talk about it. Would you tell me now?"

"I never forget. Like yesterday. Big fence with barbed wire across top. When drug out of bus they shoved me over to where other boys sit on ground crying in hot sun. Shaved heads and overalls." Bahb turned away. "So scared they wet bed at night. Army wool blankets so scratchy it hurt. So hot." Bahb was quiet a minute. "Little ones, they suffer so. No one care."

Loni never knew Bahb to express so much at one time. She stayed silent as Shiichoo joined in.

"I remember when I came. I was only five. I must have cried for months." She smiled at Bahb. "At least my hair grew back long again by the time you got there."

"How'd they catch you, Bahb?"

"My pop he die in house fire. Drunk. I stay in brush, hunting." Bahb climbed up a ladder and rolled paint on the walls as Loni finished the baseboards. "Still be out there but Ma take sick. Nurse turn me in." He climbed down and searched for missed spots. "Heard later Ma die."

Shiichoo walked over and kissed Bahb on the cheek. "The day you showed up was the best day of my life." Bahb hugged her in return.

"Good thing she there, too," Bahb said to Loni. "Hardest thing, no food unless learn English. Shiichoo would save me food."

"What food did you like?" Loni searched for happier memories.

"I liked the white bread in fresh milk with a little sugar." Shiichoo smiled. "Only time we got sugar. I used to tear off the crust and put it in the milk and hide the center. Then I put the center in book to dry flat and pretend it was Indian bread from home." She grinned. "Sometimes it took the print off the pages. I often wondered what the next person thought who got the book."

"Not matter." Bahb patted her back. "Most of us not read anyway."

"True," Shiichoo answered. "And even those of us who could, played dumb. It would get them so frustrated, but they would get tired of beating us and leave us alone."

"I remember this one teacher. Big man with bad temper and wet evil eyes. He break boy's arm when he not move fast enough."

"I remember. He was a sweet boy from my tribe. He was never the same."

Loni studied Willie, admiring the way his black head contrasted with the pale yellow of the paint. "You missed a spot," Loni teased him.

"Only spot I miss is your face." Willie reached down and painted a swath across Loni's forehead before he dabbed dots down her cheek. "Better." He admired his work with a straight face. "You good Apache warrior now."

The last pale yellow coat of paint went on the kitchen after dark. Shiichoo loved her bright, open kitchen. The beautiful brown wrinkled face beaming at her was all Loni needed as she headed out the door.

The setting sun cast deep red streaks across the sky as Loni drove home and thought about the dirt in the air that created such vivid colors. She hoped a dust storm wasn't rolling in as she did her usual check in the rearview mirror before a turn. A motorcycle following her sped on down the road toward one of the airport houses after she turned into the hangar. She lost sight of it. There were too many motorcycles around here, she thought. She rolled her shoulders to ease the tension and climbed down from the truck. Coco bounded ahead of her, a yellow blob of paint bobbing at the end of her wagging brown tail.

Coyotes yipped to one another in the distance. They were on the run, maybe about to share a supper after they took turns running a jack rabbit into exhaustion. Loni heard a high keening. She grabbed the railing to keep from falling on the stairs as Coco bolted by her. When she opened the door, the dog shoved her aside again and immediately leaped on the bed, curling up into a small ball. "Maria used to brag about how brave and protective you were," she teased Coco. "She should see you now."

So tired she felt she couldn't move another inch, Loni climbed onto the bed and pushed Coco's huddled body over, smiling at the two of them until she remembered the motorcycle.

CHAPTER FOUR

Back on patrol, Loni parked at one of her favorite speed traps. The still-waning moon high in the sky was surrounded by pinprick lights. A silvery luminescence settled on everything around her as she waited at a rest stop outside town. At peace in the hush of silhouetted greasewood and cactus, she stepped out of the SUV to lean against the warm hood. Gone were the city noises, glaring lights and smells.

Loni poured coffee from her thermos for something to do. She had seen only eight cars in the last three hours sporadically making their way home. The night was too quiet for a Fourth of July weekend.

Loni's thoughts returned to her time with Maria. In LA, all the holidays in Maria's family were events. She delighted in attending every birth, baptism, confirmation, wedding, birthday party, anniversary, and other gatherings with no reason at all. Loni got so worn out she babysat the grandchildren while Maria's older sister Sandi helped Mama cook. The rest of the family played touch football in the huge backyard.

Loni snapped out of her reverie and checked her surroundings before she let Coco out to pee. The quiet was spooky. "Where is everybody?" she asked the dog.

Coco barked a sharp retort, but Loni had no idea what it meant.

Reluctantly they got back into the car and slowly drove south, hoping to pick up a few speeders on the freeway. All she saw were a few early fireworks far in the distance. The night continued to drag until she signed out. Her sense of peace was destroyed when she met Chief coming into the police station.

"Follow me," he spit at her from a contorted face and limped down the hall.

Loni recoiled. Here it comes, she thought. In his office, she moved to sit down next to a smirking Tully. "Don't sit." Chief stared at her through blue faded eyes that popped out of his hanging face. His skin had an unhealthy purple tinge. "What's this crap about drugs?" He punched her report with his finger at every word. "Tully don't find no drugs."

"He didn't look."

"That was rhetorical." He punched the report again.

Loni thought it might be the only four-syllable word he knew. She kept her mouth shut.

Squirming in his chair, Chief chewed on his lip before he declared, "State called. Your drug sample came from a batch mixed with talc from a mine they're tracking. They're coming to work with us. You will not say one word to them, you hear! Not one word!"

"Yes, Chief."

"And another thing. Don't you ever send anything to State without going through me."

"Yes, Chief."

After a long pause, the Chief picked up the report, tore it in two, and threw it into the trash can. "You're off this case now." He sat back in his chair. "Give everything back to Tully and get back on patrol."

"Chief." Loni couldn't resist. "What'd they say about Rene's murder? And the bullet that barely missed my head?"

"There weren't no murder yet. This here valve on your report don't prove nothing. Your bullet sounds like a random robbery gone bad." Chief leaned back and crossed his arms on his belly as he watched Loni back out of the office.

Loni quickly collected her notes with the copy of the receipt for the money and dropped them on Tully's desk. "Wait 'til Chief sees the money I sent to State," she muttered to herself. "Wonder if I'll have a job tomorrow? Wonder if I care?"

Hoping for peace and quiet, she headed toward the ranch. It didn't turn out that way.

"Hey, Shiichoo, why are you cooking? It's hotter in here than outside!" She recognized the smell of mixed hot spices in the menudo when she lifted the lid from a pot filled with rolling dark stew. White and green pieces swirled around in the liquid. She smelled garlic. A great hangover cure, Shiichoo always told her. Would it help a lack-of-sleep hangover? Sticking her nose back over the pot, she decided smelling it would cure anything.

"So, whose dog did you cook this time?"

"That wasn't funny the first time I heard it." Shiichoo gently slapped Loni's butt as she pushed around her to put wood in the stove. "A sick and hungry family came in earlier. Menudo's good comfort food."

"How long have the beef tripe and pigs' feet been boiling?"

"About three hours."

"You made Bahb quarter the pigs' feet and cut up the tripe, right?" She tried to stare Shiichoo down. "Right?"

Shiichoo stared back.

Loni picked up her grandmother and carried her into the living room. She stood her on one of the rag rugs, turned her around and held her shoulders. "You! Sit! I'll finish." Loni glanced down, recognizing one of her old school dresses in the rug and chuckled to herself as she returned the kitchen.

"Don't burn the bread!" her grandmother hollered as the door swung closed behind her. She reached up and lifted down a fry pan to put on the stove. The pots and pans had hung on the board above her head as long as Loni could remember. After she greased the bottom with butter, she poured a cup of batter into the pan.

When she whirled around to pick up the spatula, she nearly knocked her grandma down. Shiichoo had slipped back into the kitchen and was opening the stove to shove in another piece of wood. "You're putting more wood in the stove? It's already two hundred degrees in here! Bahb!" Loni yelled for support. "We're getting heatstroke in here." Nobody said anything. She turned back to the stove warning her grandma. "Wait 'til Thursday."

"Shush. I don't want a new stove. They don't cook right," Shiichoo said.

"Listen," Loni said soothingly. "The old stove's staying. You can cook with it when it cools off." Loni fanned herself complaining, "Sidog! Sidog!" Fanning faster, she groaned. "Too hot to even eat."

Shiichoo sent her one of her "don't be silly" jabs as she changed the subject. "How was work?"

"I'm really beginning to hate Chief Bubba." Loni sat the dishes on the end of a long wooden counter. "Really, really hate him!" She reached into the ancient freezer for tin cans of frozen tea and left the door open. "Wow, this feels good. Think I'll stick my head in here and stay." She rubbed her face with the side of a can as she reluctantly closed the freezer.

"You haven't been home long enough to quit. Give it time," Shiichoo said philosophically.

"Where's Bahb, anyway?"

"Out," her grandma snapped. "And I don't want to talk about it. Take the pot of menudo to the second cabin. And on your way back, stop at the barn and tell him he can eat supper outside, too."

"What did he do?"

Her grandma didn't answer.

"Second cabin on the right or left?"

"Left. Russell still lives in the one on the right."

Loni said, "I bet he would like to see Coco. She's so much like her mother." Loni had great memories of watching Russell teach Coco's mother Chocolat games. His brown poodle was smart like Coco, and she was grateful that she had one of Chocolat's offspring.

Loni pushed the screen-door open to a screeching noise, holding onto the loop handle of the pot. She carefully maneuvered the narrow plank board over the ditch running in front of the cabins and knocked on the cabin door.

A very short and very round Papago woman opened the door with five children stacked behind her like dominos. As she smelled the pot, joy wiped across her face. "Gracias! Muchas gracias!"

"De nada." Although Loni spoke a little O'odham, she was relieved to hear Spanish. She smiled at the children as she left, thinking she needed to find some toys in her grandma's toy box to give them.

Loni entered the barn to find Bahb soaping down a saddle. He was three inches taller than Loni and always stood poker-straight tall. He never changed, not even when a horse tried to roll on him. While the horse was struggling, he'd step off and wait until the horse got his feet back under him before Bahb stepped back on. He never abused horses when he broke them. When she was young Loni asked him why he was so gentle. "Spirit judge how we treat all life. Want to know a good man see how he treat his dog." Then he rubbed Loni's head.

"Stop it." Loni pushed on him. "I'm not a dog."

"Prob'ly not." He half grinned. "They smarter and much more useful."

Saddles were stored on their wooden horses, and Loni's favorite, the Porter saddle, still sat freshly oiled and soft, sat in the corner. Horseshoes lay in boxes on the two-by-four bench sagging from years of use. Tack hung off the weathered walls, harnesses her grandfather Wagner used on the plow horses to grow alfalfa on the thirty acres out back. Her grandparents had replanted feed grass.

"Hey, Bahb, how come Shiichoo is mad at you?"

He snorted. "Horses got in wet clothes on line."

"And?"

"Drug them around. Had to wash again. Twice. She still mad?" He sported a hopeful half smile on his brown smooth face. Loni couldn't help comparing her wrinkles, unhappily noting she already had more than he did. "She said to tell you to eat outside."

"Do I have to sleep out here, too?"

Loni giggled with him and left him to his saddles.

Loni stopped by Willie's open door to tell him lunch was ready.

"Bahb still has trouble?"

"He might be sleeping in with you tonight."

She walked away to the sound of Willie's groan.

A full stomach accompanied Loni to her loft home as she settled in for the long night. She turned out all her lights to watch the Fourth of July fireworks shooting up from the distant rodeo grounds. Everything was black except the runway and a few twinkling lights in houses scattered across the landscape. She pulled a chair up to the window and waited.

Loni was still adjusting to the eerie silence after the constant babbling voices in LA. The phone always ringing off the wall of Maria's aunt, grandfather, cousin, relative, or friend calling for help. Maria was like a whirlwind, circling Loni with her affectionate chatter and help, even when the two of them were alone. She held Loni close to her, always included her and forced her to react with people. Without Maria, Loni lost the will to reach out and crowds only caused greater loneliness.

Earlier she pushed a kava kava pill down Coco's throat to keep the flares and explosions from bothering the dog. Flashing guns and loud reports were part of Coco's attack training so she might not have needed any medication. "Pill must be working, huh, Coco?" The dog didn't even open her eyes in response. She lay on her back in the middle of Loni's bed, long fuzzy legs straight up in the air.

The fireworks relaxed Loni. Brilliant lights spiked into explosions of blossoms before the tendrils drifted down in the hazy smoke. They boomed and echoed until the frenzied finale faded, and the last distant sparkling streams of light floated back to earth.

The dark left behind suddenly made her feel vulnerable. Moving away from the window, she flooded the room with light. She grabbed a cold green corn tamale out of the fridge and sent a quick e-mail to Sandi.

FROM: Loni Wagner
TO: Sandi@gmailyahoo.com
DATE: July 4
SUBJECT: Still here

I tried to help Shiichoo cook this evening, but it's so hot in her kitchen it made me half sick. I'm hoping the new electric stove I ordered will get Shiichoo out of this heat.

You must have forgot I grew up on an Arizona ranch. To answer your question, I'm not going to get out of "playing copper," as you call it, to ranch. It's way too hard for such little money. My grandparents barely squeak by.

They don't need to support me too, although it might help if they didn't support everybody else who came along. Every time I go to the ranch, there are new faces. Time I talked to them. I'd really hate to arrest my own grandparents for harboring undocumented immigrants."

Times like this I miss Maria to talk to about the case I'm working on. Well, not really working on, but I am because I'll probably get it back again. Chief keeps tossing the case between Tully and me to upset me. And it's working.

I know you're worried about me so I'll tell you what I can. The report I sent in? The main problem is with Rene's notebook. I've tried to match it to numerous possibilities but what fits best is a list of dates, times, and maybe milepost numbers. And, if I'm reading it right, the next date coming up is at 3:30 am on the 27th of this month at Milepost 63. No matter how stupid it may turn out, I plan to be there waiting.

Take care.

Loni

CHAPTER FIVE

Loni promised Trevor her firstborn if he would come in four hours early to cover her shift. She needed to help Bahb check on the mother cows at the Seven Mile Well. As soon as Trevor showed up, she drove straight to the ranch. The rising sun was already hot on her back as she climbed down from her truck. The day promised to be another scorcher. Nothing new there.

Ignoring Bahb's and Willie's grumbling how it was already noon, day's a wastin', now damnit, as she herded Coco by them into the house, she ran up to her old room to change out of her polyester uniform. Sighing in relief she reveled in the cool cotton feel of her old Western shirts as she fastened the snaps. How about that, she thought, they still fit.

A fast trip back to the kitchen, Loni handed Coco a dog biscuit and told her stay. Quickly turning away, she slammed out the back door to avoid the dog's censuring eyes. At the open one-inch pipe-framed horse trailer, Roani impatiently stood, stomping his hooves and switching his tail. She reached out to give him a treat, and he stretched out his nose, competing with Paint and buck for the carrot pieces in the palm of her hand as she rubbed their sweet velvety noses. She gave all of them one last bite and breathed in deeply the warming desert air. She peacefully watched the horses bobbed their heads for more carrot as Stonewall stood stock still under his lean-to, watching them. Loni's gaze continued across the desert floor to a WPA fence that ran for miles until it disappeared in the heat haze.

Willie leaned on the horn jerking Loni back to the present as he yelled at her to get into the gotdamn truck. Loni heard the engine grind into a chug-ag-ag-chug-ag-ag until it caught and burst into life as Loni reached the passenger door. "Oh, no, you don't!" Loni tried to pull Willie out of the ancient GMC pickup.

"No, no." Willie giggled like a little girl. His walnut-colored face sat under the long, spiked pitch-black hair grown out from an ancient crew cut needing a new trim. He always waited at least five months to long to get his hair cut.

"I don't wanna open anymore gates," Loni whined. "Come on, Willie. It's your turn."

"No!" Willie kept on giggling as she pulled at his rock-hard arm muscles under the blue-checked Western shirt. "I open close all time you gone."

Giving up, she got in and tried to close the door behind her. They had carried out this ritual for as long as she could remember. "What the —?" Loni gawked at the bailing wire wrapped around the door handle.

"Lock busted." Willie leaned over her and wrapped the end of the wire around the window post. "Lock fixed." She didn't even ask how they closed the window. The handle was gone anyway. And so, she quickly realized, was the window.

Bahb slowly pulled the old pickup forward until the horse trailer jerked the pickup a few times before it settled in and bumped along the ruts behind them. Loni held on tight and kept her teeth clenched as worn-out shocks nearly jarred them off their seats.

The pickup shuddered to a stop at the first gate.

"God, ol' man!" Loni cringed at the state of the worn-out pickup as she clung to the door, hoping it didn't fall apart around her. "Where you going thrashing next?"

"Think I thrash you now." Willie giggled again as he snatched at her braid. Avoiding him, Loni ducked and whipped the wire off the door post. The door fell open, tumbling her onto the ground. She picked herself up and ran to the gate, and after considerable grunting, swearing, and general complaining she managed open the gate and drag it off the road. Loni kept her eye on Willie as the pickup drove by dodging Willie's outreached hand. Closing the gate she climbed back into the pickup to be immediately assailed when Willie pulled on her long braid to prove he still could. "What are you, ten?" she complained. "Bahb, make him stop."

The two continued to bat at each other as the pickup followed a three-strand barbwire fence across the desert floor. "When did you say the WPA put that fence in?" Loni.

"In thirties."

"We should have a ninetieth birthday party for it."

Willie smiled at her suggestion. "For a fence?"

"Got a better idea?"

"Party for me?"

"When is your birthday? I don't remember."

"Because you never knew."

"That true, Bahb?"

"Either that or he would not say. Hate birthday parties I remember."

"So, Willie. I think we should throw you a birthday party."

Willie ignored her.

"Do you remember when Paint was born?"

Willie brightened up. "O' course." He turned to Bahb. "Remember old Gabby? Paint her foal?"

"Yi. Your dad's favorite mare," Bahb told Loni. "Bad time helping her foal. Shiichoo brought coffee and say it new year."

"Okay. From now on your birthday will be the first of January." She snickered at Willie. "How many birthdays do we have to make up for? Eighty?"

Willie shoved against Loni. "Maybe forty."

"Forty. Well, hey, we better get with it. I'll tell Shiichoo to bake a cake, and we'll have a party."

"Presents, too?"

"Don't push it." Loni grinned until she noticed the next gate approaching. "Damn, Bahb. Are you ever going to put in any cattle guards?"

With a sly smile he glanced over at her, his dark eyes dancing. "Shiichoo read somewhere to paint black lines across road. Cows not cross."

"I buy paint for you," Willie volunteered with a perfectly straight face.

"Ha. Ha," Loni smarted back as she got out of the pickup to open another gate. "I'll paint strips down your face." Back in the pickup, she poked her head out the window in the hot, dry breeze to dry the sweat popping up all over her. Gazing ahead she watched a windmill rise up through the heat haze and slowly grow larger as they drove up to it. "Seven Mile Well. I haven't been here for more than eleven years."

"Not much change," Bahb responded.

"Yep." Loni smiled to herself at how fast she picked up their speech patterns. "Is that new patches on the tank?"

"Lost a few cows over that."

"We saved most," Bahb reminded Willie. "Got windmill fixed and water runnin'."

"Spent the next three hours keeping them from drinking too much."

"You two never change. Glass half full, glass half empty."

"So?"

"So nothing." Loni unwound herself from the pickup, stepped out and circled the towering metal tank. "Hey, Bahb, they're still here."

"Yi."

Loni lightly traced the Indian drawings with her index finger, careful to not disturb the pencil carbon. She followed other drawings, mostly ink, as she walked around the tank. She and Maria hunted in art stories for the fine-point colored ink pens so Bahb's drawings wouldn't fade in the Arizona sun. Maria had come home with her a few times but never made it to the tank. Loni fought back tears as she mourned what they never got to do. "Bahb's are still the best drawings," she quietly said to herself as she listened to the squeaking of the horse trailer ramp lowering and the stomping of the horses backing out.

"Damn!" Willie said. "Get off my foot, Paint!" The horse grunted as Willie grunted back. Loni heard Paint grunt again as Willie tightened his cinch. "Not waiting," Willie warned Loni. But she knew he would wait when, few seconds later, Loni heard leather squeaking as Willie lifted into the saddle. "Not waiting," she heard again.

She traced her grandfather Wagner's drawings next. His pencil drawings were all cowboy: trailing a cow, riding a fence, climbing over a hill, always alone, always in the distance. Bahb's, on the other hand, were up close and detailed, dancers in dress, each feather traced, each bead outlined, powwows, children playing. All of them were full of colors and life.

"Gone!" Willie hollered.

Loni ignored him as she searched for the diary someone had written back in the Twenties. The words had almost disappeared, but she remembered them. "*J ne   2 o t of fo d. Ate t cs off dog. Ate snake. Look d for Indan wh t an mesq ite bean . . .*"

"No, you not!" The sound in Bahb's voice meant trouble. "Come."

Loni followed the voice around the tank to the windmill where her granddad was standing. "Shit," she blurted. The pump rod lay on the ground.

"They back. This time broke pump rod."

Loni knew to keep her mouth shut while he studied what to do. Her granddad never hurried. "Too many mistakes," she could hear him remind her. "Only have to do it again."

One time she asked, "Why don't you read directions when you put something together?" He was putting together a table for Shiichoo, again and then again. "Directions no good. My guess good as theys."

Jerking on the broken rod, he turned to Loni and Willie. "You find mother cows. I get rod off for Herm to fix."

Loni untied Roani and reached to tighten the cinch.

"Get that horse's head up." Willie hollered.

Loni stared at Willie. "You tired of telling me that yet?"

Willie shrugged as he told Paint to head out down the road. "Fall off with saddle. I care less."

"Roani!" Loni warned the horse. Roani finally lifted his head, turned and stared at her as he gave his tail a good switch while twitching at the tightening of the cinch.

The sun was hot on their backs as they followed the tracks for a couple of miles. Fed up with the heat, Loni got restless. She reined Roani away from stepping on a peyote plant. "Do I remember right? Didn't you once tell me peyote was only used when you celebrate death?"

"Maybe."

"Your old village still use peyote?"

"Maybe. I youngen then but remember my last."

"Last what?"

"Party." Willie searched for words. "We party death and cry over births. Suffer from birth to the ride home to happy ground." He paused. "It was medicine man who went home. Big party. Everybody high. They went fifty miles to find best horse. Belonged to some big rancher over on the Colorado." He was silent again.

"That horse was so beautiful. Took five men to push it off." Willie's voice was almost a whisper. "At night I still hear that horse scream. Took a long time to hit canyon bottom. I never go to 'nother party. Not even my pa."

"Nobody stopped them? Just let them walk away with the horse?"

"You want to tell bunch big Injin men no?"

Loni leaned over and broke off leaves from a greasewood as they passed by. No longer oily, the bleached leaves shimmered in the wavy rays from the sun. She stuck a leaf in her mouth to help with her dry mouth noting the wonderful flavor was burned away.

"Damn it Paint!" Willie swore when Paint stepped in the middle of a pissant hole on his way down into a small gully, his hoofs scattering the pissants into frenzied action.

Listening to Willie apologize to the ants, Loni questioned, "How long's the top hole been open?"

"Two days."

"Damn! Rain in four days? Monsoon's coming."

"Yi." Willie watched one cow track separate from the others. He directed Loni's attention to the tracks. "Cow running hard. Horse behind. Better follow." He pushed Paint into a running walk for a good half mile. "Hear that?"

Loni heard nothing until they reached the top of a hill and saw the jumping cactus patch spread out before them. A bawling mother cow was trapped in the center of the needle-filled plants.

"Oh, hell!" Willie said. "That's Flossie. Had her long time." He slowed down, easing around the patch to find a way to clear a path to the cow as Loni stayed back, watching. A beautiful brindle, the cow was a cross between Brahma and Santa Cruz, a mix that could travel further to forage and water than most cows. Flossie didn't move as she continued her terrified bellowing.

When she turned her head toward Loni the bile rose and she nearly threw up on Roani. "Oh, god, Willie! A ball's hanging outta her eye."

"Maybe best shoot her." Willie mournfully got off his horse and pulled a long limb from a Palo Verde tree. He used the end as a broom to sweep a path to the injured cow. "Bring me rope." Using his stick, Willie knocked cactus balls from between her legs so she could walk.

Loni untied the rope from her saddle and stepped off Roani, dropping his reins. Having experienced jumping cactus climb her leg once, burying needles through her Levis as they crawled, she shuddered as she carefully followed Willie's path to the cow and hand Willie the rope. Backing out she watched as he eased a loop over Flossie's head. Gently pulling, Willie slowly led the cow out on the cleared path until they were clear of the patch.

Freaking out over the ordeal ahead, Loni babbled, sometimes in a high annoying pitch so she could shove the horror of Flossie's tragic circumstance into a black hole. She learned at an early age that babble shoved all thoughts from her head, overriding any other emotion boiling over inside her. "Did I ever tell you about the time I found a moose up on Mogollon Rim?" The sound of her voice filling her ears also kept her from crying as she dug tweezers out of her pocket desert kit and carefully pulled needles from Flossie's face. Willie grabbed two flat rocks a bit larger than his hands and began to pull the baseball-sized yellow balls out of Flossie's legs, each ball filled with a million sharp needles. The cow moaned and quivered with every extraction, but she didn't move.

"Moose?" Willie grunted, pulling another ball from in front of a knee as Loni followed him, searching for needles he left behind as best she could. She knew Flossie couldn't walk far until they finished her legs.

"That moose acted like this cow." Loni gently continued to follow Willie. Flossie tried to lean into her, and Loni decided to finish her nose before the cow transferred the needles to her. "I saw him off the side of the road walking in a small circle. When I got out and talked to him, he lifted his head and trotted to me." She pulled up the cow's lip and yanked a few more needles from her gums. "Scared the bejesus out of me for a minute and I almost turned to run but then he stopped and tried to hide his head under my armpit."

Loni worked around Flossie's mouth and avoided the ball hanging out of her eye. "The more I talked to him and rubbed his face and neck, the calmer he got." Her stomach turned queasy again as she avoided the cow's eye. "She's going to lose her eye, Willie."

Willie grunted in agreement. "Balls like fire. Needles gonna make her very sick." He pulled off another ball and tossed it into the growing pile. "What happened to moose?"

"Oh. Somebody driving by told the forest service to bring a horse trailer. Sad thing, it was blind from some virus. Most were dead before they found them. Couldn't defend themselves. Couldn't run." Loni moved to Flossie's back legs, following behind Willie. She quivered with the cow. "They take them to the vet school in Colorado, the ranger said, to do research for a cure. As far as I know, the moose became a world traveler."

Flossie began to bawl again. "All done but tail and eye." Willie pulled three more balls from the tail before she swished the hanging cactus balls into her sides.

"Wish all the needles came out with the balls." Loni felt Flossie's pain.

"We go now. Balls gone enough. Get more needles later. Hope she no flick tail onto herself."

"You go get trailer." He coaxed Flossie into a walk. "Take Paint. We wait on road. I ride trailer with Flossie."

Loni put Roani in a running walk toward the tank with Paint trailing. The trip seemed to take forever but running a horse in this heat would kill it.

She explained to Bahb about Flossie as he jumped into the pickup and jerked onto the road. Loni watched a line of dust follow the clanging of the horse trailer hitch banging against the pickup coupler as they bounced through the potholes. She had never seen him drive so fast. She watched the pickup and trailer until they were out of sight.

Loni unsaddled the two horses and led them to the corral. Opening the gate, she stuck a hand out, running it down their backs as they passed through to join Buck. She settled in the shade of the tank and waited until she heard the clanging. "Show time," she told herself as she stood and brushed the silky dirt off her butt. Watching the pickup slow down as Willie opened the door for her, Loni leaped into a trot and jumped in so Bahb didn't have to stop. It was Loni's job to watch Flossie out the back pickup window as the cow spraddled her legs with her head down for balance and bawled all the way home.

Bahb came in honking, bringing Shiichoo out the door, waiting. Bahb yelled to her, "Call vet!" as the pickup passed her by and ground to a halt in front of the barn. Shoving each other out the door the three quickly lowered the trailer gate. "We here," Bahb repeated, love talking as he led Flossie slowly out of the trailer and into the barn. Willie helped him tie her into a cross rope so she would not move far as they pulled out needles.

Loni filled a bucket of water to give the old girl a drink. She drank gratefully as Loni held it up for her.

Bahb was scrounging around in a tool box when Shiichoo stepped into the barn with a bottle of Elmer's glue, a roll of duct tape, two pairs of tweezers, and an old-time strapping razer. "Vet is on her way." She handed Willie tweezers and the razer.

"Good" Bahb approached Flossie with a pair of long-nosed needle pliers in his hands. Within seconds they swarmed the cow pulling needles any way that worked.

"Doc said she would be here in a half hour," Shiichoo reported.

"Woman vet for big animals?" Surprised, Loni held the water for Flossie as she watched Shiichoo search for needle patches on her face and neck to pour the glue on.

Loni followed her grandma with her eyes as she waited for Flossie to drink. "Can't remember, Shiichoo. How long will it take for the glue to dry?"

"Soon."

"Good, too, so don't hit on Doc and run her off," teased Willie.

"How come? You want her?" Loni retaliated

"No. I think she two-spirit like you."

Bahb cleared away another round of larger needles along a back leg. "I not agree. I know she have big loss. Enough loss. Be careful."

Setting the bucket aside, Loni followed behind Bahb finding the smaller needles with tweezers. "How do you know?"

"In the eyes. They full of pain. Be careful," he repeated.

Loni had no answer. She settled in behind Bahb as they carefully cleaned Flossie. Beyond an occasional flicker of pain, the cow stood quietly as she seemed to understand they were helping her. Loni listened to her grandma talk to the cow. "Such a good girl you are." Shiichoo held her hand up to Flossie's nose and fed her rolled oats. "Yes, you are. Yes, you are. Yes, you are. Yes, you are."

Loni stared at her grandma.

"What?" Shiichoo stared back. "You don't love-talk animals?"

"It's a cow!"

"You talk to Stonewall. He's a cow."

Loni shrugged in defeat. "My bad."

"Get your dog before you leave, child. I hear her barking for you."

"Don't let her out here. She upset Flossie." Bahb moved to the cow's front leg, still slowly pulling out the pale-yellow elusive needles. Any left could work through her body and come out anywhere. Or end up in her brain.

Loni glanced up at the sound of an engine. The vet stepped down and grabbed a bag. Loni understood Willie's teasing. She was pixie cute. Her purposeful stride caused the short blonde bangs on her forehead to swish above her brilliant blue eyes. She frowned as she walked up. "Geez, you meant it when you said a cactus was hanging out of a cow's eye." She studied the eye a minute. "Could I get a pail of hot water."

Shiichoo hurried toward the house.

Loni stepped forward. "I'm Loni." She held out her hand. "The granddaughter."

"Willie said you came home." The vet shook her hand. "I'm Tory. Welcome back."

"Thanks." Loni indicated Flossie. "Eye's pretty bad, huh?"

Tory shook her head, reaching for her bag. By the time Shiichoo got back with the bucket of water, Tory had her tools laid out ready to use. She filled a plunger full of clear liquid. "Can somebody put a twitch on her so she won't move? And hobble her. She's going to have to be still for a while now." Bahb hobbled the cow as Willie lifted a stick with a small noose off the wall and twisted it around Flossie's upper lip to subdue the cow.

Loni wanted to hang around and watch this woman, but she couldn't stand to see Flossie's agony any longer. Loni ducked her head and walked away.

"Ask Herman to help fix windmill," Bahb said to Loni's back. "Take broken rod to him."

Loni slowly drove the back way to Uncle Herm's house along the single-track dirt road. She parked next to his pickup and found him in the kitchen. Coco followed her in, sniffing the air.

Herm was sitting at the table with Loni's Aunt Mae yammering at him. "I can come back later," Loni said.

"No, you sit." Uncle Herm ordered. "I need a referee. She's been ranting for ten minutes."

Mae rounded on him again. "How would you know? You never listen to me!"

"If you didn't talk all the time, maybe I would!"

Loni was ready to flee Mae's fury when Herm handed her a piece of toast. "Here, Mae. You need to build your strength back up."

Mae sat down with the giggles. "I swear, Herman, if you're not two shelves below a dog turd." She turned away from his puzzled expression toward Loni. "How come you're so sad, sweetie."

"Not sure who to feel sorry for, Uncle Herm here or Flossie." Loni explained about Flossie and the windmill. Mae gave her a long hug as Uncle Herm agreed to pick Loni up in the morning to repair the windmill. Satisfied, Loni readied herself to leave when he said, "Come with me."

Mystified, Loni followed him into the hall where he lowered a boot box from the highest shelf in the hall closet.

"Wow! Lucchese boots!"

"No, no boots. It's your grandfolks' letters and notes. Your dad's history. I wanted to give it to you years back, but you were gone before I knew you were even leaving."

Loni ducked her head. "Sorry."

"You might like learning about your grandparents' ways." He winked at her. "Then again, maybe not all of it." He handed her the box. "It's not a bad thing, having a soft heart. Might help you to see where it came from." As they walked to the door, he reached out his arm and hugged her. "This belonged to your dad, him being the oldest. Take good care of it."

"I'll save it for Daniel."

Her aunt gave Loni another good hug and a spank on her butt as she stepped out the door.

"Hey," Loni reminded her, "I'm not twelve anymore."

"Really?" Mae grinned. "I hadn't noticed." She closed the door.

Loni left Coco to roam outside the hangar and carried the box upstairs. She studied it for a long time as she sipped cold, bitter coffee from a cup she left on the table earlier. Carefully, she gingerly lifted the lid. On top was an old, faded spiral notebook, its cover inked with hand-drawn cattle brands and who they belonged to. Digging into the box, Loni found more notebooks, envelopes, and folded pages. She gently picked up the notebook and turned the pages, occasionally reading a few lines. All the notebooks and letters seemed to be recollections of people, pets, school, living on the desert. She stopped at a letter with a drawing of a windmill like the one on the tank she saw earlier in the day. The words Ben Wagner were written under the windmill. Curious, she read out loud to Coco.

> "The old windmills have about all gone to join the yesteryears. There were so many famous ones stretching across the Arizona desert. The old Clanton wells. They were so deep he used a tall tower with a big wheel that could be seen for miles. There was the Flowerpot, the Fourteen, the Seven Mile, Burnt Well, Surprise, Volcanic, and Winters Well, to name a few. At the Winters Well, there were two windmills stood side-by-side,

hooked to a walkenbeam. They all started to fade out of the picture in the thirties. The sagebrush mechanics were getting few and far between and no one knew how to wire them back together. Lots of cowmen went broke then due to low prices and droughts so they didn't need the mills too much.

I really hate to see them disappear. As I came toward them they were fascinatingly silhouetted against the sky, a sentinel, and above all, a beacon. Many an old cowhand going by could get a drink of water for him and his tired horse. The squeak, the squall, the clang spilled out more beauty and rhythm of the windmill and still did not disturb the solitude. The old guys that put up the windmills and pumps were masters at it. They could do more to bring water out to the top with less. When the windmills are all gone a chapter of a grand and glorious way of life will be closed."

Loni felt a connection to the grandfather she never knew. She wondered how many of the windmills were still left. Maybe she would take some time to see what she could find. He might like that. She'd see if Uncle Herm remembered where any of them were. But enough lore for today. She was tired, muscle sore, and rubbed raw from the saddle. And still hurting for Flossie. If she didn't get an e-mail off to Sandi right now, she wouldn't do it. She pulled her laptop computer toward her and opened it.

FROM: Loni Wagner
TO: Sandi@gmailyahoo.com
DATE: July 5
SUBJECT: Greetings

My granddad had his cows rustled today. And yes, there are still rustlers. When I catch them, and I swear I will, I really hope I can keep from shooting them. Since you want to know, I'm sending you my first four items on a list why I don't want to ranch anymore.
   1. Too damn hot
   2. Cattle rustling
   3. No profit when or if pays the bills at all
   I am so raw and sore from riding today I'm hunched over like an old man. I'm glad Maria can't see me now. She'd think it was pretty funny.

Met a really cute veterinarian today. What I want to know is where all these lesbians were when I was growing up? I've been back a month and I've already met three. No, make that four.

Love to all.

Loni

Loni left the door to the loft open for Coco as she fried some eggs for lunch or supper or whatever the meal was supposed to be. She was scooping the eggs onto her plate when Coco trotted in. "Gag a maggot, Coco! What did you roll in?" Loni ran out the door and down the stairs before she allowed herself to breathe.

"What's the matter?" Daniel asked.

"Did you get a whiff of Coco?"

"Nope. Rolled in something, did she?"

"I think she got a direct hit by a skunk."

"Better get her a bath in tomato juice then."

"You're kidding me? They don't make that much tomato juice."

Daniel got the giggles and couldn't stop.

"Coco!" Loni called and ducked behind Daniel.

"Get away from me, Coco! Get!" Daniel held his nose while he danced around trying not to crack up again. "I'm going home now." He jumped into his pickup and drove away, leaving Loni to avoid Coco.

"Stay," she told Coco as she went back upstairs and called her grandma. "Coco got hit by a skunk. What do I do?"

Shiichoo laughed.

"Not funny!"

"Maybe not to you."

"Why don't I just send this dog to your house?"

"Why don't you give her a bath?"

"In what?"

"I heard milk was good."

"I don't have any. What else?"

"I don't know."

"Well ask Bahb what his people did."

After a long minute Shiichoo got back to her. "Avoid." That was all she said before she hung up.

Groaning, Loni called Lola, who laughed harder than Shiichoo.

"Well shit, Lola, do you know what to do?"

"You got any hydrogen peroxide?"

"Hang on. Let me see." Loni tucked her cell phone in her chin and rummaged through her first aid cabinet. "Yep."

"Got any baking soda?"

"You mean for cooking?"

"Or smells. It's the same."

"What does it look like?"

Lola's sarcasm was heavy. "It's a yellow box that says baking soda on it

"My aunt Mae put something in my ice box I think could be it. Hang on." Loni moved food around until she found a yellow box. "Yep. Says baking soda."

"Wonderful!"

Loni couldn't miss Lola's sarcasm. "Well, I don't cook!"

"And I'm not asking you, too. Mix some peroxide with the baking soda and liquid soap. Pour it into a bucket of warm water, cover your nose, and scrub. And don't ask me to help." Laughing, Lola hung up.

Loni bathed Coco and herself in the shower several times to get the smell even bearable.

CHAPTER SIX

Uncle Herm picked Loni up from the hangar in his ancient Army jeep an hour before sunrise. They followed the trail up through the entrance to a ranch once been well tended. "At least I don't have to get out and open this one." Loni grimaced at the broken gate. Herm carefully avoided splintered boards with rusting nails scattered across the road as he swung in and out and back onto the road.

Loni shaded her eyes from the sun peering over Saddle Horn. She scanned the unfamiliar territory. "Where are we going, anyway?"

"Didn't I tell you? Part of the pump rod you brought me was gone." Uncle Herm focused on the far distance at the remains of a ranch house surrounded by a ring of green salt cedars. "We should be able to find another one on Billy Bain's old place."

Loni tried to remember the mentally slow man who lived there, but all she could picture was a dried-up old rubber inner tube, split and cracked from the heat. When he died, nobody found him for months. They said he didn't even smell anymore. He was found on a sleeping bag in a small utility room on the back of the large house barely habitable when he was still alive.

They slowly drove by the rubble of the house before they bumped a mile down the road and drove off the beaten path to circle around a crescent-shaped black hill. Loni hung on to keep from being thrown out of the canvas-covered jeep and wished for a door or even a seatbelt. Uncle Herm climbed in and out of dry washes Loni knew her truck couldn't maneuver. When they reached level ground, Loni was mesmerized by the vastness surrounding her.

Along with the beige-colored six-inch Indian wheat turned invisible in the tan dirt and rocks, greens were faded to yellows in the shrunken greasewood and cat's claw, protecting themselves from the life-sucking heat. The myriad of cactus covered with needles left sharp shadows in double imaged relief. Loni thought about the last lines of a poem by Shelley. "Round the decay of that colossal wreck, boundless and bare. The lone and level sands stretch far away. Look on my works ye mighty and despair."

Uncle Herm slowed to a stop beside a stack of wood and metal that had once been a windmill. Long ago, the water tank fell off its rotten posts onto its side. Loni followed her uncle out of the Jeep and waited as he wandered around the pile. Climbing onto the pile, he jumped up and down a few times, listening for a rattle, a dead sound like no other. Neither of them heard a thing. "No snakes." Uncle Herm smiled and pulled on his blue and white-striped work gloves. He threw angle iron pieces off the top while Loni walked around the tank, searching for writings or drawings. Finding nothing, she circled back to help her uncle pick through the pile of debris.

"The box you gave me? Read about your dad's love of windmills. Have you been by to see any of them lately?"

"Not for years. Don't travel the desert like I used to. You should ask your Uncle Kirk. He goes all over."

Loni snorted. "Like he'd speak to me."

Uncle Herm stopped and frowned at her. "It's not him, you know. It's his poisonous wife."

"And his kid."

"James'll grow up. Things have changed while you were gone." Uncle Herm returned to his picking.

"Uncle Kirk still prospecting?"

"Yep. Doing real good to. He's livin' up on Walker Heights with the rest of the hoity-toity."

Loni laughed. "Guess he knew Rene then?"

"Neighbors, I understand."

"Your dad teach you how to fix windmills?"

"Actually, no. It was your dad before your mom died and he ran off to the mines. He'd drag me with him every time he went out to fix one. Left me some tools and manuals. I wrote off and got others. Benny loved windmills as much as our dad."

"Do you know anything about the mine where he died?"

"I'll never forget it. A salt mine in Louisiana. The Belle Isle Mine." Uncle Herm paused. "Often thought of going back there for a look-see."

"Maybe we can go together."

"I'd like that." Herm returned to his search. "Meantime, we need to get a windmill repaired."

"What kind of windmill is this?" Loni wondered.

"This here's a Samson like Bahb's."

"Tell me what you're looking for and maybe I can help."

"Pump rod. One you brought was busted so bad I couldn't fix it."

"Well, shit! Why would anyone take the trouble to ruin it?" Loni wiped her face with her sleeve and dug in to help Uncle Herm search. The sun baked their heads by the time they were down to the motor parts. Uncle Herman waited to answer until he dug out a pump rod. "I guess they think it's funny to make things harder for others."

"You know, Uncle Herm, it looks like a whole windmill is here?" She tried to remember what she'd been told. Something about the old man pulling down windmills.

"Used to be. Been picked over for parts more than sixty years though. This Samson windmill was a favorite out here before the Stover Company later made the Oil Rite and Aermotor 702." He tossed the pump rod in the back of the jeep and walked over to the windmill fan. "The 702 was the most popular, especially after World War II. Lots of them still work." With a fierce grunt, Uncle Herm pulled up the fan from the center hub and stood it on end.

"My god! That thing's huge!" Loni exclaimed. "It's more than twice as tall as you are!"

"Looks like somebody else needed blades." Uncle Herm counted five missing. "Gotta be the Burnt Wells bunch. Only other Samson around here still working other than Bahb's." He leaned the fan against the bottom of the old metal tank. "Bring me the tool box from under the front seat. I need penetrating oil."

Loni opened the box and handed him a squirt bottle. He sprayed oil on the nuts connecting three of the blades to the fan and sat in the shade of the tank to wait.

"Why three?"

"Bahb said he only had three damaged."

"I was so busy staring at the tank, I didn't even look up."

"Glad you're not trying to solve a crime for me," Uncle Herm teased. He lost his smile and peered at her. "Daniel said you got shot at. Want to tell me about it?"

"Nothing to tell, though I'm working on it. Lola's helping me hunt for motorcycles in the county and who owns them. Maybe when I find out, I'll know more."

"Something's worrying James. Do you know what it is?"

His question surprised Loni. "Not the slightest. You see James a lot?"

"You forget already. He always did prefer our house to his dad's. Sure pissed off my sister-in-law even if she was never home. I swear she found more places to go." Uncle Herm wiped the sweat from his face. "Your shooting got anything to do with Rene's plane?"

"I don't know, Uncle Herm, but I'd guess so. I supposed Daniel told you Rene was murdered."

"I made him tell me so don't get after him."

"Good lord, Uncle Herm! This was published over a hundred years ago!" Loni pulled out a windmill manual and opened it.

"Well, not much changed in the Sampson since then." He reached in the box and pulled out a worn tool resembling pliers.

"What's that?"

"Pliers for the Sampson pump rod. One of the tools your dad gave me. He called it a Love Pump. He thought that was pretty funny." Uncle Herm grinned as he threw a stick at a curious lizard. It scurried to the stick and promptly climbed on. "Stick lizard. You gotta love 'em."

Loni touched the dirt in front of her. "Good. Too hot for rattlers to crawl."

"You have any snakes or cactus up in the Northwest where you went to school?"

"No. There was gorse down the coast."

"What's gorse?"

Loni was quiet a minute. "Remember the time you took Daniel and me hunting muskrats down the canal and a jackrabbit jumped out in front of us?"

"Sure. There was a field of safflower on one side of us and a canal on the other. The field was at least a quarter-mile long. The poor rabbit's tongue was hanging out before he got to the end."

Loni got temporarily lost in her memory of the huffing jackrabbit sitting under a cat's claw bush. "Gorse is like safflower. If you get in it, somebody has to find a tractor to come in and get you out."

"Sounds like jumping cactus." Uncle Herm fit the wrench on a nut, and with a grunt and jerk, removed them one by one, each one with his large body in simple fluid movements. "Only safflower don't jump on you."

"Don't let go, either." Loni thought back to Flossie, and her anger flashed. She kicked dirt on a cone-nosed beetle to watch it stand on its head. "One thing I really appreciated about the Oregon coast is that nothing was poisonous." She checked the back of a blade Uncle Herm handed her for crawly things before placing it on the backseat of the jeep. "No cockroaches there. No deadly snakes. No insects except for the brown recluse which everybody has and nobody sees. No poisonous plants that I have ever seen. Mosquitoes get blown away so fast I never got bit." Loni fanned herself. "Best of all, no goddamn heat. Did Billy Bains really take down three windmills?"

"Yep. This here's Moon Mountain. Then there was Whitehall and Old Six."

"Whitehall was that way, right?" Loni pointed north.

"Yup. About ten miles." Uncle Herm strained as he took off another nut.

"Where's Old Six?"

"Way up on Eagle Tails." Uncle Herm directed Loni's attention to the huge mountain range to the west. "Camped up there every summer. Only water for miles was at that windmill."

"Why did he take them down?"

"It was the second world war. My dad, your dad, and I dug dams on Centennial Wash to catch rain water. One dam could water a lot of cows during the winter. Of course, August thunderstorms washed the dams out, so we went back every year to fix them." He threw another stick at the lizard. "I really miss your dad." They watched the lizard jump from the old stick and clamber onto the new one. "We camped on the banks of the wash in a clump of rocks named the Shit House hills."

"You serious?"

"You bet. Even used to be on the old maps. Rocks jutting up in a square with a pointed cap on them like an outhouse. Up that high you could see everything happening in the Harquahala Valley. I must have been nine the summer the army came." Uncle Herm managed to get another bolt unscrewed and handed it and the nut to Loni. His blue work shirt darkened down the back and under the armpits from sweat.

Loni didn't dare ask if it would be cheaper to buy a new fan blade. She knew "waste nothing" was the law of the land.

Uncle Herm continued, "The army came in to train for the Africa invasion, they said. Mostly they dumped, burned, and buried. Dad called it the government's biggest cost-plus burial ground boondoggle."

"Did they really bury tires?"

"That and food and lumber and gas and oil. Stuff we needed to survive."

"Why?"

"Who the hell knows? Some Washington idiot's idea. Some said Americans needed to sacrifice to keep believing in the war. Kept them going. Others said it was corruption. I say follow the money. Been a lot of years and nobody I know of explained it." He sat a minute in thought. "Dad always said only man was dumb enough to believe in justice. Animals know better. He said too many laws were made by the rich to keep what they got until somebody bigger and richer came along and took it."

"And that can't change?"

"Too late. Soon as somebody suggests it, the greedy bastards holler socialism! Communism! Corporate America is too powerful now, too big to fail. It's like a huge vacuum, lowering prices until it sucks small businesses and farms into its bowels and shits them out in one big polluted turd not even useful for fertilizer. Families break up and scatter, working for corporate America wherever they can find a job." Uncle Herm's attempted laugh was hollow. "Can you believe it. All done in the name of family values." Mocking himself, Uncle Herm added, "But then, what the hell do we country boys know?"

Loni agreed. "I've seen lots of families try to hang on and end up in big trouble. That reminds me. I wanted to ask you about the story of a relative robbing a bank during the Great Depression. That true?"

"Oh, yes. Three of them. As soon as they walked out the front door the lock clicked behind them. They'd overheard earlier that day banks were quitting. Pissed off, they circled around to the back door and, unfortunately, took their money back at gunpoint."

"So it really happened?'

"Yep. Your grandfather's older brothers. It was in Texas. They were outlaws 'til the day they died. Hid out in the Arizona desert to race horses. Great uncle Johnny switched to racing ostriches. They were brought in originally to herd cattle. Ate next to nothing and anything, laid an egg equal to a dozen chicken eggs, had huge drumsticks, loved the desert heat." Uncle Herm tilted his head back and laughed. "Problem was, those ostriches scared the shit out of the cows, scattering 'em so bad some were never found. After that, Johnny bet his ostrich could beat any horse alive. Made a good livin' until everyone knowed about it."

He pried another nut off before he sprayed a third one and sat back down and threw another stick. The lizard ignored the stick. Instead, it picked up the one under it and ran a short way before it dropped it and climbed back on. Checking its surroundings, the lizard ran across another stick and scurried up an ironwood tree. Chuckling, Uncle Herm loosened the nut and handed Loni the last blade.

Loni followed him into the jeep. Soon they were underway again and Uncle Herm found a faint trail back to Seven Mile Well. The shade of the canvas top and the breeze blowing on her sweat cooled Loni enough she was ready to return to the previous conversation. "The windmills?"

"Oh, yeah." Uncle Herm considered a minute. "Well, Billy Bains gave the army permission to use his land, so they let him hang out with them. That was after one of them shot a horse out from under one of his wranglers. They decided to get nice to Billy."

The road turned smooth, and they picked up speed. "One August we didn't have much wind, and the windmills weren't pumping enough water to keep the tanks full. Don't know why Billy worried though, considering he had no cows since his dad died. Anyway, an Army sergeant told Billy if he took down some of his windmills, then the rest would get more wind."

"Be serious. He actually believed it?!"

"I am. He did."

"He really went out and took down windmills to get more wind for the others?"

"The two cowboys hired to take care of him even helped him. His dad's will paid those two cowboys to stay with Billy the rest of his life. He outlived both of them."

"So he died alone?"

Uncle Herm pulled his straw hat off to wipe at the sweat running into his eyes. The band was stained dark from years of sweat and dust. "Tried to get out there at least once a month or so. Took him some beans, flour for tortillas, and beer. Listened to him talk about his friends the half coyote, his skunk. His horse." Uncle Herm smiled. "Skunk lived under the house and let go every so often. Pretty hard to visit him on those days." Uncle Herm shook his big head. "I got so busy building the airport and keeping after contractors, I neglected him too long."

They were making good time. Loni counted the humps of dirt remembering what made them. "How many planes did they finally dig up here?"

"Don't know. We counted thirty piles." Uncle Herm chuckled. Loni loved listening to his stories.

"How did you find the first plane?"

"I guess over the years the rain washed enough dirt off the plane site that our cable caught on the propeller of one and drug the plane up out of the ground. Should have seen your dad's face when he jumped off the tractor and ran. I wasn't far behind."

"Cable?"

"You don't remember any of it?"

"No. Dad was pretty much gone by the time I was ready to hear stories."

"That's true," Uncle Herm said sadly. "Losing your mom pretty much killed him Why he had to leave. You Dad loved to loop a long metal cable, tie both ends on a small tractor and drag it across a space to clear the brush. Worked lickety-split. Made building temporary corrals much easier." Staring around, Loni tried to visualize the scene as she listened to her uncle's voice. "That way, when the cattle came in from Old Mexico, we could get them cut, tagged, and branded most anywhere we wanted to before we turned them out."

Uncle Herm's eyes glazed in memory. "Too many times some of them came in sick. The trucks mostly traveled at night which helped from heat stroke. Some always got pushed into the middle and others pushed to get out. Then they'd push back in and go back and forth from hot and sweaty to cold and shivering." He pointed out the wide road. "This was the landing strip for the planes. Still a good road. Too short though."

"I don't understand. Why bury them way out here? It's three hundred miles from the coast!"

"They worried about Japanese invading. Out here they had time to dig them up and get them on their way."

How fast, Loni wondered.

"The plane we dug up was wrapped in rubberized tape to waterproof it."

"So they had to dig them up, unwrap them, clean them up, gas them, and then take off?" Even though all signs they were there had long since been washed away, Loni gawked around in disbelief. "Whose crazy idea was that?"

Picking up speed, Uncle Herm pushed the jeep until they left the smooth runway behind. He slowed down to avoid the deep ruts. "Well, hell. Another thing never to be told. After the Air Force ran us off so they could dig them up, they came by the house and explained what they could. Seems the government buried them from Old Mexico to Canada. The two I seen were around ninety miles apart."

"No way! Are they still in the other one?"

"Hard to say. The plane we pulled up was already there thirty years or so."

Back at the well, Uncle Herm greeted Bahb and Willie. Thanking Herm for the help, Bahb held the rod for Uncle Herm to connect as Loni returned to re-read the writing on the tank. "Tell me again about the diary written on this tank, Bahb."

"You forget I no tell stories in day."

"You forget I don't believe the evil one will get me for telling stories in the day."

"You forget I do."

"Well, forget about your Navajo beliefs this time and tell me the story from your Papago half."

Bahb smiled.

"Come on! It's really hard to read anymore." She spoke out loud, making up things even though she memorized it a long time ago. "Day Five. Ate mesquite beans. Day Six. Coffee gone. Day seven. Ate cone-nosed bugs and threw them up. Bitter. And a lizard. Threw it—up, too. Nasty thing. Day Eight. Fought Henry for a rattlesnake. Snake bit him so I won and ate well. Only kidding. Day Nine. Thought about the bugs again. Day Ten. Fished a dead bird out of the tank. Stunk. Burned in the firepit wasn't bad. Day Eleven. Nothing. Day Twelve. Can't stay any longer. Walking out." Loni paused. "Hey, Uncle Herm, do you know what happened to them?"

"They were old men when I knew them. Dead long time now." Uncle Herm tightened the nut on the pump rod. "Part of the Hellman tribe. Seems their horses wandered off and took days to get home. It was awhile before the oldest brother finally came looking for them. Found them a day out."

"Still alive?" Loni touched the faded date. 1933, the year Bahb thinks he was born.

"Yep."

She was forming the next question when Willie hollered, "Hump, girl." Lifting a finger to him Loni picked her cell phone from her shirt pocket and took photos of the unknown people and horse tracks. Among them she found tracks from an unshod horse. One hoof had a crack in it. Beside it were prints from a tennis shoe. "In a minute!" She turned to Uncle Herm. "Why would anyone wear tennis shoes on a horse? Got a death wish?"

Uncle Herm studied the track. "Good way to get a foot caught in a stirrup for sure, especially trying to herd some of those feisty half-Brahmas you got. They run you down for the fun of it."

Loni rounded the tank and found Willie sitting on Paint under a mesquite tree.

"Nah, saw earlier. Too small. Be older colt. Rider on mama track beside." Willie reminded Loni again. "Butt it, Loni, too hot soon."

Loni fanned herself with her shirttail. Nine in the morning, and the temperature was already over a hundred degrees. "Just cool it. I'll put my butt on that horse when I'm ready." Forcing herself to pocket the phone, and leave the shade of the tank, she walked over to Roani. Groaning, she hop-stepped up, still stiff and sore from yesterday's long ride. "Let's go." She followed Willie with Roani fighting to get the lead as they trailed the rustler's tracks. "Why are we doing this? We were here yesterday already."

"We no finish." Willie ignored her complaints.

"Well, hell." Loni decided. Disagreeing wasn't going to change anything so she relaxed, forgetting who she was riding. As soon as Roani felt her relax, he jumped into his side-hop dance to let her know how much he hated following another horse. His big dipping head added to the hop dumped another level to the pain from her raw saddle-burned thighs. Letting go Loni let Roani catch up to Willie, and, to Loni's great relief, the horse peacefully fell into a rolling walk beside Paint. Loni never understood why he had to have his damn nose out in front.

"Was rustling worse in the old days?"

"No. Truck out now. Slaughter hundreds miles away. No way to find, no way to stop."

Determined to ignore her sore butt and raw thighs, Loni wanted to keep Willie talking but he was focused on the imprints ahead of them. By noon they tracked the cattle to a cut in the barbed wire fence where a set of large tire treads waited. Loni photographed the treads and followed them a half mile to the paved road leading into Caliente. Or out of depending on which way the truck disappeared. "Well, shit. Another successful day."

The overhead sun left neither shadows nor shade as Loni and Willie turned back to the tank. A few miles in Willie pointed and Loni followed his finger to a coyote following them, stealing from bush to bush. It gave up after a mile and loped away.

Following the coyote's skulking helped Loni ignore her burning misery. "Tell me how the Coyote got his yellow eyes, Willie."

Turning, he grinned at her. "You too old for stories now."

Loni wiggled in the saddle, standing in the stirrups as long as she could before riding sidesaddle. Nothing helped. "Tell me something. I'm dying here," she whined.

Willie relented. "Coyote meet Blue Bird and tell him how beautiful he is. But Bird does not understand, so he throw his eyes straight up. When they fall back in Bird's eye holes, they are much brighter. Coyote ask Bird to brighten his eyes, so Bird take Coyote's eyes out and throw his eyes straight in the air and they come back much brighter. Coyote say, 'That great, Bird. I want eyes more brighter.' 'Go away,' say Bird. 'I am tired.' But Coyote insist and so he throw his eyes back into the air."

"Wait," Loni interrupted. "I thought Bird threw his eyes."

"Making sure you listening." Willie slowed the sweating horses to a plodding walk, hoping to cool them down. "Bird throw Coyote's eyes back into air but doesn't catch. He walk away! Please, Bird. Bring me my eyes! Fed up, Bird find pinion tree, pull off sap, and roll them into balls to stuff in Coyote's eyes. That why they yellow."

The singsong cadence relaxed Loni. "Tell me why his tongue is black."

"You tell me."

"Please.

"Last one. We almost there."

They crested the last long hill, and the windmill shimmered far away in a long, wide valley.

"Ever'one like to hear Snake rattle, so they keep teasing and scratching him to hear rattle. So, Snake go to Elder Brother and say, 'Ever'one tease and hurt me.' Elder then take two hairs from beard and make two teeth for

Snake and say, 'If they tease again, bite them.' So, when Rabbit scratch Snake, Snake bite him. Rabbit die from rattlesnake bite."

Loni hung on to the view of the windmill drawing closer as she lost herself in Willie's sing-song voice.

"The village not want Coyote to eat Rabbit, but they can't figure what to do. If they put in tree, Coyote climb and get it. If they bury, Coyote dig up. If they hide, Coyote will find. So, they decide to burn. They send Coyote to sun to get fire and Elder Brother rub a stick and start fire to burn Rabbit. But Coyote see fire and return, so village circle fire. Coyote jump over and grab Rabbit's heart and eats. It so hot, it burn his mouth. That why Coyote's mouth black."

Even though the air was deadly calm at the windmill, somehow the windmill fans were slowly turning, and the pump rod was pumping. Rustlers took all the mother cows at this well, but Bahb left the pump rod connected anyway to leave water for the wild animals whose lives depended on it. Loni loved him for that.

Blistered and tired, Loni thanked Daniel for letting Coco out. She pulled herself up the stairs, and a brown wooly mass nearly knocked her down at the door. Stripping off her filthy clothes, she took a long, cold shower and stood in front of the cooler fan to dry off. She smoothed aloe vera everywhere she could reach before she forced herself to dress for Rene's funeral.

A lightweight brown and black-striped serape hid the clean black tee and black Levis she fished out of the dirty clothes basket. The serape reminded Loni of the caftan Maria made her wear to weddings. Loni hadn't worn a dress since she was in kindergarten, and she swore then she never would.

Loni substituted her boots with black slip-on shoes and left her hair to kink in braid waves almost hiding her face. She shoved a square black scarf in her pocket and rummaged around until she found large sunglasses. Carefully running a bright red lipstick on, Loni was ready to leave, hoping her disguise and pathetic limp would keep her anonymous.

"Coco, stay" Loni ordered and gave the dog a biscuit to make up for not taking her. She closed the loft door on a pitiful brown face and accusing eyes.

Loni drove along ranches and small farms on her way to Caliente. Most of them worked Native-Americans and occasional undocumented workers, weak and exhausted from their trek across the desert. Lots of them needed someplace to rest before going on, but a few found homes. Loni was gone so long most of them were strangers.

Farms around the town dotted the landscape with houses, barns, and shacks. The land was rich from years of river floods dumping fine silt. The tall hill on the fourth side was the wealthy section. Caliente Butte sheltered the McMansions on the overhanging cliffs old timers called Butt Hillers. They poked fun at the people building on a diamondback rattlesnake den especially when they found the snakes on their stoops so often their children were not allowed to play outside. Her uncle Kirk skinned them and gave the skins to James who made hat bands he sold in the bars. Loni shuddered, remembering the times he tossed skins with rattles on her hollering, "Rattlesnake! Run!"

A few houses were spread along the highway where Old Highway 85 ran through the town and fifteen blocks out the other side. Loni crossed the railroad tracks paralleling Old Highway 85 on her way to the town square. A train hadn't stopped there for decades, and the empty station turned into a seed and fertilizer store. A small Mexican community stretched out three blocks on the other side of the tracks.

Arriving at the dirty tan adobe Catholic Church in Caliente, Loni found a parking place under a eucalyptus providing some shade. She jaywalked across the street to find cover under the overhang of the buildings along the sidewalk and reveled in the cool air escaping through the screen doors of open businesses.

Walking up toward the church, she studied the mourners and the curious, listening to the gossip as they slowly gravitated toward the church. She waited for a group of teens to cross the street and edged around the last dawdling boy who was buying a tamale from Spin's cart. Loni stopped at the old wrought iron fence across the front of the church lot. Rusted posts leaned in a crazy pattern with small white crosses with white flecks of paint stuck on the tops. Their shadows made bold patterns on the parched dirt.

A few bright yellow flowers barely hung on a palo verde tree. Loni stepped under the tree and pretended to be another Indian woman waiting for her man while she watched people outside the church. After a few minutes she left the tree and felt another wall of heat on the sidewalk and steps. She pushed open the old creaky double doors and entered the whitewashed interior with small stained-glass windows in the thick adobe walls.

The smell of furniture polish and burning candles took her back to her childhood. The darkened wood backs and arms of the old benches gleaming in the colorful sunlight through the stained-glass windows provided the only friendly spot in the tired building. Loni thought about what people did to each other in the name of religion. Every time she was shunned by a church Bahb would remind her, "Christians cannot teach kindness. They have too much to lose."

The church filled up fast. Loni checked for anyone who seemed out-of-place or whose behavior didn't fit. Most of the people calm, talking quietly among themselves as they found a place to lite, most particularly a tall, stocky salt and pepper-haired woman passing by Loni appeared pleased. Not exactly a funeral expression, Loni thought. A woman and man moved over to make room for the woman and the smaller woman with long curling honey-red hair gave her a one-armed hug.

Loni rubbed at her eyes to stay awake until Rene's family entered, jarring her awake in surprise to see Larry and Dorothea on either side of Rene's sobbing wife, holding onto Ellen like family. Tears ran down Dorothea's face as she held onto Ellen's hand. What the hell?

Loni remembered Ellen as a plump, mostly blonde cutie who was her counselor in high school. She helped Loni get a scholarship. Loni never understood why Ellen stayed with Rene. Her pretty face was crumpled in agony. Loni worried when she saw Ellen try to jerk away from Dorothea and Larry but they wouldn't let go.

The murmuring ceased when the priest began the chanting. Ellen's sobbing soon drowned the priest's evocations and continued throughout the mass. Kneeling, standing, sitting with ringing bells, singing voices, and Ellen's heartbroken keening, Loni felt the mass ritual roll over her, opening into painful memories of Maria's funeral.

While she stood over Maria's grave, unable to leave, one of Maria's sisters-in-law invaded their apartment and took everything, including furniture and kitchen wares. Even the toilet paper was gone. She'd taken Loni's things, like her favorite leather jacket and her boots. Gone too were things she gave Maria. The woman even took her books. All Loni had left besides some of her clothes were a beat-up toaster, a single-person fry pan, a few mismatched dishes, and some towels in the rag pile. Enough to get by if she kept the dishes clean and her clothes washed. And the pictures.

What bothered Loni most were the pictures. All the photographs of Maria were gone. Betty had torn Loni out of the photographs and scattered them onto the floor. Thank God she still had the one picture of Maria and Coco on her desk at the station.

Loni never told Sandi or Maria's mom what Betty had done. Betty had stolen from them before, but this time was the worst. When Loni found anything missing, she would holler at Maria. Betty's been here!" If Maria knew that Loni was upset, she would go by Betty's house and get it back. But Maria was gone, and she could never bring anything back again.

After Maria's death, the walls closed in on Loni. One night she knew she had to get out of the apartment. Her head down, she didn't see the two masked men in a grocery store until almost too late. She knew then she had to get out of the city as well. Time to go home.

Loni jerked herself back to the church and scanned it for anything out of place. Nothing caught her eye until Ellen stumbled down the aisle and stopped long enough to curse the woman with honey-red hair. With firm grips, Larry and Dorothea yanked her on. Loni ignored Dorothea's wink when they passed by and she fell in behind the honey-red hair. She hoped she could overhear something, but the woman was silent. The crowd on the side walk murmured as they stopped to watch the casket loaded into the hearse. Moving among the mourners, Loni heard nothing, not even a mention of the crash.

The hearse pulled away, dispersing the crowd who wandered off, giving Loni a good look at the two people next to the tall salt and pepper woman. The honey-red hair was in her early thirties and chic in a carefully casual way. A dark grey silk dress clung close to her slender body. The man had blond wavy hair and was more a pretty boy than handsome. He wore a dark-striped suit and subdued tie contrasting with his pale flattened face and jittery eyes, all signs of a meth addict. The tall woman with them wore a full-length caftan with gaudy swirling patterns reminding Loni of a runaway circus. Her proprietary manner toward the smaller woman rang Loni's gaydar.

Loni watched the procession of cars trail its slow way out of town as the kids under the trees on the courthouse lawn piled into cars and followed. By the time she reached her truck, the town was cleared of traffic. She did not follow the procession.

Glad to be home, Loni changed into a tank top and shorts so she could slather her raw red thighs again. She was in the middle of slicing cheese for a grilled cheese sandwich when Coco rushed to the door barking. Loni opened the door to a smiling Dorothea. She didn't return the smile. "Long time, Dot." Loni said flatly. "Where'd you leave Ellen?"

Dorothea was wearing short shorts and a skimpy top. Her nipples were clearly visible through the red cloth stretching across her breasts, displaying serious cleavage. This was not the same sobbing black-clad woman clinging to Rene's wife at the funeral or the tearless purple-robed woman staring at the wrecked plane. The pretty, sexy teenager of her youth turned into a blousy, overweight matron.

"Aren't you glad to see me?" Dorothea cast an appreciative gaze up and down Loni's buff body.

"Should I be?" Loni snapped.

"You forgot already?"

"Forgot what?" Loni tried to hold her ground, but Dorothea pushed by her into the room. In disgust Loni pushed back. "What are we? Still in high school?"

Dorothea made herself home at the table and waited, still smiling.

Loni leaned on a chair back unable to sit on her burning butt, and waited.

After a minute, Dorothea spoke into the silence. "I know you remember what good times we had on those summer parties."

Loni replied grimly, "That wasn't me."

"Yes, it was."

"It wasn't me," Loni repeated. "I was never ever at one of those parties."

Dorothea hesitated. "You and I used to make out somewhere."

"Well, well. I wasn't the only girl you shoved into a corner. I always figured you did it on a dare."

"I wouldn't have done that."

"Listen, Dot, I don't look to me for some side action. I don't do married women. Or closets."

Loni watched Dorothea's face tighten. She ducked her head and reached back, coiling her dark brown hair into a knot on the top of her head. After a few seconds, she let it tumble back over her shoulders. Dorothea lifted her head, glared at Loni and blurted, "That's harsh. I thought we were friends."

"If you want a friend, buy a dog."

"When did you start hating Mexicans?"

"When did you start hating Indians?"

"I don't!" Dorothea snapped. "What are you talking about?"

"I'm talking about bullshit," Loni said firmly. "That's what we're both sayin'. You're playing word games, and it's bullshit. You're not interested in me. Why not just tell the truth? Why did you really come?"

Loni saw the pain cross Dorothea's face. "I'm afraid. I need to leave my husband but I'm afraid."

Loni's head jerked up in surprise. "Why come to me?"

Dorothea wiped a few tears from her face. "Old times, I guess. I always trusted you and I don't trust Chief or James. Most of all Chui. Don't know what he's on but he's bat-shit crazy half the time."

"Okay." Loni thoughtfully studied Dot. "Any idea what I can do to help you?"

"Yes. I'm almost positive he's into drugs." She paused, nervously tugging at her top. "He's flying them in from Mexico."

"Can you prove it?" Loni waited.

"A month ago he brought home a little suitcase. When he was in the shower, I opened it. There were packages of white powder. Looked like any photo I ever saw on drugs. I had no idea what to do so I closed it and made dinner. Last week I called his work. Can't remember why. They said he quit months ago." Dorothea's voice wavered. "When I asked him, he said he forgot to tell me he got a better job, but he wouldn't tell me where or even what. He's always gone, flying out at night or hanging out with Rene. He's spending money like a Rockefeller. Even got one of those fancy red sports cars. A Lamborghini for god's sake. I checked the price. It's over two hundred thousand dollars! For a car!" A rueful expression crossed Dorothea's face. "We didn't pay that for our house. Sometimes when he's gone, his kid takes it for a spin." Dot had a start of a smile. "Hope he wrecks it."

"How'd he explain the suitcase?"

Dorothea inspected her chipped fingernail polish. "I was afraid to ask him."

"So, what you're saying is Larry and Rene are working together bringing in drugs."

Dorothea's head jerked up in surprise. "Why'd you blame Rene?"

"We found drug residue in his plane."

Dorothea's eyes popped wide open in surprise. She took a minute before she said, "He's a real asshole I agree, but I never thought he was a dealer." She sat in contemplation before she continued. "It does explain a lot. I wouldn't be surprised the way they hung out, always planning about flying off somewhere." Dorothea paused again. "I do remember this time when Rene got really, really mad at Larry for buying the car. Said it advertised business and would get a shit load of their friends into real trouble. He wanted Larry to get rid of the car, but Larry refused."

"You close to Rene's family?"

"Well yeah, Rene was my half-brother, eleven years older. I grew up with him. You knew that, right?"

Loni tried to hide her surprise. "Do you know anyone else Larry hung out with, called or who called him? Anyone who traveled with him? Or where he went?"

Dorothea shook her head. "Nothing on our home phone bills. Or cell, that I can tell. Ever since I found the case I've been searching. I did hear him phone the O'Neal Nursery a couple of times but I never saw any plants around." Dorothea stopped as a few tears ran down her face. "Please! Say you'll help me."

Relenting, Loni agreed. "Can you give me copies of your phone bills, credit card receipts, bank statements, anything else that would tell us anything?"

Dorothea opened her mouth to speak. Suddenly she leaned forward into her arms, sobbing.

Loni waited until she calmed to sniffles. "Do you know where he is now?"

"Ask me if I care."

"What you're trying to say is you have no idea what he does, where he goes, or who he sees. Except for Rene who's now dead." Loni straightened up from leaning on the back of the chair, arching her sore back. "Life's a real bitch sometimes. You got kids now so don't let it get to you." She turned for the door. "Let me do some checking, Dot. See what I can find."

Dorothea reluctantly got up and followed Loni to the door. "Promise?"

"I really do." Loni held the door open.

Dorothea grabbed a chaste kiss before she disappeared down the stairs.

Wiping her mouth, Loni shut the door. Debating her next move while she fried her cheese sandwich, Loni was positive Dorothea knew more than she'd said. She smiled, hearing Bahb's voice. *Walk in shit, it will bury you!* Loni mentally moved the problem onto a back burner and sat down with her sandwich. Coco trailed a mouth full of dry food and dropped it on a small carpet to eat with her.

Finishing her meal, Loni searched for something to read. She missed her books. Until Maria moved in with her, she read herself to sleep. Loni decided she would go to the library after work wondering if Mrs. Hunt was still there. As she headed toward her bed with her laptop, Loni thanked Coco for cleaning up her dog food. The hard bits could be tough on bare feet and her back when she tried to exercise. Oh, damn. Exercise. Tomorrow, she promised herself. She'd get back to it tomorrow.

FROM: Loni Wagner
TO: Sandi@gmailyahoo.com
DATE: July 6
SUBJECT: Still here

Reason #5 I don't ranch is because of the long, long hours of hard, hot labor at no profit.

Have I mentioned how much I hurt, how sunburned and rubbed raw I am? I'm already dreading tomorrow. I'm having so much difficulty walking now I hope I won't be chasing anyone on foot.

We tracked rustlers all morning and found a cut in the fence where a truck loaded the cows. Without a brand, it's going to be hard to get them back. These old mother cows have been here for years, dropping calves to keep my grandparents going. Selling the steers they occasionally brought in from Old Mexico is about their only income. I'm putting a BOLO out tomorrow and hope for the best.

Remember the plane wreck? I went to Rene's funeral and watched some interesting interactions. I also had an unexpected visitor tonight, Rene's half-sister Dorothea. Went to school with her, but I forgot she was related to Rene who was my history teacher then. She said she thought her husband was into drugs but she didn't know about Rene. Knowing the old Dot, I find that hard to believe.

First time I've been hit on since I got home, though. She wants me to help her get rid of her husband. Told her if he was doing something illegal, I would arrest him. But that's as far as I'd go. Hope she doesn't get caught in whatever Larry and Rene were doing.

Write more tomorrow if I can.

Loni

The cold sheets felt wonderful on her hot burned skin. If she kept this up, she'd soon be as dark as Willie.

CHAPTER SEVEN

The only thing Loni ran into on patrol all night were thousands of bugs splattered on her windshield, headlights, and in her radiator. She squirmed in the sweltering heat and night so deadly not even her sore, burning muscles and aching butt could keep her awake. Now on her regular patrol she had circled around and was headed back onto the last leg of her night. Needing a pit stop bad, she turned off the highway, following an abandoned trail. When she drove in far enough for privacy, she parked and turned Coco loose. Grabbing her plastic bag of aloe vera, she hurried behind a bush and dropped her pants. She rubbed goo all over the inside of her thighs, wishing for her grandma's salve.

Slightly relieved, Loni drove into the growing pink on the eastern horizon as she entered the town proper. She stopped in a circle of light flowing from the open door to the bakery kitchen. The smell of baking doughnuts had her saliva running as she watched the baker through the screen door. Dressed in white, he poured a large bag of flour into the huge mixing bowl. The white dust puffed up almost as high as his white Doctor Seuss hat as he putzed about. She loved his Doughboy image. After a few minutes, Loni drove on and circled a few town blocks reassuring herself all was well before returning to the darkness.

Lights flickered on one by one in shadowed houses across the desert floor where rancher and farmer families were rising into a new day. These were people she knew from long ago, and she passed the time making up stories about what happened to their lives while she was gone. She wondered who died, who got married, who left, who was gay? Patrolling alone all night and sleeping most of the day made for lonely times. "I'm just plain weary." She told Coco who was sound asleep.

The sky turned from pink to yellow, and her slow night was almost done. Loni barely parked in a wide spot on Harper Road when a car fishtailed by her. Its tires spun as the car raced down the highway. Wide awake, she tore after the speeding car and clocked it at 120 miles per hour. When it shrank to a dot on the horizon, she called to warn Bobby the car was headed toward town. "It's a dark blue Mercedes, Bobby. Pretty sure it was an S Class."

"Oh, lord, I want one of those so bad."

"If I catch this guy with drugs, I'll get it for you."

Loni anticipated Bobby's laugh of delight as she hung up, still clutching the steering wheel so tight her knuckles turned white. She pushed her SUV up to ninety miles an hour before it danced and shimmied. Fighting the savage vibration, she felt herself losing control. Slowing down, she relaxed her grip on the steering wheel as she sped toward town.

At the first cluster of houses, she spotted the Mercedes slowly weaving onto the wrong side of the road. It lurched onto the shoulder of the road and crashed against the guardrail. She slowed to a stop behind the car and sat a minute, waiting. The back window was tinted too dark for her to see inside. "Something's not right," she said to Coco. Loni went back on her mike. "Hey, Bobby. The Mercedes ran off the road, and I don't like it. Get me some backup. And check this Mexican plate." Loni rattled off the long numbers and letters.

"I'll send James," Bobby said.

Loni flipped on the loudspeaker. "Get out of the car." Her voice blared into the early dawn. Nothing moved. "Get out of the car, now!" She waited again. "Well, shit, Coco," she reluctantly told the dog. "We better go see."

With her gun in her hand, pointed down, Loni slipped up to the darkened windows on the driver's side of the car. Her mind flashed back to a good friend who stopped a speeding car and called for backup. She found him face down in the middle of the highway in his own blood and no car in sight. They never found the shooter. Loni wished she had a partner, somebody watching her back. She rapped on the window. "Out! Now!" Nothing moved. She yanked open the door, gun ready, and found a man slumped over the steering wheel. He was alone, and he was dead.

His wrinkled Western shirt and dress pants had a travel aura about him. So did the stubble on his pasty face and food wrappers littering the floor. The blood on the grey floor mat under his feet oozed toward the door. Pulling him back, she saw a knife handle sticking out of his stomach and a large red circle on his white pearl-snapped shirt. She let him flop back and closed the door.

"Bobby. The Mercedes? The driver's dead with a knife in his stomach. I'd guess he was trying to get to the clinic."

"I'd guess he didn't make it," Bobby echoed.

"I need CSI out here now. And send me a wrecker."

"Know who he is?"

"Nope. Young, cowboy clothes, all I can tell. Didn't want to disturb the crime scene."

"Maybe you shouldn't move the car."

"This isn't the original crime scene. The man can't sit in this heat all day."

Loni followed the wrecker to the police garage. Gary Beasley, the police mechanic, was on duty. He had a baseball cap plopped backwards on his bald head. Darkened blotches of grease covered the front of his shirt and his frayed cuffs. Like a doctor, he wore latex gloves. "Allergic to grease," he told her once. She made him promise not to take his eyes off the car until the crime scene people and coroner got to it.

Her shift finally at an end, Loni signed out and returned to the police compound for her truck. Climbing in she noted the Mercedes was still in the police garage. She waved to Gary as she drove out and he pointed to the car, reassuring her he was keeping a close eye out. Her adrenaline faded, but her thighs were still burning as she drove to her grandparents' ranch. Every move only made the burn worse. As she stopped in front of the ranch house, her cell phone rang. Loni saw Lola's name. "Hey! Tell me what you want won't make me hurt any worse than I already do."

Lola's laugh was infectious. "Chief wants you back right now. I'll protect you."

"Why?"

"Because you're special?"

"No," Loni said, embarrassed. "Why do I have to come back?"

"What? I know everything?"

"Well, yes."

"Not this time."

Loni groaned. "When?"

"Like I said. Now."

"Listen. I've got to get my grandma's salve on my ass. Give me another five."

"What's wrong with your ass?"

"I spent the weekend on a horse, and I'm dying here."

Loni could hear Lola's teasing chuckle as Loni hung up and slowly climbed down from her truck.

Every step made Loni groan as she limped into the house to the bathroom and dropped her pants. She reached for the jar of homemade salve on the bathroom shelf and covered her butt and inside of her legs with the foul-smelling grease. Sighing in relief as the fire drained away, it hit her. She forgot how her grandma's crap smelled like a fresh skunk kill she couldn't avoid, and she had to go back to work and face Chief. Coco backed up and tilted up her nose, sniffing the air. Loni pulled up her pants and bow-legged, walked through the living room ignoring her smirking grandma.

"I'll be back soon," Loni told Coco.

Her grandma patted Coco on the head as the two of them watched Loni head out to her truck. "Dogs can't reckon time, child."

"Shush, Shiichoo. Don't tell Coco that. She'll think you're lying to her," Loni teased. "Would you tell Bahb to take Coco home for me?" she hollered out the window of her truck at the two standing in the doorway. "I gotta get back to work."

At the last tree under the row of clustered salt cedars overhanging the circle driveway, a banty hen popped up on her windshield and nose-dived onto the hood of her truck. Loni jerked to a stop. Please, lord, let the chicken be all right. She didn't want her grandma mad. Again. The tiny mottled brown and red bird lay still for a minute, stood, and shuddered. She gazed at Loni, wagged her tail and crapped on her truck. With another shudder, the bird flapped back into the tree.

Ignoring the brown and white poop, Loni drove to the highway intersection and waited while she counted seven John Deere combines passing. Loni envied the drivers sitting in refrigerated king cabs as they waddled to the safflower fields ahead. The sound of Western twang from a local radio station poured out of the last one as it rumbled by. She smelled the hot exhaust from the combines' powerful engines as she followed them until they turned into a safflower field, bouncing splashes of green against the blinding yellow flowers.

The field ended abruptly at Caliente's city limit sign boasting a population of four-thousand twenty-five. Outlying gated developments made the town seem much bigger. Including Caliente Butte, the reservation village near the town's southern border, and the development at the Wagner Airport to the west, all added to the population. On weekends, farmers, ranchers, and miners came to town to shop and mingle with the Mexicans who came across the border. Strangers erased the quiet, safe place of her childhood, but she wondered if the safe feeling about the 'good ol days' wasn't an illusion in the first place.

On the outskirts of town, familiar landmarks unfolded, all in the same shades of desert tan. Wood, adobe brick, sidewalks, sand-pitted vehicles stripped of color, this was what Loni remembered most about the desert, the open space and lack of color. Abandoned cars and pickups rested amid dead weeds surrounding older, unpainted houses bleached pale tan. Screened-in porches filled with rocking chairs, tables, and beds stretched across the front of most of the homes. Too poor to have refrigeration, old-time residents like Miss Mickle, her favorite grade-school teacher, spent their time on these porches, waiting for a stray breeze. The frail woman waved at her, and Loni waved back as a warm feeling rolled over her.

Loni drove by the Mormon Church, stucco white with a tall cone-shaped sphere, reaching into the sky. She remembered counting the churches and bars in town. The churches won.

An empty service station huddled next to the old abandoned movie theater popped up next. A faded yellow sign on the wide double doors read "CONDEMNED." Loni admired the marquee, pushing out in its past splendor. Carved wood with chipped gilt surrounded a few plastic letters hanging precariously from their railings. The city refused to confiscate the property because it would cost them too much to demolish. The building waited, its last owner dead and no heirs to be found.

The last owner was Old Man Jandas, mostly deaf and blind. Every night after he closed, he climbed up to a small one-room shack on top of the building. The last time she saw him, he was up on the roof wandering in his long, white night-shirt.

The movie that Halloween night was "The Rocky Horror Picture Show." She remembered the fuzzy image and the crowd chanting, "Focus, focus, focus." Finally, someone in the audience climbed up and fixed it.

After the movie, Loni found a flat tire on Bahb's old pickup. Waiting for the parking lot to empty, she changed it with an equally beat-up, worn-out tire and drove across the street to get the flat fixed. She was not about to go out on the desert without a spare. It just wasn't smart.

The station owner was a talkative fellow, always friendly to everyone, even breeds. He was telling her about old man Jandas. Seems earlier that day, the old man went to Phoenix to pick up his mail-order bride. He was in such a hurry to open the theater on time he didn't see the outhouse the football team put in the middle of the street in front of his theater. He blasted right through it, shattering lumber for a block. Without a word, his new bride got out of his car, grabbed her suitcase out of the backseat, picked her way through the shattered pieces of wood to the drugstore, and bought a ticket for the first bus back to Phoenix. Needless to say, Jandas was heartbroken.

Loni grinned over the story with the service station owner as he finished up her repair. The next thing Loni remembered about that night was the sudden shrill scream from the service station owner's wife. "Oh my god, he's going to jump! Somebody stop him!"

The few people standing around stared up at the old man as he wandered over and stopped at the edge of the roof, leaned out and pissed. Stunned, they watched the steaming stream, sparkling in the street light, arc off the roof. It seemed a very long time until Jandas turned and disappeared back into his shack.

Smiling at the memory, Loni stopped for gas at the new service station, the only one open in town and the only one for a good fifty miles. There was no service. No one came to help. She poked her credit card into the slot and shoved the hose nozzle in, filling the truck's tank. A pimply teenager chewing bubblegum in a small hutch behind bulletproof glass read a comic book as he waited to flip pump switches on and off as he pushed/pulled the cash only tray in and out.

On Main Street, she passed the general store facing the town square and turned onto B Street. Over half the storefronts were vacant, and the rest were mostly bars. Billy the Kid's bar claimed a famous fight on this spot, Last Stop Saloon was self-explanatory, and the name River Bar was a misnomer if ever there was one. Unfortunately, the water long since disappeared, trapped behind towering dams many miles upstream. This water was diverted into canals snaking across the desert floor for large farming irrigation.

Loni parked in the police lot and stepped out into oven-blasting heat that sucked the breath out of her. She ducked her head to avoid the sun's glare and hurried across the street as fast as her raw legs could move. Her boot heels sank into the soft, sun-melted asphalt burning through her soles. She waddled up the long sidewalk and pushed the button beside the heavy, reinforced door. Inside, she gingerly walked up to the counter, relishing the slightly cooler air.

Lola watched her slow approach. "You got here."

"Still no idea why I was summoned?"

"Nope." Lola patted her cheek in commiseration. "Something's got him going and he's meaner than a snake. Might help if you threw in a piece of raw meat first." Giggling, Lola nodded toward the bullpen and turned serious. "Something big. You've got lots of company."

Loni took in the bullpen. She had never seen so many town cops and highway patrollers in one place.

Lola grinned. "Makes you wonder who's minding the store, huh?"

"Hope to God it doesn't have anything to do with Rene's plane." Loni cringed. "Chief's mad enough."

She followed Tully into the sound of male laughter. She nodded a greeting to Trevor and sat a seat away from him back in a corner. Like roll call in LA, she thought, realizing she missed cop humor, no matter how black.

"What's so funny?" Tully groused. "It's too damn hot for anything to be funny."

"Well shit, Tully, ain't you used to this heat yet?" said a patrol officer Loni hadn't seen before.

"Hell, no."

"How long you lived here, anyway?"

"Eighteen summers."

"Ignore Tully," James told the patrollers. "He doesn't even know which way to go to get out of the heat. Some traveler asked him for directions to Springville, and he said, 'Head north.' The man asked him which way was north. Tully then said, 'buy a compass'. O' course, the next thing outa the guy's mouth was where to buy a compass. Then Tully says, 'How would I know?' This really pissed the guy off. 'Damned if you're not the dumbest cop I ever saw. You don't know anything, do you?'" James paused, basking in the attention. "So then Tully said to the tourist, 'Maybe not. But I'm not the one lost.'"

"Well, shit," Tully objected. "I only moved to town that week. You ever see how lopsided this town sits with the world?"

James continued poking fun at him. "My favorite is when Tully asked Old Man Phillips where the laundromat was. Phillips said, 'It's over behind where the old theater burned down.' Tully said, 'I been livin' in this town only a month then. How the hell would I know where the burned down theater was?' Old Man Phillips replied, 'I just told you where it was,' and he walked away mumbling something about all we needed was more outsiders coming in on the short bus."

"What is this, pick on Tully Day?"

"Thought you said you lived here eighteen years," Trevor drawled.

"In the desert," Tully nearly yelled. "Eighteen long goddamn hot summers in Yuma on the goddamn hot desert."

Tully stalked down the hall toward the restroom followed by the men's laughter.

A patrolman by James spoke up. Dark blue eyes, wild red hair, and big freckles splattered everywhere made him appear younger than his age which Loni guessed at early thirties. "I got a ticket story. Yesterday I passed a woman with both her feet straddling the steering wheel, painting her toenails. When I stopped her and gave her a ticket, she said, 'I wasn't doing anything wrong. I was on cruise control.'"

"Oh, god, I had one of those too," Trevor said in his slow way. "This guy put his RV rental on cruise control and went back to shit. Found hisself sitting on the side of the road, with his pants gone. Said he thought cruise control meant it could drive itself."

"Was he hurt bad?"

"Not a scratch except on his bare ass. The fiberglass bathroom saved him. Couldn't drive that RV again though. It was one of those two-by-four square jobbies. Lumber scattered for blocks."

Carl Harper stopped next to Loni and reached out and rubbed her head. "Is that hideous smell what I think it is?"

"Shuddup." Loni stood and hugged him, glad to see a friendly face. "Getting a little gray there, sport? Gained some weight, too?" She patted his stomach. "Hear you're living the good life now, playing copper. How come you're not ranching anymore?"

The lines around his eyes deepened as his brown, leathered face beamed at her. "Heard you were playing copper instead of living the good life ranching," Carl mimicked her. "How come? Forgot how?"

"She's not ranching because she gave it all back to the Indians," James said from the other side of the room.

Carl ignored him and gave Loni another hug. "Good to see you home in spite of the smell."

Backing away she sat again, owning up. "Spent the weekend on Roani. I'd forgotten how much it hurt."

"I got used to that smell years ago." Carl sat next to her. "Old Roani's still alive?"

"Yes. And obviously in better shape than I am."

Carl snickered. "So why did you become a cop?"

"Didn't own two fine Brahmas like you did," Loni teased him.

"And here I thought you loved those bulls."

"Are Big Hump and Harvey still alive?

"Big Hump died. Sold Harvey to Essey Rigall. I'm sure he would love for you to come see him."

"Yeah, well, now that I carry a gun and all, tell the bull if he gets near me again, I'll shoot him."

"Strange you were the only one Harvey ever chased."

"You taught him that just to humiliate me."

"Worked to."

Trevor joined in. "You two ranch together?"

"Nah." Carl explained. "We were neighbors. Years ago the ranchers agreed to each buy two bulls from different breeds. Every two years we traded them to keep new blood in the stock." Carl nodded toward Loni. "We had the Brahmas. Every time her granddad got them, she spent the next two years running and hiding."

"Last time we got them, I was fifteen," Loni told Trevor. "When I went outside, I had to go backwards with my eyes on Harvey every second or he would flat-foot jump the fence and be on top of me faster than I could blink. For two long years I spent my time climbing trees, hay stacks—"

"Pickups, horse trailers, outhouses." Carl chuckled at the memories.

"I even tried to climb a mesquite tree once. Damn, that hurt!" Loni winced at the memory.

"It was even funnier when we branded calves. Harvey was right there, his eyes never leaving her. She had to do all the heeling." Carl giggled. "She didn't dare get off her horse." Carl turned back to Loni. "I swear he was in love with you."

"Do you have any idea how creepy that is?"

"I believe it." James's snide voice curled behind her.

Carl ignored him again. "At least they were more interesting than those two huge white-faces you owned. Except when they met at the water trough in the evening. Now that was funny."

"What'd they do?" Trevor asked.

"They'd spot each other a half mile away and bellow. Take a few steps, stop, paw dirt, throwing it everywhere, bellow again a few times. Take a few steps, paw dirt until their backs and heads were thick with it. They had these huge hoofs as big as dinner plates and could throw a lot of dirt. They must have weighed a ton and were as slow as molasses. It took them on to an hour to finally meet. Then they'd knock their heads together, hook horns, bellow, rock a bit, bellow, back up and shudder off the dirt as they walked over to the water trough together like best of friends."

"Well, at least we could find them when we wanted them," Loni retorted.

"That's true. Those two Santa Cruz of Essey's were amazing. They simply disappeared. We never saw them the whole two years."

"Except for Willie. He could always find them." Loni smiled at the memory.

"So Bahb put your sorry ass to work this weekend checking his mother cows?"

"You didn't hear. We got rustled."

"Oh, god." Carl's eyes popped wide in surprise. "All of them?"

"All but one. They chased old Flossie into a cholla patch and left her to die."

"What'd you do? Shoot her?"

"Of course not! Bahb shoot anything? She's tied up in the barn with Shiichoo's medicine."

"So the smell tells me you haven't been on a horse in a while."

"Not for two long days at a time. I'm so sore I can barely walk."

Carl nearly fell over laughing. Catching his breath he teased her, "Good thing I got used to that smell."

"You really quit the ranch?"

Carl's face sobered. "Just wasn't worth it anymore. When the folks died, I sold what cows were left and leased the place out." He pulled on his ear, and Loni knew something was bothering him. "Somebody's leasing it now, growing rare plants in greenhouses. Can you believe that?"

Loni leaned closer to Carl and lowered her voice. "I wanted to ask you about that. The dead man I found this morning. You hear about it?"

"Sure. Who hasn't?"

"Well, he came out of the road between your ranch and Bahb's."

"Really?" Carl stared at her. "Doesn't sound good. You tell anybody?"

"It's in my report. But since nobody reads them, then no, I haven't told anyone."

"Thanks for the heads up." Carl pulled on his ear again. "I'll check on it."

"Would you let me know?"

Before Carl could answer, Chief stepped out of his office. "Carl. Tully. In here."

Loni fanned herself with her folder as she glanced up at the ribbon tied to the grate in the ceiling, hoping it would flutter, indicating the roof mounted cooler was working. No such luck. She sighed and opened the folder. The ink refused to flow on the damp paper when she tried to finish her report on the dead man in the Mercedes.

Trevor laughed. "How many times are you going to waste your time filling out forms in here before you learn?"

Loni's tan synthetic cloth uniform wrapped around her body, burning her skin. She scratched at her heat rash. "Oh, hell, I don't know. Obviously, I haven't learned yet. I hate these uniforms. I hate the heat. I hate the humidity. I'm even half-sorry I came home." A voice nearby broke into Loni's litany.

"Hey, I've been trying to find you for two days. Don't you answer your goddamn phone anymore?" Chui's voice sent a chill through Loni.

"Don't you answer yours?" James spit back. "I left you a message I had to go out of town. I just got back."

Loni wondered why he didn't show up at the Mercedes. Distracted, she hadn't noticed a sandy-haired man walk into the station. He was at the booking desk, asking for Chief.

"Must be why we're all here." Trevor fixed on the man. "He's State, head of Narc. Name's Jim Filbrite."

Loni watched the red-headed patrol officer eye Lola as she talked on the phone, ignoring Filbrite. She had a shoe off and was rubbing her foot. Placing a hand over the phone, she pointed toward Chief's office. He disappeared as she hung up and slipped her shoe back on, riding her skirt up so high on her long legs that everybody, including Loni, ogled.

"If those shoes hurt so bad," the red-headed patrol officer said to Lola as she passed by to hand James a phone message. "Why do you wear them?"

Lola stopped long enough to pinch his cheek and smile. "To get anything out of you I want."

Everyone cheered as he got on his knees, begging Lola to ask him for anything.

The hilarity stopped when Chief came out of his office and motioned Filbrite to follow him into the bullpen. Chief circled around in the bullpen introducing everyone while Filbrite handed each person a thin, yellow folder. He was complementary until he reached Loni.

"This here's Loni Wagner. Newbie from LA." Chief wrinkled his nose and pulled on Filbrite's elbow to move him on. He wouldn't budge as he reached out to shake her hand.

"I know who you are. I have a friend in LA on the Major Crime Squad. Garrad Peppard. He said to say hi if I saw you."

"Sure. Great detective. Good man."

"He says the same for you. Well. Not the man part."

"Don't be so sure," Chui sniped loud enough for everyone to hear.

Filbrite frowned. "Listen, Loni. Garrad told me you're an exceptional detective and profiler. I hear you're a desert native, too. I'm counting on your help here."

"Anytime." Loni felt good about his comments despite Chui's nasty remark.

"Listen up." Chief ignored the entire exchange. "Jim Filbrite's from the State office. He'll tell you why he's here."

Everyone quieted. "We got three dead in south Phoenix from poisoned meth. The dealer we picked up says his source was Caliente." Filbrite's faded blue eyes swept the room. His voice was so flat Loni had trouble paying attention.

"We need to find the source of this one fast because the meth was cut with ricin. We don't think it's intentional because ricin's a deadly poison and dealers really don't want to kill off their customers. For those of you who don't know about ricin, it's leftover from squeezing the oil out of castor beans. We think some castor oil processor got careless about where he put his waste. Or maybe somebody's growing castor oil plants too close to the meth lab."

Filbrite stared around the silent room again. "This batch of poison can be disastrous, especially if it gets into the schools. We don't know how much got out there before it killed the people in Phoenix. We don't know how much more is coming. Or even where it's coming from."

He walked across the room with nervous energy. "Here's what you look for. Swallowing ricin causes nausea, vomiting, abdominal pain within twenty-four hours. Inhaling it causes shortness of breath, chest tightness, and a cough within six hours."

Chief was obviously not happy as he studied Filbrite like he was a scorpion. "You saying we follow people around all day to see if they puke?"

An annoyed expression crossed Filbrite's face before he continued. "Start with the schools. Tell the administration and nursing staff to be on the lookout for a sick kid. Get to doctors, clinics, EMTs, anyone in health services. Make sure they understand what's happening. Talk to parents." He punched a fist into the palm of his other hand. "This is serious, people! Find every source you can, call in any favors, get the sonsabitches mixing this stuff."

"What about the 'shake and bakers' we find?" Chui asked. "Want them sent to Phoenix for you to question?"

Filbrite paused and frowned. "I don't think the amount of meth we found can be manufactured in a bottle in a car." A few people snickered. Raising his voice, Filbrite continued. "I can't assign highway patrol to search, but they can help when needed. Agree?" Loni and the three other patrollers concurred. "Questions, anybody?" He rubbed the side of his thin nose, waiting.

"Yes." Loni ignored Chief's scowl and the glares from James and Chui. "Are you working on the Rene Garcia murder and apparent drug trafficking?"

"I haven't heard anything about it, Loni. I'm not sure it's related to this case. What do you think?"

"I don't see any connection yet, but I got a bad feeling it is. I won't know until I see the analysis of the drug residue, and DNA results on the blood sample I sent from the plane crash along with the thumbprint on the valve to find the person who murdered Rene and shot at me. From what I'm hearing from you maybe test the drug residue for a match with yours. Maybe check out the names and numbers in Rene's notebook and cell phone. And another thing. Dust for fingerprints on the two-hundred-thousand dollars from the plane."

"What two-hundred-thousand dollars?" Chief exploded.

"From Rene's plane, Chief." Loni answered.

"Where is it now?"

"At the State lab where I had it sent."

"Well, goddamnit! Get it back. That's my money."

"Sorry," Filbrite interrupted Chief's tirade. "It's evidence in a murder charge. And probably drug money."

Filbrite turned back to Loni. "Could you fill out a report listing all your concerns and send it to me?"

"I already did it. Lola will give you a copy."

"Soon as I get your report, I'll see what I can find and get back to you." Filbrite gazed around. "Any other questions? No? Then I'll turn it back to Chief."

Chief stood. "People, what we're going to do is put together a task force. Everybody available meet in my conference room at nine every morning." He put a hand on Carl's shoulder. "This here is Carl Harper. He's heading it up so call him if you find anything. I mean anything. Nothing is too small. Let's pay attention out there, people."

Chief stepped back, and Carl took over. "Here's where we start." He jingled the coins in his pocket. "James, get Loni's report on Rene's plane and check everything. See if you can find a connection to the meth. Follow up on Loni's questions. Also, check his flight plans over the past year. Can you do it?"

"Sure." James smirked at Loni.

"Chui, talk to your buddies on the border about any new source for meth. And talk to Rosa. I bet you she knows something."

Chui opened his mouth to object, but Carl's glare shut him up.

"Tully, talk to Rene's wife. Maybe she can tell you more about why he took these trips."

Tully ignored Carl.

"Tully?"

Tully slowly conceded.

"Good. Anything else?"

Reluctantly, Loni spoke up again. "I think Larry Kildare is involved with Rene somehow."

"Where'd you get that idea?" Chief barked.

"Something he said about flying into Old Mexico." Loni wasn't ready to reveal Dorothea's suspicions about her husband. She avoided the eyes staring at her.

"Tully. Go talk to Larry." Carl scanned the room again. "See you back here in the morning. The rest of you, report anything you find." Chief hobbled out of the room back to his office, breaking up the group, some leaving as others stood around talking.

Following them out, Filbrite nodded to Loni as he passed by and pushed out the double doors of the police station.

Loni stopped at Lola's counter. "Hey, Lola? I need to sign out some drug samples to train Coco. Can you order me some?"

"Like what?"

"Ricin for one. What do you see in here the most?"

Lola shrugged. "I have to get the ricin expressed from the Phoenix labs tomorrow morning. I can get you pot, coke, meth, maybe some mescaline."

"Any opium or Ritalin?"

"Rarely. I don't have any here."

"Okay, how about some pot, coke, and a couple of buttons." Loni ticked them off on her fingers.

"You're gonna have to return them."

"Maybe."

Loni smiled at Lola's stern scrutiny. "Think I'll give you drugs with that smart mouth, think again, sister."

"I'm not your sister." Loni saw the snide expression in Lola's eyes. "Nor your brother, sister, or lover, or—"

"Okay," Lola interrupted, blushing. "Okay. See me tomorrow." She bent down to coo at Coco. "Such a sweet girl you are. Yes, you are. Yes, you are. Yes, you are."

"Judas!" Loni snorted. "Does everybody talk to animals like that?"

"You want those drugs or not?"

"Okay, okay. I'm outta here." Loni said goodbye to Lola, more than ready to leave. Her hand was on the door when a voice grated her to a stop.

"Girly!" She turned to see Chief's head stuck out his door. "Get the hell in here!"

Inside Chief's office, she waited for another explosion. Carl and Tully ignored her with expressionless faces. "Chief?"

"I'm assigning you to track down drugs."

"But, Chief—"

"Was that a period at the end of that sentence? Did I say you could talk?" Chief barked. Tully guffawed. Loni was grateful Carl hadn't joined in the fun. "I'm assigning you to Carl. He'll give you orders at the task force meetings."

"You can't do that!" Loni objected.

"Watch me."

Loni figured the extra hours were punishment for bypassing Chief with the plane's evidence and probably for being a female. Loni glanced over at Carl who raised one eyebrow a millimeter. She stood silently, trying not to breathe in the acrid body smell in the stifling office mixed with her own odor from her grandma's salve.

"You can go now. Carl, get her the hell out of here."

Back in the bullpen, Loni watched Carl open a notebook. "Sorry, Loni. Maybe I can give you some short jobs. Chief said you got a sniffer?"

"My dog Coco."

"How about you take her to the school and let her do her thing? Maybe she can find something we can follow up on."

"Sure, Carl. First thing in the morning."

"You better do it now."

"Can't. I need a sample of the ricin for her to smell. I'll get Lola to overnight it from Phoenix."

Carl agreed. "I'll do it for you. Why don't you go home and get some rest? Tomorrow might be a long day."

🌵

In the police garage the coroner had come and gone, taking the body with him. Jim Filbrite was watching a crime investigator pull packets from inside the spare tire. Gary Beasley had taken off the door panel searching for more contraband. Car seats with the upholstery ripped into shreds were scattered across the garage cement floor, and the Mercedes was in pieces. Lord, Loni thought, this is gonna break Bobby's heart.

"Whatcha got?" Loni stayed behind the yellow tape.

Gary picked up a package. "Looks like Sudafed."

"How much?"

"So far enough to cook a pound or better."

"Not real creative, was he?"

"First place I would've looked. This your collar, Loni?"

"I followed him to town," Loni explained. "He was dead with a knife in his stomach by the time I got to him."

Loni said goodbye to Jim Filbrite and Gary and walked to her truck. Before she got in, she called Carl. "You should know the dead guy had a shit load of Sudafed. You need to be careful out there. Want me to go with you?"

"Well, damn. Thanks, but no. I've got it covered."

Worried, Loni drove home and parked in the hangar. She got out and dragged herself over to the plane where Daniel was working. Black grease streaked his face and light blue work shirt as he dropped a filter into its canister on top of a Cessna Skylane's engine. "Hey, cuz, how's it going?"

"Hunky dory!" Daniel winked. "And you?"

Loni knew he was making fun of her. "So whatcha doin'?"

"What's it look like?"

"I don't know." Loni shrugged.

"You don't know when somebody's changing an air filter?"

"So I'm a retard."

"At least you're smart enough to admit it. Hand me a wrench."

"Good one, cuz." Loni punched his shoulder. "Gotta let Coco out now." She ran up the stairs.

"I already let her out. You don't have a comeback."

Loni stayed quiet.

"See," he hollered at her again. "You got so smart from college when I say something like a simple hello to you, you're stuck for an answer."

"Keep it up, and I'll sic Coco on you." Loni opened the door to the wiggling dog that almost knocked her down. They came back downstairs, and Loni wandered in to talk to her uncle. "How come you didn't farm or ranch?"

Uncle Herm closed his ledger. He stretched out his long arms and legs, smiling up at her. "When I finally got out of high school, my dad said, 'Son, you're too small to pull a plow and too big to ride the horse. Not coordinated enough to be a cowboy anyway. And you hate to dig. Best make your way somehow else with those aero planes you're so crazy about.' So, when Pa died, he willed the ranch house and Taylor grazing to your dad and the section next to town to me. He gave Kirk the mining rights. That's all he wanted to do anyway. Did good, too, with the Haley mine."

"Made him rich enough to be a Butt Hiller."

"The old man left me enough money to build the runway and hangar. I found investors to build the airpark houses. Airfield fees, maintenance, and repair pays a living. Built the loft over the offices for overnight stays when someone has to."

"I don't remember most of this," Loni confessed.

"Kids don't," he said reassuringly. "The old man always said nobody's worth a shit until they're at least thirty-five years old."

"Got a few years to go, but I'm working on it."

"You grew up the hard way. It'll either help or harm. It helped you. Anyhow, you came home to care for family."

"Hope I came soon enough. Shiichoo isn't good."

"How come you're not living at home?"

Loni paused. "Knew I'd be in and out at all hours. Shiichoo would do her best to keep up with me, and that's the last thing she needs. Between you and me? Even though I get lonely, I can use some down time."

"I get it. Well, your granddad and I arranged it. Thank him. 'Sides, keeps Mae's nephew, Junior, from asking to move in here all the time. I worry about kids wandering the hangar at all hours and the party mess up there."

Loni smiled to herself. She'd picked up more than a few condoms and empty junk food packages cleaning up the place.

"Anyway, I was planning on hiring security. You're it now." Uncle Herm hung his head. "Truth is, I wasn't able to give you a home when you were a kid, Mae sick and all. Least I can do is give you one now."

Loni was at a loss. "I don't remember you ever talking so much at one time."

"What? Don't think I know how?"

"Well, yes."

"You haven't been around enough to watch Mae train me. She talks all the time and makes me answer."

"Do you really listen to her all the time?"

"Well, I try." Her uncle ducked his head. "It only matters if she thinks so."

"No shit!" Loni laughed, grateful to be around her uncle again.

With a grin still on her face, Loni bounded upstairs behind Coco into her apartment. Coco vaulted onto the bed and circled a few times. Settling down, she tilted her head to one side, crossed her front legs, and watched Loni's every move. Loni grabbed two tamales from the fridge and decided to read one of the letters from the boot box while she ate. The envelope was addressed to her dad. "Wow, Coco. This has a Louisiana address." She remembered a trunk that had come from Louisiana with her dad's belongings. Something about a friend brought it home. She spread the letter in front of her and peeled one of the tamales.

My son,

My campfire is gettin' dimmer so I guess I'll writ you some of what I remember. My granddaddy always said a family's history should be passed on before it is forever lost.

Lookin' back on it, I believe it is best for me my life started a quarter mile above the Caliente School and store in August of 1909. It was a year before the first railroad came in and three years before Arizona became a state. I'm sure being born in territory inspired my life. I was my own king and jury, and for sure my own council.

The wild horse will be remembered by the few and he is becoming the few more and more. The dust we saw made by them from miles off has mostly settled. I say with reverence that a few of us that have rode upon a ridge to look down at a band, with their unspoiled poise and beauty, of perfect strength and freedom, you mite feel a closer touch with the divine than you've ever known before. After you have been out there around many campfires over many years, then it would grow on you, you belonged. You would feel the freedom as you watched them vanish over the skyline.

In this country for miles, the buracrats and cowmen have used every method to destroy the wild horse and the jackass. It's all been done to save the grass and browse for the cow and the deer they believed. Since they are mostly gone, I haven't seen the cow any fatter nor any cowman get richer, nor the deer count any greater.

I regret I saw the Indian become dominated and mostly sent to the reservations in such a rude and crude style. Then the Cavalry could toot their horns louder and was to benefit the supplier to replenish his larder much on the cost plus style as the government paid the bill. Many Indians drifted back to their brush and mud huts and a few horses. I'm proud I knew many of them and used their advice on how to hunt and trap and how to survive on the fruits only our God had planted and the wild meats he had created.

Loni stopped to fill her can with more iced tea and wondered what he thought of his oldest son marrying an Indian. She took a long drink and picked up the next page.

I saw the coming of the automobile and many of us regret the passing of the far western years as it drastically changed from good to bad to worse a lifestyle of too much hustle and bustle and many good medicines left with the pot they boiled them in.

I'll not linger along writen of the farms. Around 80 percent of the farms that I know about on the lower Phoenix valley floor was lost to the mortgage holders. Even some farmers had got them as a gift. After foreclosures I saw good, old, sound, and at one time, proud families leave there the best way they could. It sure wasn't in a new wagon or new car.

Son. I know sorrow drove you away and the ranch doesn't amount to much but you are needed. Come home before you can't.

Dad

But her father never came home. Loni wiped a few tears away as she folded the letter back into the envelope. She thought about Carl and the ranch he could no longer run. Loni carefully put the boot box under her desk and crawled into bed with Coco. She was in a soft dream about Maria when the alarm jerked her awake. She almost threw the damned clock across the room.

CHAPTER EIGHT

Loni ironed the clean uniform her Grandma washed for her and slowly dressed, reluctant to go out into the dark. She strapped on her gun belt and pulled her suspenders up over both shoulders to hold it up. Thirty pounds dragged down her pants. She checked the two extra gun magazines, her microphone for the mobile camera in the SUV, the collapsible baton, two pairs of handcuffs, two flashlights, a canister of pepper spray, and her taser, making sure they were all secure. Untangling the wire, she secured the shoulder microphone for her police radio. Last, she grabbed her badge out of an old ceramic ashtray shaped like the inside of a smoker's lung dotted with black blobs. It sat on the table as her reminder to never smoke again. Although she wasn't much of a smoker to begin with.

Coco lay against the door and watched Loni's every move. When Marie was alive, she played a game every morning before she went to work. She would send Coco to the front door to sit while she hid a baggie from the small batches of drugs she kept in the freezer. "Find!" Maria would order. Coco would frantically search and find the drug. Depending on the drug she would scratch once for hard drugs, twice for cannabis, three times for meth before she leaned against the door again. Loni knew she should continue the training as she rubbed Coco's head on their way out the door.

At the station, Bobby handed her a flyer. "Chief said for you to use this map tonight."

"And do what?" Loni studied it.

"Damned if I know. Bring in undocuments?"

"Sure. They're going to stand in the road, hoping I'll arrest them."

Bobby rubbed the thinning blond hair on top of his head. "Sometimes Chief's a serious fuckface. Did you hear about when he went after this black guy who didn't move his tractor out of his way fast enough?"

"Do I want to hear this?"

Bobby leaned on the counter, and his long fingers drummed to a song in his head. "He got out of his car and pointed his gun, hollering at the guy to move. The gun scared the crap outta the poor man, so he jumped off the tractor and ran out into the desert with Chief right behind him."

"Well?"

Bobby chuckled at Loni's scowl. "Thought you didn't want to hear this story."

"Bobby! What'd Chief do?"

"Don't know. Didn't find Chief until the next day, sitting under a desert willow with an empty gun in his hand. The black dude was never seen again."

Loni winced. "That's not funny, Bobby. About tonight? Don't call me, I'll call you."

"You wish!" Bobby chortled as Loni walked out the door studying the flyer. She got more and pissed.

Large letters spread across the top spelled out "Arizona Desert Invasion."

> **Mexican drug rings and 'coyotes' bring in 75% of all illegal drugs sold in U.S.**
>
> Coyotes charge up to $5,000 for each illegal.
>
> More than one million people cross each year and leave eight million pounds of trash, killing animals, and polluting the land.
>
> Illegals send $16 billion back to Mexico.
>
> 1.5 million illegals in our schools cost about $7,000 each.
>
> Last year over 800 illegals were found dead in the desert.
>
> **Hunt These People Down!**

Loni nearly cried as she reread the last line over and over. "Hunt These People Down!" Well, crap, what are they? Goddamn animals? She crumpled the flyer into a ball and threw it in a trash can on her way out the door. Miles down the road she was still fighting her anger, but it didn't work. Just numbers, she sputtered to herself. Nobody cared about the thousands dead over the years of trying to find a better life. Families destroyed by those touting good ol' family values.

This flyer would horrify Maria. She had a warm smile for everyone and a hug for people even if she'd never met them before. Homeless, hookers, druggies, and dealers—they all knew her, and she knew them by name. She'd give them a ride to the clinic or shelter, a warm coat or shoes. Loni learned to be okay when they ran out of money before the end of the month. Especially when Maria turned those huge, imploring brown eyes on her.

Loni clenched her jaw and tightened her hold on the steering wheel as she drove through the silent night. She had to do something. Maria would expect it. But she had no idea what.

Another deadly slow night, the sliver of a moon gave so little light she was unable to see into the desert shadows. Loni's headlights hit a black wall only yards ahead. She wandered desert trails, stopping frequently to shine a spot on a barrel cactus or greasewood. "What do you think, Coco? Anybody out there?"

People walking in from Mexico avoided roads and towns and looked for work on the farms if they could reach them. They would avoid her police car, too. She felt helpless knowing every night somebody was out there suffering.

Loni could smell the dust storm heavy in the air. She left the desert and drove up to the top of Caliente Butte looking for the first signs of blowing dirt. Sniffing the slight breeze, she hoped she was imagining the coolness crossing her face heralding a storm. Lightning flared across the northern sky over the freeway. She was following the direction of the flashes when a long row of lights popped up far in the distance over toward her grandpa's place. A runway? But where?

Her SUV was crawling back off the butte toward town when she heard the call she dreaded. "Freeway pileup in a dust storm. Seven cars so far reporting, no casualties they know of."

"I'm on my way, but it'll be a bit."

"You got time," Bobby answered. "Caller from a car in the middle of the tangle claims dust is too thick to see anyway."

Bobby called again as she moved traffic around the wrecker hauling away the last of the stranded cars from the freeway pileup. "Undocuments at Milepost 56. I'd guess the dust ran them off the road. Need transport."

"How do you know they're undocumented?"

"Caller said, 'Mexicans heading north.' You think?"

"Gee, Bobby, sounds like profiling to me."

"Loni, I saw how you reacted to the flyer. You be careful. If there is a coyote, bring him in, you hear?"

"Catching coyotes is the second best thing I love to do."

"I know, I know. You hate domestics, bar fights, coyotes, and drug traffickers. Around here, what else is there?"

"Can't you ever give me a plain old drunk driver?"

"Oh, boo hoo." Bobby mocked her. "You know there's no such thing as justice, Loni. Deal with it."

The last of the tow trucks rolled toward Caliente, and Loni sped down Old Highway 85 toward a huge thunderhead with lightening flashing across the top and snaking down to the desert floor, outlining the outer shell of black churning clouds like an old-time movie out of sync. Dim headlights reaching out into the desert ahead told her slow down. A pickup was stuck off the road in sand. She waited to get out of the SUV and counted three men. One had his arm around a young woman snuggling a baby. The other two sat at the side of the road quietly waiting.

She drew her gun and stayed in the dark behind her open door, listening to the whispering chatter. She signaled Coco to search for anyone hiding in the brush. After a few minutes she felt a wet nose nudging her open palm. She ordered Coco to guard and walked behind the sitting men. All she got from them was shaking heads when she asked for their papers. She handcuffed the men and searched all of them, starting with the woman.

A diaper bag held three cloth diapers, one empty bottle, a small box of dry formula, and two baby tops. Not much for a long trip. She tasted the formula No drugs.

Loni found nothing until she got to the third man. The oldest in the group, he tensed his muscles and pulled a switchblade. She shoved him face first against the hood of the SUV and twisted the knife out of his hand. Searching him for any other weapons, she found a slip of paper in his shirt pocket. Written on it was Chui's phone number. Her anger grew as she locked them in the back of her SUV.

Her search of the pickup showed no water, no food, and no drugs. Lightening flares from the booming thunderhead overhead hurried her along. Back on the highway the storm passed over them dropping gallons of water, forcing her to a crawl back to the darkened town.

With her flashlight, she herded her prisoners into the police station, grateful to see the red glow of the emergency lights.

"Lightening hit the power junction again?" Loni guessed.

"Yep. Be down for a while."

Bobby helped her lock them in the holding cells as the sky brightened in a blood-red breaking dawn. Loni sat at her desk filling out useless reports as she waited for Chui. She didn't have to wait long. Loni fished a paper from her pocket, stood and confronted Chui at the counter. "Found this on a coyote tonight. He's upstairs if you want to talk to him. After you tell me what he's doing with your phone number in his pocket."

Hatred shot out of Chui's eyes as he turned and stomped back outside through the exit door.

"Wow!" Bobby warned her, "Pissed him off good. Better watch your back."

Loni cringed in apprehension. "I've been watching my back around him since I was in high school."

Bobby patted Loni on the head as he walked around her. "On that sour note, guess I'll go home."

Lola was quiet as she took the note from Loni and put it in an evidence box. She studied Loni for a minute. "As bad as it looks?"

"Jesus, I hope not."

Loni handed Loni a small sack. "Here's the poisoned meth you wanted. Carl wants to know if you can check out the school for drugs this morning."

"School still on? What about electricity?"

"You know school opens no matter what."

"Tell him as soon as I clean up."

"Do me a favor?" Lola said cautiously.

"After the hard times you give me?"

"Please?"

"What?" Loni reluctantly agreed.

"Do you know Helen Hunt?"

"I assume you mean our town librarian and not the movie actress."

"Of course, I mean our librarian."

"Yes, I do. She was great to me. Gave me a safe place to be. Good to know she's still around." Loni remembered the tall, stately woman's kind eyes.

"I'm not so sure. It's her fault I'm in this mess."

"She's too nice to hurt anyone," Loni said defensively. "What'd she do, anyway?"

"I've got the new art teacher from the high school mad at me."

"What's that got to do with Missus Hunt?"

"The teacher came in wanting to see the 'Arizona Revised Statutes,' and I told her to go to Helen Hunt for it. All of a sudden she threw a few really bad curse words at me and flew out of here."

Loni tried to keep a straight face, but she laughed so hard she had to wipe tears off her face.

"I'm screwed, huh?"

"Pretty much."

"Would you stop by her room and explain? Please!"

"What's wrong with you going?" Loni teased.

"I'm afraid she'll throw something at me before I open my mouth."

"What's her name?"

"Agnes Hartford."

Climbing down from the truck, Loni watched Coco make a quick trip to a patch of Indian wheat. Seeing the school bombarded her with memories. The three long, flat wooden buildings were German POW barracks moved in after the war. Surrounded by chain-link fences, the putrid pink could be seen for miles. Evaporative coolers jutted out from windows like sick, green growths. The red-bricked administration building stood outside the fence like a guard house. Originally the only school, it replaced the first one, a wood shack flattened by a bad dust storm.

Taking a deep breath, Loni hurried Coco up the fiery cement walkway before her paws burned. She walked into the principal's office, thinking the only difference between a school and a jail was kids could go home at night.

The girl on the other side of the counter appeared to be all of twelve. A little lost face almost hidden under long brown hair had a deer-caught-in-the-headlights expression. Her clothes didn't belong to a twelve-year-old though. The short tank top, more like a bathing suit top, left her belly button exposed. Loni watched her texting and wondered if the school had any problems with sexting.

"I'd like to see the principal, please," Loni said.

The girl turned her head toward a closed door behind her. "Mister Swicart! Somebody here to see you!"

Loni struggled to keep from reacting to the loud, barking voice coming out of her mouth. "Wow!" she complimented the girl. Loni flashed onto the principal's name. He was her health teacher who belonged to the "passing-the-trash" club, getting promoted after he was accused of sexual assault. Like the Catholic Church, the school never fired the molesters. They moved them up and gave them more power.

A middle-aged man walked out of the office door. He wore a lightweight, white short-sleeved shirt with no tie, and a black belt held up the light-colored pants riding above his round belly. His hair was thinner than she remembered, and he'd gained considerable weight. But she recognized him as the same sick sonofabitch. His eyes skimmed over Loni. "Who?"

"Her." The girl popped a loud bubble in Loni's direction.

Loni smiled as his recognition bled the arrogance from his shiny face. He must be remembering their last confrontation. She had opened a closet door where he had trapped a scared freshman boy with his pants halfway down. The boy scurried away as Swicart pulled his pants up. He dared Loni to utter anything. "Who's going to believe a breed, anyway," he snarled.

"Yes?" The smell of garlic oozed out with his sweat.

"I'm here to search for drugs."

His face closed up. "Can't." He pulled an already damp blue kerchief from his back pocket and wiped his face and his balding head. "We got privacy rules."

"Really?" She remembered her own locker searches. "When did it happen?"

His pale blue eyes darted around the room. "Who sent you?"

"Chief."

"Aren't you State?" He stared at her uniform and badge.

"Yes." She drew the word out in two syllables.

"You said Chief?"

"Yes." She stretched out the word again.

"I'm not unlocking any lockers."

"I'm not telling you to. Yet." Loni fought her desire to shove his flat face up his ass. "I plan to let the dog take me where she wants to go."

Swicart leaned against the counter. "That a drug dog?"

"Yes."

"Just drugs?"

"No."

"No?"

"No."

"What else?"

"Fear."

Swicart stared at her a minute and finally shrugged. "Go ahead." He waddled back to his office.

Loni turned back to the gum-chewing girl who was still busy texting. "Hey, over here."

The girl ignored her.

"Where can I find Ms. Hartford?"

With a huff the girl continued to thumb her phone a mile a minute as she walked over to the schedule board. "Room Twenty-Nine. Middle building."

"Thanks. I know where it is."

"Swell."

Loni opened the gate into the yard of dry dirt around the middle school. "Well, Coco, might as well start here while we find Ms. Hartford."

Lockers lined the wide hall. She pulled out the sample of the ricin-laced meth for Coco to smell and followed as Coco moved from locker to locker. She enjoyed being on the chase again but hated the search being at a school. Occasionally Coco hesitated to paw at a locker, usually twice. Loni noted the locker number of the drug find, relieved it wasn't meth, yet.

The door to Room Twenty-Nine was open. Coco walked in ahead of Loni and wandered toward the hands reaching out to pet her. Loni rubbed the dog's side to calm her and glanced around for the teacher. A bulky body blocked her path.

"Can I help you?"

"Are you Agnes Hartford?"

"Yes?"

Wild, colorful watermelons scattered across a green background on her blouse and skirt and matching shoes jarred Loni. Even the large round glasses propped on her wild green hair had teeny watermelons. Loni pinched her nose hard to keep from bursting out in gales. She would get Lola for this.

"Yes?" The woman's high voice twanged.

"I'm Loni Wagner. Can we talk somewhere private?"

"What about?"

"Private, please?"

Reluctantly, Hartford led Loni into a small office with a glass window looking out onto the classroom. The room was so stuffed with supplies Loni told Coco to wait outside. There was no place for her to sit so she closed the door behind her and leaned back against it. She paused, not knowing how to begin.

"Well?"

Loni took a deep breath and jumped in. "I need to explain a problem."

"You a parent?"

"No." Loni felt herself shrinking, ready to run. Teachers did that to her. "A friend said something to you that came out very wrong and asked me to explain and apologize."

"Well?" The impatient voice made Loni even more insecure.

"Did you know we have a town librarian named Helen Hunt?" The expression on Hartford's face slowly changed from suspicion to horror.

"Oh my god." She turned almost as red as the watermelon on her blouse. "Please tell her I'm so sorry." The woman pawed at Loni with her long, watermelon-red talons, apologizing over and over. "I'm so sorry!"

An hour later, Loni had finished searching all the lockers. Five with drugs from middle school, thirteen from high school, and two from elementary. The last made her really sick. But nothing, thank god, from the ricin batch. She worried when Coco hesitated, cocking her head at Loni for confirmation. They needed to start training again. Loni dropped off a copy of her list with the secretary at the principal's office and left the school behind to go to the ranch.

A truck blocked her way when she arrived. The Thursday truck had come with the electric stove. She hoped Shiichoo wouldn't be too upset.

Loni walked into the kitchen where Bahb and Shiichoo sat at the table watching Bill Henry connect the stove. When he finished, he gave Shiichoo a lesson on how it worked. She grimly stood in front of the stove, turning it off and on, watching the burners immediately turn red and immediately fade.

Loni went over to stand beside her. "See the red light there? When that's lit, the stove is still too hot to touch."

"How much electricity does that waste?"

Loni smiled to herself as she closed the screen door behind her. Her grandma was going to be fine. Back at the hangar, she heated up the food Shiichoo handed her on her way out. She gobbled her food and took a long, cold shower.

Sitting buck naked in bed, she emailed Sandi.

FROM: Loni Wagner
TO: Sandi@gmailyahoo.com
DATE: July 8
SUBJECT: Hard to believe!

I saw this flyer that said more than 800 Mexicans died in the desert this year trying to get into the United States. I spent my shift searching behind everything, worrying someone was out there needing help. I can't even imagine the suffering. Any government official who causes human suffering is a criminal and ought to be in prison. But they never are. I did pick up a coyote bringing in three from Mexico. At least I got to shove him in jail. Sad to say, along with the other three. It made me sick to know that no matter how much I wanted to help, I can't. But I know Maria would have found a way, and that makes me feel even worse.

On a better note, Shiichoo's electric stove came. She acted mad, but I know she's pleased. And thanks for asking about her. I think she's better now.

Take good care of you and yours.
Loni

CHAPTER NINE

Loni kept nodding off even when she pinched her nose hard and rubbed her cheeks so red somebody might think she'd been drinking. She kneaded her neck as she pulled off the road and parked. Coco leaned against her, and she leaned back.

Startled awake, embarrassed she had fallen asleep so fast, Loni reached under her seat for the "Disney Fairy" lunch box she found in a moving box and took out a cold tamale. She peeled off the corn husk and gave half the tamale to Coco. The dog swallowed it in one gulp and begged wistfully for more. Loni pulled the tamale apart again, one piece for herself and one piece for Coco until the food was gone. She sipped her coffee and counted stars until she gave up in boredom. When she snapped the lunch box closed, she remembered how Maria made fun of her femme "fairy" lunchbox.

"But it's a collectible!" Loni retorted.

"Then put it on a shelf."

"You don't mind the fairy carrying it. So what's the problem?" Overwhelmed by her painful memories, Loni peered into the darkness.

Again Loni jerked awake. This time she had gone to sleep and nearly conked herself silly on the steering wheel. "Crap!" she said to herself. She got out of the SUV and stomped in circles around a wait-a-minute bush, carefully avoiding its cat claw-shaped thorns. Sweat rolled down her face and her back.

Back in the SUV, Loni took a swig of water and poured some into a thermos lid for Coco, dodging her turkey drinking. Tipping up the bottle, she soaked her head with the rest of the water and shook like a dog. She was on the outskirts of Caliente when Bobby's voice crackled. "Clinic called about a gunshot wound. Need a report."

"Any deaths?"

"Didn't say."

"Where are the detectives?"

"In with Chief. He said to send you."

Loni wondered why everyone was at work so early. In the emergency room, a woman was on the phone at the desk. Her nametag said "Chelsea." She covered the phone and whispered, "Gunshot victim?" The distress on

Loni's face was all Chelsea needed to know before she turned back to the phone.

Loni recognized the woman from high school. She had the same short, light-brown kinky hair and cheerful expression. She'd started dating a piece of shit during her senior year. Brad Taylor was a cocky bully, one of James's cohorts, and Loni's personal nemesis. Loni wondered if they got married.

Chelsea hung up the phone. "I heard you'd come back. Good to see you."

"You, too. It's good to see a friendly face. So where's the gunshot victim?"

"Third curtain." She pointed to a corner of the large room.

"What's her name?"

Chelsea handed Loni the file. Loni cautiously opened a slit in the curtain. "Is it okay if I come in?" Loni recognized the heavy-set bleach-blonde. She was in her fifties and worked as the bartender at the Volcano Bar and Eatery on Old Highway 85. Before the trains came through, it was a stage stop.

The woman was lying on her back with a bandage wrapped around her leg above her knee. Smeared mascara smudged under her eyes made the circles even darker. She ignored Loni and restlessly clicked the TV remote from one channel to another.

"Chastity? Want to tell me how you got shot?" The woman avoided Loni's eyes, but she took off her head phones.

"Chastity," Loni repeated.

"Not really."

"Why is that?"

Chastity put down the remote. "I shot myself."

"Really? Accidentally?" Loni waited. This should be interesting, she thought.

"Well, no. I decided to commit suicide, so I shot myself in the leg first to see if it would hurt."

Loni hoped she could keep a serious face. "Did it?"

A chagrined expression crossed Chastity's oval face. "Like a mother."

"Still thinking about it?"

Chastity glared at Loni. "Not today."

Loni handed her a "Need Help?" card. "My cell number is on the back. If you need someone to talk to or any kind of help, please call me."

Chastity turned back to the TV, speed clicking the remote as Loni laid her card on the table. She went back to Chelsea's desk. "Did you find out why she shot herself?"

"Nothing new. Her boyfriend left her for a young thing."

"She been with him long?"

"Yes. They tended bar together at the Volcano. Been there for years."

"Anybody picking her up?"

Chelsea frowned. "I'm getting an ambulance to take her home."

"Can I keep this file?"

"Sure. I copied it for you."

"How many gunshot wounds have you gotten this year?"

"Deliberate or accidental?"

"Both."

"This is our second suicide attempt. The first one was successful." She paused a minute. "Only one accidental. Last week these two guys were white-wing hunting. He said his dog shot him." Chelsea was thoughtful. "At least, I think it was accidental. He was such a crybaby I was ready to give the gun back to the dog."

Loni felt her mouth drop open. Chelsea reached over and closed it. "He said he propped his shotgun against a tree. His golden retriever was so excited about the hunt it jumped up and fell on the gun. The guy thought the dog caught a nail on the trigger and the gun fired as it went down."

"Oh shit, oh dear! What kind of damage?"

"Lucky for him the buckshot only grazed his butt. Had to dig out a few pellets."

"Chelsea!" Lu rushed in. "Somebody shot a gun in here?"

"Whoa. No. It's a gunshot victim and it's not an emergency. She needs a ride home."

Lu inspected Chelsea and then smiled. Chelsea beamed. "I was scared your asshole ex showed up shooting." Lu finally noticed Loni. "We gotta stop meeting like this."

Loni's gaydar pinged, and she teased back. "It's your fault, you know. Disasters follow you like Pigpen's cloud."

"Maybe, but I usually get there in time to help. What's your excuse?"

Loni winced in agreement and walked out of the clinic.

Leaving her SUV in the police lot Loni walked into the station with Coco at her side.

"So?" Lola sounded worried. "How'd it go with Agnes."

Loni fought to keep a straight face. "She said she'd meet you later for a showdown."

Lola's face fell. "You're kidding? Say you're kidding!"

"Okay, it was fine." Loni relented. "She said to tell you how sorry she was for the misunderstanding. Said she'd come by and apologize. I'm getting back at you for not warning me about her weird clothes."

Lola's emerald eyes brightened, and she snickered. "Wild, huh? She's one of those people who scatters bad taste behind her wherever she goes."

"God help anyone who gets behind her, then."

"How'd the drug bust go?"

"Scary, Lola. Found drugs at all levels, even in the elementary wing."

"How is that even possible?"

"I don't know. Not enough supervision? Busy hands? Too much money? Too much pressure. I have no idea."

"Any ricin?"

"Not that I could tell. No meth anyway." Loni drew herself tall to face Chief. "Hey, would you keep Coco out of sight from Chief, behind the counter?"

"Sure. Come here, sweet girl, and sit by me."

Loni tailed Chui and James into the small conference room next to Chief's office. The narrow windowless room was painted the usual prison green Loni hated. Rickety chairs of unknown ages and colors lined a long, thin missionary table. None of them comfortable or stable.

Loni took a seat next to Tully, the only place left. She could smell the garlic on him. Carl sat on her other side, penning her in. He frowned as he carefully opened the briefcase in front of him. His crisp clean tan suit and brown striped Arrow shirt with a plain tan tie were a sharp contrast to Chui's unshaved face and cotton T-shirt and dirty Levis across from her.

Next in line to Chui, James glared arrows at her. His round face belied his temper, both inherited from his mother. She couldn't remember when Aunt Ethel and Uncle Kirk had spoken to her. Loni willed herself not to think about his family and turned toward the fan on a shelf at the end of the room. Its screeches from a feeble attempt to move the dead air was the only sound in the room.

"Come on, people, let's get started," Chief demanded as he sat in his rolling plush chair with his back to the closed door. Loni had an almost uncontrollable urge to giggle at his tight face. His eyes darted around at the room seeking a place to light. "Okay, Carl."

In slow motion, Carl stood and took papers out of his briefcase. He handed a stack to Loni. She took the top sheet and passed the rest on.

"Here's what we know."

Loni read the page as Carl talked until the rustling of the papers and chatting settled.

"I'm sure you've already know, but Todd Barclay died last night. We think it's the bad meth." Carl's eyes teared. "His mother went in to wake him for school this morning. He had such promise, an exceptional artist."

Loni hadn't heard that.

"Great right end," James butted in. Everyone stared at James until he squirmed. "Well, he was."

"Another thing, and we don't know if it's related. Got a stabbing death. Young man name of Perry Abbott. Anybody know him?"

Heads shook around the room.

"Had a load of pseudoephedrine in the trunk of his car. Mexican license plates. I'm looking into this one." Carl riveted onto Chui. "Hear anything about a source from Mexico?"

"No."

"You're our drug expert here. Have you tried?"

"You doubting me?' came Chui's hostile reply.

"This is not the first time we had a meth problem where you shoulda known something, Chui."

Chui refused to answer as he stared back at Carl.

"Talk to Rosa yet?"

Chui squirmed. "She don't know nothing."

"You talk to her?"

"You got a reason I should?" Chui said belligerently.

"It was only a question, Chui," Carl replied. "And yes, we do. She must know something about Rene's activities, don't you think?" He glanced down at his notes, then back up at Chui. "I'm sure you can find time to see her today. Then I want you to check with your border friends and find out what you can about Perry Abbott and his Mexican car."

Carl moved on. "James, what did you find on the plane?"

"You didn't tell me to search the plane. You said read Loni's report. My uncle still has the plane. Want me to go take look?"

"What did Tully tell you?"

James turned to Tully. "You know anything?"

"Nope."

"Didn't think so." James turned back to Carl. "He doesn't know anything."

Jerking on his ear, Carl was beginning to sound impatient. "What'd you find out on Rene's flight plan?"

James shrugged. "Flight plan said he was going to San Diego. Don't think he filed again."

"No shit," Tully sarcastically affirmed.

Carl frowned at him. "Rene's wife have anything to say?"

Tully held his belly as he leaned against the wobbly table. "Do it today, boss. First thing."

Carl stared at Tully.

"I'm already out the door. See?"

Carl turned and stared at Loni. "You got anything to say?"

Eyes big, Loni shook her head.

"Good." Carl continued to stare at Loni. "Tully? After that, talk to Todd's parents. Find out where he was last night."

Not hearing anything from Tully, Carl turned back, staring, until Tully finally nodded.

"Guess this here meeting's over then." Chief pushed his chair out the door toward his office. Loni almost slammed into Chief as he blocked her way. "You got nothing more to say to Filbrite, got it?" he said menacingly.

"Got it, Chief." She held her breath until his body and chair rolled into his office and she hurried down the hall to pick up Coco. As she reached the counter, Tully gripped her arm. "How come you sent all the stuff to Phoenix without me lookin' at it? You made me look bad," he whined.

"You don't need any help from me," she retorted.

Lola handed Tully one of the lollipops she kept for the little kids. "Here, big boy. Suck on this." She turned to walk away, and Tully patted her butt. Lola knocked his hand away and turned back to him. "Tully. That's one!" she snapped.

"How about two? I can do that again."

"Listen, toad vomit. Think about that old joke before you pat my ass again."

"What old joke?" he sounded perplexed.

Lola insisted, "You tell him Loni. I'm too busy to waste my time with jerks."

"Nuh-uh. You tell it. You'd do a better job."

Lola's arm-waving set her bangles into musical motion. "This newlywed couple's in a buggy pulled by a mule, and the new wife keeps talking a blue streak. The mule stumbles, and the man flicks him with his whip and says, 'That's one.' The wife keeps right on talking. The mule stumbles again, and the man says, 'That's two.' The wife blathers on, and the mule stumbles again. The man said, 'That's three' and shoots the mule dead. The wife yells, 'What did you do that for?' He turns to her and says, 'That's one.'" Lola paused. "You get it, Tully?"

"Not a problem, Lola. You got no gun," Tully said sardonically, his grin revealing his brown teeth.

Lola unlocked a drawer and pulled out a pistol. "Tully, that's two."

The listening men added their own interpretations in titters and giggles as they scattered.

Loni leaned over the counter. "Is Tully really that dumb?"

Lola studied Loni. "I wouldn't turn my back him. I think he's smarter than he lets on."

"Street smart?"

"Shrewd. In his eyes." She played with the stacked bracelets on her wrist. "When he thinks somebody's watching, I swear he deliberately finds ways to make himself the bad guy."

"Maybe he's lazy."

"I don't think so. Ask him sometime for computer help. Nobody can be that lazy and know what he does."

"How long has he been around here?"

"A couple of months before you. Midwinter, I think."

"Know where he came from?"

"No. Come to think of it, I don't believe it's in his file, either." Lola unlocked a file drawer, pulled out a folder, and read for a few minutes. "Nope. Nothing there. Curiouser and curiouser."

Loni changed the subject. "Can you get me the phone numbers of the ranchers between here and the border?"

"Sure. Tomorrow okay?"

"You bet."

"Gonna tell me why?"

"You see the flyer Chief sent out?"

Lola's face saddened.

"I thought if I could get ranchers to talk to me about any sightings they had, maybe I could find a way to help."

"Can I ask you a personal question?"

Loni panicked. "Depends. What?"

"I've read your file. You've got a bunch of awards and commendations. Good recommendations, too. So what are you doing here?"

"Sick Shiichoo."

"Slick shwho?"

"Sorry." Loni struggled to explain. "That's Apache. It's my grandma on my mother's side."

"Must be more than that."

Loni thought for a minute. "I worked with violent crimes, profiling serial killers. Also did a lot of sexual assaults. One day my partner and I chased a perp into a building. Perp jumped off a fire escape with my partner right behind. It was pretty dark. Backup cop arrived and followed her around the corner. He shot her three times in the back. I worked with another partner for a while, but I was done with it. My grandma's not well, and I wanted to help her anyway so it gave me a reason to come home."

"Didn't the backup warn her? Give her a chance to tell him who she was?"

"Not a word."

"So, what happened to him?"

"Drummed out. Became a fireman."

"No shit! Listen, honey, I'm surprised you left him alive."

"The truth? So am I. The Apache in me was verging on out of control, but the Papago in me won. My granddad's voice."

"What?"

"Do no harm. Over and over he said to me as I grew up. Do no harm."

Lola understood. "Old medicine mantra." She nodded toward the bullpen. "Are you sorry you came home?"

"Every day. But if I ever get some sleep and have time to think about it, I might change my mind." Loni's lips curved upward. "Meeting you helps."

"You flirting with me?"

Carl came out of Chief's office and beckoned Loni to follow him. "You need a desk. Take one of those with a computer and stick some personals on it."

"Sure."

"I know you're tired, Loni. But can you do one more thing for me?"

"Sure." Loni knew she had no choice.

"I didn't get Todd's ceramics teacher interviewed. Can you do that now?" They walked out of the police station, and Carl squinted at the hot sun. "Damn, I'm tired of this heat." He got into his patrol car.

Loni agreed but thought he at least had air conditioning. She walked with Coco to her truck and hoped Tully would dredge up some sensitivity when he talked to the grieving parents.

The door to the ceramics room was covered with graffiti-like cartoons. The reddish blond-haired woman stood in the middle of the students. Loni recognized her from Rene's funeral. The teacher's full-length yellow apron covered a gray short-sleeved blouse, and vivid colors smeared her Levis. Catching Loni's eyes, she smiled and revealed a small gap between her two top front teeth. Loni always found it sexy.

"Hi, I'm Jenny O'Neal. Are you here about Todd?" Loni nodded, and Jenny said, "Let's go in my office." Her eyes teared. Loni left Coco in a circle of excited students to follow Jenny into a small room like the one Agnes had. It had the same large window opening onto the organized chaos of the ceramics class and the same mess.

Jenny cleared the papers from a chair and offered it to Loni. She moved with the natural grace of a dancer, Loni thought. "I'm sorry. Todd was so beautiful. The most talented student I've ever had." She stopped and wiped her light brown eyes, almost cat golden. "One of my students went to the party with Todd." She gazed out the window at the class. "Just a minute. I'll let her tell you." Jenny called into the room, "Katy, could you please come here?"

A slender girl with long, dark hair and braces on her teeth would have been pretty any other time, with her delicate pointed chin and face a heart shape. But today her eyes were swollen from crying, and her short nose was red and raw. Loni stood up to give Katy her chair. "She was home alone, but she couldn't stand it," Jenny explained. "Her friends are here."

Loni sat on the floor. "Katy Beachum?"

Head down, Katy pulled at a strand of her hair nervously waiting for Loni's questions.

"I'm Loni Wagner from the state police. I wondered if you would answer some questions about last night."

"I need to get back to my class. Talk to you later?"

Loni watched her walk out and close the door before she turned back to Katy. "Has anyone interviewed you yet, Katy?

Sniffling, the girl shook her head.

"Tell me about last night's party."

Between sniffs, Katy said, "The assistant football coach had a barbeque for the team. Like up in Caliente Butte." She stopped again to blow her nose. "Even losers like Billy Joe were there, you know? Like I remember because he and Ralph held Todd down and like made him drink something." She shuddered. "Like he never took drugs, you know? Said he hated them."

"Did they say what it was?"

"Something about come to mama. Everybody kept making fun of me when I said his mama was home, you know? Like even the coach's wife. Is that what killed him?"

She must not know anything about sex enhancers, Loni thought. "Is that Billy Joe Kildare?"

"Yes, and he's a real slime ball."

"Any adults there?"

"Only the coach and his wife. They're really nice."

"What happened then?"

"We had hot dogs and hamburgers. There were all kinds of fruit and dessert. Some kids threw oranges around until they hit this girl, you know? She tried to make them stop, but they wouldn't so she left."

"Didn't the coach make them stop?"

"I don't remember seeing him then. His wife like sort of danced around with the boys like she was having a good time, you know?"

"What was Todd doing?"

"That was the really strange thing. He, like, couldn't sit still. He was tossing oranges. Then he'd sit down a second, then he was up again." Tears rolled down her face. "He got mad at me when I tried to get him to dance with me. He jerked me up and dragged me to the car. He didn't even speak to me. He took me home and left me. He said he was going back to the party and that was the last time I saw him." Katy sobbed. "I don't understand." She wailed. "He never acted like that before."

"Do you know the coach's address?"

"Yes, it's next to Glenda's. My friend." She added. "647 Caliente Butte Drive." The bell rang. "Can I go?"

"Sure," Loni said gently.

When the students were gone, Loni said to Jenny, "I really appreciate this."

"Did she help you?"

"I hope so."

Two students walked into the room. Jenny quietly said, "I'd like to talk to you more about this. Maybe we can meet for coffee tomorrow? At the Greasy Spoon?"

"Sure." Loni agreed. "What time?"

"Noon?"

"Good." Loni nodded. Outside, she called Carl to fill him in.

"Hey," Carl answered. "I need one more thing. Tully can't make his interview with Todd's folks, and I'd like you to do it. You should take Coco over there anyway and see if the kid had any drugs." He rushed his words so Loni couldn't refuse.

"What the hell, Carl! Does Tully do anything?" Loni snapped.

"Just do it, Loni." Carl hung up.

Loni flipped her cell phone shut and drove to Todd's parents' house. She signaled Coco to stay behind her and walked up to the door. She remembered them. High school sweethearts years ahead of her, Bill ran the Whistle Stop Café trading off with his dad as the cook, and, between pregnancies, Janine waited on tables. Loni saw a closed sign on the café as she drove to Bill and Janine's house.

Both of them answered her knock. Loni said, "Bill. Janine. I'm so very sorry about your loss."

They stepped back and let Loni and Coco into the house.

"Thanks, Loni. Heard you were back. And a cop no less." Bill studied Coco.

"She's a police dog," Loni responded to Bill's unspoken question. She fiddled with her sunglasses. "I need to go through Todd's room. And ask a few questions if you're up to it. Okay with you?"

"No." Janine wiped tears off her face. "I'm not okay with it, but I know you have to do it." Long-legged and short-waisted, she was taller than Bill. Her short hair was graying, and Bill's dark-rimmed glasses partly hid his eyes. Both of them had gained weight. His recently shaved head gleamed white with the rest of his face. Loni heard people thought he was a skinhead but he said no, he hated to wear a hairnet. Bill led Janine to the couch and sat down with her. "We need to know what happened, sweetheart."

"I'll keep this short, I promise." Loni sat down across from them. "I need to know about his friends and the party he attended last night."

Janine leaned against Bill. "He said it was the usual opening football season celebration with adult supervision." Janine buried her face in Bill's shoulder. He rubbed her back as he talked. "His friends were really good kids. I don't see any drugs going on with them." He paused. "I was watching for it, too. We both were. Close to the border like this, it's easy for them to get drugs." He stumbled a few seconds. "His girlfriend is—I mean was—Katy Beachum. He buddied around with Jimmy Crowe, Fuzzy Bals, Jake Junior, and Alvin Petre." He patted his wife. "Is that about it, honey?"

She mumbled from his shoulder, "They're the ones that hung out here."

"Thanks." Loni stood up. She knew all the names. Jake Jr. was the mayor's son. Probably the pickup load of kids she hauled home after she took away their beer. She didn't remember taking Todd home that night. "Can I see his room?"

"At the top of the stairs, last door on the right." Bill pointed toward the stairs. "He shares it with his brother. Don't know what belongs to who. But Todd keeps—kept—his space neat."

Loni easily identified which part of the room had belonged to Todd. Jenny was right about his talent. Drawings and paintings were pinned on the wall above a small desk with a laptop computer. His bed was neatly made, and his bookcase was filled with science books, mostly animal anatomy. He might have been drawing animals, Loni thought. She opened his closet for Coco to sniff. Clothes were neatly hung on hangers or folded on shelves. This is a teenage boy? she wondered. All the boxes were more of the same, neat and organized.

Coco sat quietly in the center of the room. "Nothing to say, Coco? Good to know." She opened drawers and skimmed papers. They were class notes and research. Most of the anatomy terminology she didn't even know. She didn't find any drug names, but she took the papers and the computer back downstairs where Bill and Janine still sat on the couch. "We'll mail you a receipt for the computer and papers. I promise to get them back to you as soon as I can," Loni said.

"Did you find anything?" Bill asked. "Anything at all?"

"No," Loni told him. "Just class notes."

"And?"

"Nothing. Really. No drugs. I don't expect to find anything. What I found is a teenager who was serious about his art. Nothing more."

Loni let herself out. She made a mental note to find out where Todd's siblings were and tell Carl to interview them and Todd's friends.

Home at last, Loni was hungry. She fried hash browns and eggs, not caring what she ate. Glancing around for something to read, Loni wondered if Mrs. Hunt would pick some mysteries out for her. Loni opened the boot box again and pulled out her grandmother's notebook. "Come up here, Coco. I gotta' story to read to you. It says November 24th, 1917. Wow." She continued to read aloud to Coco to hear a human voice. Even her own.

> "Big day. Mama came down with the measles and also delivered Sal, the family baby and our pride and joy. Everything she did was something to ooh and ah over for my older brothers and me. She was a little white-headed, brown-eyed beauty. If she got spanked, we were all suffering right along with her. Believe me it was a clash of wills too because Mother never gave in. If she said to do a thing, we'd do it even it took a long time.
>
> Papa never whipped me, but the sad way he'd act if I disappointed him and how he'd talk and explain things to me. I'd feel about a foot high and sorry and wished he'd whip me instead.
>
> Our cousins came to live with us for a while. A girl older than me and a boy my age. Mama and Auntie were quilting and sent me down the road a mile to the neighbors where my cousins were playing with the neighbors. They were playing cowboys and Indians. Butch was tied to a post in the front yard and they were doing a war dance around him. They never asked me to play. When I got home auntie said, 'Did you see the kids?' I wasn't going to lie, but I guess it sounded like it. I said, 'They've got Butch tied to a post and doing a war dance.' I should have stopped

there, but I had to elaborate a little. I said, "I think they were going to light the fire to burn him at the stake." Thread and chalk and scissors flew thru the air. Aunt Nettie turned her chair over and mama was already out of the house. I thought I'd better stay where I was. Auntie was short and fat, but she sure got home fast and pretty soon mama came back and whipped me with the yard stick. I didn't mind that but hated the indignity of holding my skirts up so she could hit the back of my bloomers."

Loni cracked up in giggles at the image of the girl holding up her skirt startling Coco awake. She rubbed Coco on the head and went back to reading to the already asleep dog.

"Christine, Butch and I didn't do anything but fight. Hateful needless fights kids get into. Part of it was my fault when we got to the point of really fighting with our fists, sticks, or whatever. Butch and I were up in an ironwood tree and we got to pulling hair. That is one thing that never hurt me. My scalp must be leather. Anyway, mama and my aunt told us to come down at once. I didn't dare disobey, and I wouldn't turn loose first, so we both let go of the tree and fell to the ground. It knocked the breath out of us. Both mama and auntie cried. It was a climax, auntie said she'd better move on before I killed some of them. I guess I was born with an evil fairy godmother."

Loni frowned as she thought about her fights with James as they grew up together. They were like her grandmother fighting with her cousins. Loni wondered if she had an evil fairy godmother, too. Moving on from her dark thoughts, Loni pulled out her laptop.

FROM: Loni Wagner
TO: Sandi@gmailyahoo.com
DATE: July 9
SUBJECT: Still not looking

I know I told you about how much I like my cousin Daniel, but I don't think I told you about how much I can't stand our cousin James. We've always been serious enemies, and now I have to see him every day, I do worry about what he might do to me.

This town is beginning to feel like LA. We lost a great kid to ricin poison and have no idea where it's coming from. I interviewed his parents this afternoon. It's the hardest thing I've done in a long, long time.

And it just keeps coming. Looks like our little town is a holding place for drugs to pass through. Don't know where or how.

On top of that, a woman shot herself in the leg to see if committing suicide would hurt. Then our PA told me about a man earlier this week who got shot by his dog. How weird is that? I had to laugh when she said she wasn't sure it was an accident on the dog's part.

Take care of you and yours.

Loni

CHAPTER TEN

The rising sun breaking the long night and coloring the cloudless sky burned Loni's arm through the open car window. She wished for the umpteenth time for a uniform with a long-sleeved cotton shirt to stop a perpetual burn. She could hear Chief. "Good thing you drive at night, girly."

Loni carried a large box into the police station, struggling with the heavy door. She plopped it on Lola's counter.

"Don't tell me you found more evidence."

"Nope," Loni replied. "Stuff for my desk."

"Chief left a note for you." Lola handed it to her.

Loni read it with amazement. "Do you know what's in this?"

Lola's bracelets jangled as she waved her arms. "I can imagine Tully wants you to do his work. Again."

"He wants me to arrest Terrence Willard for assault. Does he still weigh four hundred pounds?"

"Yep."

Loni read the note again. "Guess I'm screwed, huh."

"Just about." Lola needled Loni. "Looks like you had a long night. You're asleep standing up."

"Nights aren't bad. It's adding on the day work that's killing me."

"Fucking bulldyke," he muttered as he stomped by.

"Jesus, Chui," Lola said. "Tell us how you really feel!"

Without turning around, Chui flipped Lola the bird.

"I'm sorry," Lola said. "How come Chui hates you so much?"

"Other than I'm Indian and gay? And he's macho Mexican male and thinks you and I have a thing going. Besides that?"

"Besides that," Lola said with a burst of laughter.

"Oh, what the hell." Loni shrugged. "One day after school, he pulled me into a classroom and tried to rape me. I hurt him getting away. But not bad enough."

"Chui might as well join the Taliban."

"Nah. He's a good Catholic altar boy. Same thing."

Lola reached under the desk and handed Loni a slip of paper. "I nearly forgot your phone message from Jenny O'Neal. You're supposed to meet her at the Greasy Spoon. Said she was running late." Lola wiggled her eyebrows at Loni. "Two-timing me already?"

"Thinkin' about it." Loni grinned, stretching the words out. Lola rolled her eyes at Loni as she picked up her box and walked into the bullpen. She set it on the desk Carl pointed to and pulled things out of it. Coco crawled under the desk and went to sleep.

Before long, she had dragons everywhere. Dragon pen and pencil holder. Dragon envelope opener. Dragon stapler. Ends of pencils. She stuck a row of tiny dragons on top of the computer.

Lola came over to Loni's desk and chuckled as she picked up a paperweight with a baby dragon climbing out of an egg. "How cute," Lola exclaimed, turning it over in her hand. She sat the paperweight down. "Is there a reason you're into dragons?" She pointed at the rest of the desk.

"I love things that make me smile." Loni showed Lola the cup circled with playful purple dragons. "How could you not feel good when you look at this?" She pulled a sack of candy out of the box and poured the cup full of malted balls.

"Cool." Lola grabbed a handful. "My favorites!"

"They were mine too before you took them all," she kidded, refilling the cup. She pulled another paperweight out of the box and handed it to Lola. "I brought this one for you." A baby dragon was curled up asleep with its thumb in its mouth.

"I love it! It's so sweet! Thank you, thank you."

"Makes a good weapon, too," Loni told Lola as she carried the paperweight back to her desk and gently placed it on the corner of her desk calendar.

The candy cup was joined by a dragon cup, its handle formed into a tail. Loni filled it with dragon pencils. Dragons crossed the pages of a calendar and desk mat. Loni added a dragon clock and last, but not least, three photos with dragon frames. One was of her grandparents and another with Roani. Her favorite was of Maria with Coco. Satisfied with the arraignment, Loni was ready for the task force meeting.

Loni scanned the hostile faces. Chief was absent, and nobody else wanted to be here. She turned to Tully and handed him back the note telling her to arrest Terrence Willard. "Tully, I don't have time for your crap today."

Tully raised an arm to object, but Carl cut him off. "Okay people." He stood up. "I'll report first. Tox report states Todd died of a powerful dose of ricin mixed with meth, like the three others in Phoenix. Todd's was also mixed with too much alcohol. Seems he partied up on the Butte at his assistant football coach's house. Last night, they found the coach and his wife dead. Could be the same poison."

Loni's head jerked up in astonishment.

Carl continued. "They had enough meth to feed a factory of people for days. Also pot, ecstasy, and other unknowns. I think he was a major dealer, especially to school kids." Carl reeled this information off with no inflection in his voice. He nervously pulled on his red tie and seemed overwhelmed. "Anything on the lockers at school?"

"Lots of drugs, but no meth."

"Well, get back to the school as soon as you can. And tell the school about the drugs you did find. It's their job to clean it up. Did you find anything in Todd's house?"

"No. It was as clean as it could get. And I already left a list of what I found with the principal."

"Good." Carl nodded at Loni. "We had a report about a camp trailer. It could be a meth lab." Carl's forehead wrinkled in thought. "It was last seen on Harper Road, but I drove out there yesterday and it's not there now. Don't have a license plate number. It's white, square, and small. I need you all to look out for it." In the silence, Carl turned to Chui. "What'd you find out about Perry Abbott and his Mexican license plate."

Chui shrugged. "Nobody ever heard of him. The plates were stolen."

"From where?"

Chui shrugged again.

"Well, find out. It should be a place he'd been. Any border chatter about a bad meth shipment?"

"Only that it's on the streets in Phoenix. They swear it didn't come over the border."

"With Mexican plates, we know better. Maybe you should drive down to the border and talk to them. Maybe cross over into Sonoyta? Make damn sure they aren't responsible for the cocaine as well." Carl waited for Chui to agree.

Carl stared each person in the eye and waited for a response. "This is important, people! We are talking about children dying!" He broke the awkward silence by asking James, "Anything on Rene's plane and flight plans?"

James checked his notes. "CSI went through the plane. Loni got pretty much what was there. I can tell you the drug residue was cocaine, like she said. No meth or ricin." James closed his notebook. "Rene was hauling something, though. The back seats had been removed. Potting soil and leaf bits from plants were embedded in the carpet." James glanced around, rubbing his face. The room was so quiet Loni could hear the scratching of his bristle.

"On his last flight, he was booked for San Diego, but he never got there. Called in to report he was having problems with stomach flu. He dropped off the radar then, but nobody said anything because he showed up a few hours later. You know how that ended." James shuffled some papers and rubbed his face again. "Anyway, it did give him enough time for a trip across the border."

"Thought you said yesterday he arrived in San Diego?"

"You know what, Carl?" James growled. "I think Loni's full of shit, and she's wasting our time. I don't think Rene has anything to do with the poisoned meth."

"Somebody must, or they wouldn't be shooting at Loni." Carl snarled back. "You got a better idea where to start?"

"I still don't see the connection." James argued.

"I read the report, too. The connection was cocaine cut with the same filler at the assistant coach's house, Carl barked. "Since I don't believe in coincidences, why don't you stop complaining and do your damn job?"

James refused react.

Carl continued. "I want you to interview Todd's siblings and friends, especially the ones at the party. Get the list from Loni."

Carl turned to Tully. "Check with State on the notebook."

"Did. They won't release it." Tully leaned back, and his chair nearly falling over. Jerking forward, he hit the floor with a loud thunk.

"Damn." Carl said. "Tully —"

"Carl," Loni interrupted. "I've got a copy of it at my desk."

"Give it to Tully." Carl thought a few seconds. "I'll bet Rosa could tell us more. Chui? Did you talk to her?"

"Tried. Swears she don't know nothin' in between askin' for a lawyer."

"Keep at her."

"Tully, Rene's wife have anything to add about Rene?"

"Not really. She insists she knows nothing about the drugs. Never even been in his plane. She hates to fly. Said she attacked Jenny O'Neal at the funeral because she was having an affair with Rene."

"What's the problem?" James interrupted. "Everybody knew it. He did it all the time."

"Apparently he asked for a divorce this time."

"Anything else?" Carl glared at the group.

"Yes," Loni said. "I was up on Montezuma and saw lights for a runway in the distance. It was over east, but I couldn't tell where. Anybody know anything about it?" There was no response.

Carl frowned. "What does that have to do with the case?"

"I don't know yet if it does. Just looking for anything out of place."

"Okay." Carl checked his notes. "I want you to call all medical and warn them."

"Lola already did it."

"Just do it, Loni." Carl snapped. "That's it for today." He ignored her as he walked out.

At her desk, Loni picked up a paper and handed it to Tully as he was walking out the main door. "The phone numbers from his cell phone are on the back."

Tully wadded the paper up and dropped it at her feet.

Loni turned away in disgust. Fuck him. She was tired of trying. Lola flipped on the radio, and the fast Mexican music cheered her up a little. She did an improvised mariachi step past Lola's counter.

"Where you learn?" Lola asked.

"Your pigeon Indian sounds like my friend, Willie."

"A Pima taught you to dance like that?"

"No, no. Willie is always saying 'Where you learn 'em?' when he's making fun of me. You know Willie?"

Lola patted Loni's cheek, setting off her bracelets. "He's been through here a time or two."

Loni cringed. "I was afraid of that."

"I think your granddad got him out the last time. Bob, is it?"

Smiling, Loni corrected Lola. "It's Bahb, actually. That's granddad in Papago."

"What's his real name then?"

Loni shook her head. "I don't know. Every time I asked him he would insist, 'Long as no one knows my name they can't harm me.'"

"Makes sense, I think." Lola sounded unsure.

Loni didn't want to talk about Willie in jail. Or Bahb's faith. "Friend in LA made me learn a bunch of dance steps."

"Oh?" Lola said with a smug expression.

Loni frowned, remembering Maria's loving attempts to remain serious as Loni stumbled through the steps. Before there was no more Maria.

"Oh, shit, I'm sorry."

"It's okay. I do miss dancing sometimes." Loni rebuffed the memories and asked Lola for the list of medical personnel. "Did everyone reply to your calls?"

"Why?"

"Carl wants me to call them again."

"Why?" Lola repeated.

"You should be asking him. I'm guessing to see if anyone else got sick."

"Tomorrow. I'll get it ready again."

Loni had to meet Jenny. She wished she could go to bed, but she changed to her casual Western snap-button shirt, Levis, and walking boots. At the Greasy Spoon, Jenny was waiting in a back booth. Loni sat across from her. "Hey."

"I ordered coffee for you. Black?"

"Good." Loni reached for the cup. "Thanks."

"So what have you found out about the drugs?"

"Sorry, Jenny. At this point I have more questions than answers. Can I pick your brain?"

Jenny shrugged in disappointment.

"You knew Rene, right?"

Jenny's eyes darkened.

"What do you know about Rene's drug trafficking?"

"He was trafficking? Really?" Her surprise seemed genuine.

"I found traces in his plane."

Jenny shook her head. "I had no idea."

"The word is he wanted a divorce to marry you."

Jenny leaned back and guffawed. "That's a good one! Who told you that?"

"His wife."

"Oh, shit." Jenny paused. "He did hit on me a few times, so I told him I was a lesbian and not interested. Come to think of it, it only made him try harder. But I haven't seen him since summer school began." She took a sip of her coffee in thought. "That explains why his wife's so pissed at me." She lifted head and brushed her reddish-blond hair off her face. "I didn't know." She was quiet another minute. "Loving someone that much. That's so sad."

"You don't believe in love?"

"Would you tell me something?"

"If I can."

"How do you stay a good person when you deal with so much scum?"

Loni had heard the question before. "It's not so bad in small towns. Most people here I deal with are basically good with short-time problems which I always hope I can help them solve. People really don't want trouble."

Jenny snorted. "That's hard to believe."

"Small towns where everybody knows you, people count. In the big city they shoot them, frame it on a perp, and be done with it."

"Oh, bullshit." Jenny pushed out of the booth and stood.

"I kid you not!" Loni got up and dropped a five-dollar bill on the table.

"You ever see anyone do it?"

"Not lately."

"I have a feeling I shouldn't believe a word you say."

"You never know." They walked out the door together. Loni turned away, heading toward her truck, wondering if Chui was right. Sometimes it was hard not to roll downhill with the shit.

Loni hadn't learned much from Jenny, but she was a new source to the kids. And she was really cute, too. Loni found herself thinking about Jenny as she drove around doing her chores in town. Her last stop was the post office to mail a package to Maria's nieces.

Standing in line, she realized this was the first time she thought about Maria today. Maybe she was getting better. Nights were always the worst though. The strong smell of garlic yanked Loni out of her reverie. She turned around to the source of the smell, a man with a long black curly beard and wide, flat-brimmed hat. He wore a heavy camouflage coat and baggy pants in the one hundred-eight degrees. "Hey, where are you from?" Loni said in what she hoped was a friendly voice. "You're going to die in those clothes."

"God! Don't I know it." The man smiled. "We're supposed to be playing war games." He pointed out the back Hummer with dark windows through the window. "At least, our wives think we are. Truthfully? We're mostly gambling over at the Mayflower Casino on the rez until sunrise. Then we go play war until it gets too hot." He unzipped his coat half way down to display his bare, black hairy chest. "Couldn't walk in here like this."

"Okay if I see some ID?"

He handed his billfold to Loni, and she wrote his name and description in her notebook. Loni indicated the package he carried. "Something fragile?"

"I forgot to mail this for the wife this morning."

Loni took it and wrote down the address. "Got a phone number for her?"

He told her, and she called the number on her cell phone. A woman answered. "Do you know a Robert Teag?"

Loni listened a minute. "Yes, ma'am. He does behave a little strange, but I can't arrest him for that. Claims he's your husband."

After another pause, Loni said, "I wouldn't go that far either, ma'am. But I'll tell him." She hung up. "You don't want to know," she said to Robert.

"Guess you can tell, if I was so inclined, she'd be the first one I'd send a bomb to."

"Dressed like that in this heat, how many times have the cops stopped you?"

"You ever been hit by a paintball?"

Loni kept the package and called Lola. "This is Loni. What do we do with dangerous materials?"

"What? Like a bomb?"

"Yes."

"Run?"

"Lola! I'm serious!"

"So am I."

"You mean we have no way to handle the stuff?"

"Not that I've heard."

"Okay. I'll get back to you later." Loni hung up and handed the package back to the man.

"You're going to get a heat stroke in that heavy clothing if you don't get out of them soon."

"I feel like I already have." he smiled boyishly. "Still better than the way those paint balls feel when they hit you."

"Learn how to duck."

"Better yet, run."

Loni mailed her packages and nodded to him as she left. She waited until he walked out of the post office, package still in his hand. He got into the passenger side of the Hummer. He hadn't mailed the package, and there weren't any paint splatters on his coat. Or dust on the car. Loni wrote down the Hummer's license number.

Loni walked into the kitchen at the ranch and spun Shiichoo around as her grandma feebly flapped her arms. She loved the feel of the spun cotton dress. "Where'd you get the new dress? I like the icy green color. Goes with your icy white hair."

"Put me down." Shiichoo wiggled loose. "Stop this foolishness, child, and maybe I'll tell you. First, go get me some eggs. I want to make a Spanish scramble for supper."

"Shiichoo, I'm not climbing those trees and getting stung."

"There are no scorpions in those trees. You know my bantys eat them."

"How come you don't keep real chickens in a coop? Coyotes won't get them there."

"Foxes will. Nothing keeps them out. Not to mention rattlesnakes and Gila monsters after eggs."

"Oh, yeah. I forgot." Through the window, Loni saw the vet's pickup parked under a huge salt cedar. "How long has Tory been here?"

"Just before you came. Go invite her to lunch."

"Okay. Soon as I figure out how to collect the eggs. How about I give Donnie and Kelly a quarter for every egg?"

Shiichoo frowned at Loni. "Those eggs are so small they aren't even worth a penny."

"It's worth it to me. Have you seen them around lately?"

"They were playing in the barn. Probably getting in Tory's way."

"Cool." Loni pushed out the squeaky screen door. In the barn, she found Tory redressing Flossie's eye. Two boys sat on a bale of hay with Willie.

"Need a hand?" Loni smiled at Tory before she carefully approached Flossie on her good side.

"Thanks, but no. Willie's going to hold her for me when I work on her festers."

"Good." Loni was relieved. "I was sent to collect eggs for supper. Shiichoo said you're supposed to stay and eat with us."

Tory smiled a thanks before she returned to the cow's eye.

Loni sat down with the boys listening to Willie telling a Pima legend. He told her the story a long time ago when she took something of his without asking.

"Long time ago, Coyote steal batch of pinole." Willie stopped to question the boys. "You know pinole?"

"Sure," Donnie said. "It has ground corn and sweet stuff in it."

Willie knuckled Donnie's head and continued. "Elder Brother chase Coyote up to sky. Coyote, such hurry, spill corn across sky until all gone. Elder Brother so mad, he grab Coyote and throw him into moon. And what Coyotes do at full moon?"

"They sleep?" asked Donnie.

"What else?"

Kelly said, "I know. I know. They howl at the moon."

"That right. They howl at lost brother. That what happen when you take not yours."

"Oh." Kelly's eyes were big and brown with wonder. "I promise not to do it again."

"Ah," Donnie said. "I'm not Pima, so you can't throw me to the moon."

Willie frowned at him. "You total sure?"

"I'm sure I'm not Pima." Donnie beat his chest. "Me Apache."

Curious, Loni knuckled Donnie's head as she jumped into the conversation. "What did they take?"

Willie held up his tomahawk. It was one of his most prized possessions from his father's side. "It was borrowed. Right?"

They both quickly agreed. Satisfied, Willie smiled.

"Good." Loni stood. "Can I take them now? I need their help."

The boys skipped after Loni. One by one, she lifted them up onto the big John Deere tractor. The questions came nonstop. "Where are we going? Why is the tire so big? What does that do?" Loni grabbed Kelly's hand in time to keep him from turning the key.

Loni held on to them as she drove to the salt cedars along the driveway and stopped under the first one. She lifted Donnie up first. Loni loved the ornery glint in his eyes. He also had the round face and gentle nature of the Papago tribe.

Kelly was a different story. His angelic smile didn't fool her. Fearless and careless, he couldn't seem to do anything right. Everyone watched him like a hawk to keep him from hurting himself or someone else. "Be careful, Kelly!" Loni lifted him up in the tree branches. "Move very slow or you'll scare them." She handed them each baskets.

Two tiny hens pecked at the two boys and registered complaints as their eggs disappeared. Kelly and Donny giggled at the hens' antics and dodged sharp beaks. Loni grinned with them when they handed the eggs to her.

They went to all the trees except the last one with the rooster. The kids called him Satan, and Loni agreed. He was a mean son of a bitch with a red head and rust-red body. Bright red feathers curled out of his tail, and his four-inch talons made him a menace. He could jump three feet and chase or fly onto any unsuspecting whatever that came near him. Loni kept warning Bahb if he didn't trim those talons, she was going to shoot the damned bird, but Bahb kept refusing. "He need for coyotes and foxes. Protect his hens."

Loni wondered if the rooster really could protect anything until she remembered the story a friend told her about a parrot someone gave him. The bird came in a five-foot-tall cage, and the previous owner said to leave the door open. The parrot won't leave. Her friend was watching TV when he noticed his cat stalking the bird. When the cat was a few feet away, the parrot hopped out and strutted up to the cat. Suddenly the bird screeched and wildly, flapping his wings. The cat took a backwards flip in the air and disappeared. The parrot walked back to his cage going "he, he, he," and climbed back in. He said he never did close the door.

Loni drove the boys back to the barn and gave each one of them a dollar. She told Tory and Willie lunch was almost ready and walked by Jack on her way to the house. He gave a feeble bark, too blind to see her anymore. "Damn." Loni helped him struggle out of his hole before she moved on. "It won't be much longer, old boy, I know. You'll be out of pain." Tearing up, she knew Willie would have to take Jack out back. She couldn't do it.

Shiichoo stuffed the eggs into the refrigerator and told Loni she needed to learn how to make Indian fry bread. She carefully dictated the ingredients, handing Loni the pots and pans while Loni measured out the portions and mixed them together. Loni sat at the table and watched while Shiichoo poured the batter into a skillet, "Here. Use these dishes." Shiichoo moved her aside. They fussed with each other over which dishes to use until Loni smelled burning. She rushed to the stove and flipped the bread. It was black.

"See!" Shiichoo complained. "It doesn't cook right. We can't feed guest burned food."

"Looks great to me." Loni took the bread out of the pan and poured in more batter. "I'll hide the burn inside the roll and use these for my lunch tonight." She dribbled honey in the burned ones, rolled them up, and stuck them into a plastic bag for lunch for her five-a.m. stop. She liked to watch the sun rise while she ate.

"Honey makes a mess," Shiichoo said. "You'll be sorry."

Loni patted her grandmother on the cheek as she picked up the plate of fry bread and put it on the table as Tory and Willie burst in the back door. Loni grabbed a can of tea and drank from it, trying not to check out Tory.

"Call your grandfather," Shiichoo told her.

"Where is he?"

"I don't know. Willie, you seen Bahb?"

"No."

"I did," Tory said. "He was in the tack shack."

Loni reached the back door noting how familiar Tory seemed with things around the place.

"Don't you dare holler out the door," Shiichoo warned her. "Go fetch him."

"Okay." Loni opened the screen door and stepped off the stoop, closing the door behind her. "Bahb! Lunch!"

"Loni!"

"You said not to holler out the door."

The four of them were passing the food around by the time

Bahb appeared. Loni filled Bahb's plate, ignoring her grandma's directions.

"Too much egg, Loni. Take some off."

Loni dropped on another spoonful as she ignored her grandma's ire and focused on Tory. "So, how long before Flossie can be put out to pasture?"

"Maybe next week. She's healing fast." Tory smiled at Shiichoo. "You've taken good care of her."

"Pasture, maybe. She never go back to desert with one eye," Willie said.

Loni considered, "Maybe she can be turned into a milk cow?"

Willie grinned. "Maybe Loni can come every morning and night and milk her."

"Maybe she can't," Loni mocked Willie.

After they finished, Loni walked Tory back to her pickup. Thanking Loni for lunch, Tory climbed in and leaned out the window. "I need to move on. I've got two more stops."

"When are you due back to check on Flossie?"

"In a week."

"Good. We can have lunch together again. Maybe dinner sometime?" Loni said cautiously.

Tory admitted to Loni, "I just had a really bad loss so I'm not the best company in the world."

"I lost someone, too. We can commiserate together and drive each other even more miserable."

Tory smiled as she started her pickup. "I don't think that's possible." She kissed the tip of her fingers and pressed them against Coco's head. Still smiling, she drove away.

Loni didn't get home until mid-afternoon. She quick changed into a tank top and shorts and went to bed. Struggling against the banging on her door, she woke up in a sweat and pulled herself out of bed.

"It's me," Daniel yelled. Coco had gone into a frantic barking dance, and she had trouble getting around her to open the door.

"I need something to drink," Daniel announced, pushing by her to the refrigerator. "It's a damned oven down there." Loni could hear him rummaging through the objects on the shelves. "No beer? How can you not have any beer?"

"You forgot, Daniel. I don't drink."

"When did it happen?"

"I never drank."

"I didn't know. What about the plane rides?"

"I wouldn't go up, remember?" Loni shuddered.

"Oh, yeah. You were a chicken shit about planes. So what's that got to do with not drinking a beer at the end of a hot day?"

"I got sun tea."

"How about I bring some beer and store it here? You gonna drink it?"

"Fuck you, Daniel." She climbed back in bed.

He opened the freezer section, grabbed one of the frozen cans of tea, and left her to go back to sleep. Of course, when he got back down stairs he had to bang a time or two on something to let her know he could.

CHAPTER ELEVEN

awn brought back the relentless sun. Grateful, Loni's shift was quiet. She stopped a few times training Coco to give her one sharp bark when she found the ricin she hid in bushes on the side of the road. She left the rock hills behind as she drove through the river-bottom farms. Along their edge was a wide border draining system that wicked alkali from the soil. A shed about the size of a large dog house housed one of the half dozen water pumps running nonstop to drop the water table in the valley bottom. The system kept thousands of acres of farmland from getting too saturated to farm.

Many times Loni rode Roani through the white salt patches along the river. She pretended they were snow. She didn't see real snow until she was nineteen and went on a ski trip up to San Francisco Peak. It took her three hours to admit she couldn't keep skis on in cowboy boots.

Loni signed out, grateful the task force didn't meet on Sunday.

A few hours later, Loni walked into the new Mormon temple for Todd's funeral. She hadn't been there before, and she tentatively pushed open the white double doors. Large blocks of light reflected off the white walls from the tall windows and skylights. Loni stood in the back of the room to scan the crowd.

Rebecca had her arm around Jenny, who was crying. The young man Loni had seen with Jenny was on her other side, holding her hand. Loni hoped to pick up some of the conversation from the last row, but she got caught up in the service. She wiped away a few tears.

At the end, Jenny grabbed Loni's sleeve. "This is my brother, Steve." His gaunt features and hollowed out eyes convinced her he was a meth head. "Coffee?"

"Sure," Loni answered.

"Starbucks?"

"Fine."

Loni turned to speak to Rebecca and was startled by the pure hatred in the woman's eyes. She pondered Rebecca's behavior while her truck idled in the line of cars trying to get out of the parking lot. Rebecca walked by and sneered. "Move that filthy thing." She was still wondering about Rebecca when she got to Starbucks.

The freezing air inside gave her some comfort. Loni walked up to the tall round table where Jenny and a cup of black coffee waited for her. She hated high bar stools, especially wobbly ones, but she thanked Jenny for the coffee.

Jenny giggled at Loni as she grabbed both sides of the quivering round table and carefully climbed up on the stool. "Good thing these cups have lids. Little insecure, are we?"

"Oh, no, I always sit like this."

Jenny's face screwed up in an attempt to symphonize. "You can let go of the table. You're not going to fall off."

"Just shows how little you know me."

Jenny leaned forward. "Well, we could remedy that."

Loni let go of the table fast. "So is this like a date?"

"Do you want it to be?"

Loni wasn't sure of where Jenny was heading. "I think Rebecca might object."

"She's only a friend."

"Sure she wouldn't like to be more?"

"Probably." Jenny shrugged. "She's not my type."

"Can you tell me a little about her?"

"Like what?"

"I saw her take off flying the other day. Does she know a lot about planes?"

"I guess. She said her dad used to own a small airport and flew charters until he gambled it away. She helped him overhaul planes as soon as she could walk. Said flying was the only time she felt free and happy."

Loni sipped her coffee. "Okay. So is this a meeting? You got an agenda?"

The playful gleam faded from Jenny's cat eyes. "I had a visitor last night. The party where Todd was killed? One of my students was raped there."

"Ah, shit. It just keeps coming. Tell me she went to the clinic."

"No." Jenny fiddled with the gold chain around her neck in general agitation. "I know what she's going through."

"I'm sorry?"

Jenny pushed her long amber hair out of her face. "I said I know exactly what she's going through."

Loni reached over and took Jenny's hand.

Jenny pulled her hand back and sat up straight. "Somebody said you were some hotshot detective in LA. What are you doing back here?"

"How come everybody's asking me that? Is it so bad around here?"

"Let me think. We've got one laundromat with three washers and dryers, one general store with no taste, one self-serve gas station, one drug store, one clothing store with nothing but snap shirts, Levis, and boots—"

"Okay, okay," Loni interrupted, "I get it. But I could ask you the same thing."

"I wanted to be with my dad and brother. And you?"

"I don't have a dad or brother."

Jenny swatted at Loni. "Let me ask in a different way. Why did you leave in the first place?"

Squirming slightly, Loni dropped her head in defeat a few seconds before she met Jenny's eyes. "I was tired of being called a breed. And worse."

Jenny's mouth dropped. "You're kidding?"

"Oh, I kid you not. Other kids wouldn't even be seen in public with me. I didn't want to be alone anymore."

"God! I'm sorry. I've taught this age level for years, but I forget how cruel they can be."

"What doesn't kill us makes us strong, right?"

"Or evil." Jenny seemed to mentally shake herself. Resting her arms on the table around the coffee cup, a mischievous grin slowly removed her sadness, stumbling to a stop at the eyes. "So how about now? Anybody interesting around here?"

Loni ignored the question. "Can you tell me what the girl remembers?"

Jenny sipped her coffee. "She thinks it was Billy Joe who gave her the drug. She remembers a bedroom, the assistant coach, Billy Joe, and one of his friends, but it's all mixed up in her head. Most of it's blank. She woke up on her porch at home in pain, with dried blood on her legs and no panties." Jenny paused, swallowing hard. "She's a good Catholic girl who was a virgin and proud of it. Her gift to her husband. This broke her heart."

"Think she would talk to me?"

"I don't know. She went to the party with friends because she liked this boy, but he wasn't there. She was heading out the door when Billy Joe offered to give her a ride home in his fancy sports car if she'd stay and have a coke with him."

"Sounds like Rohypnol."

"The date-rape drug?"

Loni nodded.

Jenny shook her head. "Damn. It's too late for a rape kit. Worse, she couldn't get the morning-after pill. The pharmacist's a real nasty Right-to-Lifer."

"Really?" Loni was surprised. "It's against the law to deny anyone the morning-after pill."

"Tell that to him," Jenny said heatedly.

"I will. He has a right to believe in whatever. He can't act on it."

"You're a Right-to-Lifer?" Jenny's voice rose in amazement.

"What I believe doesn't matter. It's the law."

"And you believe all laws are good?" Jenny climbed down from her stool. "Tell me this hurting each other is going to stop someday."

"I wish I could," Loni replied. "But I can let you know if I find anything." She watched Jenny walk out of the espresso shop, wondering what she really thought. Loni also wondered if she was ready for anything more than flirting.

Shiichoo already had the stew on the stove when Loni stepped into the kitchen. Her grandma handed her the open recipe book, and Loni read her grandmother's beautiful cursive script. "Boil corn," she read. "Put cornhusks in hot water, mix cornmeal in hot water." She read on silently for a few minutes before she put the book down on the counter. "Wouldn't it be easier to make cornbread?"

"Just do it. Good practice for making tamales."

"Oh, in that case . . ."

Shiichoo smirked. "Every time I make them, the next day they're all gone. You're not feeding them to Coco, are you?"

Loni ignored her grandmother's jab and plopped corn husks into the skillet to soften.

Bahb walked in with pipe wrenches, screwdrivers, and a crowbar as Loni took the husks out of the pan. She saw him out of the corner of her eyes and jumped.

"I swear, Bahb. You scare me to death sometimes, you are so quiet. I can't even feel your essence."

"Because you not know my name."

"Oh, barf."

"Oh, barf? What that?"

Loni changed the subject, knowing she couldn't win this one. "What are you two doing?"

"Taking stove apart." Bahb walked over to the old wood cook stove.

"And do what with it?"

"Put in barn for now. Maybe sell later."

"No, no, no," Loni and Shiichoo said together. "The stove stays."

"What?" Bahb said. "You no say that."

"I can't let it go." Shiichoo was almost in tears.

Bahb hugged her. "Stove stays."

They finished eating Loni's lunch before she saw a flash of lightning through the kitchen window. "Willie and I saw ants uphill Monday," Loni told Shiichoo. "Gonna rain today."

Shiichoo jumped up from the table. "Why didn't you tell me? My wash is on the line." She rushed out of the house with Loni close behind her. They threw the clothes into a basket as the wind kicked up. Loni took a long, deep breath and smelled rain in the air.

Shiichoo poked her. "You'll be sleeping on gritty sheets if you don't help. It's here."

"Dish'ah." A few sprinkles splattered as Loni grabbed the last group of towels off the line and ran into the house behind Shiichoo. Sudden torrential rain came sideways with the wind blowing and clanging everything that was loose. The tin roof sounded as if the rain was stripping off layers.

The downpour was over in minutes and left behind a glorious clean smell of wet greasewood brush permeating everything. Loni walked out into the desert, enjoying the feel of the cool breeze on her skin. The chirping birds bathe in puddles, and the quail with their scurry feet and topnotch feathers bobbed up and down as they ran. A white wing close by repeated COO COO three times over.

Loni collected Coco and got into her truck to drive home. She felt better, but the truck was filthier than she thought possible with the rain mixing days of accumulated dust into mud. The boiling sun melted the rubber off the windshield wipers, and the broken pieces left streaks of dark brown goo to block her view. The water in the windshield reservoir was empty, and she drove slowly back to the loft with her head out her window. Tomorrow, Loni thought, I'll clean it tomorrow.

Loni had one more thing to do before she could climb into bed. She closed the door on the heartbroken dog and walked back out into the searing heat of midday. The high humidity popped sweat out all over her body. She ducked her burning eyes down and away from the blazing sun Her sunglasses were missing again. The asphalt was so soft she felt like she was slugging. At Dorothea's house, she knocked on the door.

A small girl opened it. She called out, "Mama, somebody's here!"

Dorothea's pissed-off expression blossomed into a smile when she recognized Loni. "You've got news? Or maybe you changed your mind about the two of us?" She opened the door wider and eyed Loni up and down. "Let's go to the kitchen. I baked."

"No thanks. I'm on my way home to get some sleep." Dorothea ignored Loni and headed into the kitchen. Loni reluctantly followed her.

"It's quieter in here. We can talk."

Loni stood beside a round, retro-Fifties Formica kitchen table with bright swirly colors and chrome trim.

Dorothea sat a plate in front of Loni. "In case you change your mind." Loni finally sat and watched Dorothea pour a cup of coffee and sit across from her. She spooned in four sugars and stirred it before she sipped the brown liquid and refocused on Loni.

"Anything from Larry yet?"

Dorothea was disappointed. "You want to talk about Larry?"

"Yes," Loni said flatly.

"Carl was by yesterday, asking me the same thing. And no, I haven't seen him. And I don't know where he is." Dorothea took another sip. "Sometimes he goes to this private hunting lodge with a landing strip. Talked about the all-night poker games and all the money he won."

"Do you remember where?"

"Montana. Somewhere close to Lincoln, I think." Dorothea said. "I remember Larry said his cabin was practically next door to the Unabomber."

"Thanks. I'll tell Carl." Loni decided to move on. "I have another reason coming over here."

"About us?" Dorothea attempted to reach for Loni.

"No!" Loni held up her hand in warning. "I need some hair with a skin tag from Billy Joe."

"Why? What has that little shit done now?" Dorothea slumped. "I guess I could get his hairbrush."

"It'll work."

Loni waited until Dorothea reappeared with a brush. Loni pulled hairs from the brush and dropped them into an evidence bag. "Thanks." Loni handed the brush back to Dorothea before she sealed and labeled the bag.

"He's quite a preener." Dorothea ran her hand across the soft bristles. "Spends more time in front of the mirror than I do." She grinned at Loni. "Don't say it." She playfully poked at Loni with the brush.

"You look good, Dot. You always did." Loni leaned against the back of a chair. "Did Carl tell you about the three drug deaths from poisoned meth?"

"He talked around, that's about it."

"You do realize, Dot, the next kid to die could be one of yours. I know Billie Joe's mixed up in this so you really need to talk to me."

Dorothea's head jerked up, and she almost spit coffee on Loni. Her chin quivered as she wiped off her mouth. "Damnit!" She replaced her coffee cup in the saucer and stood. "You need to go now, Loni."

"If you hear from Larry, you'll call me?"

Dorothea closed the door in Loni's face.

At the loft, Coco made her usual circles of joy around Loni before she rushed outside. Loni finished her tuna sandwich before she heard Coco bark to be let back in. She gave Coco a playful rub and hug on the floor before she stripped for a quick shower. In bed, Loni grabbed another letter from grandfather Wagner sent to Loni's dad. She snuggled close to Coco. "Ready Coco? Looks like this letter continues where the last one left off." Loni took a deep breath and read aloud.

> "Our life was slow growen up. We spent the summers underbrush sheds. Ma had a stove, table and benches, and beds all out there. Very little ice and for sure no coolers. The water pump was in back of the brush shed. You had to keep a toe sack to wrap the handle as it would burn the hide off your hands. There was room also under the shed for a marble game. Marbles were made of clay and weren't too round. We tied sister out on the ruff string of the jackasses wandering outside the shed. One bucked her off, and she sailed out thru the air like a butterfly, landed on her bottom like a sack of . . . She rite then hung up her surcingle for all time.
>
> We had a little old mean mare called BoBo. Sis could ride or drive the old buggy more. Her and I made a trip up to the main road and mailbox. Got 100 lb of ice off a freight wagon. On the way back she wanted to hurry home so she hit the old mare with a line. The old mare had been on green feed. She throwed up her tail, backfired green second hand hay all over us and the ice. The dashboard was worn out so no protection. Her with a mini skirt on, Ma had to come out and swab her off as she was too embarrassed to go in to meet company.
>
> Our grandmother Sutton was a half-breed Choctaw Indian and half Jewish."

Loni suddenly stopped reading and gawked at the word. My God! Choctaw? James was part Indian? Boy, is he gonna shit!

"She stayed with us most all the time and was most necessary as ma was sick so much, lots of kids and sometimes many men to cook for. I can remember holding on to her skirt and sitten' on her lap many hours. I remember she left one time for a spell and I had gotten a mile from home when Mrs. Wish stopped me at the church and asked me where I was going. I told her after my grandma. Was pullin' my wagon which was the only toy you could buy in those days. I was five.

I hurt my thumb bad when I was five. Dr. Rubel had moved into a tent house on the canal bank as he had come down with tuberculosis back east. A remark he made scared me and I broke and ran down the canal bank. Brother Lem overtook me. Before I got back, grandma took over. She dared anyone to hurt or whip me. So Doc put on some salve and wrapped it and sent us home.

Ma's sister Aunt Mabel moved near us. She didn't seem to be too fond of some of us kids and Ma and Pa would leave us there sometimes. We couldn't talk, have a drink of water, and at the table we had to wait for the blessing and Uncle Knoll was way too slow. Around 1918, Aunt Mabel knew she had professional daughters. Her son George didn't count and they were barely eeken out some groceries and had a Model T Ford. Uncle Knoll drove it in the barn, took the back wall out with him holleren' whoa. They moved on into northern California where Aunt Mabel believed it would be a higher culture for girls that weighed 250 lbs and more. Uncle Knoll soon worked himself into the grave to offer all this for them that turned out common like most of us.

Loni folded the letter back into its envelope and dropped it on the stand beside her bed. She hugged Coco's soft wool body, and her tears rolled into the dog's wiry wool. She longed for her yesterdays with Maria. Accepting the changes in her life was too hard, and death gave no do overs.

CHAPTER TWELVE

Loni was in time for breakfast. She dropped into a chair and leaned back, watching her grandma cook. "How do you get rid of the thorns without your wood stove?" She watched her grandma dice the prickly pear pads.

"Willie singed them outside." Shiichoo dumped the cut cubes into a pan half full of boiling water. "About the only thing I miss anymore cooking on the wood stove. Can't singe on these burners."

Loni ducked her head to hide her smile.

"Don't you say anything!" her grandma retorted, slapping her across the back of her head with the towel.

"Whatcha cooking?"

"Nopalitos," Shiichoo reached for a fry pan. She sat it on a burner and splashed in olive oil. "Bring me the chilies."

Loni struggled up out of the chair. "How many?"

"How hot you want it?" Shiichoo replied as she quickly chopped an onion.

"Without the seeds?" Loni handed her ten and watched her chop them without cleaning out the seeds.

"Good for your digestion," her grandma said.

"Not worried about my digestion, thank you. I'm worried about my mouth."

Shiichoo dried her hands on her faded rainbow apron and dropped a pinch of salt and pepper in the fry pan. "Get me eight eggs and go tell your grandpa and Willie breakfast is on."

Loni didn't move.

"Now," her grandma insisted.

"Oy. Dish'ah."

"No. Not later. Now!" she insisted again.

Loni struggled out of the chair, got the eggs, and sat them on the counter. She opened the screen door and hollered, "Bahb! Willie!"

"Nice."

Loni laughed as she stepped out onto the screen porch and broke off a large chunk of aloe vera.

"You take too much leaves and desecrate the plant." Bahb said.

"You mean decimate."

"No. I mean desecrate. It has good spirit."

"Right now, it's all about my spirit."

"Told you again to wear hat."

"That's not what hurts."

"Still need hat."

"I never did before."

"Yi. But you younger then."

"Bull crap."

Bahb shook his head as he banged into the kitchen. She dropped the leaves into a ziplock bag and slipped it into her shirt pocket. "It's to rub on my driving arm when the sun burns it later." She explained to Shiichoo, who was giving her a skinny look. "Can't drive around all the time with your stinky salve."

Shiichoo drained the prickly pear pods and returned them to the fry pan. She quickly stirred in the eggs until they cooked. Slathering them on top of pan-fried bread, the nopalitos made a Loni's mouth water. Shiichoo handed Loni the brown plate.

"Tell me about your folks. Did you ever get to visit them?"

"The school knew we were scared and lonely. They also knew if we went home, our folks would hide us out, and we would never go back." Shiichoo filled a plate for Willie, who was washing his hands and face at the kitchen sink. "They were right." Setting the plate on the table, she filled one for herself. "I had a favorite older brother they never did find."

"What happened to him?"

"Last I knew he went to the Oklahoma oil fields. He was only thirteen last I saw him, but big for his age. Cherokees taught him enough English so he got by. Married a Cherokee."

"Do you know what happened to your folks? How they died?"

Shiichoo shrugged. "Families around there said they got caught in an ice storm. Everything was lost."

"Jesus, that's some kind of hurt."

Shiichoo handed her a bar of soap and pointed at her mouth. Pushing Shiichoo away in jest Loni fought to kept her tears at bay. She turned to watch Bahb wash his hands. He had been repairing fences, and his light blue work shirt had streaks of sweat down the back. "Hey, Bahb? How long were you at the Indian School?"

Sitting back down at the table he turned to her with sad brown eyes. "Forever. Truly a prison."

"I felt unsafe until your grandfather came," Shiichoo added. "So many of the girls were abused by the older boys and male teachers. But your grandfather protected me. I don't think I would have survived without him."

As Shiichoo drifted into sad, Bahb sat down. "Remember basketball team?"

She smiled back. "You mean the team famous for losing every game?"

Bahb turned to Loni. "I on team. I tall Indian. But we all from different enemy tribes so nobody speak to other."

Shiichoo explained. "They also spoke different languages and couldn't understand each other."

"I remember this story. Didn't you know any English?"

"Little. Around fifteen when caught. Still, hard to be team player with enemy."

"They tied them to the goal posts if they spoke anything but English." Shiichoo patted Bahb's arm as she sat his plate in front of him.

"Court outside in sun, too. But your grandma taught me fast."

Shiichoo smiled at him. "They had never played basketball before either. I wonder if that's why you had a new coach every few weeks?"

"That would be it for me."

Loni cleaned up after breakfast while her grandmother gathered a pile of corn, pots, and pans. "Good lord, Shiichoo! You got the Sell Village moving in?"

"Nope." Her grandma frowned at her. "Making enough green corn tamales so maybe you'll leave me some."

"Don't count on it," Loni snickered.

"That's today's cooking lesson. Maybe you will cook some and bring them to me."

"Hah! You're so funny. Besides, tamales are Mexican."

"Child! Who do you think taught the Mexicans to cook?"

"Well, I'm not sure Mexicans would agree with you. I always heard green corn tamales were created in Globe by the Borquez family."

"Just start hulling and cutting the kernels off the corn." Shiichoo swatted at her and pointed at the pile.

Loni drove into the hangar before noon and carefully hid her tamales from Daniel. He had a habit of raiding her refrigerator, and she had seen him eat a dozen in minutes. Loni settled in and called ranchers between Caliente and the border, asking each of them to call her if they saw any recent signs of travel.

As Loni headed for work, she saw a dark car behind her. Get paranoid much? Maybe nothing, maybe . . .

Loni turned into a driveway and watched in her rearview mirror as the car sped by. She quickly backed out, but the car turned the corner and disappeared by the time she got there. She forced herself to drive slowly to the station.

CHAPTER THIRTEEN

As dawn broke, Loni found herself babbling to Coco. They were parked on the side of the road, hidden by a curve where the road wound around Mariner Peak, a good place to pick up speeders and drunks. A short passing lane pushed drivers to speed up to pass cars, but they didn't slow down after they passed. Bored, she combed her fingers through the wavy wool on Coco's long ears. "You could help me stay awake!" Eyes drooping closed, Coco ignored Her.

An hour later, an ancient truck slowly meandered by, its taillights so dirty they faded to purple and no license plate. Here we go, she thought. She pulled in behind the truck, turned her flashing lights on, and followed it for a mile. It wandered over the white line on the road's edge, tires singing on the white stripe, before it jerked over the center line and back again toward the edge. She drove another mile before she hit the siren.

The truck hiccupped to a stop in the middle of the road, and Loni pulled in behind. She kept her flashing lights and headlights on and stepped out. A hulk of a man struggled with the pickup's door as he swung out, hanging onto the swaying door. God, please don't be a mean drunk, Loni thought. "Coco, come." Coco stayed close beside her as they walked up and waited for the drunk to struggle upright onto his feet.

When Loni shone her flashlight in his face, she recognized Charles Baker. Longtime rancher on a small place that barely made it, he did a little rustling of unbranded calves and milked a few of his own cows. He wore a cow-milker's hat, the crown flattened from leaning into the cow's side. He had a grunge look without trying, and he smelled as if he drank the entire bar. He let go of the door and waved his arms wildly, trying to stay upright on wobbly legs. Loni figured he was too drunk to know he was going in the wrong direction to get home.

Loni flicked off her flashlight but kept her distance in the light of her SUV. "Hey, Charles, how you doin'?" Age etched deep creases into his long face, and too many bar fights left him with a bumpy, crooked nose. She guessed his beard at about five days. He was fatter than she remembered, and he kept the gander attitude of a cocky bully. Bare-footed, he wore a holey undershirt under faded bib-overalls. Even at five-foot-ten, Loni had to tilt up a long way to see his face.

"Did you see that sombitch that was driving?" He waved his arm, vaguely pointing into the desert. "He jumped out and ran. Why ain't you chasing him?"

"Well, hell, I heard that one before, Charles."

"Well! It weren't me driving." His voice was slurred. He stuck out his arm to lean on the truck and fell flat on his face.

Loni tried to not touch much of him as she shoved him into the back of her SUV. She'd grown up with the smell, a mix of grease, cow barn and butcher. Forcing herself into his truck, she took a deep breath and left the door open for fresh air. She parked it on the side of the road and hoped his tools would still be in the back when somebody picked it up. "Hey, want me to call anyone to come get your truck?"

He shouted, "You lettin' him git away! Where you going?"

Loni didn't answer.

"I got cows to milk and kids to feed."

"Oh, shut up. Your kids milk the cows." Loni stopped talking to him. By the time they got to the jail, he was asleep.

"Charles," Loni shook him awake. "Get out." Stumbling around a few steps, she finally got him headed in the right direction toward the jail doors. "Take your hat off," she snapped at him as she pushed him into the station.

Long hunks of his salt and pepper hair crossed each other in long greasy spikes in need of a haircut. And a wash. "Looky here what I brought you, Bobby."

"Well gosh, oh darn, Loni. I'm so overjoyed I'll just pull on my suspenders and shoot straight up."

She poked Bobby in the ribs loving his brand of humor as she helped him book Charles. All the way into lockup he moaned and bitched about somebody else driving.

"He got away with that the last time he was picked up." Bobby's sardonic expression said it all. "Guess he's decided to try it again."

"Think the judge will buy it again?"

"Would you?"

Loni chuckled all the way back to her SUV.

Back on Old Highway 85, she pointed the SUV toward the border across the desert plateau. She parked at her favorite speed trap upwind from the Oasis Bar. Finishing her last cup of coffee, Bobby's voice broke into her dejected thoughts.

"Got a home disturbance, Loni. Woman. Said she brought a guy home and when she woke up to go to work at the Whistle Stop, her purse and car was gone."

"Car description?"

"Greenish to grayish to bluish. She said it depended on time of day. Late model Buick."

"License number?"

"She didn't remember, and her registration was—"

"—in her car," Loni finished for Bobby. "Oh, god, poor woman."

"Here's her name and address." He reeled it off as Loni wrote it down. "I'll call for the license plate when the Phoenix offices open in the morning. Meanwhile, get her statement."

"Don't suppose you could send Tully?"

"Only if I don't want it done this year." Loni grinned at his sarcasm as he hung up.

When she finally got back to the station to sign out, Lola was already on duty. Loni handed her the evidence envelope with Billy Joe's hair. "Can you get a priority DNA on it? I really want to pick up this little bastard as soon as I can."

"I'll do my best." Lola sounded upset. "Think he's the rapist?"

"I'd bet Coco on it."

"You get it legal?"

"Yes. Dorothea let me in and gave me the hair. That's his step-mom."

"Dorothea Kildare?"

"Yes."

"Didn't you guys have a thing in high school?"

"Who the hell told you that? And no. We did not have a thing in high school. And before you ask, we're not having a thing now nor am I ever planning on it." Loni decided to tease a little. "Not that we couldn't." Loni gave the counter a knock with her knuckles and turned to leave.

"Wait a minute!" Lola stopped Loni and handed her a fax with the DNA results from Rene's plane.

Loni stared at the fax. "Well, shit! A woman sabotaged his plane? That doesn't make sense." She rubbed her eyes in confusion. "Anything come in on the fingerprint? Or anything else?"

"Some. Carl got it from me yesterday."

Loni thanked Lola and dropped the fax on her desk. She grabbed her notebook and followed Tully into the conference room.

Carl turned to Loni before she sat down. "Since you missed yesterday, I'll update you during the reports."

"Sure." Loni opened up her notebook.

"State sent findings from Rene's plane debris. Remember? He'd removed all the seats from behind the pilot's seat? They found potting soil mixed with cocaine residue and exotic plant leaves. They think he was delivering drugs with some sort of rare plant shipments he got out of Mexico. He must have already dropped them and collected the money when he went down." Carl paused, studying Loni. "I know you think Rene's drugs and the meth are related, but nobody's found any connection yet." Carl patted Loni's shoulder. "We may have to leave Rene to State and stay with the meth."

"Wait! I agree his death and the meth might, and I emphasize might be coincidental. I think whoever killed him had an entirely different motive than the drugs. But I still think Rene's drugs and the meth are tied together somehow."

"How do you figure Rene's death was unrelated to the drugs?"

"Because I got shot at. And because somebody was very worried about the valve yet didn't take the money."

Carl leaned back and pulled on his ear. "I still think we should leave Rene to state."

"What about who shot at me?"

Chui jeered. "Hopefully, next time he won't miss."

Loni reacted to Chui's hostility before she could stop herself. "It was a she, you ass!"

Chui chortled in glee. "Pissed off an ex, did you."

"I expect she was after the valve." Carl cut off Loni's retort. "You got in her way."

Loni turned to Carl. "And the second time?"

Carl studied Loni a few seconds, his long arm snaking across his balding head until his fingers reached an ear. "I don't think she'll be back."

"But if she is?"

Chui jumped in with his odious voice, needling Loni. "Don't worry about it. You'll never feel a thing."

"Enough Chui!" Carl reprimanded. Turning back to Loni he fast rubbed on his ear. "Maybe you better wear a vest."

"In this heat?" Loni fiercely shook her head. "I'd rather dig the bullet out than die of heat stroke."

Carl scrutinized Loni an interminable time before he backed off and let go of his ear. "Suit yourself."

"What about the thumbprint? Might answer who killed Rene and find my shooter."

Carl shook his head. "No hits yet."

"Okay. Maybe Rene got the exotic plants from your renters? Didn't you say that's what they were growing?"

"How's he going to fly it out of there?"

Loni shrugged. "There's an airport over your direction somewhere. I saw the lights, remember?"

Tully jerked into attention, his belly bouncing once above the table top. "What exotic plants? What airport?"

Carl wiped the sweat from his face with a clean, white handkerchief. "A guy by the name of O'Neal is growing some kind of rare plants on my ranch. Built himself greenhouses." He shoved the handkerchief into his back pocket. "Good question, Loni. I'll check that one out myself and see what they're selling and who to."

"Did you check with State if they found any exotic plants anywhere near the meth deaths?"

"I don't think anyone checked, but it's worth a look." Carl turned to Tully. "Call on it."

"And see if they identified the thumb print yet, please?" Loni added to Tully's phone call.

"Maybe you interrupted the shooter before he got a chance to grab the money," James sniped. "Or maybe the shooter was really there for you."

"Or he's afraid of getting ratted on." Loni retorted. "I still insist it's somebody we already know and know pretty well. Somebody who seems to know everything before we do," Loni added as everyone stared at her. She knew the shit would hit the fan with that one, but it had to be said.

"Who?" asked James and Tully in unison.

"If I knew, I'd arrest his sorry ass."

"Bullshit!" Chui said, in his usual raspy nasty tone. "You're just a coward or you would've got the somobitch. Or maybe you concocted this crappy story to cover your own ass."

"Chui," Carl interrupted.

"She can't go around accusing one of us, Carl. It ain't right."

"Is that a confession, Chui?" Loni rasped back.

"Chui!" Carl stopped him. "I thought I sent you to Mexico?"

"Today, Boss. Had to pack first."

"Did you talk to Rosa?"

"Rosa lawyered up, and somebody must have tipped off the border patrollers I was working with. I can't get a hold of them."

"That's what I'm talking about, Chui. Who tipped them?" Loni glared at him. In return, he tried to stare her down. With a snort he turned away.

"What about their families?" Carl asked.

"They live in Mexico. So far, Mexican police haven't reported."

"Drive down there today, Chui. Try to find them." Carl turned to James. "I need you to go to Phoenix and interview the meth dealers. They obviously know who they're buying from. Find out what they know about exotic plants at any of the meth sites. Get State to deal."

"Sure, Carl." James complied as he reached over and took Loni's pen and notebook, writing a note on the bottom of her notes. "I always appreciate it when you type up my notes for me," Loni cooed. The men sniggered, triggering a deep red blush on James. Tearing the bottom off, he crumpled up her notes and threw it at her.

"Eyes over here, please, children. Playtime's over." Except for James, everyone turned back to Carl. "Tully, keep checking Rene's list. Maybe he's got a meth dealer on it we can pick up. Also get long-distance phone calls to Phoenix. See if anybody here called them. Access anything you need."

"But I've done what I can, Carl."

"Then do it again. Maybe State will give you something new. Ask. We need to find a trail to the source." Carl turned back to Loni.

"Chief wants you to go check out a report from a rancher. Says he found dead Mexicans. Thinks they had drugs with them. Find out if the drugs are related to this case. Lola can give you directions."

"Can I ask something here?"

"Yes." Carl sounded cautious.

"The guy who was knifed. Did he have a cell phone?"

"No." Carl picked up his papers with quick jerks. "That's it for today."

Loni waited for Carl outside. "About the two dead on the butte. Did you get a blood sample?"

"Yep. Sent it to the lab already."

"Did you send the drinking glasses with the debris?"

"No. Why?'

"I think one of them had rohypnol in it. I'd like to know who put it there."

"Interesting."

"Did you send the bed sheets to the lab?"

"No. Why?"

"Girl claims to have been raped there. Is it okay if I collect the glasses and sheets and send them in?"

"Sure. After your assignment."

Loni stepped aside as Chief walked by into his office. Seconds later he came roaring out. "Goddamnit! Who's the jokester? It ain't funny!"

"Whoa, whoa, whoa." Carl grabbed him as Chief tried to push by. "What's wrong?"

"Somebody robbed me!"

"What do you mean robbed you?"

"What the fuck do you think I mean," Chief spat at him. Loni saw a mix of fear and anger flushing his face. "My God. I'm gonna be the goddamn laughing-stock of this town. Do something, Carl!"

"Okay." Carl said calmly. "Tell me what they took."

Chief jerked away to confront Loni. "If you had anything to do with this, your ass is grass!"

Carl focused on Loni, a questioning frown on his face.

Loni shook her head. "I know absolutely nothing. Honest to god!"

Carl turned to Lola. "Anybody been in Chief's office you see?"

"Nobody gets by me. Check graveyard."

"Okay, Chief, what's missing?"

Chief kept his eyes on Loni. "My gun. It was on a hook by the door. My taser and keys to the cruiser. They were on my desk."

"Anything else?"

"Ain't that enough?"

"When did you leave your office?" Carl calmly steadied Chief.

"I got here early and went over to Whistle Stop for breakfast."

"Lola, put out a BOLO. Make some calls." Carl moved into Chief's space.

"Why don't we go back and search? Maybe try fingerprinting some areas?" Carl kept talking quietly as he slowly led the loudly protesting Chief back into his office.

Lola struggled to cover her giggles.

"Maybe you should call the garage. Make sure no one took his cruiser. Time for me to get out of here," Loni said. "I'm in enough trouble."

Loni traded the SUV for her truck. She sped down to Milepost 72 and stopped behind the coroner's SUV. The flashing white-box ambulance was parked in front of it. She left her motor running and the refrigeration on for Coco as she scrambled down into a wash and scrunched her way up to a stand of mesquite trees. Carl told her she wasn't in time to help anyone, but she didn't want to keep anyone waiting in this heat. Loni hurried to the scene. "Find any drugs?"

Both EMTs and Doc Benjamin sadly shook their heads. The bodies were covered. They were waiting for Loni to release the scene.

"How many, Doc?"

"Three adults and two kids this time."

Loni followed the tracks a short way, checking the direction they came from. They must have been carrying the children. She returned to take her photos and search the victims, the toddler first. Blisters covered his nose and cheeks.

Doc Benjamin slumped against a mesquite tree. He wore a white cotton shirt with lightweight dark blue pants. His bald head and face were shiny from sweat as he fanned himself with his wide-brimmed hat. "Been dead almost a day," he said. "Rigor's already disappearing in the adults." He peered up with sad eyes. "So close to the highway, but afraid to stop anyone for help."

Loni instructed an EMT to take one of the children as she knelt beside the tarp over two of the adults and uncovered the bodies. The man's shoes were old cut-up tires held onto his feet with leather thongs threaded through holes and wrapped around his ankles. They matched the trail she had followed. His head was turned toward her, and his cloudy eyes seemed to mock her in reproach. She checked his faded Levis and found a hand-stitched cloth billfold with nine American five-dollar bills and three green cards. "Not very good forgeries," she said, showing them to the doc.

"Bet they spent everything they had to buy them." Doc Benjamin noted the money in the billfold. "They didn't have enough to pay a coyote."

Loni walked around to the woman curled up against the man. Dressed for the desert, she wore a large floppy straw hat, full white cotton blouse with long sleeves and a full brown skirt allowing air to circulate and cool the sweat. She found no ID on her.

"No water jugs and food bags?" Loni searched.

Doc Benjamin shook his head once.

Loni released the two bodies to the EMTs and moved to the last body. When she uncovered it, she fell to her knees and stopped breathing. The girl was the spitting image of Maria when Loni met her at the Police Academy ten years earlier.

"Oh, god, not again." It seemed a long time before Loni responded to a voice in her ear. Someone was shaking her, and she wanted it to stop. An acrid smell of the dead's evacuation hit her nose, jerking her out of a deep hole.

"Are you all right?" she heard Doc Benjamin repeating.

Loni forced herself back into the real world and stood up stiffly. She gently pulled the baby from the young woman's arms and followed the EMTs carrying the woman up to the ambulance.

Feeling gutted, Loni turned onto Airport Road and headed back to her loft. She hugged Coco and cried in her soft brown wool before she made herself eat a bowl of vegetable soup. She picked up her grandmother Wagner's notebook to read while she ate and tried to disappear in the words.

"When old man Reed hung up his spurs and moved to town, he turned his two pet saddle horses loose on the desert. With feed and water and their old familiar stomping ground, it would seem horse heaven for the two old pals. They weren't entirely happy. They missed people, petting, and the old gunny grain sack. Every time we made camp, and night fell, the fires going and the good smells of coffee and food, we would hear a soft nicker, and here they'd come, sure of their welcome. Santa Claus and Dime. Santa was a little bay with black points. Dime was a roly-poly gray dappled. Both small, about 14 hands and gentle as dogs. How they knew where camp would be was one of the mysteries, as we made camp at so many wells, Old Cut, Volcanic, Surprise, Willow and Red Tank. That covers a lot of desert, but they always showed up. If we were short of mounts, we'd use them until we gathered and then a big feed of grain and bid them farewell. Just parted like friends who expected to meet again soon.

Loni tried to remember what she knew about the windmills. Most of them were gone, Uncle Herm said. In others, the water level dropped so far they no longer pumped. Billy Bains destroyed three of them. She remembered when they camped at two of those same wells. Her patterns were the same as her grandmother's, breaking off dead mesquite branches for fire and using the same cast iron skillets for cooking. She closed the same gates and listened to the same windmill sounds. A smile on her face, Loni finished her grandmother's story.

"One night, out of the shadows came Dime, alone. We knew Santa must have gone to the Big Range as they never separated. We never found his body, tho we looked. Dime was with us three more years.

One day we found him standing in the water at Old Cut. His front legs were swollen and the screw worms had done their work. Some rope hobbles on him told the tale. We tried, but it was hopeless, so little Dime got the mercy shot. Later on we heard that he had stopped at a sheep camp. The herders, not knowing he wouldn't leave, had hobbled him and left him like that. Why they didn't release him we never knew, but decided it was just low mentality. Shortly after that, a band of sheep camped at Winters Well. They had reported to the deputy in that district that two wild cow men had broken up their camp, ran the burros off, disrobed the sheepmen down to their underwear and took their shoes and rifle, and destroyed their food. I believe this to be true, as I heard the story with much laughter and some grimness. I never asked the names of those 'ruffians.' I thought it was better to not know. But I seemed to see a white cloud floating above in the starlight and it looked mighty, like a horse head uplifted, the mane flying back, and I seemed to hear a horse laugh. Could have been my beloved Dime."

She had to stop reading. Dime reminded her of all the Mexican coyotes and the evil they had done. Loni replaced the notebook and closed the box. Feeling hopeless, she pushed the box to the back of the table and climbed into bed with Coco.

Loni tossed and turned until she fell into a restless sleep. Again she dreamed of moving limbs so intertwined she could not tell where Maria began and she ended. Skin on skin, they moved all over each other, tasting everywhere until Maria's sweet juices turned into the taste of blood. Loni woke calling Maria's name. She sat up and grabbed the edge of the sheet, wiping the sweat from her face and body.

Unable to sleep anymore, she got up and wrote on sticky notes, slapping them all over the loft. "I want Maria." "It should have been me." "The wrong one died." When her alarm rang, she peeled them off and stuffed them in the trash so Daniel wouldn't find them when he raided her refrigerator for his beer. In an oppressive fog, she got ready for work.

CHAPTER FOURTEEN

L oni bumped through her shift with only three speeders and no drunks. The last speeder was in a hurry to get back home to LA and complained bitterly about the Arizona heat. Loni stared after the car even when it disappeared and thought about how she no longer wanted to take the highway to LA. She couldn't remember when that changed.

Early for the task force meeting, Loni checked at the front desk. "The fax on the cattle rustlers come in yet?" she asked Lola

"No." Lola sounded upset.

Loni quickly decided to drop it. Moving on, she walked into the conference room and sat next to Carl. Tully's eyes silently followed the oscillations of the tired fan. Nobody else was there.

Carl stood and cleared his throat, waiting for Tully to pay attention. Tully kept watching the fan, and Carl cleared his throat louder. Tully's scraggly beard quivered as he muttered to himself about a computer problem. Carl said, "Tully? Got anything?"

"Only a peanut candy bar." Tully held up an eaten-on mush mess. "Want me to tackle the dispensary thingy machine for you?"

Carl sounded disgusted. "Here's what I want you to do. Ask around who visited at the couple's house, talk to the neighbors, check phone calls in and out, find who they hung out with who needs to be interviewed. And do it now." Tully got out of his chair slowly and gave a deep sigh before he took his time walking out the door. Carl waited until he left before he turned to Loni. "The fingerprint from the valve is not in the criminal database. They said they would keep looking. You find any drugs yesterday?"

"No." Loni was disappointed. "The undocumented workers were clean."

"See you tomorrow."

Loni worried about Bahb's cow troubles. She beat Carl out the door and hoped Lola was in a better mood. "Anything for me?"

"Yes. They ID'd your fingerprints from the windmill. Here's the fax."

Loni concentrated on the face of Calvin Miller. "I think he was in my freshman class in high school. I don't remember him after that." Loni noticed Lola's concerned face. "What!"

Lola shrugged. "I used to date his brother. Hope he's not involved."

Loni was surprised at her flash of jealousy. "Which one?"

"J.R."

"What happened?"

"Nothing." Lola's response was curt. "Other than he was really a bore. Nice. But boring."

"Well, there's a lot of that around." Loni said, relieved.

"Nice or boring?"

"Not for me to say. They're your dates."

Lola stopped sparing and returned to the problem at hand. "If he's part of this, you should look to his old man. His attitude toward minorities was really sick. He's one mean sonofabitch."

"I'll do what I can, Lola. Don't know what though." Loni checked the fax again. "This his right address?"

"Far as I know."

"Hoping Coco was trained enough Loni spent an hour watching Coco sniff each locker. Back out to her pickup Loni nearly dropped to her knees in relief. So far they found nothing on ricin.

Loni got to the ranch in record time and within an hour she was driving with Bahb and Willie on a rutted desert road with a barbed wire fence on one side. They kept giving her a hard time about the climb into her truck, their nose bleeds from how high it was in the air, and the rough ride. "The fence remind me of the way you tried to teach me to drive, Bahb." Loni tried to get them to talk about something else. "You put me in that old pickup and said, 'Just keep it between the fences.'"

"I 'fraid to ride with you," he said, totally poker-faced. "You go in ditch."

"Crap! You didn't know how to drive yourself. I gave up and had Daniel teach me."

She saw his mouth twitch. "Hope Shiichoo not hear you. Turds in dirty mouth."

"Soap, Bahb, soap." Loni slowly pulled to a stop. "What the hell?" she blurted, watching the scene unfold in front of her. A shirtless and barefoot man perched bareback on top of a jackass. He was flapping his legs in an effort to herd a mother cow and two calves out of the road and back through a hole in the fence. His arms waved in time with his legs as he yelled, "Move! Goddamnit! Move your sorry ass! Move!" Loni couldn't tell if he was talking to the jackass or the cows.

His bare feet dragged the ground and caught weeds between dirty toes as he rode over to the truck. "Look at this." He pulled on the jackass to stop. "My empire's falling down all around me."

Loni would have laughed if she hadn't been so pissed about Flossie. And her raw, sore butt. She took a deep breath and straightened her back. "Hey, Cal. I'm trying to find Bahb's cows. Know who took them?"

"Well, don't look at me. I swear I had nothing to do wit it. Alls I knows is my brother took 'em."

"J.R.?"

"Nah. Not J.R. He's so worthless we have to do his stealing for him."

Fighting a grin, Loni was relieved. "You know who did take them?"

"It were Peewee. He did borrow J.R.'s truck though. Boy, was J.R. pissed at Peewee. Thought he was gonna beat the shit outa him. Wouldn't even take a cow for it. Last I know'd, Peewee left 'em behind my dad's house."

Loni nodded and drove up the road to Cal's dad's farm. "He's lying," she said to Bahb. "It was his fingerprint on the rod. Both he and Peewee are in on it."

"Whoa," Willie said, and Loni stopped on the side of the road. They had found their cows. Standing with heads down, clicking their ears and swishing their tails, they made hungry and thirsty noises.

Loni listened to Bahb and Willie talk about the cows, each by name, as if they were people. When she pulled in front of a sagging farm house, she interrupted them. "Old Man Miller. Is he as mean as I remember him?"

"Probly." Bahb got out with her. A large, short-haired, brown mutt greeted them with wild, out-of-control barking and body slams against the gate.

"Wow." Willie grinned. "Guess he no like you."

Loni gave Willie a skinny look. "Maybe it's you he doesn't like."

Watching the dog slam against the gate again, Willie shook his head. "Only one thing worse than bad dog."

"I know, Willie. You've said it before. It's the sonofabitch that would own one."

Loni clanged the cowbell hanging on the gatepost, and the dog went more berserk. "Think he knows how to get out?"

"Not yet." Willie cracked up as Loni's eyes widened.

An old man opened the screen door and yelled, "Wha'dja want?"

"I'm after those cows out back," Loni shouted back between dog snarls.

John Miller shuffled out, kicking at the dog.

"Shaddup!" The mangy dog cowered and limped, crawling back under the porch.

The pale and emaciated man ran a swollen hand through his thin, stringy hair to wipe away the sweat. Tired, gray wisps of chest hair stuck out around his dirty undershirt.

"Find happy hunting ground soon," Bahb said. "Man sick."

"You mean go to hell. I wish I could send him there now." Loni fumed.

Bahb gently placed his brown hand over Loni's fingers resting on her gun butt. "He already in hell. Been there a long time." They watched him shuffle down the walkway toward them. "Leave him be."

"So?" John opened the gate and glared at them. "You want to buy them?"

"No," Loni snapped. "I want them back."

The old man sneered. "They ain't branded. Prove they're yours."

Loni muttered, "I really want to shoot him." She felt Bahb squeeze her hand. "I need your bill of sale."

"Why?"

"Because you can't prove they belong to you without one."

"Don't have one."

"You admit you stole them."

"From who?"

Loni was out of patience. "I just told you. From Bahb here."

John guffawed. "Good one. You know you can't steal from an Indian. Bob doesn't own anything worth stealing."

"It's Bahb, not Bob. He's my granddad, Mister Miller."

"I know who you are."

"Then you know those cattle belong to him."

"Fine. Take them. Told those worthless boys to sell them, not leave them there," he snarled, turning away. "Can't understand anyone who won't brand a cow, anyhow."

"Well, guess what? You're under arrest, Mister Miller."

"Ni, ni." Her granddad pulled on her arm. "Leave him be."

She turned to him in exasperation. "They left old Flossie in the cactus patch to die!"

"It okay."

"Damn it, Bahb." She turned back to Old Man Miller. "You tell Cal and Peewee to take the cows to Bahb's ranch. Today. Or I will be back, and I will arrest the lot of you."

He gave a submissive wave over his shoulder as he went back to the house.

Angry and frustrated, Loni got into the truck and waited for Bahb and Willie to climb in beside her. "He shouldn't get away with it!"

"He do bad. But I never knew man who try harder."

"Not that I ever saw."

"He work hard for his lord and he thought on his investments."

"What does that mean?"

"Years back he buy motel, and new freeway bypass it. Remember? He buy laying hens, and virus kill them. He buy Shetland ponies. They so mean, kids no near them. He buy cotton farm, but price fall out bottom. Cheaper from India. His wife die. He sick, broken man. Leave him be."

"I know one way he was successful. He gave the church a new member every year."

"Yi." Willie's stoic voice oozed irony. "Wonder he know what cause it?"

"Bet his wife didn't." Loni snickered. Feeling disapproval from her grandpa, Loni couldn't quit. "Shit, Bahb! His kind would have scalped you a hundred years ago."

Bahb lifted his hat. "Still have it." He had a tiny upturn to his lips as he dropped his hat back on his head.

Loni gave up and silently drove Bahb and Willie back to the ranch. She wondered what they thought about during their long, quiet rides across the desert, what pictures were in their heads. She couldn't even imagine how they had grown up.

Past the last gate, Loni smiled. At least today's Thursday, she reminded herself. The truck should bring something else. The dishwasher and hot water heater were due.

Three trucks blocked her way when she got to the ranch, and Ralph was pulling big boxes out of the back of one of them. Speed had taken out three of the old canvas-covered screen windows and was working on a fourth. She wasn't sure about the third truck idling in the middle of the road.

Bahb and Willie commented on the activity when Loni parked her truck under a salt cedar. At the house, she heard whining through the screen door and let Coco out. She thought about the poor, beaten dog at the Miller's ranch and imagined Maria's angry face. She would insist they take the dog and find it a good home. It didn't matter how many times Loni reminded her the animal belonged to someone else, Maria would bulldoze her way in until the owner gave up the animal or she charged them with cruelty.

Loni gave Coco one last hug and continued on into the kitchen to face Shiichoo's ire. Time for Loni to go home.

Loni opened her laptop and wrote a quick email.

> FROM: Loni Wagner
> TO: Sandi@gmailyahoo.com
> DATE: July 14
> SUBJECT: Not Ranching
>
> Still listing reasons I don't ranch.
> Reason #5: Cattle rustling again. Bahb's still missing some yearlings, but I'm glad we found the others. That loss would devastate him. More than money, it's losing old friends. I am always amazed at how much love he and Shiichoo have for all children and animals. Wish I could say the same for most of the whites I know.
> Not much going on with the case. It's as though everybody's being sent to the wrong place at the wrong time on the wrong day. I don't want to believe that Carl is deliberately misleading everyone, but I also don't understand how anyone could misread the leads so badly. Funny about that! Seems I've gone full circle.
> Missing you all.
> Loni

Finished, Loni rummaged in a kitchen drawer for the sack of drugs she got from Lola. Watching Coco sniff the drugs reminded her of a story Trevor told about a group on a campout he ran across during last winter.

A high school coach from a neighboring town had dug up plants and replanted them next to the camper. Trevor asked him why, and the guy said they were in his way but he didn't want to kill them. He couldn't believe the plants were peyotes. "What really gets me," Trevor told Loni, "is how very ignorant our educators are. He couldn't even recognize a drug when he saw it."

Loni thought about the coach and his wife who died at the party while she left Coco in the loft and wandered the hangar to hide the drugs. Chief quietly shipped them back to Fresno to be buried. In fact, everything was too quiet. She felt as if the task force was being shut out, kept from accomplishing anything.

Loni let Coco out of the apartment. "Hunt, Coco."

Daniel watched her follow Coco around. "Never saw a grown person play hide-and-seek."

"Oh, shut up, Daniel. Go back to your toys."

Coco took longer than she should, but Loni had never trained Coco on her own before. She had to learn to do a lot of things on her own now.

🌵

CHAPTER FIFTEEN

The night was so pitch black Loni couldn't see her hand in front of her face. Determined to find undocumented immigrants before they got into worse trouble, she inched along. Spotlights strung across the top of the SUV snaked along indistinct trails. She knew they would rather die than go back to the brutal life across the border. Accepting they were too afraid to ask for help, Loni gave up and returned to Old Highway 85. She drove on, mile after mile though the black night until the dawn lightened over the horizon and outlined Saddle Peak. At Harper Road, she thought about the travel trailer and flipped onto the dirt road to search the site one more time.

Loni hated the washboard road. Five miles in her jaws grew sore from clenching against the slamming of the uneven ruts, and dust sifting in through the open windows coating her face and everything else in the SUV. Between coughs, she spit out into the dust, only to have it blow back on her. Between sneezes, Coco crawled out of the floorboard onto the seat only to be flung back down again. Slowing down didn't help. She rolled up the windows, not knowing which was worse, suffocating from dirt or heat.

On her left, Carl's fence separated his ranch from Bahb's. The country road was rarely graded and never mended until flash floods washed it out. Ahead, a locked gate was posted with NO TRESPASSING and NO HUNTING signs. "What the —?" she muttered to Coco. "Where did that gate come from?" Other metal signs were anchored to the fence.

After seven more brutal miles, she came to the dead end where Carl said the trailer was camped. Under an ironwood tree, she let Coco out to help her search. Neither one of them found anything, not even human trash. She turned back after a quarter of a mile to see a black Hummer drive out of another gate. It stopped beside her, and Loni felt the cold air rushing out of the window through the open window.

"Well, Robert Teag. How's your wife? Did she like your package?"

"You're trespassing," he said. "I have to insist you move on."

Loni smiled and shook her head. "This is a county road, Robert. Anybody can travel it." Loni pointed to the distant hill. "This side of the road you and I are on? Belongs to my granddad's ranch. Guess if anybody's trespassing, it would be you."

"What are you doing here?"

"I'm standing on my own land, and you ask me what I'm doing here? You're kidding, right?"

Teag impassively waited.

Loni finally explained, "Looking for a travel trailer someone said was camping here."

"Not here. I've got surveillance on this road, and I can tell you no trailer's been around here."

"You part of Carl Harper's renters?"

"Security."

"Security for what?"

"Plants."

"What kind of plants. Rare plants?"

Robert shrugged. "You have to ask the boss."

"Do you fly them out of here?"

"Sometimes."

"You have a runway?" Loni watched Robert's face close down as he rolled up the window.

The Hummer turned around and sped back to the gate. Teag punched in three numbers, and the gate quietly slid open. The Hummer drove through and the gate slid shut as he disappeared over the hill in a cloud of hot dust.

"Let's go," Loni told Coco. She got both of them a drink of water and poured some on her kerchief and wiped at her face. Reflected back at her in the SUV rearview mirror was the smeared mess of sweat and dirt she left still streaking her face. She fought a losing battle against her anger and disappointment. Carl lied to her about the camp trailer, lied about drugs on the undocumented immigrants. If she couldn't trust him, who could she trust? she thought sadly. If Maria were still alive, she'd turn this damn car around and head back to LA.

Loni left the filthy SUV at the police shop with a note on the windshield for Gary to wash it. She was glad he wasn't there so she didn't have to hear him rebuke her with "That ain't a cow. You can't rope and jerk it around like that!"

Bobby was at the front desk when she stopped to sign out. "Chief find out who robbed him yet?"

"No. Maybe when I was releasing this kid who rents from Carl. He got drunk at Billy's Bar and beat the crap out of a woman, and his dad was bailing him out. Steve O'Neal. I was upstairs a few minutes getting him down." Bobby's long face was screwed up in thought. "Maybe you can drive out there? See what they know?"

Loni was still futilely searching for information about ricin on her computer when the task force gathered.

Chui grabbed malt balls out of the bowl on Loni's desk and stuffed his mouth full.

"You enjoying them, Chui?" Loni crossed her arms and leaned back in disgust.

His mouth full, Chui mumbled, "You bet."

"Good." Loni ducked her head. "I picked them up off the floor of the drunk tank." With a shit-eating grin, she watched him spit them out.

James snorted.

"That's three, Loni," Chui spit at her.

Loni shrugged along with the smirk.

Lola laid her head on the desk and pounded her fists in laugher.

Chui turned and glared at Lola. "You know what's wrong wit you wimen?" His accent was heavier when he was angry. "What's wrong wit you wimen is that you're a bunch of flat-petered cowboys wit penis envy." Chui grabbed his crotch and shook it, staring at Lola.

Isn't he done with that old line yet? Loni thought. She turned her back on him.

"Chui, Chui, Chui." Lola said. "You're such a silly boy." A flourish of her arm sent her bracelets jangling. "You know that's not true. We girls can get all the penis we want!"

Chui furiously stalked toward Lola. "Why you defending that bulldyke? You sleepin' with her now?"

"Not yet, but I'm thinking about it." Lola stared back at Chui with a serious expression.

"I know you lie," Chui said. "I seen how you love men."

"You know what? I'd rather sleep with her than you."

Loni regarded Lola in amazement as Chui fled into the conference room sputtering about goddamn dykes. James followed him in, eyeing Lola with a speculative expression.

"I know you put up with a lot of crap in school from Chui," Lola said. "What about James?"

Loni shrugged.

"You gonna answer my question?" Lola insisted.

"James was in the same year with me and my biggest tormenter. He and his friends loved to grab my breasts and butt, play tricks, call me names. He wasn't happy with me being a lesbian, but he hated me even more for being a breed. I don't know which embarrassed him the most."

Loni smiled sadly at Lola. "You know defending me is going to get you into trouble?"

"Why? Think I care if someone calls me a lesbian?"

"Well, don't you?"

Lola shrugged. "Maybe when I was younger. Not anymore." Lola's expression became thoughtful. "Growing up, did you hate yourself for being a lesbian?"

Loni shook her head. "No. I believe what my grandpa taught me. He said I was a two-spirit and that was an honor. I was equally male and female, which gave me greater wisdom. But what really got me through high school was hearing his voice repeat to me over and over. I can still hear him. 'Our spirit God made no mistakes. Just keep think on that.'"

"God made no mistakes. I love it." Lola walked away smiling.

Nearly colliding with Tully as he came around the corner Loni jumped aside. Apologizing, she followed him into the conference room.

Carl was already talking as Loni walked into the smell of sweaty bodies. "I'm sorry to do this to you, but I need all of you to work Saturday."

His voice was drowned out by "No way, Jose." "Well, shit on a stick." "I got a sick mother." "I got a sick turtle."

He waited until the loud voices quieted. "Here's what we know, people. We got three more dead in Phoenix. They caught another dealer who pointed to Caliente as his source. Said it was a squatty white guy who said his name was Jimmy. Couldn't get a better description. The dealer was a young Mexican kid who said all gringos looked alike. Oh, yes. He did say his source drove a dark Hummer. Anybody seen a dark Hummer around?"

"Dark what?"

Carl stared at Tully. "Dark, dark. How would I know?"

Someone would shoot her down, but Loni had no choice. "I saw a Hummer at the post office earlier in the week."

"You see the driver?"

"Absolutely. He was mailing a package. Or so he said." Loni patted the notebook in her shirt pocket. "He gave me a phone number. He was mailing it to his wife, so I called her."

"Was that legal?" James asked Carl.

"He had heavy camouflage on," Loni said defensively. "Too heavy for this time of year. I didn't believe him."

"What'd his wife say?" Tully sounded curious.

"Aside from insisting she'd shoot him if he ever showed up again? You don't want to hear what else she said, but she convinced me he was who he said he was." She took her notebook out of her pocket and opened it. "I got her name, phone number, and address plus his name and address off his driver's license. His name's Robert Teag. I also got the Hummer's license plate."

"Good. I'll handle this one."

"Wait a minute," Loni interrupted. "I'm not through. Saw him again this morning in the same black Hummer coming out of your place, Carl. Said he was security. I asked him if they were growing rare plants. He didn't deny it. Didn't deny they had an airport there either."

Carl ducked his head and jotted something down. "I didn't know." His voice sounded stressed. "But it's time we found out." Carl turned to James. "You find anything out from the Phoenix dealers?"

"Wait. One more thing," Loni interrupted again. "Bobby said only people around when Chief lost his gun were O'Neal and Teag. Bobby said he went upstairs to get the O'Neal kid out of lockup and left the two at his desk."

Everybody stared at Loni, who turned red and shrank down in her seat. "Just saying."

"Chui, find Teag. We can get a warrant." Carl turned back to James. "The dealers?"

"They lawyered up." James insisted. "I couldn't get another word out of them."

"Okay. Tully could use some help with the couple. See him after." Carl turned to Tully then. "Find anything on the couple?"

"Previous drug arrests, but no convictions. Arrest sheet from Fresno indicated they were probably dealers there."

"Any connection to anybody here?"

"No. Still looking, though."

Carl nodded. "Tell James what you need."

"Isn't Chief from Fresno?" James asked. "Maybe he knew them."

Carl shrugged. "I doubt it. He's been here more than five years, but check with him anyway." Carl continued around the table. "Chui? Rosa talking yet?"

"No."

"Why are you still here? Thought I sent you to Mexico."

"I'm going!" Chui complained. "I was waiting for a contact to get back to me. He said Rene flew out of San Luis the day he crashed, so that's where I'm headed." Chui paused, tapping his pencil on the table. "My friend, Sergeant Ruiz, said he'd make it a point to find out who Rene met by the time I got there."

"Good, Chui. Keep on that."

"So, Loni, here's what you do." Loni noted the change in Carl's voice.

No longer tentative, he sounded like any other bureaucrat making stupid decisions. "I want you and Coco back at school checking lockers."

"Did anyone check out the lockers I already found?"

"Can't tell you what I don't know."

"And I'm going back because?"

"Maybe the meth has shown up by now." Carl gave her a harsh look, and she shut up.

Loni caught up with Tully as they reached the door and she walked out of the building with him. "Tully, could you research ricin for me?"

"Research how?"

"Any report of castor bean trees growing and where. Any animal deaths due to eating the beans. Same for castor bean oil production. Orders for plants or beans. Anybody making ricin for commercial purposes." Loni thought as they walked to the police lot. "I guess any possible source that contaminated the meth. Could you do that?"

"I've already done it," Tully said. "I'll leave the information for you in the morning." He turned and walked into the drugstore as Loni stared at his back in amazement.

Loni finished searching for the poisoned meth. Sighing in relief, she stopped at Jenny's classroom at the ringing of the last bell. Jenny glanced up and gave Loni a broad smile. "Lunch?"

"Great!"

"My house?"

"Sure!"

Loni followed Jenny into the parking lot and ordered Coco into the truck. Driving out of the parking lot after Jenny, Coco's head fixated on the floorboard at Loni's feet and she barked. Something hit the back of Loni's leg so hard it knocked her foot off the gas pedal. She grabbed Coco's collar to keep her from hitting the dash and slammed on the brake. Something hit her leg again. Through the steering wheel, she saw the head of a rattlesnake. Loni was up on the seat and squatting before she even realized she had moved. "Coco, stop barking!"

Loni slowly opened the driver's door and cautiously reached past Coco to open the passenger door. A kid stood outside the truck staring at her. "Get me the shovel out of the back." He kept staring at her. "Now!" she yelled.

He climbed up the tailgate and grabbed the shovel.

"Now! Careful! Stand out there and hand it to me, handle first."

His eyes were huge when he handed her the shovel.

"Now. Run like hell and take the dog!"

"Why?"

"Because a big old diamondback is coming out from under my seat and you don't want to be in the way."

The young man scrambled away, Coco in tow.

Loni tried to get the snake to strike the shovel by waving the blade along the bottom of the seat. Nothing. She used the shovel as a shield and carefully checked behind the seat. Nothing. Undecided, she waited. A flat head reached out the driver's side, weaving up and down with its tongue flicking in and out. Loni stepped out the passenger's side, shovel in hand and ran around to face the snake. They stood, staring at each other until the snake undulated down to the ground. Loni came up behind the surging snake and chopped off its head. In a cold sweat, she dropped the shovel and slid down the side of the truck, leaning back against a tire. When the adrenaline dissipated, she found herself trembling. Reaching for Coco, Loni wrapped her arms around the dog and hung on until her shakes subsided as the dog nuzzled up to her and licked her face. Someone seriously wants me dead, she realized, too frightened to move.

She was still sitting there when Jenny walked up. "What's wrong? You weren't behind me so I came back to check." Before she could answer, the large woman from Rene's funeral pushed through a small crowd of students and came at her. "How dare you kill my snake?" she demanded.

Pissed off, Loni yelled back at her. "What? You want one of those kids to get struck?"

Rebecca swore at Loni. "Next time I won't miss."

Jenny said, "What did you say?"

"No. No. I didn't mean it that way. I meant next time I won't miss finding my lost snake," Rebecca babbled.

"That was your pet rattler, wasn't it? The one you cut the rattles off?" Jenny insisted.

"She can't prove it."

"I guess she doesn't have to." Jenny's voice raised an octave.

"Do you own a motorcycle?" Loni asked Rebecca.

"No."

"Yes, she does," Jenny said.

"You shot at me Tuesday night!" Loni yelled.

Jenny gaped at her in horror. "You were shot at?"

"Well?" Loni demanded.

Fear flashed across Rebecca's face, and she stormed back into the school.

Loni spoke quietly to Jenny. "If you don't mind, I'd like to take a rain check. I've lost my appetite."

"I understand," Jenny said between clenched teeth, "and I need to talk to Rebecca."

Loni wondered about the female DNA from Rene's plane. She wondered if any of Rebecca's fingerprints were on the bumpy smooth skin of the snake. She gingerly picked up the snake's body and coiled it up into a corner of her truck bed, half smiling to herself. Bobby was gonna love this.

Loni slowly drove home, adrenaline spikes alternating with the shakes. She could no longer believe in Carl, and now she was worried about Jenny.

The handful of saltine crackers in the tomato soup made Loni think of white pieces floating in blood. She pushed the bowl away and opened her laptop.

> FROM: Loni Wagner
> TO: Sandi@gmailyahoo.com
> DATE: July 16
> SUBJECT: Still here
>
> Yes, I'm sure Lola is straight. I think she'll be a good friend and boy do I need one, especially around the station. She's got good common sense and street smarts, and, hopefully, a set of eyes at my back.
>
> I think I know who's trying to kill me. One of them, anyway. I found out the hard way when I climbed into my truck and a rattler from under the seat struck my foot. I think it belonged to a crazy jealous teacher who thinks I'm hitting on her girlfriend. Can you imagine?
>
> That's the second time a rattler has hit me. Thank god for high top boots. The first time, the rattler nearly knocked me down. God, they hit hard. This time he couldn't get the height. Had to kill it. It was at the school and children could have been hurt.
>
> I think our poison ricin answer is at Carl's ranch. With Teag's Hummer and Chief's robbery. It should be enough to get a warrant, and I can't understand why Carl

hasn't searched the place. If I can figure out a way to get in quietly, maybe I will!

Take care of everyone.

Loni

CHAPTER SIXTEEN

The task force had settled in the conference room by the time Loni joined them. She sat beside Tully and thanked him for his research on the ricin. "You're sure Carl's renters are selling castor bean seedlings?"

"I'm a cop, aren't I?" Tully muttered out of the side of his mouth as James came in.

Carl followed James into the meeting. He appeared tired and drawn, his wrinkled brown suit showing signs of neglect. Carl fidgeted with a pen. "I'll start. Talked to O'Neal who said the Hummer belonged to him. Said he fired Teag for taking things. Didn't know where he went, didn't care."

"Can we get a BOLO on him for theft?"

Loni watched Carl's temper flare. "I tried. He said he wanted to forget it, said he hoped he went straight to hell." He leaned back in his chair. "He offered me the guy's job. Pays more than this one, too." Carl shook his head. "If we don't find Teag soon, I might have to take it." He checked his notes and turned to James. "James? Any connections to the couple yet?"

"No more than yesterday." James shifted in his chair and shoved a boot into Loni's leg.

"Tully?"

Tully shook his head no.

Carl closed his notebook and stood. "Call me if anything breaks. Otherwise, see you all Monday."

Loni sat behind the booking desk listening to Lola talk sweet things to Coco as everyone else scattered. The brown fuzzy ball on the end of the dog's stubby tail swept the floor in short half circles, as her head rested on Lola's knee, he eyes staring up in adoration. Loni relaxed. "It's nice around here with the boys gone."

"Cops do tend to be heavy on the testosterone."

"Hey, Lola. I heard you work with Habitat for Humanity."

"Whenever I get some time off. It's fun."

"You can really use a saw and hammer?" Loni had to grin at the image.

A flash of anger sparked in Lola's eyes. "You got something against girls in construction?" she snapped.

Loni laughed at her reaction. "God no! I think it's great!" She paused. "You doing anything Sunday morning?"

"Who's asking?"

"I am. Wondered if you were up to an adventure."

"Depends on the adventure."

"Pick you up about eight?"

"Is this a date?"

Loni blushed, too stunned to react.

Lola gigged at Loni's reaction. "You've never had a breakfast date?"

"Not like this. How about you?"

"Only when I was still in bed." Lola patted Loni's red face, jangling her bracelets as she reached for a telephone message slip for Loni. "Third time she's called. She wants you to call her back. Sure you don't have a new girlfriend?"

"What? Two-time you? Am I crazy?" Loni snickered, taking the paper.

Loni was quiet a minute, watching Lola with Coco. "Can I ask a personal question?"

"No." Lola frowned at her.

"How come you're not married?"

"How come you're not?" Lola countered.

"Not legal yet?"

"That's true," Lola admitted. "I was once but never again. He was one mean sonofabitch."

"He hit you." Loni nodded goodbye and walked out the heavy doors into a wall of heat. She left the door to the truck open after Coco hopped in and called Jenny.

"Aren't you ever going to ask me out?" Jenny said before Loni had a chance to respond.

Dumbfounded, Loni forgot to close her mouth.

"Well?"

"I guess," Loni stuttered. "When and where?"

"How about tomorrow night? You don't have to work then, right?"

"Right."

"Good. See you at six. I'm cooking."

Hanging up, Loni got in her truck and drove in a daze back to the ranch.

Six o'clock found Loni back in town, shopping with her grandparents. Everybody went to town on Saturday night payday. People visited, jostled one another, had fun buying their kids ice cream while an occasional woman pulled a man out of the bars before the wages were gone.

Loni and Shiichoo meandered along the sidewalks following Bahb in and out of stores. "Hey, old man. You're not too old to carry," said Loni and joked about the sacks they piled in her arms.

"Been on earth much longer than you."

"So?"

"Stop it," Shiichoo told her. "You are too old to tease him."

"Well, crap, you buy heavy stuff."

"Stop! How can you put that awful word in your mouth, child?"

"If I have to stay behind him, he can at least help carry." Loni could see the sly smile on her granddad's face.

"How many times have I told you he walks ahead to protect us. I'm tired of saying it."

"But I'm the one with the gun, Shiichoo."

"And God help us when they give girls guns."

"Shiichoo! You're a chauvinist!"

"Not either. You know I'm Apache."

Loni hid her grin knowing they were both putting her on when her granddad stopped and spoke softly to a homeless man as he dropped a twenty-dollar bill in his box. The young man's tan, medium-sized, nondescript-looking dog licked Bahb in return for his pat on the head. The Navajo was dressed in a reservation homemade cotton shirt without sleeves, faded blue Levis, and hiking boots. His swollen and crooked knees and elbows indicating a bone disease.

Loni stopped beside Bahb. "Don't give him any money. He'll end up drunk on it."

Bahb took Loni far enough away so the man could not hear him. "What do you see?"

Loni glanced back. "The same things you do."

"Ni. You don't look."

"I saw you drop a twenty in his cup. I suppose that makes you the good Indian?"

"That to make me feel better, that true. But what is good I don't take like you did."

"Take what?"

"Your attitude disrespect him. Took his dignity. That the worse you do."

Ashamed, Loni returned to the beggar and dropped another twenty before she followed her grandparents into the store. Still balancing her packages, she wandered around picking up a few items for herself.

Arriving at the meat counter, she stood behind her grandmother watching Pat talk to a short, plump woman while he wrapped hamburger for her. A tall, skinny white woman with her gray hair twisted into a tight bun pushed in front of Shiichoo. Loni remembered her as the Baptist preacher's wife who had complained about an Indian who was passed out on the sidewalk. She said it was her duty to help keep the town clean.

"Just look down there." The woman pointed to the south wall of the Last Chance Saloon where a pair of boots stuck out onto the sidewalk. "Look at that dirty drunk!"

Loni walked to the corner of the building and peeked around to see a young Pima asleep in the sun. She kicked his scuffed boots, waking him up. "Hey, you know where you are?"

The young Pima finally sat up, lifting his head. "Ain't I in Caliente?"

Loni fought a giggle as she turned back to the woman. "Sounds sober to me."

The woman harrumphed and stalked away as Loni helped the young man up. "Listen." She pointed down the side road. "Go down to the corner. You can get a meal and a bed." She grimaced. "You could use a shower, too."

"Know where I can get a job?"

"Where you from?"

"Sacaton. And no, I ain't related to Ira Hayes."

Loni laughed in understanding. "What kind of work do you do?"

"Know how to weld."

"Heard the blacksmith shop was looking for somebody to work on windmills. Go on and clean up. Hester will tell you where the shop is."

"Thanks." He ambled off.

Loni came out of her reverie to watch the woman elbow Shiichoo out of her way.

"Good thing you don't care." Shiichoo smirked at her as Loni mumbled her anger. "You carrying a gun and all."

"Not funny." Her grandmother chucked until the preacher's wife, cruising the case, pushed on her grandmother again but Shiichoo didn't budge this time. Huffing, the woman gave up and circled around Shiichoo. Reaching up, she ran her finger across the counter and stared at her finger. Loni laughed to herself at Pat's expression as he watched her finger travel over the countertop. "Find anything?" he asked her.

"Not yet." Loni stared him down. "What's your freshest meat today?"

"Got a nice cow tongue just in."

"Ech! I can't eat anything that came out of something's mouth!"

"Well then, I got some fresh eggs in this morning. Rangers, too." Pat pointed to the next cooler. "How about a nice Spanish omelet for supper?"

Loni watched the woman stomp out of the store. Giggling, Loni exchanged knowing looks with Pat. He said, "She'll be back unless she wants a long drive to Tucson. Her husband's a really good guy. He helped some people, but I swear he should throw his wife out with the rest of the trash."

Loni kept eye on her grandparents as she flipped through some board books while they shopped. She thought they would make a good birthday present for Maria's niece who turned two in a couple of weeks. They reminded her of shopping sprees with Maria and her sisters. Loni preferred getting a Pap smear to shopping, but she had no choice. Maria especially loved shopping malls. So many more choices of clothes and appliances to marvel about.

The two of them played games guessing the uses for unusual cooking utensils. Loni remembered the citrus fruit knife with two sharp blades on both sides and at both ends of the handle. She lost the game but won another one when Maria couldn't guess the cherry pitter. Her reward for winning was always amazing. Lost in her memory of tangled bodies moving in the dark of the night, Loni didn't hear someone talking to her.

"Hey, looks like you could use this." Loni turned around to see Jenny standing there pushing a grocery cart lightly into her, jarring Loni back to earth. Astonished at her feeling of excitement, Loni dumped her bundles into the cart. "Hey, thanks." She grinned back at Jenny as her grandma walked up and handed her a package. "This is my grandma Shiichoo. And my grandfather, Bahb." Loni opened up a space for Bahb to join them. "This is Jenny O'Neal. She teaches art at the school."

"Hello," Jenny said and turned back to Loni. "I'm shopping for dinner tomorrow night. Chicken sound good?"

Loni grinned, a fast nod in agreement, avoiding her grandparents' stare.

"Good." Jenny's smile included only Loni as she turned and walked away.

Glad to be back at the loft for even a few hours, Loni opened the door of the refrigerator. "Damn," she said to herself. "Daniel's been here again." All her tamales were gone along with half her milk. She slammed the door and searched through the cupboards. "Shit!" She opened a can of chili con carne and poured it into a pot to heat up. A few minutes later she grabbed the pot off the stove, and the burning handle made her drop it. Chili spattered all over the stove and floor. "Shit, shit, shit." Another reason to miss Maria who was a fantastic cook.

Loni was no longer hungry by the time she cleaned up the mess. She nibbled on saltine cracker so soggy it almost fell apart in her hand as she settled in bed with her laptop.

> FROM: Loni Wagner
> TO: Sandi@gmailyahoo.com
> DATE: July 17
> SUBJECT:

Granddad can't drive in town any more. Chief told him they would take his license if he did. As long as I can remember, he never stopped at stop signs or looked either way when he pulled out on a street. Last time he drove through a stop sign, my friend Trevor stopped him. Of course, Bahb insisted he was a very slow and careful driver. I accept he is slow, but, like Trevor said, when he finally stopped laughing, honking his way through stop signs does not make him a careful driver. So I'm driving them to town to shop.

I can't believe how old-school Bahb is and how much he used to embarrass me. He always insists on walking in front of us wherever we go, on a sidewalk or into a store, making sure it's safe for us to enter. When I remind him I'm the one with the gun, he gives me this inscrutable stare and waves me back. Honestly! I think it's sweet. God help me if I ever tell him that.

And I have a date with Jenny tomorrow night. She's cooking for me. That's a good thing, right? Do you realize how long it's been since I dated? Oh, wait. I don't think I've ever had a date. Maria and I skipped that part. What does that say about me? Also, I think I'd rather date Lola, but since she's straight, I can forget about that.

The best news. Shiichoo is feeling much better these days and nothing makes me happier.

Take care of you and yours.
Loni

Loni thought about the last thing Bahb said to her as she helped put away the groceries in her grandparents' kitchen. "Your friend in store? She has empty eyes."

CHAPTER SEVENTEEN

Loni followed Lola's directions and stopped in front of a two-story house surrounded by large eucalyptus trees. The limbs reached across the roof and shaded the wide porches circling three sides of the house. Its roof served as a deck for the second floor. Loni liked the color combination of newly painted yellow house with the teal trim. Beside the house, tall date and fig trees lined a ditch running along a lane. It led to a barn and a long row of flat-roofed buildings with garage doors. She was staring at the bright red front door when Lola banged out and trotted up to her truck. "Where's the ladder?"

"Pretend you're mountain climbing," Loni retorted. "You can do it."

"Not gracefully." Lola grimaced and reached for the handle. Loni watched her pull herself up into the truck and admired the cleavage revealed by Lola's sleeveless red blouse. Her tight dark blood-red pants flared over short white boots.

"You could quit ogling half a minute and help me."

"You might wear bigger britches. What are those, size six?" Loni grinned as she grabbed Lola's hand and pulled her in.

"How sweet." Lola patted Loni's cheek. "I haven't seen size six since I was ten years old." Lola strained to close the reluctant door as Loni tried to coax the truck to start. "Are you sure this thing has an engine? Where did you ever find it?"

Loni glanced over at Lola as she waited to try again. "Butch belonged to my partner. I needed something to move my crap home in, so I sold my car."

"Butch?"

"Don't look at me. My partner named her." A few choice words helped to start the engine, and Loni pulled slowly onto the road.

"The one who died."

"Yes."

"She the reason you left here?"

"Nope. Met her at the Police Academy in LA. We went through school together."

"So why did you leave here?"

"Thought being Indian would be easier somewhere else." Loni shifted into fourth. "I moved to Portland, Oregon, first to go pre-law. I mostly wanted to live close to lots of water. Seemed a good place to go to school."

Lola didn't speak until Loni turned onto Old Highway 85 and the truck bounced along on the badly patched cement, sprouting more rattles and bangs. "Aren't these things supposed to be dangerous? Something about a bad rollover rate?"

"Only to the people riding in them."

"I feel better already." She crossed her arms over her chest. "I should have worn a bra."

Loni chuckled. "Ah, crap. Just roll 'em up and hang on."

"What's that knock-knock-knocking noise?"

Loni smirked at her imitation of the sound. "I think Butch is about to throw a rod."

"Exactly what does that mean?"

"It means I better get an overhaul soon or I'll be walking."

"How soon is soon?" Lola sounded a little panicky. "Don't these things have guarantees for years?"

"Some do."

"How many miles is your guarantee?"

"Fifty thousand, I think."

"How many miles do you have?"

Loni read the odometer. "Fifty-thousand, eight-hundred and two."

In the midst of laughing, Lola managed to say, "Well, it made it."

"Bite me."

An abandoned motel was a blight on the main approach to town, but the light-red adobe walls glowing behind the graffiti stood strong. So did the roof. The tile made from clay in Old Mexico ran across the roof in red even waves, and the old adobe wall surrounding the motel had only a few crumbled places and holes.

Loni parked in front of what had been the office and eyed Lola. "You ready for this?" They wandered through every room. Fixtures, cabinets, and bathrooms were stripped away. Ceiling boards were missing, and the wood floors were badly scarred. The windows were either broken or gone. But it could be fixed.

"A very long time ago I stayed here a week one night."

Loni frowned in her in confusion.

"Well, it seemed that way." Lola halted a few seconds. "I had walked out on my husband. He beat the shit out of me, and I needed to heal before I went home."

Loni stared at her with horror.

"So." Lola was matter-of-fact. "It's gonna cost a pile, but I think it would be cost effective to rebuild."

"Labor's a big problem, but we don't have to have all the rooms ready to open. Maybe get the office area first and let a family live there to help with the grunt work. Shovel the rubble out and clean it up for construction."

Lola pulled a small notebook from her pocket. "Get bids from electricians, plumbers, sheet-rockers. Count the windows and doors. Figure fixtures for bathrooms and kitchens."

Loni added, "Cabinetry. Refinish the floors. Paint. Find cheap furniture. Clean out the swimming pool and repair it. Fence it." Lola began writing. "How many rooms are there?"

"Twenty-four."

"Twenty-four bathrooms and kitchenettes."

"How many doors and windows in each?"

"Two doors and four windows."

Lola kept writing. "Add one more door. The garages in between could be turned into bedrooms. Too small for the cars now days, anyway. Probably put in windows."

"Good idea."

"Only dry rot is the window frames. They need to be totally reframed. And we need to make a couple batches of adobe bricks. I have a kiln in my backyard to bake them in."

"How did you learn so much?"

"My dad and brother are contractors." Lola turned and accidently stepped on Loni's foot.

Loni caught Lola to keep her from falling and held her a few seconds. This feels too good, she thought, wondering what it would feel like to kiss her. Loni backed up a step, mortified at her thoughts. The first time since Maria died, and she had to react this way to a straight woman. Loni tried to replace Lola's face with Maria's, but her features were dimming in Loni's memory. She couldn't feel Maria's skin or hear her voice anymore. She knew what Maria looked like from her photo, but she didn't have a recording of her voice. Loni tried to push the thoughts out of her mind and focus on Lola.

"Sorry." Lola unwound from Loni and moved toward the open door back to the truck. "Are you really up to this?"

Loni wondered if Lola meant the motel or something else. Probably the motel. "Figure the cost first and we can decide then."

"Guess this means we'll have to spend a lot of time together."

"Think you can put up with me?"

"Sure. As long as you do it my way!" Lola laughed at Loni's expression of dismay.

The truck pulled out of the motel driveway and picked up speed. Loud noises ratcheted up as the large tires sang on the cement road.

"That was thirsty work," Lola shouted.

"Where do you want to go?"

"How about McDonald's?"

"Sure." Loni drove back up Old Highway 85 and pulled into the drive-through. "A medium Coke, please, and a —?" Loni turned to Lola.

"Diet Coke."

"And a medium diet Coke."

A girl with stringy brown hair handed Loni the Cokes. Loni searched for the indentation on the lid before she turned back to the girl. "Which one's the diet?"

The girl stared back at Loni with a blank expression. "The one with the pushed in star on the lid."

"Which one? No indents here." Loni showed the Coke lids to the girl.

The girl leaned out the window and pushed on one of the lids. "Now it does."

Loni handed the indented Coke to Lola, and they collapsed in laughter. As she drove off, they tasted their Cokes, sputtered, and traded cups. "Good thing I left my gun at home."

"Do you hunt?"

"Only people."

"Get serious. How many people have you actually killed?"

"Well. None."

"So? You're desert bred. Why don't you hunt?"

"I remember Uncle Herm taking me hunting for white-wing. He used me for a bird dog. I got to this one bird, and it was still alive. I saw the fear and terrible pain in its eyes as his life faded. Something in me left with that warm creature and never came back." Loni got lost in the memory. "Never hunted again."

Lola was quiet a minute. "Do you really live in an airport hangar?"

"Doesn't everybody?"

"Seriously."

"Well, yes. But I spend a lot of time with my grandparents."

"Where do they live?"

"Up Wagner Road a few miles."

Lola snorted. "I forgot you have a road named after you."

"Not me. It's my great-grandfather Wagner who homesteaded."

"Well then. Let's go up Wagner Road. I want to see where you live."

Loni blurted out, "Now?"

Lola arched her eyebrows. "Why? You didn't make your bed?"

"I don't remember. Which bed do you want to see?"

"Describe them and then explain why anybody would live in two places in a teeny, tiny same town. I can't keep up with one." Lola paused. "Come to think of it, I'm not sure I made my bed, either."

"The bed I mostly use is in a loft apartment above my uncle's office in the airplane hangar. I spend my spare time at the ranch."

"You own a ranch?" Lola arched her eyebrows.

"Well, sort of, but I really feel it belongs to my grandparents. It's like I've been a visitor since I left for college."

"But it's in your name?"

"It belonged to my dad. He inherited the ranch part, and my uncle inherited land for his airport. My mother died when I was born so my dad talked her parents into coming off the rez to take over the ranch and raise me. Since he was German, he wanted me raised at home, but he hurt too much to stay around. My aunt Mae was too sick to take me. My dad wandered a few years, prospecting but mostly mining. The times he came home were the best days of my life. Right after my fourteenth birthday, we got a telegram he was killed in a mine cave-in. They sent a few of his things home. Never found his body."

"Have you been to the mine?"

"Not yet."

"Well then, maybe we should do that someday."

Stunned into silence by the "we," Loni turned off Old Highway 85 onto Wagner Road. She pointed to the ranch headquarters in the distance.

"Why aren't you ranching?"

"Among other reasons, running enough cattle to survive in today's market destroys the desert. I didn't want that."

"You're serious?"

"Of course." Loni pulled into the barnyard and parked under a salt cedar tree. The salt dripping's eating the paint off her truck was bad enough but getting back into a burning cab was worse.

Lola followed Loni through large double sliding doors into the barn. Tools, tractors, carts, and wagons lined one side of the building with stock pens on the other. In the center, Willie was hauling hay out of the loft with a pulley and settled the bales onto a small trailer behind a John Deere tractor.

"Hey, Willie. You know Lola?" Willie ducked his head with a shy smile. Loni searched around for Flossie. "Where's Flossie?" Her voice rose in panic.

"Out in last corral."

"She's better?"

Willie leaned on a bale. "Still some sick."

"I'm driving, Willie." Loni climbed onto the tractor. She reached over to pull Lola up beside her. "Fenders make great seats." Willie climbed up on the hay trailer, and Loni headed through the open back barn doors onto the lane between the cattle pens.

Loni inched the trailer along the lane between the feed pens, as Willie broke up the bales and tossed sections of hay into the troughs. Huge cow heads stuck out through the board fence into the troughs and pushed at each other to reach the feed. They shoved their noses in the hay, worrying holes in it, feeding from the bottom up.

Willie talked to the mother cows as he fed them, and Loni explained the process to Lola. "In a good spring, Bahb buys a few half-Brahma steers from Old Mexico. Profit's in the weight gain, so he mostly raises his own and sells the steers at two years." Loni could see Lola calculating again. "Desert cows can produce eight to ten calves in their lifetime. In the bunch the Millers took, there were fourteen two-year-old steers ready for market we didn't get back. Those steers were probably a twelve-thousand-dollar loss. It's money that helps pay the bills through the year. I always sent them something every month to help them get by."

"But you caught the thieves?"

"These are the mother cows they took, but they already sold the steers. Without a brand, they're long gone."

"Why aren't they branded?"

"Bahb won't inflict pain on any living thing unless it's absolutely necessary for its well-being."

"What about the slaughter house?"

"It kills his soul but he does it for me so I can keep the ranch."

"What about the loss?"

Loni shrugged. "I'll help them deal."

"How big is the ranch?"

"The house sits on a section of titled land with twenty-two sections of Taylor grazing attached to it."

"Taylor grazing?"

"In Arizona, most of the land belongs to the government."

"Does the government charge you?"

"I think I heard it's about a dollar and fourteen cents a month now for every cow that grazes the desert."

"That's not much."

"Maybe not. But all the little things whittle away."

Lola watched Willie as the cattle tossed and nosed the hay. "Isn't he too old to do that?"

"Does it look hard for him?"

Lola watched him heave another bale down and break it into sections. "Well, no."

Loni stopped in front of a pen filled with cow manure pushed into a pile nearly ten feet high. Lola gripped Loni's shoulder and laughed as she pointed to a large black and white-spotted bull spread out on the top of the pile. He flapped his big ears while he gazed down on the cows. "Do you suppose he thinks he did that pile of shit all by himself?"

Loni cracked up. "Nah. That's Brutus, Bahb's Beefmaster bull. He's just surveying his kingdom."

Lola turned and pushed at Loni. "My line was funnier."

The huge bull turned his head and benignly stared down at them. "He may look like he's full of shit," Loni warned Lola. "But don't turn your back on him. He was mistreated when he was young, and he's a mean sucker. Bahb's working to gentle him, but he's not turned around yet."

"I've never heard of a Beefmaster. Looks Brahma to me."

"He's a mixture of Hereford and Brahma. This breed can travel further for water and food and gain the most. Really good for desert travel."

Loni spotted Flossie across from Brutus and climbed down before helping Lola off. "Willie, take the tractor back, okay?" She opened the gate for Lola. "Walk real slow right behind me. Don't make any sudden moves." She abruptly stopped, and Lola bumped into her.

"What?"

"Just waiting for her to see us." Loni listened to the cow's mournful bawl.

"Why is she crying?"

"She's hurting. The Millers left her in a jumping cactus patch. We've been shaving places and pulling needles for days." Loni talked to Flossie as she slowly walked up to her. The cow watched from her good eye and shied a step away as Loni checked her over for festering bumps on her legs and chest. "Much better." She showed Lola the shaved places scattered in the brindle overcoat plugged with black patchwork. Flossie's bad eye had been removed, and a bandage covered the empty socket.

Loni led Lola through a solid wood gate bleached grey from the sun, stuck her fingers in her mouth and whistled. Three heads shot up, and three large bodies trotted side by side toward them as if they were shackled together. Loni untied the wire on a bale by the gate and spread out the hay.

The three grew bigger with each step, especially Stonewall. Lola quickly backed to the gate. "My god, he's big! Should we run?"

"Where to? If he wanted, he could jump flat-footed over any fence here."

"Fine then. I'll get behind you so he'll get you first." She clutched the back of Loni's shirt.

"What's the old joke?" Loni grinned. "All I have to do is outrun you."

"Not if I beat you to the gate and shut it in your face."

"Hey, Stonewall." Loni kept talking as he came, head down to an abrupt stop at the hay. The two horses joined Stonewall, and Loni rubbed all their heads.

Donnie and his little brother Rolfe ran up. Donnie sidled up to Stonewall. "Can I get on him? Please!" he begged.

Loni gave him a leg up while Lola panicked. "Don't put him up there. What if he gets hurt?"

"This bull's a Brahma. Be kind to them, and they're the gentlest creatures in the world. The opposite happens if they're mistreated." Lola hid behind Loni and watched Donnie climb onto Stonewall. He sat on the bull's hump for a minute before he slid down over the tail. With huge eyes, Rolfe hid behind Lola and stared at the bull.

"Is his name really Stonewall?"

Loni wondered why she asked. "Well," she said cautiously, "he's built like a stone wall, and he looks like a stone wall so he must be a stone wall."

"Who named him?"

"I did."

"Really? No other reason?" Lola had a small knowing smirk as she reached out. Stonewall raised his massive head. Lola jerked her hand back but didn't give ground. Rolfe screamed and held onto Lola's leg as his brother giggled.

"Look, Rolfe." Donnie climbed over Stonewall's hump and patted his neck.

"Remember to rub, not pat. Animals think you're hitting them if you pat and they worry they did something wrong. "Feel." She held Rolfe's hand up to the bull's nose. "It's like velvet. They feel through their noses, so let him sniff you."

"No!" Rolfe jerked away from Loni and scooted back behind Lola again.

Loni rubbed Roani's ears. "This ugly thing belongs to me. I really missed him while I was gone."

Stonewall shook his massive head, and his huge ears made a whapping noise. Hay flew everywhere, and Rolfe began to cry. Lola held onto his small body as Donnie slid down Stonewall. He took Donnie's hand and gently pulled him through the gate. Holding hands, they ran for home.

Loni's cell phone rang. Jenny. "No, I'll take a rain check. Are you okay?" Loni hung up beaming. "My date cancelled!"

"You sound happy about it."

Loni didn't make eye contact. "I like where I am."

"It's hard to date again after a loss." Lola stuffed her hands in her jean pockets and watched Willie turn the tractor around. She waved at him as he disappeared down the lane. "Wait a minute. Isn't that our ride?"

"One of them." Loni reached for Stonewall's halter and led him to a wooden fence. "It's time to get out of the sun. We can ride Stonewall back to the barn."

"Oh, goody." Lola watched Loni climb the fence. "I always did want to ride a Brahma bull."

Swinging onto Stonewall, Loni reached her hand down to Lola.

"You ride. I'll walk."

"Come on. Even Donnie gets on him."

"That's because he's young, stupid, and a boy."

"It's better than getting cow shit on those pretty white boots."

Lola winced with dismay. "What the hell!" Lola climbed the fence and held onto Loni's hand as she gingerly slid on behind Loni.

"If this doesn't work out, you owe me your firstborn."

Trying not to groan, Loni sputtered, "There's no chance of that."

"You don't want children."

"I never thought it was a good idea," Loni admitted.

"Did your girlfriend want kids?"

"Maria? Thousands. She came from a big family." Loni's eyes misted.

"So what happened?"

"You're a straight girl. It's a whole lot easier for you."

"Who said I was straight?"

Loni tried to not let her surprise show. "Everybody."

"Maybe I go out of town to play."

"I understand you like camping," Loni teased.

"In the summer? Are you crazy?"

"I heard you have a boyfriend working as a fishing guide in the White Mountains."

"I have a cousin working as a guide and I camp with him as often as I can. It's beautiful up there."

"So what are you saying?" Loni turned to see into Lola's eyes to find out if she was teasing her.

"Just because I don't wrap myself in rainbows like you—"

"What? I don't even have a rainbow on my truck," Loni said in mock anger. "I did stand in a rainbow one time."

"You are so full of it, I never know when to believe you."

"It's true. Really. I was sliding down a sand dune and it was right in front of me. I thought it would disappear as I slid into it, but it didn't. The colors almost faded away, but the water shards sparkled all around me like tiny stars."

"How did it make you feel?"

Loni stared at Lola. "You're the first person who ever asked me that." Loni hunted for words. "Special. Very, very special."

"I suppose you've seen the famous green flash from the sun setting on the ocean?"

"Twice." Loni smirked.

"You really loved the ocean, huh? Why did you leave?"

Loni sighed. "Following my tail."

Lola patted her shoulder. "Of course, you were." Stonewell automatically stopped at the barn door. "We could have walked back faster than he moved."

"Need help getting off?" Sorry to lose Lola's warmth, Loni was surprised at the tingling down her body. Lola hung on to her leg while she dropped to the ground. She rubbed Stonewall's nose and thanked him for the ride.

"So. About our conversation earlier—"

"Fine. I'm bi, okay?"

"Works for me."

Inside the kitchen Coco jumped up and tried to lick Lola in the face. "Shit, Coco never greets me that way. She introduced Lola to Shiichoo.

"I see where you get your beautiful eyes, now." Lola admired Loni's grandma.

"She used to have my hair." Loni reached to pat Shiichoo on the head. "But I was never that skinny."

"Piffle." Shiichoo stuck a potato peeler in her hand. "You best get to peeling and slicing those potatoes," Shiichoo muttered. "Shouldn't fun an old lady."

"Piffle? Is that Apache?"

"Now, child!"

For the next hour, Loni stayed out of the way while Lola and Shiichoo cooked mam-stuffed chicken, Apache Indian bread, Gesatho, Apache wojape, and rosemary blue-cheese scalloped potatoes, the last a concession to Loni.

Lola went to the bathroom before they ate, and Shiichoo smiled at Loni. "I can tell you like Lola. So do I. Have you asked her out?"

Loni wasn't ready to answer and was saved when Bahb and Willie came in and Lola came back. Everybody talked at once, and Loni took a deep breath. For the first time, she felt she had truly come home.

🌵

In the heat of the setting sun, shadows of the saguaros' arms were stretched out across the desert like an army in retreat when Loni stopped in front of Lola's house.

"Your grandma is really glad to have you home."

"Not entirely. She knew why I left. She held me often enough while I cried." Loni was quiet for a few minutes. "I asked her one time if I went to the Catholic church, could I be a Mexican. I reasoned since Mexicans were a mix of Indian and Spanish, I was half acceptable. They had friends and lots of fun. If you want to go to church, go, she told me. Bahb will take you. I went a few Sundays, but I didn't make any friends. I didn't go back."

"Clans are fragile. Let one new person in changes the dynamics, and somebody can get resentful. Like a dog pack circling the new one."

"I know what you're saying. They'll either invite you to sit at the table or make you the main course."

"I think you should kill this truck and get it out of its misery." Lola struggled with its door.

"It got you there." Loni watched Lola slide down onto the driveway.

Lola rolled her eyes at Loni. "Not without damage."

Loni felt a warm glow as she waited until the red front door closed behind Lola.

🌵

On her way home, Loni wished she had been brave enough to ask Lola if she was putting her on. She slowly got ready for bed and started an email to Sandi, hoping it would distract her from thinking about Lola. Loni's mind felt like a rat spinning in a cage, but she couldn't stop feeling hopeful. Bahb was right. Hope changed everything. And somehow she knew Maria would approve.

> FROM: Loni Wagner
> TO: Sandi@gmailyahoo.com
> DATE: July 19
> SUBJECT:

> I had an outstanding day with Lola. We explored an old motel I might renovate where immigrants can stay

until they're able to move on. We have an agreement with Mexico that reads anyone who helps catch a coyote can apply to stay in the U.S. I'm going to find many ways to use that law. Won't the conservative right shit? I am so tired of their family values crap when it is so obvious they don't believe in helping any family but their own. What kind of value is that?

The day ended having supper with the family. Shiichoo even let Lola help her cook. Willie actually talked to her, eye contact and all. I nearly fell off my chair.

Kiss everyone goodnight for me.

Loni

That night Loni's dreams turned back to Maria, loving in the night. Sweet talking, tongues locked and hands moved over soft breasts, down stomachs to the dark triangle of ecstasy. She lifted her head in her climax and was shocked awake when she found Lola smiling back at her. When her breathing finally settled, she hoped she was finally climbing out of her pit of despair from losing Maria.

CHAPTER EIGHTEEN

L oni was bent over, putting on her boot, when a bullet exploded through the window over her head. Glass shards shattered everywhere. She crawled to the wall and flipped off the light switch. Loni peaked out the window to see a single headlight turn onto the road to town. A motorcycle again! But too far away to chase. She dropped back into the glass and waited for the shakes to stop.

With the lights back on, Loni ordered Coco to get on the bed while she swept up the sharp glass fragments. The bullet was buried in the wall over the bed, its path close to where she had stood. She dug it out and bagged it.

Finished dressing, Loni checked her gun one last time and re-holstered it. She grabbed a tamale and slipped out into the dark. Anyone could pick her off anywhere, anytime, she thought, especially on patrol. She sent Coco out to sniff around before they drove out of the hangar.

Loni told Bobby to dust for fingerprints from the snake when she signed in. "Got shot at again. It's getting old."

"Think whoever's fingerprints is on that snake is your shooter?"

"Who knows?" Loni tried to shrug it away, but she was still worried. "I really hope we get Rebecca's fingerprints off the snake." Loni thrummed her fingertips on the counter. "Still nothing back on Rene's plane stuff? Nothing on the blood or fingerprint in the epoxy?"

Bobby shook his head before Loni finished talking. "Nothing yet. I'll call in and nag again for Rebecca's prints, though, before I leave."

"Thanks, Bobby. I still think Rene is involved with what we're working on."

"Listen." Bobby sounded upset. "you be careful out there. Don't take your usual route."

"I won't." She nodded goodbye.

Loni was soon driving through the dark night with Coco her only company. She rubbed the dog's head affectionately. "So, Coco, how do you like living on the desert so far?" The wiggling dog tried to lick her face. "Good to know."

With no moon to help the desert was a black hole around her. Frazzled from worrying about when the next attack against her would come, Loni took Froggy Bottom Road to an abandoned airstrip where she could see for miles and track any approaching light.

The runway had been an old American Airlines emergency landing strip. Loni wondered if the beacons were still up on the mountains. All one winter her grandfather and his brother had snaked poles between two donkeys up the mountains to build the airline beacons. Her granddad wrote about how his feet got so bad from the snow he took off his boots and pissed on them. He swore it saved his toes from frostbite.

Loni slowly drove onto the triangle runway. It must have been built sometime in the thirties. She watched for potholes on the ancient tarmac and decided the runway was so badly damaged planes couldn't use it, even to bring in drugs. Certainly not at night.

Along the edge, Loni found recent tracks that might be from kids racing. She came out here with Daniel years ago. He thought she'd like riding in one of the small planes the Butt Hiller kids flew. Headlights from the cars lining the runway provided landing lights for the three small planes that landed one right after the other. Everybody passed around jugs of Thunderbird wine during their midnight rides. Hell of a fun place to puke from, they said. Loni remembered shaking her head at Daniel and going back to his car. She worried herself sick about Daniel up in the sky and never went with him again.

Back on Old Highway 85, Loni was passing the intersection to Taylor Road when a black hulk came out of the dark and rammed into her passenger side. Loni's SUV was forced down the embankment into a spin ending up against a saguaro cactus. Airbags popping open imprisoned her. Heavy arms of the shattered cactus fell in large thorny hunks reverberating off the top of her SUV. One crashed into the windshield immediately before she heard the sound of a gunshot. Coco's frenzied barking penetrated her haze, and Loni forced herself to focus. The airbags deflated enough so she could take hold of Coco's collar. She opened the door and fell out, pulling Coco with her.

Loni scrabbled to her feet hanging onto Coco's collar. She pulled the dog away from the sound of slamming doors as flashlight beams snaked out. When a light swept across her, she stopped to shoot at one of the flashlights. The beam jiggled and went out.

"Damn." She heard a holler. "That was close."

"She can't run from this," another voice shouted.

Loni stumbled into a boulder and felt her way around it as a repeater splattered around her, the shooter sweeping in half circles. She toggled her shoulder mike to call Bobby, but it came off in her hand. Her cell phone was in the SUV.

Coco dragged her away in the dark from the voices, and Loni felt sand crunching under her feet. They staggered up a wash as fast as they could. She hoped the loud voices of two people, one of them close to her, would cover the scrunching sounds of her boots. When voices grew more indistinct, she stopped to catch her breath. Both of them panted in the heat.

Loni found a large outcrop along the side of the wash. She cautiously pulled Coco around it, and the dog tugged Loni out of the wash.

A man's voice shouted, "I found her tracks!"

A light swishing back and forth reached below her.

"Toss your gun." She flashed her brightest light at him. Dressed in black, he was gigantic in the flashlight's beam.

He turned toward her, gun raised.

She fired a shot at his feet, and he jerked and dropped the gun. "On your face and spread."

The other light bounced further and further away as Loni climbed down, warning him again not to move. "Not even a twitch." A Dirty Harry stupid prattle, she knew, but it seemed to work. She cuffed him before she turned him over and flashed her light in his face. "Hello, Robert Teag. I heard you quit your job and left town."

Loni stuck her gun between his eyes and searched him. She found a cell phone. He refused to answer her questions. In the distance a car started up and raced away. "Shit! Shit! Shit!" he shouted at the car. "You fucking coward!"

"Coco, guard!" Loni lay the flashlight on the ground and angled it at Teag who was face down with Coco standing over him. Loni dialed Teag's phone and called Bobby for a pickup. She spent the hour waiting for Carl and ragging on Teag until her adrenaline high finally dissipated.

Loni left Teag with Carl to book as she raced home. By the time she showered and got back for the task force meeting, he was already bailed out.

"Damn it!" Loni said to anybody who would listen. "The man tried to kill a cop. Who let him go?"

"Chief did," Carl answered. "O'Neal came and bailed him out."

"Thought they fired his sorry ass."

"That was the father. Steve was who bailed him out."

Deflated, Loni sat and watched Tully hurry toward them through the door.

"Sorry," Tully apologized. "Had to go to court."

"Tully? In court? You never go to court," said James.

"Well, he rear-ended me."

"Tully got hit by one of our regular DUI drivers," Carl explained.

James laughed. "What happened in court, Tully?"

"He was whining about needing to get back to work to pay alimony. Judge Sal asked him, 'How many times you been married now?' Guy says five. 'Got any kids?' the judge asked. 'No, Judge Sal,' my man said to her. 'Fed them all to the pissants.'"

"What did Judge Sal do?"

"Three years for smart mouth, one year for DUI." Tully sat down with a large bearclaw.

"Dropped by the bakery, I see."

"Court's hard work." Tully turned to Loni. "Heard they refused to dust for fingerprints on your snake and threw it away."

"Oh, shit. How am I going to get fingerprints from Rebecca now?"

"Ask her out." James grinned. "She's family ain't she?"

"Listen up," Carl interrupted. "Loni got attacked last night. Seems Teag is back and already out on bail."

A mumbling of "well, shit" and shaking heads were the only responses. Carl grumbled and frowned at his notes. "One got away, probably Steve. I figured he's running south so I got border patrol looking into it." He kept reading from his notes. "State called. They want us to find somebody growing sex enhancement plants. Anybody know anything about it?"

"I told you already. That's what those exotic plants are at your ranch, Carl."

Everybody stared at Carl. "Say again. What are they growing on my ranch?" Carl sputtered.

"Sex enhancer plants. It's in my report on the rape at the couple who died."

"They said it was exotic plants. They didn't mention sex enhancers."

"Like what?" Tully actually sounded interested.

"What do you care, Tully? Nobody would go out with you anyways." James's laugh was nasty.

Loni ignored Tully and James. "Come to Mama, ginseng, and Horny Goat Weed. At least according to Billy Joe who was at the party. I don't know what else. Also castor bean seedlings. I think they got our meth lab out there. If they're storing caster bean seeds to grow, it's easy enough to smash a few accidently and leave ricin behind."

"If that's not enough for a warrant, I don't know what is." Carl's voice rose a notch. "James, you and Tully pick up the O'Neals. It's time we had a talk." Pausing a few seconds, Carl gathered his folders. "I'm skipping these meetings until we interrogate the O'Neals."

Loni followed Carl out of the conference room. "Why did Chief let O'Neal bail Teag out?"

"Don't know, Loni. I'm going to find out right now."

Loni sat with Lola and soaked in her warm, healing essence. Lola had the cost analysis for the motel ready. "I'll call the Phoenix Food Bank and find out how they provide food for a homeless shelter," Lola said.

Getting back to everyday business was a relief. "Ask your brothers for a bid, okay?"

"Sure. We could request help from churches, but they're usually a controlling a pain in the ass."

"I know. Most do-gooders are so judgmental that they more often make bad situations worse." Loni remembered the Baptist preacher's wife.

"Let's skip them for now. I'll call some shelters and ask for setup advice. I think I've got someone to help run it. I'll introduce you to her and see what you think." Tired of waiting for Carl, Loni stood. Lola's hug held Loni very close for a long time. Loni breathed in a slight citrus scent from Lola's hair, not wanting to let her go. Lola released her and pushed her out the door. "Remember what I said. Be careful."

Searching for a safe place Loni retreated to the ranch. She started with cleaning the corrals, kicking dried-up cow patties into pieces as she pitched manure into piles. Filthy dirty, she felt salty sweat soaking up cow pucky, sliding and burning into every crevice and orifice before she put the snow shovel away. The afternoon was hot when she headed home and her cell phone rang.

"James needs help at the Oasis Bar, Loni. You close?"

Crap. "I will be. I'm on my way."

Beside James's patrol car, Loni untied her hair and tangled it and mixed dirt with water to smear on her face. She shoved through the door and yelled, "Puta. Alquien desear puta?" At the bar, she demanded, "Beer!" Two Mexicans were on either side of James and threatening him.

"Get out of here, you filthy bitch. Nobody wants to fuck you!" a cowboy yelled at her.

Loni muttered and backed off. She plopped down at the table closest to the door and yelled again, "*Puta. Alquien desear puta?*"

"I do," said a swarthy man at a table. "How much?"

"*Cinco dinero.*"

"No way. You're not worth five dollars. How about two?"

"Cinco! Cinco! Cinco!" Loni chanted.

"Barkeep," one of the Mexicans at the bar called out. "Give her a bottle of beer and shut her up. And keep her down wind."

The two men pulled James off the bar stool and started for the door. Loni stumbled forward and grabbed the bottle from the bartender. "Asshole!" she said to the nearest man as they passed. He turned toward her as she swung the bottle in his face. He went down. She shoved her gun into the butt of the other one and snarled, "I'm a cop. Let him go or you'll lose your dick and most of your balls." James spun around and disarm both men. He handcuffed them and shoved them out the door and into his patrol car. Loni followed them out. "I owe you. I thank you."

"De nada." Loni smiled.

James stepped back to his car, got in, and drove off with a last wave.

"Wow," Loni said out loud to a tree she was standing beside. "Did you see that? James thanked me and he waved at me. That was almost fun."

CHAPTER NINETEEN

H ey." Bobby held out a message to Loni. "You're late." He peered down at her with his light-blue eyes. "This call came in at two-thirty this afternoon. Looks like a theft out in Sandhills. Somebody stole a pig."

"Why didn't day-shift take it?"

Bobby's Adam's apple bobbed like a nibbled float on a fishing line. "It's in Tully's writing. Chief initialed it though. Apparently it's not an emergency. They know who took the pig. Tully said you could pick it up and take it back on your last run."

She read the note, wadded it up, and threw it back at Bobby. "Damn. A pig in my car?"

"Tully would claim you already have a pig in the car, so what's your problem? Anyhow, it's a pet. Pot-bellied, I think." Bobby caught the note and tossed it in a trash can. "Guess he thinks he's overworked."

"He is." Trevor stepped up behind Loni to sign out. "Why, I saw him sharpen his pencil twice last week."

Loni felt cheered by Trevor's joke and headed out on patrol.

Checking on a badly beaten drunk outside the Oasis was Loni's last stop. Caught cheating in a card game, the barkeep told her. He didn't see who did it. She carefully helped him to his feet and drove him to the clinic.

Ronald, the other nurse practitioner following Chelsea's shift at the clinic, held the drunk away from him and fanned at the reeking booze. "How's your car smell?"

Loni groaned. "He threw up twice. Gotta go hose it down now." She left the SUV for Gary to clean as she dodged the handful of gravel he threw at her.

Coco hopped with Loni into her truck, and they sped out of the police compound. Gary shouted Spanish/English gibberish she couldn't decipher. She headed to the grocery store but couldn't remember what Shiichoo wanted.

"Shiichoo? I'm at the store. Shin'a' silgg."

"Do you want Apache bread or fry bread?"

"Am I cooking tonight?"

"Of course," Shiichoo said. "The workers around here are driving me crazy. When is it going to end?"

Loni ignored the question. "Dahidgg' ch'ikaagi?"

"What leftovers? You already ate them."

"Ch'ik'eh doleel'. I'll cook."

"So you pick." Her grandmother hung up.

Loni snapped her cell phone shut, smiling at Shiichoo's abruptness. She got tamales at Spin's Mexican food stand.

At the ranch, Bill Henry was hoisting the new evaporative cooler up on the roof. He'd already dropped the old cooler in his flatbed truck. She noted the cooler pads were black from mold, and the bottom almost rusted through. Wow, she thought. Just in time.

Loni could hear the whirring from the Hyster lifting the new evaporative cooler onto the roof. It would wait there to be used whenever the humidity decreased due the monsoons rendering the evaporative cooler useless. She studied the already working refrigeration unit squatting on a pad by the back door under the overhang of the roof. It fed into the new tubes buried around the house to side vents cut through the adobe into each room.

Shiichoo joined her under the tree. "Look heavy to you?"

"Not as heavy as the old one. Bigger though." She took Shiichoo's arm. "I see the refrigeration working. Don't tell me you don't like the cool air?"

"Getting there."

"Let's go enjoy it some more."

Loni followed Shiichoo around to the front door and into the house. Shiichoo glanced up and deliberately avoided walking under the old evaporative cooler vent. "What if it falls through?" she worried.

Loni kept a straight face. She spent the night in her old room and wallowed in comfort, no longer sticky from the humidity. Still she couldn't sleep. She went to the window when she heard a boom in the distance. A massive thunderhead cloud forming an anvil boiled high into the sky and sent lightning flashes circling overhead. Thank God for the refrigeration unit, Loni thought. Suddenly a quick flash and boom took the electricity out. And just as suddenly the fucking monsoon fucking humidity joined the fucking summer heat.

CHAPTER TWENTY

Bobby's voice shattered Loni's peace. "Sounds like a domestic at four-seven-six-one-zero Calvin Lane. Passerby called in fighting and screaming."

"Isn't that Chief's address?"

"Yep. Maybe the TV's up too loud."

A strange sound rustled in Loni's ear. "Something else?"

"Oh, yeah. Forgot to tell you earlier. Your DNA from the blood on Rene's plane came back. You know a Rebecca Childress?"

"Shit, shit, shit," Loni yelled as she turned her SUV back toward Calvin Road.

"Guess I better send someone to arrest her, huh?" Bobby interrupted her tirade.

"Hell yes!" Loni raced up the highway in time to see a car hurtling out of Calvin Road. It whipped out in front of her and sped away. She recognized Jenny's bright yellow Mustang convertible.

Killing her lights and engine, Loni coasted into Chief's driveway behind a farm utility truck. She motioned Coco to heel and left the door slightly ajar. On the side of the utility truck was a sign, O'Neal & Son. Jenny's dad? Or brother? Softly stepping onto the porch, Loni slipped up to a window. The blinds were down, and she couldn't even see a sliver of light.

The sound of crashing and banging followed by silence jolted Loni into action. She stood to the side of the door, rang the bell, and called out "Police." Five rapid shots flew through the door. Loni pushed the switch on her shoulder mike and whispered, "Shots fired. Officer needs help."

The door crashed open. A man waving a gun ran out and nearly fell down the porch steps.

"Coco, attack." A brown blur hit the runner in the knees, and the gun flew out of the man's hand as he hit the ground hard. The dog's jaw at his throat and her vicious growl paralyzed the man. Loni snatched the gun from the ground and shoved her own gun in his face. "Coco, back." The dog lifted her head but kept growling. "Hands behind your back," Loni directed him, "before Coco changes her mind." She kept an eye on the open door while she handcuffed him.

The man glared at her as Loni searched him and found his billfold. His driver's license read Colin O'Neal. "You Jenny's dad?" she asked. Loni saw no resemblance. He was emaciated with a translucent pallor on his drawn face and bald head gleaming in the light of the open door. His work shirt hung on him as though it belonged to someone else. She asked him again if he was Jenny's father when she shoved him into the back of her SUV. He grunted a yes.

Back at the door, Loni peered inside. No sound, no movement but she saw complete destruction. Bookcases were face down, pictures were thrown on the floor and stomped, and furniture was ripped and broken. Wall insulation hung out of huge holes like pink cotton candy at a fair. Loni crept carefully through the debris. She couldn't order Coco to search because of the glass shards everywhere. Nothing in the kitchen and bathroom.

The bedroom was where she found Chief nailed to the wall. His intestines were wrapped around his feet, and his blood-soaked shirt hung in tattered strips. Chief's mouth was open in a silent scream, and his eyes had the empty gaze of death. Hundreds of child porn photos scattered on the floor were covered with bloody footprints.

Bile rose in Loni's throat from the horrible sight and the foul iron smell of blood mixed with bowel waste. She backed out and rushed to the porch railing. Grabbing on, she gulped fresh air. When her shakes almost stopped, she called Bobby.

"Chief's dead. Send the coroner and call the Phoenix crime lab. Tell them we need the full crew. It's really bad, Bobby."

"Bad how?"

"He was tortured." Loni took another deep breath. "I need Carl, too."

"I called him. James, too."

Loni pulled O'Neal' gun out of her belt and bagged it before she sat on the porch steps to wait. She recognized the gun. Chief's initials were in the fancy silver scrolling on the handle. Mustering up courage, she went back to search for the Taser. Chief told her somebody stole it. She found it at his feet, almost hidden in the intestines.

The coroner arrived first. Loni stayed outside until Doc Benjamin came out to sit with her.

"Do you know who did it?"

"Oh, yes. Colin O'Neal. He's locked in my SUV over there."

"Any idea why?"

"Not a clue."

Loni watched the flashing red and blue growing larger and dimming in the billowing dust. James ran up first with Carl not far behind.

"What happened?" Carl asked.

Loni watched Doc. "Chief's dead. Tortured."

"Who?"

"The perp's in my SUV, Carl," Loni said. "It's your tenant, Colin O'Neal."

Carl's face registered shock. "You talked to him?"

"Not yet."

He swore and stomped toward Loni's SUV.

"Carl, he's mine." Loni blocked his way.

"Fuck you, Loni. That bastard's mine." He reached around her for the door handle. He pounded and kicked at the locked door. "Give me the goddam keys, Loni," he threatened. "Now."

James towered over Carl and grabbed him. "Calm down, Carl. We'll sort this out." He pushed Carl back against a tree. "Loni, why don't you go on?"

Loni scrambled to her car. "Good idea." She opened the back door of her SUV and motioned Coco in with O'Neal. Loni backed out slowly and left the flashing lights behind. Her cell phone recorded her recitation of the Miranda.

"Get this dog out of my face," O'Neal begged. "He'll kill me."

"Do you understand these rights?"

"The dog, goddamnit."

"Do you understand these rights?"

"Shit, yes. Back your dog off now!"

"Coco. Release." Loni watched her back away from O'Neal and sit. She kept her growl dark and low.

"Would he really kill me?"

"He's a she. And yes, she would really kill you." Loni's anger spiked. "At least she wouldn't torture first."

"He deserved it!" O'Neal spat. "He was a neighbor. A good one I thought until I found out he raped my Jenny over and over. Started when she was only ten. O'Neal banged his head against the metal screen in front of him and rattled Loni's seat. "When she was no longer young enough, he accused me of raping my own daughter. He couldn't take a chance she'd talk. I spent ten years in prison for his crime. He destroyed my family."

Loni saw the despair on his face in her rearview mirror.

"I thought killing him would give me some relief. It didn't. My Jenny's a mess, so angry. My son's a meth head. My wife's gone. Committed suicide."

He started to cry. "She always believed I did it."

Loni didn't ask any more questions. The sky was turning pink as she walked O'Neal into the station. Bobby saw her face and stayed quiet. He helped her book O'Neal.

"You should go home. I'll get him to lockup."

"Thanks, Bobby. I'm so tired maybe I better." Loni glanced around. "Chui back yet?"

"Nah. Carl told him to call in every day but nobody's heard from him."

Loni struggled to her feet and called Coco out from under her desk. "I got patrol tonight. Maybe I better get some sleep." She gave Bobby a tired smile and headed for the door. "One last thing? I saw Jenny leave the crime scene. Get a BOLO out on her, would you?"

Bobby nodded. "Carl called the tactical assault team from Tucson. Said he and James were waiting for them to search his ranch later on this evening. He hoped to find Robert Teag and Steve O'Neal still there."

Loni snorted. "Good luck with that. By now, if they have any brains, they're in the wind."

"Probably not, especially Steve. He's a meth-head. They got no brain left."

"Good. Maybe Jenny is with them." Loni shrugged. "I don't suppose Carl wants me to go help him."

"No, Loni. It's not your job. You really need to get some rest and get back out on patrol."

The sun had climbed high in the hot sky by the time she drove to the hangar. Heat poured onto Loni's head as she parked and let Coco out to wander and sniff. Daniel was working on an airplane engine, and she slumped against him for a little comfort.

"Hard day, turkey?"

"If I gobble, will you shoot me?"

"Tell big brother all about it."

Letting go, Loni leaned against the fuselage. "I lost someone I thought was a friend."

He patted her shoulder. "Who'd you lose?"

"Jenny O'Neal. An art teacher at the school."

"Yeah? I know her. Recognized the car. She just drove by here. Stopped at Rebecca's house."

Loni snapped to complete awareness. "Oh, shit. Call the station for me and get me some help." She called to Coco as she hurried to Rebecca's house and huddled against the wall of the plane's garage. She listened to the groan of the huge garage door rolling up as an engine roared to life winding a propeller into life. A spinning propeller appeared, followed by the fuselage. Loni shot out both front tires as the plane cleared the garage.

The plane stopped, and the engine shut down. Loni waited as the propeller slowly whirred to a standstill. As she and Coco slipped behind the plane a shot whizzed by as Loni and Coco jumped and ran behind a cabinet. Coco nuzzled Loni in warning. Peered out Loni saw Daniel running toward her. "No!" she shouted. "Go back! They'll shoot you!"

Daniel dashed to the side of the garage. A minute went by before Loni heard Jenny's voice. "Is that you, Loni? Rebecca has a gun on me."

"Hang on, Jenny. Police are on their way."

A bullet whizzed by Loni again.

"Help me, please!" Jenny cried.

"Rebecca, throw out the gun!" Loni yelled.

Loni heard Rebecca scream. "Dammit, give it to me." The gun went off again. Rebecca opened the door to the plane and slid down, hit the cement floor and collapsed. Blood ran down her arm. "She shot me." Rebecca moaned, holding her shoulder.

"Jenny, throw the gun out and climb down!" Loni demanded. She walked to the passenger side of the plane keeping out of Jenny's sight.

Slowly a door opened, and Jenny stuck out a foot, feeling for the step.

"Jenny, I've got a gun pointed at you. I won't hesitate to use it. Throw your gun out before you climb down."

"But she kidnapped me. Why are you being so mean?"

"Jenny, for the last time, throw out the goddamn gun."

A gun flew out and clanked on the garage floor as Loni moved in to catch Jenny climbing down. She handcuffed her before Jenny realized what happened.

"I need an ambulance at—Daniel? What's the address here?" Lola's voice jarred Loni. "Are you alright? Are you shot? Talk to me!"

"I'm fine," Loni interrupted her. "I have a vic with a shoulder wound. I'm at the Wagner Airport. Resident Number nine."

Lola sounded relived. "Got it."

Loni drove Jenny to the police station as Daniel waited with Rebecca for the ambulance. "Don't let her move," Loni warned Daniel. "She murdered Rene and tried to kill me."

"How the hell you figure that?"

"Later."

Jenny screamed and kicked against Loni's seat the entire way to town. Loni drove onto the sidewalk to the door of the police station. She dragged Jenny out of the SUV and into the station. "Tully! A hand here!" she shouted at the snickering man sitting back, all casual in the bullpen.

"You pussy. She's handcuffed behind her back. What can she do?"

"Really?" Loni shoved Jenny at Tully. "She's all yours."

Tully laughed and tried to pull her down the hall. Three steps in, Jenny kicked him in the back of the knee, taking him down. She almost got Tully's gun when Loni slammed into her. They both landed at Bobby's feet. He leaned over and put his gun barrel into Jenny's face and grimly smiled.

Loni struggled to get back on her feet and helped Tully pull Jenny up. Bobby's gun in Jenny's nostril followed her as she rose to a standing position. "Worthless pig," Jenny sneered. "Pull, you coward!"

Bobby whispered, "Get this crazy bitch out of here." Fifteen minutes later, they got Jenny, screaming and kicking all the way up the stairs and into the jail.

"You bitch, you goddamn worthless breed," were the last words Loni heard as she and Tully shoved Jenny into a cell next to her father. Seeing her father finally shocked Jenny into silence.

Loni left Tully with the prisoners and slowly hobbled down the stairs. She limped around the corner to sit behind the booking desk with Lola.

"She was kind of rough on you, huh?" said Lola, watching Loni rub her ankle.

"She even tried to bite me!" grumped Loni.

"Still want her for a girlfriend?"

Loni glared back and tried not to laugh. "Haven't decided," she flipped back. "How do you know I don't like rough?"

Bobby's slow voice interrupted them. "She part of it?" He pushed his long blond hair back to cover a bald spot.

"Probably. She was there." Loni closed her eyes. She felt drained. "Someone needs to go to Jenny's house and search for bloody clothes." She thought a minute. "Tell them to look for a tube of epoxy matching Rene's valve at Rebecca's house."

"Forensics should find plenty of evidence at Chief's house," Bobby said.

"Did you send someone to the clinic to watch Rebecca?"

"Trevor's there. He met the ambulance. What are you charging her with?"

"Rene's murder and Rosa's attempted murder when she took down Rene's plane."

"Right. The thumbprint on the valve in Rene's plane."

"And her DNA in the blood on the tubing on the engine. Also attempted murder on me. She's the one who shot at me the first time and sicced the rattlesnake on me."

"Wow! That's some kind of mad." Bobby shook his head.

"Crazy jealous, I figure. She saw both Rene and me as competition."

Loni rubbed her shin once more before she pulled her smart phone out of her pocket. "Would you lock my phone in evidence? O'Neal's confessions on it."

Tully wandered in. "O'Neal wants a priest."

"I don't think we have one around here right now, Tully," Lola told him. "I think he moved back to Phoenix."

"What happened to the Catholic priest who lived in a trailer house on Rankin's ranch near the Indian village?" Bobby asked.

Lola glanced up from her typing. "Jimmy Rankin ran him off."

"Why?"

"Well, Jimmy said he asked the priest to help with the lice and fleas in the village and he said it wasn't any of his business. Said he was there to teach about God. He went to the village and asked Red Feather what they learned from the priest. Jimmy said Red Feather told him, 'He just talk about God and the devil. Then he passa da pot.'"

"Well, hell!" Tully shook his head.

Loni closed her eyes, feeling drained.

"Damn Chief." Lola hung her head. "If I weren't so angry, I'd bawl."

Patting Lola on the shoulder, Bobby was quiet a minute before he turned to Loni. "Who shot at you the second time?"

"Don't know yet." Loni stood up. "Can't say I even care right now. I gotta get home before I fall down."

CHAPTER TWENTY-ONE

After a slow drive home Loni was more than ready for bed. She wished she didn't hate drugs so much because she could use a knockout pill. She picked up one of her grandmother's notebooks and crawled into bed, trying to fight off the terrible images in her head.

Coco hopped up with her, and Loni curled herself about the dog. The title in large, bold letters on the first page was "Headlight." "You ready for this story, Coco?" The dog huffed once and closed his eyes. "Just try and ignore me, you're still going to listen." Loni opened the notebook.

"Headlight was a blazed face desert colt, bright sorrel and stocking legged. I always believed no horse was naturally mean; the same with boys but mishandling or environment made them so. I don't know what happened to Headlight, the five years on the desert developed him physically into a beautiful animal. Maybe someone caught him and abused him, maybe he got enough loco weed somewhere to damage his brain. No amount of kindness or food seemed to change him. If you tied him up he'd fight the rope until he fell exhausted. If you came in the corral, he'd charge you biting and striking.

We decided to geld him and maybe he'd change. That operation in itself was a story. Tied down he beat his head on the ground so I tried to sit on his head to hold him still. He threw me off like a wet sock, so Ben said, "You finish the cut and I'll hold him." So I castrated my first colt, got the bleeding stopped and smeared on his bruises and Ben let him up. We made it to the top rail, and here he came, squealing and striking. He was crazy mad. We put feed and water in the corral and left him to quiet down. He never did, just the sight of a man would make him charge at you.

Ben said, "That's enough. He'll kill someone." So he took him back to the desert and shot him. I didn't protest, because he was so mean he'd never change. We tried for months. Most of the colts were working good by then, but he only had two saddlings. He didn't buck so hard he couldn't be rode. It was when he was loose that he went haywire. Maybe a "head shrinker" could explain that.

Maybe horses have insanity, but I'll always think it was loco weed and that if it doesn't kill them outright, it affects their nervous system. So they are ruined, unpredictable, and a danger to themselves and others. Poor old Headlight, another tragedy of the desert.

Loni closed the notebook and kept hearing Bahb's voice. Do no harm. But Jenny was like Headlight. She was too badly damaged.

The vibration of Loni's cell phone jarred her awake. Carl's voice sounded pleading. "Can you come in tonight for a few hours? I need someone to protect Rosa. She's getting threatening calls."

"Who from? I thought we were done here."

"We think it's Robert Teag and Steve O'Neal. We didn't find them at the ranch, and the money's still missing. Seems Rosa might know something after all, but she wouldn't talk. Now she claims it's not safe. State is moving her to a safe house as soon as possible. I'll be in to relieve you later."

"Okay. You find enough evidence out there to prosecute?"

"Oh, yeah. There's a shit load of everything here including the meth lab."

"Chui ever call in?"

"No. Why?"

"Just asking." Sitting with Rosa or patrolling in her SUV all night didn't matter much to her, she thought.

Rosa was in rehab at a new retirement facility seven miles south of Caliente, built since Loni left home. Loni sat in a chair next to her bed and studied Rosa while she slept. Her long blond hair had dark roots. One broken leg was in a light cast, and the other was hanging in traction.

Two hours passed before a nurse beckoned Loni outside. The young Pima woman, grandmother soft, had been in and out, checking on Rosa. Loni gave Rosa a glance and followed the nurse. Her name tag read "Josie."

"Admittance wants you. A call from a Carl Harper?"

"Thanks, Josie. Can you watch Rosa while I'm gone?"

"Sure."

"Guest bathroom is where?"

Josie pointed to the end of the hall. When Loni came out of the bathroom, she saw a man in a long white coat disappear into Rosa's room. Her hackles went up, and she dashed back to her charge. A bearded man was leaning over Rosa with a pillow in his hands.

Rosa was whimpering. "Leave me alone," she said weakly. He pressed the pillow over Rosa's face.

Loni pointed her gun at him and yelled, "Police!" He threw the pillow at her face as he pushed by her. Loni stuck out her foot and tripped him. She pulled his arms back to handcuff and flipped him over. "Well, Teag. You again? Why'd you run?"

"Figured you wouldn't shoot in here."

She called Carl. "Hey, Teag's here. He tried to kill Rosa."

Loni forced the sitting man to stretch out his legs. She put a stool from the nurses' station over his legs and climbed on hassling Teag until Carl hurried up to her.

"You all right?"

"I am." Loni stared down at the prisoner. "He's not."

Shaking his head, Carl hauled him off down the hall. "I'll be back as soon as I interrogate him."

Loni joined Rosa. "Sorry," she said. "I should have been more careful."

"I'm so tired of this. I want it over." A determined expression settled on Rosa's face. "Got a tape recorder?"

"Sure." Loni took out her cell phone. "Can you hold it?"

"Yes," Rosa declared.

"I'll give time, date, and who we both are first. Then your rights. After that it's all yours."

Rosa replied she understood her rights, finishing her statement. "I kept warning Rene not to crap in his own bed." She was asleep by the time Carl got back. Loni gave him the phone and explained what she recorded on it.

Carl slid the phone in his shirt pocket. "James and Tully are out looking for Steve O'Neal now. The team from Tucson is still searching the ranch for more evidence, but I guarantee you that prosecution's a slam dunk."

CHAPTER TWENTY-TWO

Rosa sat up reading as James lightly snored in a recliner chair. His long body was stretched out in the chair across the door, and Loni pushed her way in. He didn't stir.

"How long's he been asleep?"

"All night."

"I have not." James defended himself as he finally stirred in the chair. "Got an allergy so I'm resting my eyes."

"Go home, James."

James grumbled about long nights, yawned, and struggled out the door.

"Coco, guard," Loni said. Coco took James' place across the door.

"James doesn't talk much," Rosa commented, watching Coco. "How about you?"

"Not so much either, Rosa. Carl put out a warrant for Larry's arrest. They've been at the O'Neal ranch most of the day flipping the place and looking for Steve O'Neal. I don't know any more, but Lola promised to call if anything happened.

"Do you think I'm safe yet?"

"I do. If you told us everything. You said the money is all you knew about, and State collected it. Should we know anything else?"

"What about the Mexican connection? I told you about the Mexican cops we dealt with. Did they get picked up?"

"I don't know. Maybe that's the reason State is moving you to a safe house."

"It's been four weeks. The doc said I could travel now."

"I know. The helicopter is scheduled for ten o'clock."

The room filled up with nurses and a doctor to get Rosa ready to travel. Loni and Coco sat outside and questioned each person thoroughly. They could hear the whirring of the helicopter as Rosa was signed out. A male nurse used a gurney to keep Rosa's legs elevated. Loni watched as they loaded her, gurney and all, and belted her in. The helicopter slowly disappeared on the horizon.

Loni ordered Coco into the truck and they drove to the hangar. She spent the morning putting Daniel's tools away and hosing out the hangar while she listened to Daniel and Uncle Herm argue about who was going to fly the plane they repaired. The Cessna Caravan was a lot like the one Rene crashed.

Coco entertained herself by attacking the water spray with her turkey drink until both she and Loni were soaked. It felt good in the stifling heat of the hangar. Coco made a trip to a patch of dead grass and followed Loni up to the loft.

Loni warmed up some stew Shiichoo made her and joined Coco for lunch. She fell asleep on a full stomach and slept until time for work. Before she left, she finished the cold stew and scanned down the numbers in her copy of Rene's notebook. She found what she was looking for and read, 7/28/330a/63. Today was the twenty-eighth. 3:30 was a few hours away. She climbed into her truck with Coco and drove down the highway toward milepost sixty-three.

Picking up three speeders headed for California helped fill the time, but she let them off with warnings. Time was her enemy as the waxing moon followed her down the road until she got ready. She laughed at herself, wondering exactly what she was getting ready for.

Loni parked in a thicket of mesquite trees as close to Milepost 63 as she could safely get. She and Coco hid behind a large catclaw bush. Forty minutes later a pickup truck with a camper shell pulled off the road several feet in front of her and crawled into the desert and hid. She saw soft lights go in the cab and the back of the camper open. A man said, "Todos fuera!" Five men climbed out whispering nervously to each other.

Another twenty minutes passed before Loni saw headlights appearing in the distance. Loni watched a SUV pull over on the side of the road and the driver got out. "Jose! Estas ahi?" the man called.

"Si." The camper's backup lights illuminated the waiting group. The driver trotted down into the light of the camper shell and chattered to the men.

Loni gasped as she recognized him. It was Chui. He handed an envelope to the coyote and herded the men to his SUV. The pickup, empty now except for the coyote, circled around back to the road and sped south.

Chui pushed the men into his SUV, hollering at them to hurry. He slammed a door on the last man as Loni shoved her gun into his back. She grabbed the hand moving from the door handle and twisted it behind his back. He swore in a mixture of Mexican and English and kicked out at her. Coco bit him hard in the leg, and Chui froze.

Loni cuffed Chui to the door handle of his SUV and spoke for the first time. "Coco! Down!"

"Goddamn you, Loni. I'll kill you for this!"

"Maybe so but not today," she growled as she took his keys out of his pocket. "Nice of you to lock up my other prisoners." Watching one of them pound on the window at her, Loni smiled. She knew they couldn't get out and Chui couldn't get in without a key. She called call for transport.

CHAPTER TWENTY-THREE

Everyone in town turned out for Chief's funeral in the Baptist Church. The shakes on the building were bleached a light gray in the heat, and the main building was protected by large eucalyptus trees. The church's towering cross rose toward the sky. Those who couldn't squeeze inside clustered outside the main door waiting for the casket. A few of them marveled at how such a terrible thing could happen in their own town. Others cursed or cried. Some even smiled or hugged themselves, swaying to a tune no one could hear.

The casket finally appeared. The city council pallbearers were led by the mayor. The men silently loaded Chief into the mortuary van before somberly going to their cars and following the hearse to the graveyard.

After the funeral the cops gathered at the station.

"It's really hard to believe Chief was going to run," James said. "I didn't think he had it in him."

"Can't say it worked out for him." Carl said. "Jenny found out before he got away."

"How'd she figure it out?" James asked.

Loni sat at her desk, rubbing her temples as she fought a headache. "I asked her. Seems she drove by his house on her way home from work to make sure he was there. Three days ago she saw him shoving suitcases in his car. He had a fire going in his yard burning all kinds of stuff including furniture. She must have guessed he was leaving. In Chief's house, I found a plane ticket to Bucharest."

Carl pulled at his ear. "Seems Chief was headed to some eastern European country where children are cheap and easy to find. I think something got him spooked and he moved up his leaving time. Jenny ran out of time. She knew he'd be a bitch to find over there."

"They really did plan all this? Setting up a drug trafficking scheme on Carl's ranch so they could murder Chief?"

"It was a big part of their plan, but I don't think they planned on getting caught. Jenny worked her way through college and teaching, always keeping track of Chief. Then her dad met this guy in prison who was looking for a partner in a nursery to cover a drug trade. Seems the guy once worked with Rene selling drugs, and Rene was willing to help them set up. He told them about Carl's ranch being for rent. Jenny's dad owned a huge nursery in Fresno he lost trying to defend himself. So when her dad got out, he found her brother, and they joined her in Caliente. As far as Jenny was concerned it was a deal made in heaven. Her dad and brother could reestablish the nursery business and she could take her time in designing the perfect murder."

☘

CHAPTER TWENTY-FOUR

Loni dragged into the station exhausted from driving all night on little sleep.

"Hey," Tully said to her as he turned to leave. "Last task force meeting today. You gotta be there cuz I'm in charge."

"What the hell, Tully? Where's Carl?"

"He's in Phoenix getting sworn in as interim chief."

"Is Chui still at the station?"

"Yeah. They're packing him up now for transport to Phoenix."

"I hoped he might be undercover. Guess not, huh?"

Tully shook his head.

"Guess I'm in a spot of trouble with the boys."

"Probably." Tully saluted Loni and walked back in his rolling gait to his car.

☘

Loni's stomach was tied in knots, and she barely got back to the station in time for the meeting. She ran by Lola and scurried into the conference room where James and Tully were waiting. She caught sight of Tully and almost dropped her coffee

Tully's suit was clean and pressed, his face was close-shaved, and he lost his gut. He winked at Loni and reached over to shut her mouth for her.

"Holy shit!" Loni burst out and then ducked her head in embarrassment. He was still chuckling when she jerked her head back up. "Who the hell are you?"

"Just your everyday cop."

"Jesus, Tully." Loni said sarcastically. "How long did you have to go to school to learn to say that with a straight face?"

"Nobody pays attention to a fool, right?"

James worked a few words out between giggles. "Where'd you leave your belly, Tully?"

"Fat falls. Don't ya know?"

"Not your fat." Loni was trying not to laugh. "It went up and hit him in the head. It's called fathead."

"Nah," James jumped back in. "He had the baby. What was it, Tully? Boy or girl?"

"What I really got was a bad case of heat rash." Tully paused. "Before we begin, we need to talk about Chui. As you might know, Loni arrested him last night. Caught him transporting undocumented workers for Carl's ranch. Before anybody tries to excuse him, he also transported young girls for Chief."

"Oh, god, Tully, are you sure?" James groaned.

Tully skipped over the question. "I'm glad it's all over. I'll miss you guys, but I don't mind that this is our last task force meeting." He stopped and seemed to collect his thoughts. "By now you may have figured out I'm from State. Carl suspected drugs were going through his ranch helped by a dirty cop so he called us in. We didn't want to raid his ranch until we found all the players. It was big. We raided his ranch last night, so now I can tell you what I know."

Tully didn't sound a bit ashamed as he grinned at Loni. "Sorry we stuck you in the middle of this, but we needed to feed information to someone we knew was clean."

"You were my secret admirer." Loni started laughing. "Why did you send me on so many shit jobs?"

"Carl and I were afraid that between your work and your grandma's illness you'd be too tired to be careful. Don't get too mad. I did get Rebecca's fingerprint for you. You owe me twenty-eight dollars, too. I had to take her to lunch to get it."

"It's worth it." Loni picked the money out of her billfold and dropped it in front of Tully, who shoved it in his pocket. "At least I wasn't in the way, right?"

"No, but it's a good thing I read your reports. You didn't pass on much in the meetings."

Loni ducked her head.

Tully stretched out his long legs. "We had lots of requests for permits to grow and sell sex enhancement plants in residential areas, but when we busted a dealer selling cocaine to kids, he led us to one of these home businesses. We found cocaine packed in the bottom of the plant containers. Seems the dead coach and his wife helped financed the deal and hired O'Neal. They knew him from Fresno where he ran a nursery."

James shook his head in amazement. "Who would have believed it? Anybody pulling leaves from these plants were so curious about what it'd do for them sexually, they never bothered to search any further."

Tully scratched his chin. "Thing is, the drugs were added where the plants were actually grown. We finally located it."

"On Carl's ranch!" sputtered Loni.

Tully shrugged. "We tracked it to Caliente where we hit a dead end and got a call from Carl. The residue you found in Rene's plane, Loni? It matched one of the cocaine batches. But we still didn't find the source of the bad meth."

Loni said, "What did it have to do with me?"

"When you stirred up the O'Neals, Steve and Teag went after you and gave us cause for a warrant. Seems Steve was a meth head and decided to make and sell a little on the side since he had plenty of help, thanks to Chui. Remember the report I gave you about castor bean growers?"

"Sure. You told me they grew seedlings on Carl's ranch."

Tully nodded. "It was their main crop." A somber expression crossed his face. "Seems one of the workers accidently swept ricin dust left from castor bean seed sacks stored in front of his lab. Or so Steve claims. He said when he learned about the deaths, he intended to dump the bad meth and clean up the lab, but he was so fried, he never got around to it."

"So Rene was part of the cocaine trafficking, not the meth."

"Right."

"What about the money?"

"We don't know. The feds took it over. As you know, Rosa gave us the account numbers, and we got the names of the people who had the accounts from Rene's little book you sent to the lab."

James laughed. "We already did the hard work. All they had to do was arrest people and collect the money."

Loni said, "Just a couple of questions."

"Sure," Tully turned to her.

"Why did Teag leave with the box he was supposed to mail to his wife?"

"There was nothing in it. He used is as an excuse to hang out at the post office to meet Chui. When Chui saw you there, he didn't go in."

"And another question. Who stabbed the guy in the Mercedes?"

"Teag did. The kid was part of the Mexico connection."

"Just one more thing," Loni added. "Do I get a reward? I need a new SUV."

"No, you don't." Tully smiled at her with warm exuberance. "Unless you don't want Carl's job."

"Carl's job? I don't understand."

"You're the new city detective if you want it."

Loni hesitated a minute before she leaped out of her chair and gave Tully a bear hug. "All right! Can I have a vacation between jobs?"

"Yeah, yeah. You can have a few days," Tully said. "James is taking two weeks after that. Enough time for a honeymoon."

Loni stared at James. "When are you getting married?"

"Just as soon as you can come, partner."

Loni felt like the grin on her face was so big it would fall off. Hugging James was good. He smelled exactly like their cousin Daniel.

CHAPTER TWENTY-FIVE

Loni and Lola walked out into the cool evening to watch the blue moon rise. Enlarged and yellowed by the dust in the air, it rose in a huge ball as twilight darkened, painting the desert in shades of purple and grey.

"Wow!" Lola exclaimed. "I've never seen anything like this."

"Likely never will again."

"Did you know a blue moon is magical?"

"Why? Because it brings out the crazies?"

"No, that's just a superstition." Lola pushed Loni and took her hand. "This is the time to decide what you want your future to look like."

"And that's not a superstition?"

"Not if you're very careful how you word your wishes."

"Know what? Maybe the magic in the moon can make the magic in the hard road easier."

"What does that mean?"

"Bahb believes the magic is when you walk the hard road and are still true to yourself. It'd be good if the blue moon could stick a little magic wadding on that road. Or better yet, maybe I could use you for a cushion."

Lola walked on, her face toward the moon. "I wonder how often we have a blue moon rising on the perigee?"

"What? Peri what?"

"It just means the moon's cycle is at its closest to the earth."

"I have no idea. I'll ask Bahb."

Lola reached over and took Loni's hand again as they silently walked down the old desert road. Together they watched the bottom of the moon clear the horizon and silhouette saguaro and barrel cactus in silvery tinges. Turning back, Loni nearly stepped on Bahb's old barn cat, pure white and deaf. "He can't catch rats so he's decided to follow Coco."

Lola leaned down and rubbed his head. "Good luck."

Loni said, "I wish that cat would stay out of the road. I nearly ran over him this morning."

Lola smiled. "Still has eight lives left."

"How come we get only one life and a cat has nine?"

"Well. We have more than one if we count the times we thought we would die of shame."

"Or love."

"Or boredom."

"Or fear."

"We could go on all day."

"Why'd you bring it up?

"I was thinking about that cat using up one of her lives." Loni paused. "I feel like I've used way too many of mine this month."

"You know what?" Lola stopped Loni and forced her to listen. "You have. Every time you walked out your door I swear you deliberately put yourself in harm's way."

"Was that faint praise or were you calling me stupid."

"I haven't decided." Lola leaned forward and kissed Loni. Loni tried to follow the softness to deepen the kiss but Lola stepped away again and opened the door to her car. "Where's your cat? I'd hate to be the one to use up her last life."

Loni picked up the cat and held him as she watched Lola's taillights fade into the night. She waited until the lights were gone before she walked back toward the house. Cuddling the purring cat, she absorbed the light around her. The slow, open flow of the desert was pulling her back in.

FROM: Loni Wagner
TO: Sandi@gmailyahoo.com
DATE: July 31
SUBJECT: Guess I'm staying here

Lola and I watched the blue moon a long time tonight. It was so big it felt like it was coming down on top of us. We held hands while we walked out on the desert talking about its magic.

It felt so good to feel close to someone again. Lola knows all about things in the sky. She said she spent a lot of time staring up when she was with her husband. She was pretty much a prisoner and couldn't even shop. Why is it so hard to be good to each other?

I asked her to go out with me, but she said I still had some grieving to do. She did add that I should asked her again when I'm ready. That's not a no, right?

Lots of love to all of you,
Loni

About the Author

Sue Hardesty was born and raised on the Arizona desert where she was either following her prospecting mom around, watching her pick-axe rocks, or riding horses with her dad helping him trail cattle. After college she moved to the Phoenix area and taught English and Communications for many years. Retirement took her out of the desert heat as she moved to the beautiful Oregon Coast where she and her partner now run their dog on the beach every morning. And where she even takes time to write a little. You can find her website here: www.SueHardestyBooks.com.

Author's Disclaimer

What is that old saw? Fact is stranger than fiction? I do say this is a work of fiction. Mostly. Names and places are the product of my imagination or are used fictitiously, mostly, and any resemblance to actual persons, living or dead, businesses, companies, events, or locales is entirely coincidental. However, with the exception of the plot line, characters, and some of the places, the stories are based in fact and actually happened to the people I know. They are about life on the Arizona Southwestern desert and, hopefully, they illustrate the difficulty of surviving in such a harsh and cruel environment. It is what it is, the desert at its worst and best.

This book is my talking stick, each desert story a cut on a cactus rib because I was always told that, unless you understand your past, you cannot find your way in the present. And if you know your way in the present, the future will take care of itself. Mostly.

www.ingramcontent.com/pod-product-compliance
Lightning Source LLC
Chambersburg PA
CBHW061615100726
47898CB00002B/677